CHILLING EFFECT

Valerie Valdes

HARPER Voyager

An Imprint of HarperCollins*Publishers*

CHILLING EFFECT. Copyright © 2019 by Valerie Valdes. Excerpt from PRIME DECEPTIONS © 2020 by Valerie Valdes. All rights reserved. Printed in the United States of America. No part of this book may be used or reproduced in any manner whatsoever without written permission except in the case of brief quotations embodied in critical articles and reviews. For information, address HarperCollins Publishers, 195 Broadway, New York, NY 10007.

HarperCollins books may be purchased for educational, business, or sales promotional use. For information, please email the Special Markets Department at SPsales@harpercollins.com.

Harper Voyager and design are trademarks of HarperCollins Publishers LLC.

FIRST EDITION

Designed by Joy O'Meara

Chapter opener art © happy_fox_art/Shutterstock

Library of Congress Cataloging-in-Publication Data has been applied for.

ISBN 978-0-06-287723-9

19 20 21 22 23   LSC   10 9 8 7 6 5 4 3 2 1

CHILLING EFFECT

To Eric, the other lost soul swimming in this fish bowl
And
To Jay, who carries me across the cold, cold river

ACKNOWLEDGMENTS

I have so many people to acknowledge for helping, supporting and encouraging me that it seems almost inevitable that I'll miss someone. If it feels like I've forgotten you, rest assured that it has nothing to do with you, and everything to do with sleep deprivation. I'll remember you one day when I'm pooping or showering or trying to sleep, and I'll feel absolutely mortified about the omission.

And so, in no particular order, a universe of thanks to:

Eric, my husband, the other pea in my pod, for doing laundry and washing dishes and singing to babies and all the other millions of little things that are actually much bigger than they appear. We'll play Warcraft III again, eventually.

My agent Quressa Robinson, for believing in my characters and my story and my future, for patience and professionalism and knowing when and where to push, and for being the Slytherin to my Hufflepuff. Go Team World Domination!

My editors Tessa Woodward and David Pomerico, and everyone else at Harper Voyager, for taking a chance on me and my book, and for helping me mold it into the best version of itself. My space cats thank you!

My mother, Nayra, for spending hundreds of Sundays watching me hit people with swords, and hundreds more Sundays taking care of my children so I could write about fictional people hitting each other with swords. I know it was hard. I hope it was worth it.

Jay Wolf, for being literally the best. I can't imagine what would have happened to this book if you weren't there holding my hair while I vomited feelings all over the place. I'm still at the base of Space Smut Mountain, but someday I'll reach the tip!

Matthew, Rick, Amalia, KC, Jeff and all my other TWB peeps, for your endless support and toilet reads and tear-absorbent shoulders and brioche. Without you, I would have given up a long time ago.

All my VP Twen-Tea (and beyond) comrades and instructors, for critiquing my work, for pushing me to query when I was still hesitating, and for encouraging me every single day. Go Cheese Weasels, 'til hell won't have it!

My NaNoWriMo folks, for writing with me every Sunday afternoon, and more every November, and for raging with me about movies and anime and video games and life. Always be sprinting!

Jilly and the Brainery crew, for pushing me to turn a short story into a novel and then to fix what didn't work, and for continuing to root for me long after.

My sister Laura, for getting my *Casablanca* references, and for sending me pictures of potential future bed-and-breakfast options so I have something to daydream about when the writing is too much.

My family-in-law and also in love, Aimee and Luis and Vanessa and Ashley and Erik, for being the best extended family I could ever dream of having, and for always making me feel welcome and loved and enough. (The Setzer is just for you, Ashley; I hope I did him justice.)

My dad, Keith, and stepmom, Jackie, for reading everything I write even if it's not your cup of tea, for assuring me this will definitely be made into a movie someday, and for making all your friends buy this book. Apologies to their friends!

My siblings and stepsiblings, Tasha and Kirk and Jennifer and John, and all their extremely lovely spouses, for all the kind words conveyed in person and online. Your faith sustains me and humbles me.

My other friends and family, in person and online, for asking how my book is going and patiently listening to me ramble about it, for sharing my Facebook posts and Twitter threads, for continuing to invite me to parties even when I can never make it, and for all the other little things over the years that have kept us moving within each others' orbits. You all keep me going in ways I can't express.

CHILLING EFFECT

Chapter 1

SAVE THE CATS

Captain Eva Innocente crept down the central corridor of *La Sirena Negra,* straining to hear the soft rumble of her quarry over the whine of the FTL drive and the creak of space-cold metal.

((Getting warmer,)) Min pinged over her commlink.

Min would know, since the ship was essentially her second body when she was connected to the piloting interface. But the critter Eva was tracking wouldn't stop moving. It had gone from the cargo bay down below, up through the mess, and was now somewhere between the crew quarters and the head. If it got to the bridge—

((Warmer.))

A hiss of steam sprayed Eva's hair. Startled, she nearly dropped the vented box she carried onto her foot, juggling it awkwardly before settling it against her hip. She resumed her barefoot tiptoeing with a scowl. Vakar would have to fix that leak later, once the more immediate problem was taken care of.

((Red hot!))

Eva crouched, held her breath, and listened. At last, in a gap between two panels, she heard it.

A lone kitten, purring.

Eva reached in, grabbed it by the scruff of its neck, and dropped it into the box.

((Got it,)) she pinged back at Min. Eighteen down, two to go. Her arms were covered in scratches and her black hair was a mass of tangles from being woken up in a hurry, but on the plus side, she'd gotten pretty good at catching the little mojones.

On the minus side, they were only a few hours from their drop point on Letis, and she wouldn't get paid unless she delivered the full cargo.

The kitten mewled, and Eva lifted the box to glare at it. "Don't start with me," she said. "This is the third time you've escaped and I'm ready to throw you all out the airlock."

Green eyes stared her down, the slitted pupils dilating to black discs.

"And stop trying to hypnotize me," Eva muttered. "It's rude." Fucking psychic cats.

The cat yowled in reply.

Eva carried the box down to the cargo hold. The tall ceiling allowed for multiple stacked containers, with catwalks near the top that had earned their name repeatedly over the past cycle. Metal plates were bolted onto the ship's frame, some hinged to allow access to the guts underneath, with no exposed pipes or wires to break the monotony. A blocky passenger cabin sat in the corner, for the occasions when someone hired them for transportation instead of delivery. Mostly it transported broken parts Eva hadn't bothered to sell or scrap.

Leroy stood in the middle of the room, sweat beading on his upper lip, his curly red hair sticking up at odd angles like it had been licked into place. Since she'd found him on the floor covered in cats earlier, that was to be expected.

Eva was almost a half meter shorter than him, and each of his pale, tattooed arms was thick as a steel beam, but he stiffened into the straight-backed pose of a soldier about to get chewed out as she came closer.

"I'm sorry," he said.

"I heard you the last ten times. Relax."

His shoulders hunched. "I thought maybe, just one, for a minute—"

"I know, Leroy. They're hypnotic." And you're prone to suggestion, she added silently. One of many unfortunate side effects of his years as a meat-puppet soldier, being thrown into whatever corporate war needed warm bodies instead of tactical nukes, controlled remotely by people with an eye in the sky and no skin in the game. Other side effects being anxiety, nightmares, and the kind of sudden, extremely violent outbursts that turned an asset into a liability.

Eva knew how those nightmares felt. She was also good at turning liabilities into assets, and Leroy was no exception. He'd been responsible for managing supply chains and tracking inventory when he was deployed, so handling smaller, less-frequent cargo logistics came easily to him.

She dropped the cat into the spacious, climate-controlled shipping container from whence it had escaped. It had food, water, self-cleaning litter boxes, toys, tiny hammocks, raised platforms on which to run or recline—anything a cat could want, or so the person who designed it had thought.

Apparently, what a cat really wanted was freedom.

Eighteen balls of fur sat, or splayed out, or licked their butts, most of them studiously ignoring Eva and Leroy. A few glanced up and blinked languidly, as if they had not been slinking around the ship getting into trouble only minutes earlier.

This was what she got for taking on live cargo. If she weren't doing this for her former captain Tito, and if he weren't paying better than their last four jobs combined . . . That smiling come-mierda hadn't told her the critters were genetically engineered mind-controlling geniuses. It was exactly the kind of casual not-quite-lie that had made her quit his crew seven years earlier, over her father's objections. Given that her father preferred whole-ass lies, and given that he was Tito's boss back then, his opinion had mattered as much as a fart in a hurricane.

Fuck 'em both, she thought, not for the first time.

"Found another one trying to get into a supply cabinet in my med bay." Pink sauntered in holding a kitten to her chest, rubbing its face absently with one dark finger. Her dreads were tucked under a sleep cap, and her eye patch was flipped down to cover her cybernetic eye, while her organic one took in Eva's scruffy condition with a raised brow. "You're looking splendid," she said.

Eva examined her welt-striped arms. "I look like I wrestled a needle-bear."

"Are those real?" Leroy asked.

"No," Pink said.

"Says the lady who hasn't wrestled one," Eva retorted.

Pink rolled her eyes. "I'll clean you up and synthesize you some allergy medicine when I'm done making my hormones. How many cats left?"

"Just one." Leroy paused for dramatic effect. "The leader."

"Cats don't have leaders, honey," Pink said.

"Tell that to . . . the leader."

Pink may have been right, but Eva knew who Leroy meant.

The one who kept busting everyone out was the smallest cat, a calico with mottled brown and black fur with patches of orange, and hazel eyes that looked like they had seen some shit. They probably had. She didn't know what it took to make the kittens more intelligent, but she doubted it was nice.

"Viva la revolución," Eva said. "But not on my ship. Min, can you pinpoint its location?"

No response.

"Min? Can you hear me?" The silence grabbed her stomach and slid it up to her throat.

((Bridge, help,)) her commlink pinged, the limitations of the mind-to-mind communication feature more frustrating than usual at the moment. It was Vakar, who for some reason made the cats nervous. Maybe it was the quennian's pangolin-like skin, or his twitchy face-palp things, or the fact that his smell changed to match his mood. These particular psychic cats probably weren't designed to work with nonhuman people.

"Me cago en la hora que yo nací," she muttered. If the cat had gotten into the bridge, there might be more trouble than lost wages. "Leroy, stay here. Pink, with me."

Pink shook her head. "I'm not leaving Leroy alone with these babies when we're so close to docking." She punctuated this by placing her kitten in the container and closing the lid firmly, then standing next to Leroy, hand on hip.

"Fine. I'm sure Vakar and I can handle one damn cat." Eva stalked out of the cargo bay, back up past the mess and crew quarters and head, past her cabin and the med bay, all the way up to the short hallway that led to the bridge. Min's neural implants—originally meant for controlling repair mechs on her family's solar farm, later used for the bot fights that had earned Min her reputation—let her control and monitor *La Sirena Negra* from anywhere on the ship, but the pilot still preferred to be near the physical controls. Eva had told Min to ping her if a cat made it inside, and she had assumed the comm silence meant good news.

She should have known better.

Vakar waited outside the door, smelling like tar. Nervous, Eva's scent translators supplied. He had taken off the gloves he normally wore and was trying to dig his four-fingered claws underneath the handle of the emergency door release.

"You know your hands are too big," Eva whispered. "What's the situation?"

"I tried to reason with the cat," he whispered back. "It ran in and the door locked. I managed to bypass the security protocol, but the manual override engaged. I must say, for creatures without prehensile extremities, these cats are remarkably—"

"Later." She gripped the handle and tugged it out, then twisted it clockwise to disengage the dead bolts. Each unlocking pin made a loud grinding sound as it moved.

"When was the last time you lubricated this?" Eva snapped.

"I would have to check my maintenance logs, but I have been rationing lubricant and this was lower priority than other items."

Eva suppressed a joke. Vakar was always so sensible, and it wasn't his fault she'd been denying his requisitions.

"On three, you open the door and I bust in," she whispered. "Ready?"

He shrugged assent.

She moved aside and drew her pistol, loaded with tranq rounds for the occasion. Hopefully she wouldn't need them. Hopefully they weren't strong enough to kill a cat. Hopefully she wouldn't miss and hit something that would blow up the ship.

Hope in one hand and shit in the other, and see which gets full first, she thought. She leaned against the bulkhead next to the door and pinged the countdown silently at Vakar.

On three, he slid the door open and she leaped in, scanning the room with her pistol leading.

Min lay in the pilot's chair, black eyes open, short dyed-blue hair in disarray. Because she was connected to the ship's systems wirelessly, she didn't have to look at the instrument panel in front of her, so her chair was reclined as far back as the small bridge allowed. Where some ships had holographic controls, *La Sirena Negra* was all old-fashioned buttons and switches and blinking lights—less fancy, but cheaper to maintain and not as prone to sudden catastrophic failure. Above that, the display connected to the fore hull cameras was turned on, projecting an image of the dizzying streak of stars passing them as they flew through the red-tinged blackness of space.

Sitting on the instrument panel, pawing at the manual control override, was the calico cat.

It hissed at Eva, hazel eyes flashing. She felt a sudden vertigo, as if the artificial gravity had shifted. Shaking her head to clear it, she leveled her gun at the critter.

"Get down from there, you cabrón revolutionary," she said, "before you break something."

"The little cuddly-poof accidentally blocked my commlink access, Cap." Min spoke through the speakers in the bridge instead of her human mouth, as usual.

Eva snorted. "Accident, sure. You okay?"

"Yeah, comm's almost back up."

"But are you okay?"

"A few bites and scratches in random spots. Nothing Vakar can't fix."

"I meant your— Never mind." Eva was going to say "real body," but after four years the ship was as much Min's body as the one she'd been born with.

The cat crouched, its butt shaking in the air. Then, in a fluid motion, it jumped onto another part of the panel.

"Idiot," Eva hissed. "Get away from there. You'll jettison everything in the cargo hold."

It raised a paw threateningly.

"You're seriously going to kill all your little cat buddies? Flush them right out into space?"

It hesitated and cocked its head at her.

"Cap," Min said, "you're talking to a cat."

"I believe it can understand us quite well, Min," Vakar said, peering around the edge of the door.

"Right, okay." Eva hunkered down and stared at the cat, face-to-face. "Listen, kitty. I'm taking you to a nice new home somewhere. A café where millions of tourists will come every year to pet you and feed you canned meat. I don't even get to eat canned meat."

The cat's tail lashed back and forth.

"Yeah, I don't know, maybe that's not your idea of a good time." Eva ran a hand through her tangled black hair. "What do you want me to do? Someone is paying me to take you to another planet, and if I don't deliver, I don't get paid. And if I don't get paid, I lose my ship, so pretty please with sugar on top, get in your cabrón crate already, coño!"

The bridge was silent for a moment.

"That did not sound like a compelling argument," Vakar said.

Eva made a disgusted noise and threw her hands in the air. As if in response, the cat leaped onto Min's human lap, where it settled down and began to lick its paw.

"Okay, what the hell," Eva said.

"Ooh, I think it likes me," Min said. She scratched the cat's ears with a pale hand.

"Too bad. Twenty kittens, cash on delivery. We don't get paid for nineteen."

The cat yawned, showing tiny sharp teeth and a throat pink as a guayaba.

"It is arguably cute," Vakar said.

"It broke out of its cage, locked itself in the bridge, and tried to take over the nav systems!"

"Cap, come on. How would it know how to use the nav systems?" Min scratched the cat's chin and made soft cooing noises at it with her human mouth.

"Psychically," Eva said. "Mira, cute or not, I want these sinvergüenzas off my ship as soon as we dock. If that cat isn't in its box in the next—" She glanced at Min. "How far out are we from Letis?"

"We'll hit the nearest Gate in about an hour, then two hours to orbit, plus docking time and customs."

"Madre de dios. I was supposed to call Tito to find out who we're meeting and where." Eva cast one last snarling look at the kitten, which had the gall to wink at her. "I'll be back for you, cat, so don't get comfortable. Vakar, keep an eye on them."

She stalked past Vakar, back straight, fighting the urge to scratch her welted arms until they bled. Could one thing go right for her this cycle?

"You're shitting me."

Eva sat in the mess room, clenched fists resting on the big oval table in the center. The smirking face of Tito Santiago, patron saint of smug assholes, floated in front of her. His dark, wavy hair was precisely tousled and his brown eyes twinkled with barely suppressed amusement.

"Shit happens, Beni," he said, his holo image crackling slightly. "It's not my fault the buyer went bankrupt."

"Cómetelo. Now I know why you convinced me not to take the usual half up front."

"I'll owe you a favor."

"My ship runs on fuel, not favors."

His smile didn't change, but his eyes narrowed. He was getting annoyed. Back when he was her boss, it had worried her; now it just pissed her off more.

"No es pa tanto," he said. "You can sell the cargo on the black market for triple what the buyer was going to pay."

She ran her finger along a scratch in the table's metal surface. "You know that's not my game anymore. Not to mention the damn things are a righteous pain in the ass."

"You wouldn't know anything about that, I'm sure." He ran a hand through his hair. "Decídete, mi cielo, I haven't got all cycle."

Mierda. It wasn't like she could return the cats as defective, either; the sellers would credit the original buyer. And probably reprogram them, whatever that entailed. Animal protection laws got flexible in certain sectors.

Eva thought of that stupid little ball of fluff curled up on Min's lap and sighed.

"A big favor," she said finally. "An expensive favor."

"Claro que sí, mi vida. You know I'll take care of you."

"You take care of your boyfriend. Me, you just fuck."

He glanced at someone over his shoulder. "Bueno, speaking of boyfriends, te dejo. I'll let you know if any more jobs come in that will fit your . . . particular preferences. Adiós." The holovid flickered off.

"Particular preferences." Only Tito could make her desire to avoid illegal or unethical work sound perverted. Hell, he'd probably given them the job in the first place because legality shit all over his bottom line.

Why was it so hard to make a living without killing strangers or screwing people over? Seven years of cargo delivery and passenger transport, of building up a reputation from nothing, and what did she have to show for it? A few regular clients, a handful of shell companies under various aliases, and a message box full of unpaid bills.

Eva forced herself to unclench her hands, placing her palms on the table. ((Mess room,)) she pinged to the whole crew. Time to deliver the bad news. Not to mention—

"The fuck am I going to do with twenty cats?" she muttered.

Everyone sat around the big table in the mess—even Min, who was flying the ship remotely while curled up in a chair, drinking a misugaru shake. Pink munched on a protein bar, her dreadlocks tied back from her face. Leroy leaned forward, hands clasped together under the table in his lap, his hair still a frizz of red and his tattoos programmed to look like barbed wire. Vakar sat on a stool, his double-jointed legs straddling the metal seat, smelling like incense but with a faint undercurrent of something else. Vanilla? Eva couldn't place it, but her translator told her it was anticipation.

Eva stood, bent forward so her palms rested on the table. "Do you want the good news or the bad news?"

A chorus of "Bad news" answered her.

"The bad news is, Tito shafted us, so we're not getting paid."

Pink chewed slowly, pinning Eva with a glare from her visible eye. Leroy groaned and dropped his forehead to the table.

Vakar's smell transitioned to cigarette smoke with a hint of fart.

"What's the good news?" Min asked.

"We can do whatever we want with the cargo, and Tito owes us a huge favor."

"Favors are delicious," Pink said. "I ask myself, 'Dr. Jones, what do you want to eat for lunch?' and favors are the first thing—"

"I told him that, but there's nothing we can do to him, and he knows it." She squinted at Pink. "Unless your fancy lawyer brother might be able to help?"

Pink scowled. "He's still up to his nose hairs in our habitat's lawsuit."

"Assholes." The only thing worse than scummy freelancers like Tito was corporations. In Pink's case, a Martian megacorp had encouraged a bunch of idealistic people to take out big loans to set up a habitat on an unclaimed world and do all the hard work of making it self-sustaining, then started shipping tainted seed and faulty tech to sabotage them. Inevitably, the settlers sold off their assets dirt cheap or had them seized to cover their debts, then the corporations rolled in, slapped on a coat of fancy, and resold everything at a huge profit.

Where most people gave up on fighting an impossible enemy, the Jones family got mad. And when they got mad, they got busy.

"What will we do now, Captain?" Vakar asked, interrupting her dour thoughts.

Eva straightened, her hand creeping to the back of her neck to pick at a scab. "Since we're already about to Gate to Letis, I say we dock and see if we can find a cat buyer or pick up a new client. Or both."

"I'll post an ad on the q-net," Min chimed in. That meant she would also steal some time to play a VR game with her friends, but Eva didn't mind. Pretending to shoot and stab imaginary bad guys was much safer than dealing with real ones.

"Use the Gato Tuerto Enterprises q-mail address," Eva said. "And keep an eye on the box in case someone responds while we're there."

"Any chance of shore leave?" Leroy asked, perking up.

"Sure, but take Vakar." She pointed at the quennian with her free hand, still scratching her neck with the other. "Vakar, start making a list of the damage the cats caused so I can send Tito a bill he can wipe his ass with, and pick up anything you need while we're there." She winced as her neck scab gave way to blood. "Anything we can afford, that is. Pink, same for you."

"Aw, that's work, not shore leave," Leroy whined.

"Make it a game. Whoever finds the cheapest rations that don't taste like shit gets to eat them." Her crew wore expressions ranging from dismay to anger. "Any questions?"

"Yeah," Pink said. "Next time I see Tito, how many times can I punch his sweet little face?"

"Once for every cat we still have in our hold." She pursed her lips and squinted. "In fact, if you need me in the next twenty, I'll be beating the shit out of a heavy bag with his picture on it. Dismissed."

The others stood and left, but Vakar lingered. "Would you like company?" he asked.

Eva opened her mouth to accept, then shook her head. "You need to get that parts list together. Next time, though."

"Of course." He stood, his disappointed smell making her feel inexplicably guilty.

"I'll help you with the list," she said. "It will get done faster, and then we can—"

"No, that is all right. I still have the scar from the last time we sparred when you were angry."

She grimaced. "I'm still sorry."

"That was not an admonishment. It was my fault for being careless."

He smelled less distressed, but she flapped a hand at him anyway. "You take aft, I'll take fore. If we finish early, we can hit each other until I feel better. Deal?"

"Terms accepted." He left, humming softly. Another smell snuck in under the others, dark and vaguely fruity. It had started a few months back and it was driving her up the wall. She'd even had the scent translators installed to supplement the rest of her translation suite, but the damn things were still learning.

Well, she'd figure it out eventually. Eva grinned, feeling cheerful despite herself, and got to work.

The inspection took longer than expected, so they were almost to the Gate before Eva finally crawled out of the last access tunnel and went back to her cabin to change her clothes.

It had been a long time since her every waking moment was spent in a spacesuit. Its impermeable quick-rigid material doubled as armor in a pinch, and the isohelmet that popped into existence with a thought could deflect projectiles and scrub bad air. And, of course, there were the gravboots, perfect for kicking asses when she didn't care what anyone's name was.

She'd just finished pulling on her boots and activating the pressure seals when Min poked her voice in.

"Hey, Cap, you have a call on the emergency frequency."

Eva froze. The only people who knew that frequency were her crew, who were all on the ship, and her family, who had barely spoken to her for years. A tickle of unease slid up her back like phantom fingers.

"Send it in here, and give me privacy," she said, sitting on the lone chair near the closet.

The lights in the room dimmed to allow a better view of the holo image that projected from her closet door. At first, nothing happened, and Eva leaned forward as if she could reach into the transmitter and pull the person through.

Then, a crackle of static appeared, formless and vague. Eva's eyes strained to turn the visual gibberish into a face or a body.

"Captain Eva-Benita Caridad Larsen Alvarez y Coipel de Innocente," a voice said. It sounded gravelly, like it was being modulated.

"Who is this?" Eva demanded. Not many people knew her whole name, and she'd dropped Larsen permanently after her father—

"I am an agent of The Fridge," the voice said. "We have apprehended your sister, Marisleysis Honoria Larsen Alvarez y Coipel de Innocente, and will hold her until her ransom is paid."

The Fridge? The intergalactic crime syndicate? Yeah, right. And she was a secret Martian princess with millions in frozen assets.

"Fuck you," she said. "Prove it." This couldn't be real. It had to be some twisted joke. But they knew her name, the emergency frequency—

The quality of the sound changed, and a blurry image of her sister took the place of the static. "Eva, it's Mari. Please, you have to help me."

She sounded scared, and Mari had never been scared of anything except her wild little sister getting lost or hurt. Eva's stomach shriveled like a freeze-dried fruit.

"They said to tell you something no one else knows but us. Remember when you were eight, and I was eleven, and you climbed into Abuelo's closet and found his gun safe?"

The memory rose in Eva's mind. She'd thought she would be able to crack the code, because she'd seen a holovid where someone did it and it looked so easy.

"You couldn't get it open, and you accidentally pulled the shelf down and everything fell, and you didn't want to get in trouble. I never told anyone, Eva. Never."

Mari had told their mom that Eva was with her the whole time, reading about alien cultures. Abuelo had said something about shoddy construction, fixed the shelf, and forgotten all about it.

Mari always did have her back, even when Eva didn't deserve it.

"I'm not buying this," Eva said, but she was already half-convinced. Only a handful of people knew the frequency they were using. Spoofing someone's identity wasn't impossible, but only her family used their full name—it was shortened on legal documents, and Eva operated under enough aliases to form her own fútbol team. She also doubted Mari would have a reason to randomly drop that story on someone, then for them to concoct a wild plan to use it like this.

Mari's face faded to static and the modulated voice returned. "You may ask one question for proof."

One question. She had to make it good. What was something only Mari would know, something that couldn't be found on the q-net quickly?

"How did you almost die while you were doing your dissertation?" Eva asked.

Mari's face returned, her voice trembling. "The Proarkhe ruins on Jarr. I still have the scar. A cabrón giant spider took a bite out of my leg while I was trying to dig up an impossibly well-preserved metallic container. Mom was so mad, she almost didn't come to my graduation ceremony."

Mierda, mojón y porquería. That was Mari, no doubt.

"Are you all right?" Eva asked, feigning a bravado she hardly felt, but Mari disappeared and the sound changed again.

"Your pilot will be provided with coordinates at which you will meet your assigned handler," the modulated voice said. "You will receive more information when you arrive. If you ever want to see your sister again, you will do exactly as you are instructed. Tell no one, or she will be terminated."

The transmission flickered off. Eva stared at the space behind the projector in disbelief.

Equal parts rage, fear, and determination fought for supremacy inside her. How dare these assholes fuck with her family, her flesh and blood? Especially Mari, sweet Mari, who used to save snails from hot sidewalks because she couldn't stand the thought of someone stepping on them. What if Eva couldn't do what they asked, and they killed her sister? How would she ever face her mother again?

No, she wouldn't let that happen. She'd play their game, bide her time, and figure out some way to free Mari in case honor among thieves turned out to be less applicable to kidnappers.

Min spoke through the speakers. "Cap, someone sent me coordinates for—"

"Set a course."

"But Cap, what about Letis?"

"Forget Letis," she snapped. Then, more calmly than she felt, she added, "Don't worry, it'll be fine. Send those coordinates to my commlink, please?"

Tell no one, the message had instructed. How would they even know? Was that a chance she was willing to take? Not especially. Acid climbed her throat at the thought of lying to her crew. Maybe this was all a setup, and she could blow in, bust heads, and get back to her real problems.

The Fridge was like the chupacabra: everyone knew of someone's cousin's friend's acquaintance whose goat had been sucked dry, but no one really believed it. Secret organizations didn't actually go around kidnapping people and throwing them into cryo, or running illegal labs and asteroid mining operations, or stealing artifacts from ancient civilizations for mysterious evil purposes. Only conspiracy theorists like Leroy believed in that nonsense.

And yet. Her father had warned her about The Fridge years ago, after one of his best clients suddenly sold every spaceship they owned and ran off to casa carajo. They wouldn't tell him why—got extremely nervous when he asked—but he'd looked into it. He'd found people going on mystery vacations or suddenly quitting their jobs, their loved ones liquidating assets or, if they were big shots, throwing their weight behind causes or projects they hadn't previously supported. Some of those people came back from wherever they had disappeared to, only to move away for good after a few cycles. Some stayed gone, and some, well . . . Not every culture published obituaries. Still, he told Eva, it was more void than substance. It might all be coincidence.

Also, he had told her not to fuck with The Fridge.

She stared at the fish tank on the panel above her bed, her only real luxury, and a reminder of the family she had left behind when she went into the black for good. One fish for every family member: a brilliant green one for her mother, dark red for her father, striped ones for her grandparents on each side, yellow and blue respectively.

And one for her sister, of course. Indigo and black, it tended to hide among the rocks and corals, avoiding the light. Mari, who finished schooling two years early. Mari, the brilliant historian and scientist with the cushy government job studying ancient ruins. Mari, the quiet one, whereas Eva was like their mother, loud and outspoken, quick to laugh but also quick to shout.

But Eva remembered their last big fight: her at twenty-three, thinking she knew everything there was to know about everything since she'd already been in space for five years. Mari telling her to stop being so selfish, to stop letting their father drag her into his line of work, the work that had pushed their mother into leaving the man after a decade of marriage even though it meant raising two young kids on her own. "Think of Mom," Mari had said. "You're breaking her heart." Eva had stood there and let her scream, let her vent, like she was a barnacle and her sister was a wave. She'd even let Mari hit her, once, and then she'd left.

Mari had been right, of course. And here Eva was, trying to do what she'd been told so many years ago, only to have this happen. Mari would see the irony, perhaps, but she wouldn't like it. She'd always thought Eva had it in her to do better, to *be* better, and Eva had resented the endless pushing.

Still, maybe she could unload the cats, get paid, keep to the straight and narrow path.

And maybe she'd find a café that sold some actual pastelitos de queso. Or a chupacabra.

The Fridge was bad news. She couldn't drag her crew into this, but until her handler gave her instructions, she could only guess at what to expect. What a genteel word for it: "handler." As if she were some famous person who needed a combination supervisor and assistant. Nicer than "master," or "controller," or "overseer." And yet it made her feel like an animal instead of a celebrity.

Maybe those cats had the right idea after all, wanting to escape their cage.

There was a polite knock at the door, and Eva realized she

had stood up at some point and taken a fighting stance, hands curled into fists. She forced herself to relax and sent a mental command at the door to open it.

Vakar stood outside, his gloves back on. "I was thinking, are you sure you want me to go with Leroy? I can find anything we need myself, and he can—"

"Never mind," Eva said. "Something came up. We're diverting to . . ." She checked her commlink. "Station U039F." Even as she finished saying it, she stifled a groan of realization.

"Omicron?" Vakar asked incredulously.

"You've been to worse places. Can you stock up there?"

"Probably. Are you well?" He smelled of incense. Concern.

She met his gray-blue eyes long enough to feel like she'd licked a battery, then looked away.

"I'm fine," she said.

"Are you sure?"

"As the night is long." She didn't feel like sparring anymore, but she plastered on a smile. "Come on, your ass needs kicking and I've got my boots on."

The incense smell strengthened even as he stepped aside to let her take the lead. She thought of her one time in a church, with her abuela, that heady, dizzy sense of something watching her, invisible and dangerous.

Just as she had then, she stared at her feet and prayed.

Chapter 2

WOMAN IN THE FRIDGE

Eva scowled at the collection of cats that had taken over the cargo bay. It wasn't as if they needed to be confined anymore, since they weren't going anywhere soon, and Min said they weren't getting into trouble like they had before. But more importantly, right now, it gave her something to look at besides her crew standing in front of her.

"I need to run an errand," she told them. "I'm not sure how long it will take, but you're all free to have a few hours of shore leave after any resupplying. Make sure your comms are open. Any questions?"

There was a moment of silence as they traded glances, and Vakar's incense smell took on an acrid cigarette note.

"I am fit to burst with questions," Pink said, "because this all stinks to high heaven."

Eva wished she'd spent more time coming up with a good

cover story instead of sparring with Vakar, as enjoyable as that had been. Of course Pink, of all people, would be suspicious; they'd served together under Tito, left together, freelanced together . . . Pink could see right through Eva, even without her cybernetic eye picking up on any subtle physical signs of bullshitting. And after Tito, they had promised each other: no lies.

Her conviction wavered. Choosing the sister she had barely spoken to for years over the crew who'd lived with her the whole time felt slimy, but she didn't even know what The Fridge wanted yet. For now, this was a small lie that could save a life. Pink was a doctor, so saving lives was high on her priority list. She would understand.

Probably. Hopefully.

"It could be something, or nothing," Eva said. "I don't want to say too much yet."

"You dragged us all the way to Omicron for a big ol' question mark?" Pink crossed her arms and jutted out a hip.

"Omicron isn't that bad."

Leroy raised his hand. "Last time we were here, someone hacked my tattoos. I was walking around with 'delicious meat candy' on my arms for hours and wondering why everybody was laughing at me."

"Right, okay, but Vakar was able to—"

"You got arrested for drunk dancing on the station commander's table in Limbo," Pink added.

"In my defense," Eva said, "I did not know that was Armida's table. Also, that was my fault, not Omicron's."

Vakar smelled incredulous. "There was a plague lockdown in the lower levels. They almost did not permit us to leave the station."

"Yes, but—"

"Someone tried to sneak on board and steal the ship," Min said, her tone less cheerful than usual. "I had to set them on fire!"

Ugh, the smell had taken ages to clear the filters. "Fine, yes, Omicron isn't my favorite, either. If you want to stay here while I conduct my business, allá tú. Otherwise, get the supplies we need, take your shore leave, and be careful. I'll fill you all in later."

"You certainly will," Pink said, both a threat and a promise. She stepped forward and held out a hand, which Eva took, drawing the woman in for their usual hand slaps and fist bumps. They'd been doing it for so long, Eva managed the complicated routine on autopilot, though the final hip bump was less well-aimed than usual.

The cat leader rubbed against her leg and looked up at her, eyes eerily intelligent. "Miau," it said.

"Stow it, mija," Eva replied. "I'm still selling your ass as soon as someone answers Min's ad."

The creature sauntered off, tail raised, its prim little butthole suggesting it did not believe her any more than her crew did.

Eva stepped into the umbilicus that led from the ship to the dock of Omicron. It ran the usual decontamination protocols and tweaked her blood-gas nanites as she rechecked her gear. Pistol, knife, garrote. Gravboots. She doubted the handler— there was that stupid word again—would be there to kill her, because why bother? If Eva didn't comply, her sister was a popsicle. Or dead.

Or worse, if the stories were true.

She checked the coordinates on her commlink and overlaid a map of the space station. The contact was waiting in a q-net café near the least grubby arm of the ever-rotating spindle. Easy to access the galactic quantumnet from there in an instant, always full of people coming and going, and with food that probably wouldn't give her immediate gut problems. And that arm tended to be more heavily guarded than the others; the higher class of criminals were nothing if not oppressively polite.

To get there, she had to walk through the main merchant drag with its collection of ramshackle junk stores and food carts and secondhand purveyors of parts that magically fell off passing ships. The shops backed up against the walls of the station, which rose about three stories to accommodate the taller species that sometimes wandered through, like the occasional large todyk. None of them were around this cycle—probably off negotiating breeding contracts instead of slumming it in fringe space—but it was still crowded with off-duty miners, smugglers, mercs, and the station rats who'd grown up in the nooks and crannies a place like this inevitably had.

Humans were in the minority, as usual; Omicron attracted more buasyr, with their four arms and multitude of eyes, or doglike truateg, or furry chuykrep waggling their proboscises at everything as they waddled around. There were some kloshians, which were the closest thing to humans in the galaxy so far except for their color-changing skin, tentacle hair and pointed teeth, but no quennians aside from Vakar. They rarely seemed to venture to these grubby stations for some reason; maybe it was the excess of confusing, contradictory smells. Then there were the toad-like vroak, the eac, a few tentacled ahirk . . .

Eva had loved the novelty of it all when she was younger, exploring new places and meeting people from galaxies that would be impossibly far away without Gates to close the distance. Every time she touched down on a planet or strolled into a space station, it was like she'd unlocked a door, shined a light onto a dark place on her personal map, checked off an accomplishment on a secret never-ending list. Back then, the universe was still huge and amazing, a present waiting to be unwrapped. In truth, it was still huge and amazing, but she had seen too much in the fifteen years since she'd left home to become a spacer. A present was a treat on your birthdate, but when you got presents every single cycle, it became harder and harder to be excited by what was inside.

Also, a lot of the presents ended up being a box of shit wrapped in more shit.

Eva arrived, blinking a few times as the sign outside was translated from its original language: QUANTUMNET CAFÉ, STANDARD RATES. The q-net access was restricted to small booths with chairs and an array of available jacks depending on the user's commlink model and physical preference. There was also an actual café component, with tables and seats, and a servbot floating around taking orders while the customers waited for their turns in the data closets.

Eva sighed, wishing she were there to see what commodities were trading for, or to meet a client discreetly. Then again, she rarely made it to this area, since she usually had better things to do than tirar peos más alto que el culo. It worked for other people, pretending to a level of success and wealth they didn't actually have, but she preferred to manage expectations—even if they were only her own.

She didn't know who to look for, so she took a seat at one of the tables, overlooking a light installation that changed colors and configurations every few seconds. She wondered who was responsible for it, and how long ago it had been installed. If anyone still remembered.

The universe was full of that kind of stuff: beautiful, strange, and mostly forgotten. Her sister, the historian and scientist, loved it all. Eva supposed she did, too, in her own way.

She tried to relax, letting the sounds of the other patrons wash over her like waves on some distant shore. She caught a few snippets of conversation here and there—mostly gossip about people she didn't know doing stuff she had no reason to care about. Colonies starting up or shutting down. Ships going missing, probably because of pirate attacks. Cops chasing criminals. Soldiers getting medals. Humans trying to finagle a seat on the High Council of the Benevolent Organization of Federated Astrostates—BOFA for short, to Eva's eternal amusement—which was the biggest coalition of star systems in the galaxy for now. They'd been around for a few thousand years, but that was a fraction of a second in the cosmic calendar, and the stability of their rules and regulations was only as good as their ability to enforce them.

The current human government was eating that shit with a spoon—the most cohesive one, anyway, given how far-flung humanity was since discovering Gates. A seat on the High Council meant a bigger voice in BOFA affairs, which meant power, which meant money for someone other than her. Humans had only recently gotten a representative elected to the massive General Assembly, and Eva had voted for the other lady, so her interest in galactic politics was limited to whether it made her life harder.

As if most of the species in this galaxy gave a whistle what humans thought about anything. Sounded like they were getting close to the council seat, though, trying to use some commander named Schafer as leverage. The name was familiar—right, Leroy had posters of the lady in his bunk. Spacer military brat who saved some colony from raiders, single-handed if you believed the stories.

Eva didn't, but maybe that was jealousy talking.

A shadow fell across Eva, moving as the one who cast it sat down. Eva turned her head slowly, faking a relaxation she didn't feel. Her new companion was a tuann, green as an emerald, the layers of their head ruff lying like a wimple around their narrow skull. Their mouth was a set of overlapping folds, like the petals of an unopened rose, and they had no eyes. They wore thin clothing that could best be described as a dress, though they seemed to have multiple pieces that clung together by a mechanism Eva couldn't identify. The fabric was transparent in places, opaque in others, and had a pattern that shifted as she tried to make sense of it.

"Captain Larsen," they said. Their soft voice was amplified by a device around their neck, and sounded like the rustling of leaves.

"I go by Innocente, not Larsen." The tuann had no hands, not that Eva would have wanted to shake them under the circumstances.

"Apologies are tendered. Pholise Pravo is my personal identifier. Your case was assigned to me."

Eva laughed. "My 'case'? You people are something else."

Pholise sat up taller, as if whatever passed for their spine had stiffened.

The servbot hovered over, round and white with a single huge lens. "Your order?"

"Cortadito," Eva said.

The servbot didn't move, but its lens dilated as if in confusion.

Eva sighed and rattled off the chemical formula, hoping she hadn't forgotten it, and that the translators would get it right. Espresso, milk, and sugar were easy enough to find in certain human settlements—though coffee beans had almost gone extinct at one point, and nonhumans had a strange obsession with keeping cows as pets without milking them—but everywhere else she had to rely on the whims of molecular chemical gastronomy.

"Nothing will be had by me," Pholise said, and the servbot flew off. "The instructions of our superiors are to be conveyed, that a mutually beneficial relationship might be entered into."

Our superiors, hah. "And I'm here to convey that I don't have any money." Eva's stomach turned as she said it, but it was the truth. All it had taken was a few bad trips and an increasingly depressing choice to do only legal work. "Have you tried asking my dad, maybe?" She hated to throw him into the proverbial rocket booster, but he could afford to take the heat.

Their head ruff fluttered. "Your male progenitor was contacted first. His assets have already been included in the fee calculation."

Madre de dios, Eva thought. Tito had said her dad was retired from all but his standard mostly legal ship trading, which was why Tito had gone freelance. But either dear old Pete was worse off than she thought, or The Fridge was milking this for all it was worth. "And my mother?"

"The assets and limited professional exploitation potential of Regina Alvarez were deemed insufficient to warrant her involvement."

That didn't surprise Eva. While her mom had always been frugal, there was only so much you could save up on a galactic bank auditor's salary. And "limited professional exploitation potential" meant either her mom's job was too closely watched for them to take a chance asking her to do illegal work on their behalf, or they had figured out she had a diamond-hard reputation for honesty. She'd sooner get spaced than lie, though if it meant saving Mari's life, maybe . . . It was a relief to know she wasn't involved, at least.

"What do you want, then? My cargo? It's not much, but it's yours. My ship is—"

"Your ship is considered less valuable than your service, Captain Innocente."

Eva froze. There it was. The Fridge didn't want money from her, because they already knew she didn't have it. They wanted someone to do their dirty work. They wanted indentured servitude.

"Eat shit and die," Eva said. "I'm not working for you filthy bastards. I won't even work for my own father, and he's a saint compared to you."

The servbot returned with her drink, placing it on the table in front of her and blinking red to indicate it had deducted the cost from her account. She ignored it, and the cortadito, such as it might be.

"If you do not, then your sister will remain in cryo sleep until after your demise, and will then be awakened and put to work mining an asteroid until her own conclusion." The tuann said this mechanically, as if they had rehearsed it many times. No emotion, no inflection. Just that amplified susurration.

Eva wanted to punch them until her fist bled.

There had to be a way to wriggle out of this, to convince them she wasn't worth their time.

"Why me?" she asked. "I deliver stuff. There are plenty of other people with bigger ships, faster ones. People with fancy guns and armor. People who don't care where their money comes from."

"Those people are not the Hero of Garilia. Or the Butcher, as some would say."

Eva recoiled, looking around to see whether anyone was listening. As if Omicron weren't full of people talking about worse shit.

"The fuck do you know about that?" Eva snarled. Even the Garilians had kept a lid on it, for a variety of reasons. "Who have you been talking to?"

"Others are responsible for conducting research," Pholise replied. "Their sources of information are not known to me. But it is believed you are adequate to the tasks that will be set to you."

Garilia. Madre de dios. If they knew about that, of all things, then playing the meek freight jockey was a waste of time. Garilia was the reason she and Pink had finally cut ties with Tito, the reason she'd stopped talking to her own father for years, and she'd never wash the stink of that fucking mess off her soul. She touched the scar on her cheek, the one she'd gotten that cycle, then lowered her hand as casually as she could.

She thought quickly. "I can't run a ship by myself, you know. And I can't run it on no money. While I'm busy playing your disgusting game, I'm not getting paid, and I can only buy so much fuel on credit."

Pholise sat lower. Relaxing? "Compensation will be provided for your services. How much will be put toward your obligation is for you to determine."

"And my crew?"

"Your crew is your own concern, Captain Innocente, so long as you do not disclose the nature of your business. Our superiors are confident in your ability to execute their instructions competently."

The light installation near their table had frozen, by either design or malfunction, forming what seemed to be words in the shadows on the wall. She blinked rapidly, her translators straining, but it was only shadows.

"It's not like I have a choice," she muttered.

"A choice is always available," Pholise said. "It must be noted that The Fridge is not in the habit of procuring assets who are willing to make an undesirable choice."

"I'll bet they aren't."

"If your cooperation has been secured, our superiors must be informed. Subsequent assignments are typically issued swiftly." They stood, their shadow once again falling over Eva. "May you benefit from a surfeit of good fortune, Captain Innocente." With that, the tuann left, their movement nearly as quiet as their voice.

Eva sat in silence, and after a few moments, the light sculpture began to shift again, to a deep crimson. She reached for her coffee and took a sip.

"Me cago en diez," she muttered. "This is actually good."

Life was never fair.

Eva left the café a few minutes later. She fielded a message from Min about a buyer for the cats ("Cap, they want to know if the kittens are fresh? Do I have to answer?"), then wandered back to the seedier side of the station.

The following hour was spent trying to murder her sobriety with cheap sim-rum and something that tasted almost like soda in a grimy cantina whose name roughly translated to "Stay Hydrated" in a language Eva didn't recognize. She'd been there once or twice before; it was about the size of her ship's cargo bay, with a row of self-serve machines dispensing whatever fluid combinations the tech was capable of synthesizing, for the cost of materials plus a "reasonable" surcharge. A long bar on one side had seats for bipeds, while smaller tables accommodated other physiologies, all kept moderately tidy by an automated hydrosonic system that only occasionally glitched and sprayed cleaning fluid into its customers' faces. With the base layer of acrid decontaminant, the competing drink smells that varied in toxicity levels, and the natural aromas of creatures who didn't communicate with body odor, her still-learning scent translators had given up trying to keep the conversations straight.

A single attendant who doubled as a bouncer sat in one corner, wearing the slack-jawed expression of someone linked into the q-net or a game instead of paying attention to the world around them. The other patrons either sensed Eva was in a foul mood, or were caught up in their own personal dramas and had no interest in hers, so they left her alone with an empty seat on either side of her at the bar.

All except for the guy with the big bodyguards who swaggered in like the second coming. He was bipedal, greenish-gray, and his suit made him look muscular, but he was maybe a meter tall, with a face like an excited anglerfish. Eva's tastes encompassed a broad range of humanoids, but she wasn't into big teeth, so she didn't give him a second look.

Her forehead was finally starting to feel numb when the guy climbed into the chair next to hers. She assumed he wasn't smiling like a creep on purpose, but it was still annoying.

"Hello, human female," he said. "Your facial scarring is very exotic. I desire to solicit you for sexual gratification."

Eva slow-blinked at him. "M'not a sex worker," she mumbled.

"Your profession does not concern me," he replied. "Only your ability to pleasure me to my satisfaction."

Normally she ignored people like him, or she assumed cultural differences and cut them some slack—humans had a reputation for being willing to fuck anything, even if the truth was more complicated. But between psychic cats and kidnapped sisters and her own booze-addled temper, she was ready to unload on someone. If he wanted to paint a target on himself, who was she to stop him?

"My name is Captain Eva Innocente," she slurred. "You can call me Captain, which is safe, or you can shut up, which is safer."

Maybe it didn't translate correctly, or the tonal nuances were lost, but the guy didn't budge. Robotic hands gripped a metal flask—his own, presumably, since the dispensers used recyclables—which he used to pour trickles of fluid into his enormous eyes. "That is a splendid name. I am the Glorious Apotheosis. I want to rub my sex organs on you."

Eva couldn't help it: she laughed, loud and hard. Drunk jerks were bad enough, but this guy, in this cycle, was a rain of Jovian diamonds.

Glorious wiggled his teeth and his skin flashed bright green. "Are you making a mockery of my advances in a condescending manner?"

"Claro que sí, mijo. Get spaced."

"For challenging my supremacy, you must now be legally bound to my—" The translation came in as "collection of sexual objects and broodmares" instead of "harem" or something similar, which told her everything she needed to know about how he planned to treat her.

Her buzz receded with distressing speed, which doubly sucked since she had neither the time nor the money to get it back. "You're not my type. Take a walk out an airlock."

His bodyguards began to earn their paychecks by looming with gusto. She considered reaching for her pistol, but if she shot first she'd be liable for any damages and disposal fees.

"You dare?" Glorious asked. "I will own you, you worthless offspring incubator." He was neon green and black now, with iridescent lines between his eyes. And that grin. That big, shit-eating grin.

"Eat. Me." Eva raised her middle finger like a beacon.

"Guards!" Glorious cried. "Seize the human!"

She didn't even stand, just leaned against the bar and kicked him in the teeth with her gravboots. He toppled off the stool with a squeal, landing on the sticky floor in a heap. One of his goons bent to retrieve him while the other made a deep croaking sound and launched himself at her. She sidestepped, using his momentum to drive her knee into his stomach in the hopes of hitting something vital. Given his sharp wail, it seemed to work.

No me diga, Eva thought. I don't have time for this shit.

Before the goon she'd hit could recover, she pivoted away and ran out the door.

With any luck, Pink had finished refueling, and Vakar and Leroy had found any necessary supplies instead of, well, doing what she was doing. Min should still be on *La Sirena Negra*. Eva shot them a quick location-query ping as she jogged away from the cantina, toward the bustling market area.

Pink and Leroy were back on the ship, but not a whisper from Vakar. She tried to tell herself not to worry, that he was fine, but her nerves were already jangling too loudly to be soothed. She pinged him again, then again, and was just about to set up a timed auto-ping when he finally responded.

((Errand. Surprise.))

The hell did that mean? Eva was in no mood for cryptic shit.

Then again, she had told him he could have shore leave. It wouldn't be nice of her to drag him back now.

Since when are you worried about being nice to Vakar?, a tiny voice whispered in her head.

I'm nice to all my crew, she thought. Not just the cute quennians. Super nice. And the longer he took, the longer she could delay having to lie to him about why she was going to fire everyone.

Because she was going to, wasn't she? She couldn't tell them about Mari, not if it meant risking her sister's life, and she couldn't drag them into her problems. The thought made her queasy. That, or the questionable alcohol she'd been drinking, or the adrenaline rush of kicking someone in the face and running away. Or all of the above.

She decided to head back to that q-net café and sober up with another cortadito. She could wait there until Vakar—

"You will attend me, unworthy vermin," a voice boomed over the station's loudspeakers.

She recognized that asshead tone. It was Glorious. How was he doing that? Nobody but station security should have access to those systems. The people around her seemed to be thinking the same thing, because the usually loud main merchant drag fell almost silent.

"I demand the immediate apprehension of the human captain Eva the Innocent," he continued. "Fail to obey my command, and my fleet will convey your ashes to the womb of the blessed mother void."

Yeah, right. The various species' equivalent of laughter rippled through the assembled crowds. Omicron got threats like that all the time. If he were actually dangerous, the station alarms would have gone off already.

The instant that thought completed itself, emergency lights began to flash in different spectrums. Alarms piped through the speakers, a series of triple notes along with a curt message: "Security threat. Please proceed to the nearest evacuation facilities."

Eva's jaw fell open. He was threatening to kill everyone? Thousands of people? Because she wouldn't fuck him? Alabao . . . She had no words. And he wanted them to catch her and turn her over to him? No chance.

Why the fuck did you give him your name, comemierda?, Eva thought bitterly.

"On second thought, no coffee," she muttered. Time to make like a flea and jump.

Chapter 3

UNIVERSAL CONSTANTS

The crowds around Eva morphed into a screaming mass of flesh, flailing tentacles, and fluids from the more sensitive types. Visitors, mostly, the miners and smugglers and pleasure-seekers who didn't see much action in their daily lives; this wasn't the first time the station had been threatened, so those who lived here were slower to panic, and the freelance mercs with any experience finished their drinks and shopping before they even thought about evacuating. The stores that had four walls and a door locked down quickly, but the vendors with carts were caught in the tide, trying to move to the sides of the tall corridor without being knocked over. The commlink skimmers and warez peddlers and other station rats disappeared into their hidey-holes, taking whatever they could grab in the confusion while the security mercs were conspicuously absent to guide traffic flow.

Eva sighed at the churning river of motion and odor that stood between her and the docks. Better get moving.

Pings flew in from her crew, but instead of responding, she sent an all-channel disembark signal with a ten-minute timer. Ignoring a merchant's high-pitched whine, she clambered onto the second level of his shop and jumped to the next one over, hopping from one scrap-metal roof to another until she couldn't go farther. With a click, she set her gravboots humming and leaped to the adjacent wall, clinging like a spider.

It was slower walking this way, since her muscles were engaged in keeping her vertical relative to her feet, but at least she didn't have to deal with the howling press below. Still, she pulled her pistol from its holster under her coat as a precaution. Glorious's goons were nowhere in sight, but she had a feeling they weren't going to say hello before making a grab for her.

"Captain Innocente," said a voice on the ground.

Eva caught the eye, singular, of Gargula Sinh, second-in-command to the administrator of the station, Armida. He gestured for her to come down with one of the four arms of his exoskeleton.

"Can't talk now, Garg," she said, still walking. "Some maniac is threatening to blow up the station."

"Which he has said he will not do if you are brought to his ship," Garg said, blinking his inner eyelid. "Come now, Captain, even you cannot be so cold as to trade thousands of innocent lives for your own."

"I'm as innocent as they are." He wasn't wrong, though. Hell, if she were in his place, she might have—no, this was ridiculous. She had to get to her crew and get gone. "How about you power up your fancy station defenses instead of lecturing me about math?" she snapped.

Garg flipped a mechanical hand in her direction, and one

of his mercs sauntered over with a mag knocker. He rested it against the wall, where it hummed, clicked twice, then hammered a piston at the metal, sending a gravitomagnetic pulse up to Eva's black-red boots that neutralized them. She fell in a heap but came to her feet quickly, pistol raised. The odds of her winning a firefight against so many were bad, but—

"Isolate her," Garg said. Another merc held out an isosphere that projected a cone of blue light, surrounding her in a shimmering bubble that would protect her from harm even as it kept her from doing more than running futilely like a hamster in a wheel. She could stick herself to the ground if she activated her gravboots, but they would just use the knocker again to move her.

"You can't sell me off, you bastard!" Eva shouted.

"In fairness, Captain, I am not profiting monetarily from this transaction." His security merc dragged her along like a fish in a frictionless net, her bubble tethered to the sphere he held by a thin cord of energy.

The bustling plaza was now practically empty as almost everyone had retreated to their respective ships or escape pods. Some folks lingered, apathetic or opportunistic; Garg ignored them, though once or twice one of his mercs fired a warning shot near a looter.

A blob-like fellow to their left extended a tentacular mass and turned charred vermin over a spit, where juice or fat escaped to sizzle on the hot metal beneath. Eva had heard of her ancestors cooking lechón outside in a hurricane, but this was a whole other level of ridiculous. Then again, she couldn't move much, but maybe if she timed things right . . .

She flopped onto her back, aiming her gravboots at the guy's cooker as they passed. Sure enough, it was pulled closer, smacking into the bottom of her feet—not that she could feel the heat through the shield.

"What are you—" said the merc holding her, followed by an inhuman screech as she rotated and hit him in the head with the cooker. He dropped the isosphere, which bounced twice against the ground and rolled away, the blue shield around her winking out of existence. Eva fell onto her butt and scuttled around a corner as the merc pinwheeled his arms.

She didn't wait to find out whether they'd seen her crawl away. Eva raced toward the end of the alley, taking a left at a T-junction and then another left farther down, assuming it would bring her somewhere closer to the docks. What it did, however, was lead her to a ramp that went down to a lower level of the station, where the smells of organic waste mingled like a combination toilet and perfume store. Exhaust vents from the floors above piped in more exciting aromas of fear and anger, as well as the increasingly muted sounds of escaping ship crews like hers.

"Unworthy seekers of death," boomed Glorious through the speakers again. "My patience evaporates like the seed of an ice flower in starlight." He paused as some transmission burbled through his comm, too dim for Eva's translators to pick up. Status report? Probably Armida trying to calm him down. It must not have been enough, because as soon as it finished, he said, "Your incompetence will be your doom. As a token of my ill will, I give you the gift of decimation."

Moments later, the station keeled sideways like a drunk, sending Eva stumbling into the wall that was now the floor. The alarm shifted to a series of triple notes, and the emergency message changed: "Shield efficacy is diminishing. Proceed to evacuation centers."

"Madre de dios," she murmured. "All this because I turned him down?"

A few half-hearted exit signs flickered on in floors and walls.

Meanwhile, she pulled up the map on her commlink, which indicated that the docks were farther along the corridor she'd entered. She pinged her crew with a stern ((Stand by)) and started to run again. She didn't want to get them killed waiting for her, but she wasn't keen on being stranded, either.

And where the hell was Vakar? If he died on this station, she was going to kill him.

A series of response pings came through from Pink. ((Can't leave. Ships maglocked. Armida's orders.))

Eva cursed thoroughly and with relish. Their ship's own highly illegal mag knocker had been damaged a year earlier, and she hadn't gotten it fixed because other expenses had taken priority. And now here she was, stuck on a shitty backwater space station being blown to pieces by a jerk with delusions of grandeur, while a bunch of mercs chased after her with an isosphere and—

A mag knocker. Convenient. But how to get it away from them?

She started back up the ramp to where she'd left Garg. Naturally, the mercs weren't there; must have gone down the other branch of the junction and ended up somewhere else entirely. And that stupid alarm was getting on her last nerve.

"Captain, what are you doing?"

She spun around, pistol raised. Standing in the middle of the empty bazaar, holding a small black box like a lost street vendor, was Vakar.

She wasn't sure whether to kiss him or kick him in the crotch. Not that his crotch was sensitive; his genitals were closer to his abdominal area. And they weren't external, per se.

Why was she standing there like a comemierda thinking about his genitals?

"What are you doing?" she retorted. "Where the hell have you been?"

He released a smell like fresh-cut grass. Bashful. "You were so upset about the cats, I . . . That is, I thought perhaps . . ."

His box was the kind of indestructible material used in vaults or to protect fragile cargo. "Vakar, did you get me a present?"

His palps twitched. If her heart weren't mechanical, it might have skipped a beat.

"We have to get to *La Sirena Negra*," she said. "She's locked down, but I have a plan. Most of a plan. Garg was chasing me with his mag knocker, and I lost him, but now I need to find him. Any ideas?"

Vakar wagged his head in the equivalent of a shrug. "If I were chasing someone trying to escape a space station, and I lost them, I would simply—"

"Wait by their ship," Eva finished. "Of course. Come on, let's get off this hunk of scrap." She ran toward the docks, Vakar beside her.

"Is there anything I should know?" Vakar asked as they went.

"Like what?"

"Who is so angry with you that they took over the station communications and are attacking with disproportionate force?"

"Some comemierda I shut down in a bar. The Glorious Apotheosis."

"Is that who it is?"

"Yeah." She rolled her eyes. "What kind of a name is that?"

"It is hereditary," Vakar said. "He is emperor of a thousand worlds in the Triskel cluster. Very powerful, and rich."

"And an asshole. He wants me for his collection of, uh, broodmares? Something shitty like that."

Vakar didn't respond, but his angry wildfire smell gave her step an extra bounce.

She heard the crowd before she saw it, all the people who had rushed to escape now crushed together on the docks, screaming at security mercs who ignored them or waved their weapons to maintain an order getting more ragged by the minute. When the station had listed, many of them had fallen onto each other, leading to awkward tangles and fights.

As frosting on the crap cake, a few gas pipes had cracked in the middle of it all. Helium, Eva guessed, because everyone with lung equivalents sounded like a hamster having a temper tantrum. And methane, because it smelled like the hamsters had all eaten beans for lunch.

La Sirena Negra was about five ships down on the left, but Garg and his mercs weren't there. They could be hiding in the crowd, or watching from the control room, or they could have boarded her ship to ambush her. Luckily for her, Eva was a head shorter than many of the people milling about; even the ones who normally slithered around were standing on tip-tentacle to look more intimidating. Anyone trying to find her from above would be hard-pressed to see her.

She ducked and weaved as best she could through whatever gaps she could find, sometimes making room with a well-placed elbow or stomp. Every few steps she made sure Vakar was behind her, and as if by magic, he always was. Him and his indestructible box.

A present for her. Hot damn.

Four ships to go.

The loudspeakers crackled. "Insolent waste disposal units, you believe your inferior defenses will overcome the might of the Glorious Apotheosis? You shall tremble at my awesome power before the black envelops you."

Chunks of debris pelted the station, few large enough to cause damage, but with disturbing frequency. More screaming commenced in earnest, piercing Eva's ears until she sent a thought to engage her helmet. It popped into existence around her head, the outside sounds dulling to a whimper. Even the bean-fart smell disappeared once she calibrated the air filter.

Three ships to go.

The mercs abruptly lost any semblance of authority. The crowd frenzied, so that now Eva found herself unable to move forward.

Someone grabbed her hand: Vakar, whom she couldn't smell, which was more unsettling than she cared to admit. He tugged her through the crowd as if they were both ghosts. Even though she was watching him do it, she couldn't quite figure out how he managed to move people aside, to find spaces between them that hadn't appeared to exist a moment earlier. She'd have to get him to teach her that trick later.

The booth that held the lockdown controls was being attacked by a gang of pirates and residents who had found a common purpose. Anyone with a knocker had already escaped, though by the looks of things outside and the continued pitter-patter of ship pieces hitting the station shields, they hadn't gotten far.

Two ships to go.

"There she is," a voice said. "Step aside immediately."

The crowd parted around Eva and Vakar. Bobbing gently in front of *La Sirena Negra,* glowing a vibrant purple, was Armida. The administrator of Omicron rarely descended from her seat of power in—well, no one knew where it was, for security reasons. Eva had heard it was Limbo, but that was ridiculous. Nobody could administer a space station from a giant bar and strip joint.

In one swift movement, Eva found herself upside down, tightly wrapped in tentacles thin as wire but twice as strong. Vakar was grabbed by appropriately beefy goons, one for each of his arms, and dragged a few meters away.

"Captain Eva Innocente," Armida said. Her voice was smooth as a surgical knife through skin, piped directly into Eva's head since she was basically psychic gas in a suit like a huge jellyfish. "I have prepared a shuttle for your delivery to His Gloriousness. Please convey to him my gratitude for his hasty and permanent departure."

"Go fry ice," Eva retorted.

"I am sure we will miss your colorful personality," Armida replied, towing her captive along.

Eva struggled, but Armida only tightened her tentacles further. To one side, her ship's airlock; to the other, continued chaos.

Maybe Garg was right. Maybe this was the right thing to do. The station shields were weakening, who knew how many ships outside had been reduced to shrapnel, and this guy clearly wasn't going to stop until she was under his thumb, figuratively speaking. Maybe The Fridge would even let Mari go if Eva was out of the picture. All she had to do was give up, give in, and let Glorious win.

But there was Vakar, flanked by mercs, holding his ridiculous box.

She didn't even know what was inside. That made her angry. He had never bought her a present before—one just for her, not for a holiday or birthdate celebration when present-giving was a social expectation—and she wanted it. Maybe she was broke, and The Fridge owned her ass, and she was hanging upside down in the grip of a psychic alien's myriad tentacles, and a crazy megalomaniac was killing people because she laughed at him, but she wasn't going to sit around fanning her privates while there was a chance she could find out what was in that box.

That small, black and, most importantly, indestructible metal box.

Once more, with feeling, she thought. "Vakar, throw the box at the ship!"

He stared at her, blinking both sets of eyelids as if wondering what on earth she was thinking. Then, without a word, he wrestled free of the goons holding him and did as she asked.

It arced beautifully, right toward the airlock behind Armida. The mercs raised their guns but hesitated, unsure what it was. Eva powered on her boots and prayed to the Virgin for luck.

One boot pulled some of Armida's tentacles up, while the other snagged Armida's helmet as well as the box as it began to fall. It rushed toward her, but Armida's helmet container was in the way, so it hit the glass like a missile as it tried to reach her boot. A tiny spiderweb of a crack formed.

"You wretched smuggler," Armida boomed in her mind, whipping up some tentacles to pry the box away. "I should come out there and destroy you myself."

The pressure on the glass increased as the boot kept pulling at the box.

"Your fate is sealed, craven defiers of—" the Glorious Apotheosis said, but Eva didn't hear the rest, because Armida's helmet shattered into thick fragments that rained on Eva as she fell to the ground. The tentacles collapsed, and Eva immediately reached for her gun.

"Please, fool," Armida said. "You can't shoot me. I have no physical form."

Not shooting you, Eva thought, inching backward toward a broken pipe. The air shimmered in front of it.

Bean farts.

She shot the pipe, and the methane inside rushed out in a gout of flame. Armida's scream echoed in Eva's mind as her mingled gases burned.

Eva crawled toward the airlock while Garg and the other mercs struggled to put out the fire and deal with whatever other crap that jerk of a galactic emperor had been spewing. The station rocked again, and Vakar's box slid toward her a few meters away.

Vakar was past it, sprawled on the ground. The angles of his head and limbs suggested he was unconscious. Fallen? Shot?

Her anger flared again, but this time it burned cold.

She crouched and dove, rolling as she landed, her momentum taking her to within arm's reach of the box. One more step and she had it, cradling it under her arm. She ducked behind a dislodged sheet of metal to avoid shots from the mercs who were once more after her ass.

And, more importantly, between her and Vakar.

((One minute,)) she pinged to her crew.

((Maglock!)) came the reply.

((I know!)) she thought back. But she had to get Vakar on board first.

The mercs charged. Unfortunately for them, they were easier to pick off that way, and her hand was steady with purpose. She darted past their writhing forms to Vakar, whose inner lids were closed, giving his gray-blue eyes a filmy look.

"Stupid stinkbug," she whispered. With a groan, Eva maneuvered her arm under his back and strained to pull him up, but he was half again as heavy as she was. Gritting her teeth, she slammed the box onto his stomach. Right in the ol' cloaca.

He gasped, eyes opening, and gave off a pained rusty smell.

"Sorry," she said, firing a few cover shots at mercs who had spotted her again. "I'll buy you dinner next time."

With her help, he staggered to his feet, and they limped through the umbilicus to the airlock of *La Sirena Negra*. Min opened it just wide enough to let Pink and Leroy pull the two of them inside. Pink immediately began examining Vakar, flipping up her eye patch so her implant could scan for injuries.

"Fix him," Eva said. "I'm getting the maglock off."

"How?" Pink asked. "I tried to cut the cord, but it's thick as your stubborn-ass skull."

"I have a plan."

Pink took a good, long look at Eva with her cybernetic eye.

"I have components of a plan," Eva said.

"Ingredients are not a cake, Eva."

"Be ready to jump when the maglock is off," Eva said. "Fix him!"

With a wave and a thought, she reopened the door and headed back out to the station. Garg had reformed enough of a squad that when she emerged, a dozen guns were trained on her. He was holding four of them. She walked to the end of the umbilicus, arms raised.

"Here I am," she said, voice magnified by her helmet. "I've seen the error of my selfish ways. Sorry about the mess."

Garg lowered one of his guns. "That is the second most ridiculous thing I have heard this cycle. The first being that anyone would consider you worth the trouble of destroying an entire space station."

"Some people like to set your toys on fire when you won't share them," Eva said. She inched sideways, gaze flicking from Garg to the other mercs, looking for the mag knocker. If they didn't have it, this plan was dead on arrival.

"And some people share their toys in the first place," Garg said.

Eva snorted. "Bad analogy, since I'm the toy here."

"Your analogy, not mine." He held out an isosphere. "Let us finish this, Captain."

"What about my crew?"

"None of your concern. Your ship will be commandeered for any necessary repair efforts." He sneered, as much as someone without lips could. "Likely broken down for scrap."

"On second thought, I'm rather attached to her." Eva turned and dove off the edge of the platform, toward the grav barrier that separated breathable air from the vacuum of space. Cursing behind her, Garg activated the isosphere, its shimmering blue bubble surrounding her as she clicked on her gravboots.

With a clang that vibrated through her feet, she landed on the side of her ship, waving merrily at the mercs as their shots hit the field around her and fizzled or bounced off. She prayed to every saint she could think of that he had the mag knocker, that he was distracted enough to use it without thinking . . .

Garg gestured at one of his men, who brought the device forward.

This would work. It had to work. Except for one tiny problem: the isofield. She was attached to the ship now, sure, but when the mag knocker hit, she'd be screwed.

But her ship would be free, at least. Her people would escape. They still had to get away from the Glorious Pain in the Ass, but Min could handle that. And with any luck, The Fridge would give up on Mari and let her go since their newest involuntary recruit was no longer available.

If Eva had known it would end this way, she might as well have just gone with that jerk in the first place and saved the whole station a big fat plate of arroz con mango.

No, Glorious didn't deserve the satisfaction. The station didn't deserve this, either, but she wasn't the whiny baby firing plasma cannons, so anyone with grievances could take it up with him.

Keep telling yourself that, she thought, and maybe you won't feel guilty later. Assuming there is a later.

Eva patted the side of *La Sirena Negra*. Then the mag knocker hit and she drifted off, back toward Garg and the isosphere he held, as her ship lurched and began to reverse. For the longest moment of her life, she watched it go.

"Adiós, my friend," she whispered, her hand reaching out as if she could catch it.

"I always preferred 'see you soon,'" a voice said in her helmet comm. Standing in the open airlock was Vakar, his head bandaged, his hands clutching something she couldn't see.

Another isofield surrounded her, white as a pearl, and the blue isofield shorted out and vanished. Vakar reeled her in as she let out a string of curses that would have made even her mother blush. He would never let her live this down. She could practically smell his smugness already.

Eva took one last look at Garg and his mercs; for what it was worth, she hoped they'd make it out of this alive. She still flipped them off, though.

Once Eva was inside, Pink escorted Vakar back to the med bay and Eva made her way to the bridge. Min was in the pilot's chair, her pale skin speckled with lights from the instrument panel.

"I assume you can outmaneuver this idiot?" Eva asked.

"Faster than you can do twenty push-ups," Min replied, her voice coming through the speakers.

They slid out of the dock, debris pinging their shields, and Eva finally got a good look at the might of the Glorious Apotheosis. It was . . . substantial.

"That is one serious manhood joke waiting to happen," she said.

They dropped as if they'd fallen off a cliff, Min angling *La Sirena Negra* to put the station between them and the emperor's ship. A shot from the plasma cannon cut another line through Omicron, and more things exploded behind them. In a few seconds, they'd be clear to power up the FTL drive.

"Incoming transmission," Min said.

Eva closed her eyes. "Let's hear it."

"Eva the Innocent," said Glorious. "You will not escape from me. I will bend you to my will."

"Not happening, guy, so move along," she replied, imagining his furious needle-toothed smile.

"I will pursue you to the ends of the universe if I must!" he shrieked.

"Then it's a good thing the universe is expanding," she said. "Jump, Min."

In a streak of red light, they did.

If only every problem were so easy to run away from, Eva thought as they sped off into the black. For particularly loose definitions of "easy" that she'd have nightmares about. As if she didn't have enough nightmare fuel in the tank already.

Now came the harder part: dealing with The Fridge. And for that problem, there really was nowhere to run.

Chapter 4

DE TAL PALO, TAL ASTILLA

La Sirena Negra didn't slow down until it came up on the nearest Gate. Eva stared at the huge metal ring on the bridge screens, wondering not for the first time at the mystery of an ancient alien device that could open holes in space, that people used every cycle to get from one end of the universe to the other, and that nobody knew a damn thing about.

Except how to operate them, of course. Which was its own brand of uncomfortable, since the Proarkhe hadn't exactly left instructions for their tech before they disappeared to nobody knew where eons earlier. Still, the Gates worked, and that was what mattered.

"Where to, Cap?" Min asked.

"Stand by for now. Did a message come for me while I was out?"

"Yes, sorry, everything was all woo-woo, pew-pew, so I forgot. You got one about the cats, and another one on your private—"

"Send it to my cabin." Her lips curled into a scowl as she walked to her quarters on the starboard side, across from the med bay.

No doubt the message was the instructions for her first assignment. Sounded more like schoolwork than blackmail, but she doubted it was going to be simple deliveries. Not that her line of work had ever been simple; back when she'd navigated the dark spaces between the points of light that were law and order in this galaxy, things tended to get complicated in a hurry. But she had promised the crew stability, and safety, as much as anything could be safe out in space. She couldn't jeopardize that.

She had to cut them loose.

Or did she? She didn't relish the idea of finding a new crew to pilot her ship, keep it in good repair—keep Eva from being alone and going space-mad, if she was honest. She needed people she could trust.

But she couldn't tell them about Mari. The Fridge agent had said they would kill her sister if she said anything. How would they even know, though? She didn't think they were monitoring her commlink, and they couldn't have a bug on board—Min would feel it. It would come down to whether she or one of the others said something in a place where The Fridge had eyes, ears, or some other sensory appendage. That meant not only Eva lying, but everyone else, every time they left the ship, maybe even every time they made an outgoing comms connection.

Was it a chance she was willing to take when Mari's life was at stake? She thought back to her father's warning, to the story about his client who sold their stuff and ran away. She thought about her mother crying over the casket of her favorite daughter, just because Eva couldn't bring herself to lie about this one thing.

So she wouldn't tell them about The Fridge. The irony of lying to the people she trusted was not lost on her. Nor did it escape her notice that she'd struck out on her own seven years earlier because she was sick of dishonesty. Working for her dad, running with Tito, had been one long stretch of peddling bullshit to clients, enemies, friends, even family.

She had been good at it. It had made her feel smart, confident, powerful. Until it didn't. Then she and Pink had left, and here they were, trying to prove to themselves that they could do better. That the galaxy wasn't a scattered collection of sentient races dedicated to fucking each other over at every opportunity.

This cycle, that all sounded like a shitty motivational ad in a public toilet, and Eva was about ready to flush. She took slow, deep breaths.

With luck, she'd have The Fridge's debt paid off within a few dozen cycles and her sister would be free. And then things would go back to normal. She wished she felt luckier. As it was, she felt like she'd just escaped from an insane egomaniac with more power than sense, and if her heart weren't mechanical, it would probably be pounding like a conga.

((Vakar?)) she pinged at Pink.

((Resting,)) Pink replied. ((Fine soon.))

Eva sighed in relief. She pulled up The Fridge's instructions, the opaque image seeming to float a foot in front of her.

CAPTAIN EVA-BENITA CARIDAD LARSEN ALVAREZ Y COIPEL DE INNOCENTE. PROCEED TO SPECIFIED COORDINATES. OBTAIN PASSENGER MILES ERCK. DELIVER TO SECONDARY SPECIFIED COORDINATES. PAYMENT UPON COMPLETION.

This was followed by details about the passenger and pay. It sounded simple enough. Pick up dude, deliver dude, collect money. A lot of money, really, for what they were doing; she'd expected them to cheap out on her. For a moment, she felt more chipper at the prospect of not having to leave her crew behind, and then she mentally slapped herself.

Her sister was in danger. This wasn't some stupid chicken run, this was Mari's life at stake, and her crew's. This was a group of criminals with absurdly vast resources, some of which were around to provide the muscle for the organization. She needed to get in, get out, and get paid.

Keeping your crew together is only delaying the inevitable, the voice in her head whispered. She mentally gave it the finger and checked the cat message next.

Greetings Gato Tuerto seller identity. Can your product operate heavy machinery and can it tolerate zero-grav environments?

Probably yes on the first, she thought, given how they'd tried to take over the ship. A quick codex search on the q-net told her the second was a definite no, including uncomfortable video evidence. With a scowl, she closed that message and headed for the mess, sending a mass ping for everyone to meet her there.

Leroy was mid–food prep when she arrived, turning protein powder into a slurry that was supposed to taste like scrambled chicken eggs when cooked. Pink sat next to Vakar, who looked better, but moved more stiffly than usual, clutching his abdomen in a way that made her wince.

"So, that happened," Eva said, pouring bullshit instant coffee powder into a mug. "In other news, I'm giving up alcohol, and you're all getting a raise."

Leroy cheered for a moment, petering out when no one joined him. He returned to his not-eggs, his freckled face turning pink.

Pink put her feet up and crossed her arms, leaning back in her chair. Vakar stared at her in silence, but his smell said it all. Even Min gave a short, nervous laugh through the speakers.

"Eva, the fuck is going on?" Pink asked.

Eva smiled at them like she hadn't just dragged them halfway across the galaxy for no apparent reason. Like her stomach wasn't full of rocks and acid fighting for supremacy.

"Gato Tuerto Enterprises has a new job," she said. "A new regular client, in fact. We're being put on retainer." It sounded so reasonable. So abysmally fucking possible.

The best lies were the kind people wanted to believe.

Pink sucked on her teeth. "I meant that whole Omicron thing, but okay."

Eva's smile melted. "Short answer: asshole won't take no for an answer, asshole gets kicked in the teeth, asshole escalates because he's an asshole." And people died. And it was her fault because she— No, it was his fault. He threatened her, she reacted, he escalated beyond reason. She didn't make him do what he did.

"Should have kicked him twice," Pink said.

"The Gmaargitz Fedorach is known for holding grudges," Vakar said. Underneath the rusty tang of his pain was a mild burning smell. Anger. Yeah, she was pretty pissed about it herself.

"It was either a grudge or my ass, so I guess I'll have to sleep with one eye open." Eva stared into her mug as if that would make the powder dissolve faster. She remembered the coffee on Omicron and scowled.

"Where are we going now?" Min asked.

"Here are the coordinates." She pinged them over to the pilot.

"We're playing sky cab for some scientist. Quick and easy. Five thousand credits apiece."

That got their attention. Leroy whistled softly, and Pink put a finger on her pursed lips. But now Vakar smelled like a fart in church, literally.

"That is a high price for such a simple assignment," he said. "Is this an extraction?"

Eva waved dismissively. "The client didn't say anything about trouble. We're passing through contested space, but that's only illegal if you're smuggling goods. Which we aren't."

Vakar didn't smell convinced.

"Quick and easy," she repeated. "We deliver the passenger and get our money." She stood up and laid her palms on the table, leaning forward. "Come on. New client. Retainer, which means steady work. If they screw us over, we'll pass through that Gate when we reach it."

Eva waited, looking at each of them in turn. They couldn't know what it would mean if they pushed back. She steeled herself for the worst, for having to fire them all, for running a whole ship by herself or finding a new crew who didn't care enough about her to ask questions.

Leroy didn't object. But then, he'd never much cared how they earned their money, provided he didn't have to kill anyone. And five thousand credits would buy him some choice memvids, or new tattoo designs, or presents for his moms back on Earth.

Min was also silent. Her opinions of laws varied but were generally ambivalent at best, so long as there was no chance of her family finding out if she'd broken them. And she had never been afraid of a fight, if she was controlling a few tons of metal and malice.

Vakar's gray-blue eyes met hers. He smelled like hot cooking oil, which her translator tentatively indicated was suspicion, but he broke eye contact first. He had trusted her since they met, and she still wasn't sure why, but she was flattered. It made her want to be worthy of that trust, usually; now, it just deepened her shame.

That left Pink. Pink, who had literally watched Eva's back through her sniper's scope more times than Eva could count, who spoke her mind but always supported Eva in the end, who sometimes knew what Eva was thinking or feeling when Eva was still struggling to figure it out herself. Pink, who had once pulled shrapnel out of Eva's chest as she lay gasping in pain, and had told her matter-of-factly that if she wanted to run with the big dogs, she had better stop whining like a little bitch. That had made Eva mad enough to live, and while she was lying in recovery after a handful of surgeries and a new mechanical heart implant, she realized that had been the idea.

Pink's cybernetic eye was hidden—the tech was delicate, and she'd always been a little sensitive about it—but her natural one considered Eva as if it could see inside her head, to her thoughts, better than any machine could. Eva wanted to squirm; it took every ounce of self-control to leave her palms on the table and return Pink's stare.

With a click of her tongue, Pink shrugged. "Whatever. You're the captain."

Which meant the consequences were on her head, whatever they might be. El que la hace, la paga. Hopefully the price wouldn't be unconscionably high.

Eva slapped the table and straightened. "Great! Off we go." She pointed at Vakar. "You. Sit tight. The rest of you, get the probes ready so we can scrape some fuel together."

Vakar waited for her to finish making her coffee, then followed her, limping, past the crew quarters to her cabin. She opened her door and gave him a mock bow, waving for him to go in first, then shutting the door behind them. Sipping her drink, she gestured for him to take the one small chair in the room, but he declined, so she sat down and crossed her ankles as he fidgeted next to her bed.

"Where did you get an isosphere?" she asked. They weren't impossible to find, but they weren't common as croquetas at a party.

He wagged his head in the quennian equivalent of a shrug, but didn't answer.

"Is that what was in the box for me?"

"No." The smell of grass again—bashful—and that other one she still couldn't place. "Let me retrieve it."

She waited, watching her fish drift aimlessly in their water, until a minute later Vakar returned with the black cube. It had a special combination lock that took him a few tries to open, but he finally managed and the top slid sideways with a hiss of air.

The contents were, sadly, a big red mush, but the smell . . . Eva nearly fell off her bed. She dipped a finger in and licked it clean.

"You son of a—" She shook her head. "Pastelitos?"

"They are difficult to make properly," he said. "That is what you tell me, anyway. These were certainly expensive enough."

"Really?"

"Really."

She scooped more up with her hand and practically inhaled it. Guayaba. Cream cheese. People used to think heaven was up in space somewhere, but it was a place on Earth, and that place made Cuban pastries. How the hell he had managed to get them on Omicron was beyond her, but she didn't care.

Vakar was staring at her as if he'd never seen her lick her fingers before. Maybe he hadn't.

"You don't want to see me eat the rest of this," she said. "It's not going to be pretty."

He shrugged again. "I will be resting in my quarters if you require anything of me." He left, that weird smell of his trailing after him.

Licorice, that's what it was. A strange sense of relief fell over her at finally figuring that out. She'd eaten it only a few times, and she didn't really like the taste, but the smell was kind of nice.

Her translators still didn't know what it meant, though.

She forced herself to chew slowly, to savor every bite. And most importantly, not to think about how many people had died on Omicron, how many she herself had killed before that, and all the ways everything in her life might fall apart at any moment until The Fridge was finished with her. That thinking led to insomnia, to sleeping and waking nightmares, to the feeling that her lungs couldn't suck in enough breath, that her chest was too tight and her skin was on fire and she might as well give up because everything was fucked.

That thinking wouldn't get Mari back. She needed to keep it together for her sister's sake, and to shield her crew as much as possible from whatever sketchy shit she might end up doing.

Something did stick in her mind, though: Her handler, Pholise, had said her dad was already involved. Which meant he knew what had happened and hadn't told anyone. Or at least, hadn't told her. Not surprising, perhaps, if The Fridge went around swearing people to secrecy. And given how their last conversation had gone, neither of them had been particularly pressed to make contact.

Maybe it was time to give him a call.

Eva routed the link through a dummy relay, in case The Fridge really was monitoring her outgoing comms somehow. The low buzz of the connection attempting to resolve made her head ache.

Finally, the sound cut out, replaced by a distant radio playing jazzy music.

"Eva-Bee, is that you?" Her dad sounded tired, but he had always managed to sound tired when she called him.

"What's your favorite color?" she asked.

He paused. "My what now?"

"Favorite color."

He sighed, and she could picture him rubbing his nose as he thought. "Let's see, it's . . . chartreuse?"

"Right." She wasn't sure whether she was relieved he had remembered the countersign; part of her had wanted an excuse to hang up. The dark red fish in her tank swam out of its coral cave, as if it knew who she was talking to, its mouth opening and closing as it moved.

"Well, gosh, it's been a while, hasn't it?" he asked.

"Yeah," she replied. "A while."

"It's nice to hear your voice. Things are good here. Weather has been a big mess, coldest summer we've had in ten years."

"How's the market for used spaceships? Still selling them as soon as they land on the lot?" The red fish swam in lazy circles through the kelp, eyes black and empty.

"No, no, not anymore. Harder for my customers to get financing, the way our damn government is tightening regulations to get ready for BOFA compliance."

Eva gritted her teeth. "And how is Mari doing?"

If he hesitated, she couldn't hear it. "Mari is good, last I heard, still working at that settlement on New Albany, running tests on old pottery and whatnot. With that boyfriend of hers, the one in the skin ads?"

"I think she broke up with him," she said. "I've heard it's

pretty cold where she is, too. Super cold. Frosty the fucking snowman."

Now her father did pause. "Yeah, huh. Hey, hold on there a second, I was just going outside to fill the bird feeder."

Her dad did love his birds. Some of them were even real. The rest were just really attentive, sometimes with lasers or proximity mines.

"You ready yet?" Eva asked. She toyed with the coffee cup on the table next to her bed, wishing she'd gotten a refill before calling.

"Hold your horses," he said, his easy demeanor rubbing thin. "I know you're relayed, but let me run a scrubber real quick." The quiet of his front yard was broken by a squeal of static that lasted a dozen seconds. "All right, that should be good."

"How long has she been gone?" Eva's voice was soft, slick as a buttered knife.

"They contacted me a month ago," he answered. "Damn it, Bee, I'm sorry you got dragged into this. Business has been bad since the regulators got proactive. The timing couldn't have been worse."

Eva's lips thinned as she pressed them together. Bad timing. Her sister was in cryo and her father was griping about business. Typical.

"Did they take the *Minnow*?" he asked.

"*La Sirena Negra,*" she said reflexively.

"Right, right. That's a shame. I'll see about getting you a new ship on good lease terms. It's the least I can do."

It really is, she thought. The absolute least. "They didn't take my ship."

"But you don't have any—" He stopped. "I see. Well, you always could take care of yourself. Tito wouldn't have tolerated any less."

He had nice things to say about her when it suited him. She tried not to let it get to her, just as she tried to ignore the ways in which her hazy reflection in the fish tank resembled him— same black hair, though his was going gray, same brown eyes that were dark enough to look black in most lighting. Same fucking mouth, right down to the shit that came out of it when she wasn't careful.

Compared to him, she was much less careful.

"Is there anything you can tell me about them, anything at all that could give me any leverage?" she asked.

Now it was his turn to fall silent. A snippet of birdsong trilled in the background, and she wondered whether it was a real one or a warning.

"They know what you're capable of," he finally said. "You're no good to them dead, but you're also expendable. They like their money quick and dirty, and half of what they do is for favors and secrets anyway."

The real galactic currency. Eva thought of the impending job. What kind of favor might they get out of mystery passenger Miles Erck?

"They'll let your sister out, eventually," he continued. "No one would deal with them if they didn't. But they'll squeeze what they can out of you, like a lemon."

"And then they'll pulp me and zest me," she murmured. "But none of that is dirt. Leverage. Something I can use to my advantage if I have to." If they ask me to do something and I can't bring myself to do it, she thought. If I end up with another Garilia situation on my hands. She leaned against her closet door, pressing her forehead to the cool metal surface. No time to worry about the past now, or a future she couldn't predict. Stay in the present.

"No one even really knows who they are," he said. "It's all

agents who report to other agents, and none of them are connected and all of them are under the same invisible thumb. But I'll tell you my opinion, and you know what I always say."

"That and ten credits buys you coffee."

"Exactly. I think maybe, it's like a game of Reversi. You remember playing that with me, when you were little?"

She did. It had taken her forever to figure out the rules of the game. They'd play over the q-net, light-years away from each other, and she would make a move and the pieces would change color and she'd have no clue what she'd done, really. And then her dad would make another move and all the pieces on the board would cascade from white to black in an instant.

"I hated that game," she said.

Her dad laughed. "But you got the hang of it. Now, in this case—" He stopped, and she heard another call ringing in on a different comm.

"Listen, Bee, I have to go. But you think about what I said, okay?"

"Yeah, sure." She'd have to, because he hadn't bothered to explain it.

"Love you, girlie. I'll talk to you later."

"Bye, Dad." The call disconnected, though perhaps she imagined it took a second longer than usual. Perhaps not. If nothing else, The Fridge was good at making you more paranoid than ever.

Eva threw herself into her chair with a sigh. Damn that man. She wasn't even sure why she had bothered to call him. To argue? To scream? To tell him what a selfish prick he had been? They'd had that fight years ago, when she quit Tito's crew after Garilia, and dear old Dad had given her the ship to shut her up about the trail of dead they'd left behind. He somehow managed to deflect her every time, like they were playing dodgeball and she was trying to hit him, but he wasn't there anymore, he was behind her, and did she really want to play this when they could be playing laser hockey instead? And before she knew it they'd be so far past the point of confrontation that she was almost embarrassed at how mad she'd been in the first place.

It was what made him a great criminal, frankly. But a shitty father, and an equally shitty husband.

And Eva had played the same game with other people, and every time she did, it left a fresh stain on her soul. She was supposed to be finished with all that, but here she was, letting herself be dragged back in.

Mari would do the same for me, she told herself. For all that they had fought, Mari always had her back when it counted. Love wasn't an outfit you slipped in and out of when it suited you; it was your skin, your bones, your blood. She'd sooner open a vein than let Mari die.

Eva thought about Reversi. Turn the pieces. Pick the right ones and soon you'd have an army. Maybe she could find more of The Fridge's agents, the ones who were being blackmailed themselves? But then, she'd never been good at making those choices.

And anyway, she could handle this. She'd be careful.

Eva sat on her bed and watched her fish swim in their tank, bright and oblivious.

Vakar and Leroy were already in the mess when Eva stalked in, still annoyed from the call with her father. She didn't look at either of them, just went straight for the cabinet with the protein powder to make herself a shake, intending to take it back to her room to continue misery-wallowing in private.

"Okay, so what about Sergeant Eagle and Momoko?" Leroy

said. His chair was pushed back until it touched the bulkhead, but he was sitting on the edge.

Vakar crossed the three steps between table and counter to pull a cup from the sanitizer, which he handed to Eva. "Is Sergeant Eagle the one who announces he is going to kick you?" he asked.

"It's not an announcement, it's the name of his signature move. Eagle Kick!" Leroy leaned back to demonstrate, thumping the underside of the table, which was, thankfully, bolted to the floor.

"Would it not be a more effective signature move if he did not shout it before—"

"Naw, man." Leroy waved his hands in front of him. "You're missing the point. And the question is, who would win in a fight?"

"If Momoko does not warn her opponents of impending attacks, then she would be the logical winner." He looked to Eva as if for confirmation, and she shrugged, stirring her shake.

"Not a chance!" Min's human body wandered into the mess, but her voice still came from the speakers. Her fine blue hair framed her oval face, the round, dark eyes slightly vacant, as if she weren't using them at the moment. "Momoko is super fast, and she does this awesome butt move, but the Eagle Kick would knock her into orbit." She dug into her secret stash of black bean sauce and noodles and started to prep it as Eva watched enviously.

"Would she not know the kick was coming and simply avoid it?" Vakar asked.

It was Pink's turn to stroll in. "You all know that *Crash Sisters* stuff is fake, right?" she said. She pulled a meal bar from the cabinet next to Eva and leaned against the counter.

Leroy and Min exploded into an indignant tirade about the

athleticism required and the different fighting styles the competitors specialized in and how they would all definitely beat Pink in a fight, for sure, so she shouldn't talk.

Pink smirked and tore her food open, taking a bite and cringing. Eva sympathized; they were out of every flavor but seaweed and lentil.

The crew continued to bicker as Eva finished making her drink. It was so nice to hear them be themselves, be normal, but knowing she'd have to keep up a shield of lies between her and them until Mari was safe sucked any pleasure out of the situation.

"What's with the grouchy face, Captain?" Leroy asked. "Did the protein powder get bricked again?"

Eva wavered between brushing him off and throwing him a bone. Pink raised her eyebrow, which Eva could ignore with some effort, but Vakar's worried smell got to her.

"Just talked to my dad," she said. "He's still a jerk."

A chorus of sympathetic noises and smells responded.

"It's been what, five years since you and Pete had words?" Pink asked.

"Three," Eva said sourly. "I had to call him when the auxiliary port hazcam stopped working and we couldn't source the part." And he'd made sure she knew what a huge favor he was doing her.

Vakar smelled puzzled. "Why did you contact him now?"

She hesitated, scrambling for a plausible lie. "Because of Omicron," she said. "In case Glorious traces me back to him somehow. He's a jerk, but he doesn't deserve to be a dead jerk."

"Well," Pink said, pursing her lips.

Right, fine, he probably did deserve it, for Garilia if nothing else, but by that logic Eva did as well. She liked to hope forgiveness was in reach of most people in the universe, even herself.

"Did you call your mom and sister yet?" Pink asked. "You haven't talked to them in a while, either, have you?"

Shit, of course. Certainly they were higher priority than her dad in terms of who she didn't want to get spaced.

"I couldn't get through," Eva lied. "Going to try them again later, or send them messages at least." What would she even tell her mom? She could already hear the lecture about hanging around seedy bars with strange men, as if there weren't plenty of strange men everywhere else. Her mom had even dated some of them, which she was only too happy to talk about in unpleasant detail as a deterrent for her daughters. And yet she always wondered why Eva hadn't settled down and started popping out kids.

I don't want to talk to her, Eva thought. Not now. I'll send her a q-mail and hope she doesn't start forwarding me inspirational chain letters again.

And Mari, of course, was beyond messaging at the moment.

"I miss my moms," Leroy said suddenly, and Eva hid her relief at the subject change. "I should see what they're up to."

"They sent you that care package a few weeks ago," Min said. "With the sweater."

"Yeah, and the gum I like, the one that sparks. What about your family, Min?"

Her human body shrugged and took a bite of food, talking through the speakers as she chewed. "They're still running the solar farm on Seugawa. I hear more kids are leaving, though. Not everyone wants to pilot a boring old repair mech ten hours a cycle on a boring old rock in the fringe."

"Now you just pilot a boring old freighter from one boring old rock to another in the fringe," Pink joked.

"Hey, it beats having a dozen aunties ask how much weight you've gained since they last saw you. How's your brother's baby?"

Pink grinned, her eye staring into the distance. "So cute I could eat her."

"You eat infants?" Vakar asked, smelling concerned.

"It's an expression. What do you say to compliment a baby?"

Vakar wagged his head. "That it has smooth scales and good scent control for its age, I suppose. People always said such things about my sister, at least."

"I bet you were a cute baby," Eva said, smirking. "The smoothest scales."

Vakar's smell was a cross between licorice and embarrassment. Eva chuckled.

"I was totally the cutest baby," Leroy said, leaning back in his chair. "My moms have so many holopics. I had little butt dimples and everything."

"And red hair?" Min asked.

"Oh for sure. And I was always doing silly stuff." Leroy pulled on his beard and smiled. "It's like one time, I was taking a bath with one of my moms, and—"

Shit, that reminded Eva that she needed to prep the passenger cabin for her Fridge mission. She finished her shake and excused herself, and within a few steps toward the cargo bay her mood had soured again.

Fucking kidnappers. Fucking dad. Fucking seaweed-and-lentil meal bars. Fucking stupid situation making her lie to her crew like this.

Fucking you making that choice, she thought.

Still, the Fridge job was a simple passenger pickup. Get the guy, take him where he needs to go, drop him and leave. How bad could it be?

Chapter 5

WELL, ACTUALLY

This is where you'll be bunking," Eva said, opening the door to the passenger cabin in the back of the cargo bay. It was maybe a six-by-ten space, with a bed at the end and a small cube of stasis gel next to the door for storing gear. The other corner had a waste disposal unit and a sanitizing station, but that was it. She and Leroy had spent hours clearing junk out of the room, so it still smelled vaguely of ozone and grease underneath the sharp tang of cleaning products.

Their passenger, Miles Erck, took it all in solemnly, but Eva could tell from the way his mouth twitched that he was suppressing a smile. The guy was human, young enough that Eva would feel awkward hitting on him, and not her type regardless. Skinny, pale as protein powder, thin blond hair combed sideways, with the twitchy eyes of someone running too many AR visualizations at once.

And so far, he had the personality of an unreasonably arrogant mold infestation. Eva wondered if her sister had to deal with this kind of comemierda on a regular basis, or if non-Fridge scientists were generally less irritating.

"Let me know if you need me to demonstrate the sanitation fixtures," she said.

"Well, actually, I know a lot about ship sanitation," he said.

"Great," Eva said. This was probably his first space flight, but she wasn't going to be a jerk about it. "I'll let you get settled, then. Thanks again for choosing Sweet Papaya Transport. If you need anything, Leroy will be right outside."

"Well, actually," he said, "I did have one question."

She smiled with her lips closed, widening her eyes.

"Why do you have so many cats?" He leaned sideways to look past her at the furry infestation sprawled in every available square of space.

"Unclaimed cargo," she said. "Why, are you allergic?" Or did the cats smell? Leroy said some of them did, like maple syrup or that reclaimed protein stuff they ate, but their container kept any toilet aromas from escaping.

"No. Are they for sale? One of my colleagues is doing experiments on—"

"Not for sale," she said, her smile losing some of its luster. "Anything else?"

"Well, actually," he said, "no. Not right now."

Eva turned as sharply as a soldier, marching straight to the med bay.

Vakar was already there, being examined by Pink. He smelled antsy, but not so much in pain anymore, which was a relief.

"Humans do something like your crystals," Pink said as she smeared a minty glaze onto a patch of his arm scales. "It's called bonsai. Tiny trees that grow in little pots."

"Are they challenging to cultivate?" Vakar asked.

"Yeah, and the point is to keep them trimmed really carefully. Supposed to be relaxing." Pink shrugged. "I prefer sewing. Feels more useful."

Vakar smelled pensive. "I believe there is utility in beauty, even if it serves no other purpose. But many beautiful things can—" He stopped, apparently noticing Eva for the first time, and his smell shifted to ozone and grass.

Eva leaned against a cabinet, pressing her thumb and forefinger into her clenched-shut eyes until her vision checkered.

"What kind of headache you got?" Pink asked, glancing at Eva with her mechanical eye.

"It's about this tall and incredibly full of shit," Eva replied, holding a hand just above her head.

Pink smirked. "I'd prescribe some of my brother's secret stash, but you're off the bottle."

"Yeah, and no amount of bourbon would make that come-mierda tolerable."

"Did you say secret stash?" Min piped in through the speaker. "Can I—"

"Not for you, either, baby girl," Pink said. "Not while you're flying. Maybe next time we dock, as long as Eva doesn't piss off any more emperors with big guns."

Eva rolled her eyes and gave Pink the finger. "Vakar, are you healed up enough to help me and Leroy sort through the stuff formerly occupying our esteemed guest's room?"

"Certainly," he replied, his smell perking up. Pink gave a slight nod that Eva took for approval.

"No heavy lifting," Pink said. "And no sudden movements."

Eva grinned. "Great. Whatever we can't salvage, we'll scrap. Come on."

They returned to the cargo bay, where Leroy was already

engaged in the process, which mostly consisted of staring at the piles of junk and singing to himself. The theme song to *Crash Sisters,* if she wasn't mistaken. She smiled; it was good to see him so cheerful. His last nightmare episode had been weeks earlier, which was a new record for him, and he hadn't full-on lost his temper since the time he'd rented a particular memvid that was a little too close to a real memory. Vakar and Eva had to take turns distracting him until Pink was able to tranq him from the catwalk.

"Cavalry's here," Eva said.

"Let the party begin!" Leroy raised his arms and shook his ass. Min giggled through the speakers and turned on an upbeat retro tune, to which he started doing a line dance. Eva shook her head when he tried to drag her in, laughing at his absurd gyrations.

"All right, enough," she said, still grinning. "We have work to do."

Leroy brought his dance to a close and bowed. Min responded with an applause sound effect and Vakar smelled amused.

"We'll start at the bottom corner and work our way up and over," Eva said. "Two piles: scrap and salvage."

"Salvage may be possible in most circumstances, Captain," Vakar said.

"I'm not doubting your ability to fix things, mi vida. It's a matter of time and cost. If you're not sure about something, ask me."

Vakar shrugged assent and they all dug in. Eva almost couldn't believe how much crap had accumulated since the last time they'd done this. Now that she thought about it, the last time had been before they brought Vakar on board. The previous engineer, Connor, had been meticulously organized, always kept a clean station . . . which Eva had eventually discovered was because he was selling the ship's parts every time he had an opportunity. It had taken every trace of willpower she had to keep from beating him senseless in a fit of rage.

And then, of course, she'd found Vakar.

She watched him rifle through the parts, humming softly to himself. He'd been a ridiculously lucky find, considering they'd met by chance. Life was funny like that: one cycle Pink was explaining yet again why throwing people out the airlock is not a good idea under any circumstances, the next Eva stumbled into the best engineer she'd ever worked with.

He caught her staring and she pretended she'd been looking at something behind him. He smelled bashful, grassy, with a hint of licorice.

"How about this, boss?" Leroy asked, holding up a capacitor. "Looks burned all to hell, but the casing is platinum, right?"

She took it from him and examined it. "Hmm, we can probably melt that down for patching, at least. Vakar?"

Before Vakar could answer, Miles Erck emerged from his cabin, covered in a fluid that she was generously prepared to assume was water.

"Everything all right?" Eva asked.

"Well, actually," he said, "I think your sanitizing equipment is malfunctioning."

She suppressed a snicker. She'd checked that herself before they picked him up, so she knew it was fine.

"Vakar, could you look?" she asked.

Vakar stood and stretched, sauntering over to the cabin.

Miles bent over and picked up a random junk part. "What are you doing?" he asked.

"Purging," Eva said.

"I'm a bit of an expert on technology," he said. "I'd be happy to offer my services in an advisory capacity for a small fee."

Warning sirens went off in her head. This guy worked for The Fridge, presumably, or she wouldn't be ferrying him around on their orders. The last thing she wanted was for them to get a better working knowledge of the guts of her ship. Plus, if he thought he was going to charge her for a damn thing while he was on board, he was more full of shit than she thought.

Then again, maybe she could pump him for information. He wasn't likely to be too deep into whatever layers of secrecy The Fridge cultivated, but the more puzzle pieces she could collect, the better chance she had of guessing at the bigger picture.

And, possibly, of finding Mari.

"I'm sure we couldn't afford an expert like yourself," she said coyly.

"That's true," he said. "Prominent technologists can earn thousands of credits a cycle if they're diligent."

"What's a technologist?" Leroy asked.

"Someone who studies technology." His tone suggested an unspoken "obviously" at the end of the statement. "Well, actually, I'm a paleotechnologist. I study ancient technology, primarily artifacts uncovered during surveys of potential colony worlds."

What could The Fridge want with that? Eva wondered. "Sounds fascinating," she said, giving the word a sultry lilt. "I'd love to hear more about it. Maybe after I finish here, we can chat in my bunk."

Miles blushed, and from his cabin came a strange cracking sound and a curse from Vakar that translated to "wretched spawn of a dung heap."

"I shouldn't," Miles said. "It's classified."

Leroy's eyes lit up. "Is it old human stuff?" he asked. "Ooh, or todyk? Or those guys who built the pyramids on Earth, the giant ones with the big animal masks—"

"Those weren't aliens," Eva said. But Leroy wasn't listening.

He must have worn Miles down, or sufficiently buttered him up, because the guy finally let his pride overcome his good sense. "Well, actually," Miles said, "it's the Proarkhe."

Eva groaned inwardly, and from the cabin came another strangled curse.

Leroy's obsession with the mysterious aliens was even worse than his thing for *Crash Sisters*. When he'd found out Mari wrote her dissertation on them, he had grilled Eva for hours even though she had no clue about any of it. She'd finally wangled a copy of the book out of Mari, to shut him up. It didn't help that whenever someone found anything that might possibly be Proarkhe tech, BOFA swooped in and cordoned off the sector until it was determined to be safe. It's like they wanted to breed enough conspiracy theories to populate the entire q-net a million times over.

None of the tech ever worked, though, except for the Gates. Or at least, that's what BOFA claimed. Her sister had told her once that all the pieces in museums were replicas anyway, just in case.

"I know," Leroy said, "damn near everything about the Proarkhe." He practically vibrated with excitement.

"Well, actually, most of what is commonly known is believed to be quite inaccurate."

"Oh," Leroy said. For a moment, he looked like a kicked puppy, and Eva fought the urge to, well, actually, kick Miles in retaliation. But Leroy recovered his enthusiasm quickly.

"So did they come from another galaxy?" he asked. "Why did they disappear? Did they really make the Gates or was it someone else? Did you find any of their secret artifacts? Decrypt their secret language? Did they leave any secret messages for us that would take us to their secret—"

"I'm contractually obligated not to disclose any details of my investigations." Miles had begun to look nervous, like he finally realized the depth of the hole he'd dug himself into.

Unfortunately, he started to dig sideways instead of climbing out.

"Oh, come on." Leroy picked up a cracked coolant control valve and idly tossed it from one hand to the other. "You can't say anything? Not even what they looked like? This one guy on the q-net says they were giant and had five different faces and—"

"It's classified, like I said," Miles repeated. "Highly classified."

"Everything's always classified," Leroy muttered. "Big shots keeping things quiet so regular people don't get any ideas. It's not fair."

Eva watched his skin mottle, going especially red near the roots of his bright orange hair. He was getting angry. Not good. Even the cats took notice, pausing in their bathing and eating to stare in unison at Leroy.

"Well, actually," Miles said, "information is typically classified to maintain safety and order."

"That's the kind of snobby attitude that gets innocent people killed, man!" Leroy exclaimed, spiking the control valve like a sportsball. If it hadn't been cracked before . . . "'Oh, this planet's ecology is classified, sorry if your best friend gets eaten by a sentient fungus, shit happens but that's not your fucking problem!'"

"Leroy," Eva said quietly. "Tranquilízate." She threw a look at Miles, who was too busy staring at Leroy to catch it.

"Well, actually, most people aren't equipped to properly understand the—"

"You think everyone's an idiot except you and your technobuddies, man? Maybe if you listened to the people getting shot at and shit on every cycle, you'd learn something for a change!"

The cats began to purr, a bass rumble just inside the edge of hearing. An attempt at hypnosis, presumably, but it wasn't working. Eva inched closer to Leroy, hands raised, praying to all the saints that Miles didn't say—

"Well, actually—"

Leroy picked up another piece of junk and squeezed. It crumpled in his grip like an empty tin can. The cat purrs intensified, but Eva suspected it was way too late for that.

Eva pinged Pink. ((Leroy's mad.))

((Shit. Coming.))

"You don't know what it's like, man," Leroy growled. "Your kind never does."

"Well, actually—"

Miles didn't get to finish, because Vakar tackled him from the side. The piece of scrap thrown at his head bounced harmlessly off the plating behind him instead of cracking his skull open like a bird's egg. The cats scattered, yowling unhappily.

"Min, *Crash Sisters!*" Eva shouted. The theme song started playing through the speakers immediately. Sometimes that calmed Leroy down, helped him find a happier mental place.

Now, apparently, it was going to be fight music.

Eva threw herself on Leroy's back, getting him in a headlock. "Chill," she told him. "He's a stupid little prick, he's—"

Leroy grunted and tried to throw her, but she had a tight grip and practice, and he didn't think so well when he was like this. Unfortunately, he was twice her size and pissed.

Leroy managed to get a handhold on the bottom of Eva's shirt and yanked, the material digging painfully into her neck. She fought to keep her arms locked, unsure which would break first, her skin or her clothes.

"Leroy, stop!" Vakar yelled.

Leroy reached up this time, grabbing Eva's shoulders to pull her off. Vakar tried to pry Leroy's fingers open from the back, but the man's grip was too tight.

If she could hang on for a little longer, get her arms into the right position—

Now Leroy went for her forearms, and there was no chance of her beating him in a pure strength contest. She released him before he could break her wrists, landing awkwardly on one foot and stumbling into a pile of broken pumps and inducers.

"Move!" Pink strode in like a pissed-off lady Moses about to part some shit.

Leroy spun to face her, giving Eva the opportunity to kick him hard. In the junk. It barely fazed him, but all it had to do was buy Pink the time to jab him in the neck with a sedative. He took a swing at Pink anyway, which she ducked smoothly.

Within seconds, Leroy's color dialed back from ripe tomato to guayaba, and he slid to the ground with a grumpy, mumbled "Owies."

The *Crash Sisters* song cut off and silence settled on the cargo bay. Even the cats had the good sense to keep their opinions to themselves. Pink held up her injector, Eva rubbed at the raw skin on her neck, and Vakar pressed a hand to his side, smelling pained.

Fuck, Eva thought. Leroy was dancing a minute ago. Everything was great, and now . . .

"What did you do?" Pink asked Eva, who responded with a look that could have melted steel beams.

"It wasn't her fault," Min chimed in over the speakers. "It was the passenger."

Miles Erck emerged from behind the cat container, his thin blond hair in disarray. He surveyed the situation and cleared his throat nervously. Eva was already crossing the room before he had opened his mouth.

"Well, actually—"

Eva grabbed his face with both hands, firmly but gently, and stared straight into his eyes as if she were preparing to kiss him.

"Well, actually," she said, "if you say 'well, actually' one more time, I will actually throw you out the actual airlock and you will actually die before you can say 'well, actually' with your bloated, frozen tongue."

He stared at her. His jaw moved, so she gave it an extra squeeze for emphasis, smiling with closed lips and raising her eyebrows.

His eyes widened. Hers narrowed.

He swallowed, his lower lip trembling. She tilted her head.

A bead of sweat formed on his forehead near his hairline and slid down, down, between his eyebrows and off to the side of his nose, nestling in the small fold of flesh next to his left nostril.

"Wellactuallyitwouldtakemelongertodiethanthat," he said in a rush.

Eva sighed and closed her eyes, a feeling of deep serenity flooding her body. "Pink," she said, "get his legs."

Miles Erck spent the rest of his journey locked in the cat container, which the cats weren't too pleased about. At this point Eva figured they owed her one. It wasn't quite big enough to fit him comfortably, but once the cats had done their hypnosis thing, he was in too good a mood to care.

Eva, meanwhile, sat with Pink in the mess and watched with envy as the medic enjoyed some of her brother's secret stash of bourbon. Eventually Min joined them, and Eva took over piloting duties for a while so the two could share a little free time before Leroy awoke from his medicated slumber.

Eight hours later, Eva landed *La Sirena Negra* on Suatera, sixth planet from the yellow star Fugit, which Eva was familiar with only because everyone pronounced it hilariously wrong. Twin moons watched like giant googly eyes as she and Vakar used an antigrav belt to carry one hypnotized paleotechnologist toward their drop point. Their destination was the only structure on the whole world, though Min's sensors had picked up a few random debris sites that Eva had neither the time nor the inclination to explore.

The door to the squat, round shelter was locked, so Eva kicked it until an intercom near the door whined to life.

"Who is that?" a voice rasped. "Is that Miles Erck?"

"Yeah," she replied, rolling a shoulder to stretch the muscle.

"Is he damaged?"

"Not yet, but there's still time."

The door slid open and they stepped inside, Eva walking backward so they could fit through the narrow opening.

The antechamber was filled with cargo containers, stacked two high in most places. The walls, floor, and ceiling were made from uniform gray panels, probably flash-welded together by the kind of robot that cheerfully disassembled itself when it was finished. An old computer interface was bolted to a far wall, hardline only to make hacking harder—from the outside, at least. Eva itched to see how fast Vakar could bust it open like a piñata.

Another door in the left-hand wall slid open, revealing an older woman wearing a red-and-white tunic, dark pants, and a deep frown. Two guards flanked her, carrying rifles Eva had only ever seen in the hands of top-tier merc outfits. Behind them was a hallway with another door at the end, beyond which lay mysteries someone would no doubt pay a pretty penny for, if she could figure out who the hell that someone was.

"What did you do to him?" the woman asked. She sounded like she ate carbon and shit diamonds.

"Hypnotic cats," Eva said. "He'll be fine soon."

"Well, actually," Miles mumbled. He smelled vaguely of fish.

With a disgusted noise, Eva dropped his feet and tucked her hands into her armpits to keep them from involuntary violence. Vakar lowered the rest of Miles gently to the ground, then removed the antigrav belt.

"This is unacceptable," the woman said. "I am on a strict timetable, Ms. . . . ?"

"Captain. Innocente. And you are?"

"Dr. Lambert."

"A pleasure." Eva cast a sour look at Miles. "Dr. Lambert, frankly, I'm not responsible for his comemierdería or your timetable. You want me to leave him here, or does he have a bunk?"

"The rest of this facility is off-limits to unauthorized personnel."

"So here, then. Great. Enjoy."

As she spoke, the door behind the doctor opened and a younger man in the same outfit rushed out. Eva caught a glimpse of the room at the other end of the hallway beyond—more computer terminals, people bustling about. In the center, some kind of tank or stasis field containing a large metal object, rectangular like a box. Then the far door slid shut.

Eva raised an eyebrow.

"Dr. Lambert, you're needed urgently," the young man said. "The artifact appears to have activ—" He stared at Eva and Vakar, then down at Miles, then back up at the doctor, eyes wide.

"Why didn't you— Ping silence, of course." Dr. Lambert scowled at Eva. "Go on, then, Captain. Our business is concluded."

Without another word, Eva left, Vakar close behind.

A herd of cow-like critters ambled down from a nearby hill-side, apparently oblivious to the strangers in their territory. Eva wondered idly whether they were edible, and if so, delicious.

"Did you see that thing in there?" Eva asked.

"Which one?" Vakar replied.

"Nothing, never mind." She shouldn't have said anything, not when it might make him curious, or suspicious. As it was, he started to exude a light incense aroma.

"Artifact," the man had said. And Miles Erck was a specialist in Proarkhe stuff. It wasn't hard to do the math on that one. But it had activated, whatever it was—what did that mean? What had they found and what could it do?

A ping came in from Min. ((BOFA ship.))

Eva swore under her breath and turned her leisurely stroll into a hustle. BOFA must have figured out The Fridge had found Proarkhe tech, unless there was something else going on that she didn't know about. Something even worse . . .

"Is there a problem?" Vakar asked.

"Not sure, don't want to find out." She made a beeline for the bottom hatch, climbing up into the decontamination tube as fast as her clunky boots would allow.

"They've dropped a baby recon vehicle," Min said through the speakers.

"Is it armed?" Eva asked, gesturing at Vakar to hurry.

"For sure."

"And you're good to fly?"

Min scoffed. "Pink gave me a thing. You know she wouldn't let me pilot drunk."

"Bottle us in and get out of here, then." The last thing she needed was to end up on BOFA's shit list, especially in connection with The Fridge.

The hatch closed beneath Vakar, trapping the two of them

in the small space as the chemical scrubbers did their work. Eva looped one arm around the ladder and turned on her boots, securing them to the side of the tube so she wouldn't fall on the quennian below her. He swung a leg through the rungs and clung tight, smelling uncomfortable.

"Just you and me until we hit the black," Eva said, shooting him a smile that she hoped his translators would parse as reassuring. "I'll try not to fart."

His smell went all nervous, with a weird, spicy undercurrent. She sighed.

"Are our BOFA friends giving us the stink eye?" she asked Min.

"No incoming transmissions yet, Cap. Should I be worried about pew-pew happening?"

"I certainly hope not." BOFA agents tended to shoot first and ask questions later, assuming they had any questions. And given her circumstances, any answers she might have for them would put Mari in worse danger.

Eva pictured Miles Erck staring down the barrel of an assault rifle. She was glad to be rid of him, but the idea of delivering him to an impending combat zone didn't sit well with her.

You have bigger fish to fry, she told herself. Like making sure Leroy is okay. And getting paid. And getting your damn sister away from these sinvergüenzas resingados before she ends up on the wrong end of a BOFA raid. She glanced down at Vakar, who was staring at his own feet, apparently lost in thought.

"Everything is fine," she said. She wasn't sure whether she was talking to him or to herself.

Chapter 6

JUST IGNORE IT

The next assignment from The Fridge came in as they approached the nearest Gate a few hours later. After the last one, Eva wasn't sure what to make of it. She called everyone into the mess to share the news, including Leroy, who was recovered but chastened after his involuntary nap. She made a mental note to assure him that what had happened with Miles was not remotely his fault; she'd been ready to throw something at the comemierda as well.

"Cap, this location is on the planet Dalnulara," Min said. "These coordinates will land us just outside their monastery in about a cycle and a half."

Eva nodded, petting the cat that she hadn't realized was on her lap until that moment. It purred as it gazed up at her with slitted eyes, and she scowled.

Meanwhile, Pink had brought her sniper rifle with her and

was field-stripping and cleaning it, the sharp mineral tang of the chemicals making it harder to smell Vakar. Eva couldn't remember the last time the affectionately nicknamed Anthia had been fired, but she suspected Pink was sending her a message: the medic expected trouble.

"That's pretty fringe territory, even for us," Pink said, pensively sliding the bore brush in and out. "Even BOFA doesn't bother sending patrols to the Hyova system unless they're short on their arrest quota."

"That's because the Dalnularan monks try to convert anything sapient once they hit comm range," Eva said. "If it weren't for the ridiculous alcohol they make, nobody would go there."

Leroy whistled, blue eyes gleaming. "We're going to pick up booze?"

"Pure and unfiltered," Eva said. "You'll have nightmares for cycles while you sober up, but for a half cycle you'll be able to speak just about any language, even ones that don't exist. No translator nanites needed. And they don't give it to just anyone, so we need to be extra careful with it." What did The Fridge want with the stuff? Whatever it was, it probably wasn't good.

"You are aware of what the monks do to visitors?" Vakar asked slowly, smelling concerned.

Eva waved dismissively. "That's a myth."

"I do not believe it is."

"How do you know?" Eva shot back, regretting it as his smell turned sour. He didn't respond, but Pink laid her brush on the table and looked down the bore at Eva, eyebrow raised.

"What do they do?" Leroy asked.

"Nothing," Eva said. "Don't even worry about it." She hated keeping anything from Leroy after what had set him off earlier, but he was the last person who needed to hear this particular rumor. With any luck, they wouldn't be planetside long enough to find out whether it was true.

The Righteous Sanctuary of the Eternally Echoing Warble, the only structure on the otherwise abandoned planet Dalnulara, was, to be blunt, kind of a shithole. Mostly on account of the enormous hole nearby, through which a semisolid brown substance was being slowly but constantly ejected by an unknown source. The mucus-tinged material was then collected by what Eva presumed were monks, who were using it to build a monument that, when completed, would hopefully look—and smell—like something other than a huge pile of poop.

Sadly, that wasn't the most unsettling thing Dalnulara had to offer.

"You have got to be kidding me," Eva said, staring at the thin-tentacled ahirk in front of her.

"All visitors to the monastery must tolerate our ministrations," the Dalnularan monk replied. As they spoke, tendrils waved on the left side of their round body.

"I warned you," Vakar said. He smelled like lavender and cigarettes—smug, but not happy about it.

"Tu madre," Eva muttered. Bad enough Vakar had been right; now she had to deal with Leroy knowing precisely the thing she had hoped to avoid.

"I'm not letting them stick that thing on my neck," Leroy said. Whatever excitement he'd had for this glorified beer run had vanished as soon as he saw the creatures the monks brought out with them.

The monk held an egg-shaped white critter, about the size of one of the kittens in her cargo hold. The underside was presumably where its suckers or talons or whatever were located. It seemed to be vibrating, pulsing, like it was taking rapid breaths through some unseen nose.

"No harm is intended," the monk said. It might have been soothing if they didn't have a voice like a mosquito pitched low enough to hear.

Eva tried to consider the situation logically: The Fridge wouldn't have sent her to do this if they really expected her to fail, because they presumably needed the booze for something, so this couldn't be a suicide mission. The stories of this place had gotten around, which meant someone must have survived. Ergo, it was likely that this . . . parasite could be removed later, as they claimed.

"All right, let's be done with this," she said. Taking a deep breath, she turned around and lifted her hair.

"Captain, no!" Vakar said, reaching out a gloved hand to intercept the ahirk monk as they slid over to her.

Eva brushed him off. "I'll be fine. You and Leroy wait for me on the ship."

"You cannot go in there alone," Vakar said. Now he smelled like suppressed anxiety, which was weirdly minty.

"And you can't come with. You're still not fully recovered from Omicron and saving Miles Erck from his own stupidity, and I'm not having Pink bust out the expensive nanotech for this."

"I am completely capable of—"

"I'll go," Leroy said.

She studied his face, the nervous way he bit his lip, then followed his gaze to the monk wriggling their tendrils and to the egg-creature they held. For a moment, she could have sworn it flexed a row of tiny legs like a centipede's.

Leroy had probably seen worse—killed worse—during his time as a corporate merc, cleaning out worlds for colonization even if those worlds were already settled, but she didn't want to add another nightmare to his screaming menagerie. Meat puppets usually died in a war zone or flamed out and landed in fight clubs, punching other broken soldiers in exchange for enough drugs to forget all the shit their controllers had made them do. Hell, Leroy had washed out of one ship's crew after another for years before Eva hired him, because no one else gave enough of a shit to try to help him get his angry outbursts and nightmares under control. And the corporations cared exactly as much as they were legally obligated to, less if they could get away with it.

Regardless, once they left the service, meat puppets tended to get really antsy about connecting anything to their spinal columns. Leroy was no exception.

"Fuck no," Eva said. "Get back on the ship."

Another monk, this time a muk, appeared from nowhere with a second creature held in their oversize lobster-claw hands.

"Vakar is right," Leroy said finally. "You shouldn't go alone."

"I'm not alone. I've got two perfectly good fists and boots that can break bones."

He cocked a weak grin. "I owe you, anyway, after what happened with the passenger."

"Not even. I was ready to mangle him myself." This was a terrible idea. Leroy didn't need to make amends or prove anything to her. But maybe he wanted to prove something to himself? Sometimes you fucked up and you wouldn't feel better until you did something right to balance it out.

"Please?" he asked.

Eva sighed. "Fine. Vakar, go prep the cargo bay." She gestured at the monk to hurry up, bracing herself for the shock of pain she was sure would come when the thing latched on with its . . . whatever it had.

There was a gentle pressure as it was placed on her neck. Then—nothing.

"Huh," she said. "That wasn't so—"

A rush of images hit her like a bad dream. Ocean as yellow as a dandelion; still, glassy surface unbroken by movement above or below. The taste of brine, then air, thick and murky. Something warm, like blood.

Eva fought the urge to vomit.

Leroy had also obtained a new neck ornament. Its myriad legs lovingly caressed the sides of his neck. Eva couldn't feel the thing on her, but if it looked anything like that, she'd try to avoid any mirrors for the duration of this job.

"Now can we collect our cargo?" she asked sourly.

"Certainly," the first monk said. "Follow me."

The small entrance door of the monastery was set into a larger door that remained closed. Both were made of a reddish metal, or possibly the brown stuff everything else was being built from. The aesthetic was austere, remote, perfect for a holy place.

Inside was the opposite. Garish colors decorated the walls, textured to form different geometric shapes depending on the placement of each piece. Strange submerged gardens, like a mixture between coral reefs and tiny underwater volcanoes, seemed to be creating more rock. She thought some of the parasites were lounging in the gardens, but she couldn't be sure since they weren't moving and they matched the environment. Also, the water was a cloudy yellow.

Too much protein, she thought.

And the inhabitants . . . This place was almost as mixed as Omicron, for all that it was much smaller. Truateg, walluk, even a tall watery yf wandered the halls. Not to mention a few humans here and there. They all seemed to be in a mighty hurry, but Eva couldn't figure out where they were hurrying to, exactly.

{{Isn't this delightful?}} Eva thought. Only she didn't think that. More like someone whispered it into her brain.

"Aw, seriously?" she said out loud. Ministrations indeed.

Leroy shot her a nervous glance. "Are you hearing things, boss?" he asked.

She nodded. "It's the parasites, I'll bet. Just ignore it. We'll be out of here soon." She resisted the urge to rip the thing off Leroy; if a cat could melt him into a giddy puddle, a critter latched onto his spinal cord was bad news.

Past the strange gardens were a series of tunnels that sloped gently downward. Set into the packed earth walls of the tunnels were small plaques next to opaque glass containers. They were mostly the same size, roughly two meters long, but a few were smaller or larger.

"What are these?" Eva asked.

{{They are the Redeemed,}} the voice in her head said. It was louder now, which made her nervous. {{Have the wonders of redemption been explained to you?}}

"Nope." Why was she talking to the thing? She should ignore it like she'd told Leroy to do.

{{Redemption is wonderful,}} the creature said. {{We lived in the warm dark once and redeemed who we could. But then the Great Voice told us of the Above, which was filled with the Unredeemed, and so we came.}}

"I'm not in the market for a new religion, thanks." She wasn't exactly practicing anything, but she respected the saints, more or less, and she prayed to the Virgin out of habit when things looked ugly.

The tunnel spilled into a huge room encased in a transparent shell. It was like looking up from the bottom of the sea, the way the sunlight danced on the ceiling. Eva reached a hand up as if she could touch it, as if she could rise and break the surface and take in the warm air outside. She lowered her hand, embarrassed, and found Leroy standing slack-jawed in the same posture.

"Leroy," she said. His attention snapped to her. "I think the parasite is doing more than talking. We may need a full scrub when we get back to the ship."

He nodded. "I got tagged by a beagelian spore cloud once. Thought I was a sunflower for a week. I can handle this."

"A sunflower?"

"A painting of a sunflower. But that makes even less sense, so I don't usually bother explaining."

"How much farther?" Eva asked the monk who was leading them.

{{Not far,}} her parasite replied. {{We are almost to the room of redemption. First we must pass through the room of communion.}}

"I wasn't asking you," Eva snapped.

{{There is no need to take that tone.}}

She focused on the walls of the tunnel they had entered. More of those opaque windows with their plaques—no, they were screens that gave information about . . . what?

The room of communion was dark where the other one had been light, the inside visible only thanks to the open door.

Until the door closed behind them.

"Qué rayo?" she said. With a thought, she called up a light from the collar of her suit. Leroy did the same, and the two of them stood back to back in the middle of the room, weapons drawn.

{{You need not be alarmed.}}

"The hell I need not."

The monk who had been leading them was gone. It was just the two of them and the neck suckers.

{{Do not be unreasonable. Redemption is not painful. Subsuming your will to ours requires only your silent complicity.}}

She ignored the voice again, searching the walls for a way out. They were seamless, smooth stone like the volcanic rocks in the garden pools at the entrance to the monastery.

"There must be a control panel," she told Leroy.

{{Our arguments for redemption are highly logical. For example, you will enjoy the nutrient pastes prepared under our careful supervision to sustain your biological functions.}}

"I think the controls are on the outside," Leroy said. His tone was calm, detached, and she hated herself more for bringing him. He'd be in PTSD hell later and it was all her fault.

Assuming there was a later.

{{Why do you refuse to discourse with us? You are very rude.}} There was a tightening at the nape of her neck where the fingers gripped her.

"Did you bring an EMP?" she asked. Leroy nodded, reaching for the pack slung across his broad shoulder.

{{It would be very unethical of you to damage our holy room.}}

"It's not going to damage your room," she snapped. "It'll disrupt any electronic locks temporarily."

{{How good of you to speak with us again. Surely we can maintain a pleasant and open dialogue. For example, we are happy to inform you that the locks on the room are not electronic.}}

"I thought you said not to talk to it," Leroy said. "Mine has been pretty quiet."

Eva sighed. "Don't waste the EMP. It says the locks are mechanical."

Leroy put the device away, crossing his arms over his chest. "What now, then? Wait in here until the bugs drive us crazy?"

{{We are not bugs. We are the Redeemers. There is no need to address us using pejorative terms.}}

"Shut up," she growled. "If you don't shut up, I'll tear you off my neck so fast, you'll redshift."

{{Threats are not very ethical. We have done you no harm. We are only talking.}}

"Boss, you want me to break down the door?"

She stared at Leroy in the dim light of their commlinks. "What, with your hands? Or did you get explosives in here somehow?"

He grinned. "I can rig the EMP to blow if you give me three minutes and one of your gravboots."

{{That would be very unethical.}}

"You don't like it, open the door." She sat down and unsealed the gravboot from her space suit.

{{We will be unable to conclude our business transaction if you damage our holy room.}}

"Oh, now it's about business." Her fingers groped for the place where the boot material overlapped her suit, and she pulled the boot off and tossed it to Leroy. He immediately got to work on his rigged EMP.

"All right," he said finally. "I'll set it up, you wait on the other side of the room."

{{Why do you persist in rejecting redemption? You have not offered cogent arguments against our generous offer.}}

"I'm a person, not an exosuit!" she shouted. "I don't want you riding around on my neck telling me what to do. Madre de dios, how is that so hard for you to understand?"

She froze. Leroy had closed his eyes and was breathing in a controlled way. Shit. She'd probably triggered him hard with that line.

{{We understand the words you are using, we simply reject them as false and invalid.}}

"Nothing more to talk about, then. See you on the ugly end of a blaster." Eva punched Leroy's shoulder. "I'm sorry," she said quietly. "I know this is a hot mess, but I'll make it up to you as soon as we get out of here."

Leroy continued to inhale and exhale rhythmically.

"Leroy?"

{{Perhaps we might negotiate favorable terms.}}

The room began to feel warm, cozy, like someone had flipped a switch from crazy to Christmas and handed Eva a cup of coquito. Probably manipulating the dopamine levels in her brain, she thought. Sneaky bastard.

She ignored it, wondering how many monks they'd have to blast through to escape. Wondering how she'd explain to her handler exactly how this whole deal had gone to the crow's nest and then taken a dive. They had fronted her money for fuel and supplies so she could make it here to get the cargo, and that would be added to her debt if she didn't succeed. More debt meant her sister was stuck in cryo longer, and Eva would have more chances to screw up as badly as she had on this job. More chances to let her crew get hurt because of her poor choices.

{{None of your concerns would continue if you would simply be redeemed. There is safety in silence.}}

Eva was so tired. She hadn't even noticed; she'd been busy dealing with one crisis after another. First Mari, then Glorious, then Miles Erck . . . It was all too much at once. The stress of it had finally caught up with her, but if she gave up, accepted that she would inevitably fail . . . Some of the tension slipped from her shoulders, first one breath, then another coming more easily. Everything would be fine if she'd give up, thanks to the annoying, invasive, kind, concerned spiritual guide humbly imploring her to stop fighting its attempts at communion and embrace redemption.

"Tu madre," Eva said. This thing was sneaky, and very tempting. "Leroy, you okay?"

He didn't answer.

{{He has begun his communion. Are you prepared for yours?}}

Gritting her teeth, Eva raised her pistol. "I'm going to prepare a communion for your buddy over there if they don't leave my crew alone."

{{We are not a hive mind. We operate individually for the greater good. You may speak to them yourself if you like.}}

She shook Leroy's arm. "Leroy, or alien dude, listen up. I'm going to put a hole in you if you don't back off."

Leroy dropped the rigged EMP and grabbed Eva's wrist. She tried to wrench out of his grip, but he had a hand like a power loader's claw. He shook her until she dropped her gun.

"You will not harm us," Leroy said.

"That's debatable," she said.

"We will wait with you until your communion is complete. If you attempt violence again, we will respond in kind."

Eva didn't want to hurt Leroy, though she was pretty sure she could take him if necessary. Maybe if she could get the door open . . . But then she'd have to fight her way through Leroy and a whole lot of monks by herself. Assuming they fought, which they might not, but she couldn't take that chance. And then how would she get the stupid liquor they'd come for in the first place?

{{There is no need for violence.}}

"You do realize that what you're doing to me and my buddy is a form of violence, right?" she snapped.

{{We are not harming you physically in any way.}}

"That's not the only kind of violence," she said. "You go on and on about being unethical, but you're forcing your will on people."

{{Redemption is entirely voluntary. It is your choice to accept communion.}}

"But what's the alternative? You're not giving me the choice to go back to my life as it was before, and that's unethical. It's unreasonable. You're treating me like an object instead of a person. If that's how you want to play it, then why bother with the bullshit choice? Why pretend this is anything but you keeping me locked up until I do what you want, no matter what I want?"

{{You will be released as soon as our communion is complete. Is that not what you desire?}}

She let that thought sit like a stone in her hand. All she had to do was give up, and she'd be free. Not a chance; she hadn't rolled over for Glorious, and he didn't live in a literal shithole. But how long did she have? Could she hold out in hopes of rescue?

What was the thing doing to her, anyway? She didn't want to end up like Leroy, but how else would she get out?

How else indeed. She replayed what the parasite had said to her earlier and grinned.

{{No, that will not work.}}

Eva tilted her head sideways and let her mouth fall open. She unfocused her eyes, crossing them slightly.

"Our communion is complete," she said, trying to match the phrasing and intonation of the parasite. "We may now depart for the room of redemption."

{{Stop what you are doing. This is highly unethical.}}

A rustle of clothes. Steady breaths. Then Leroy knocked at the door, a staccato pattern using the tips of his fingers rather than his knuckles.

After a long pause, locks moved outside the room. The door

opened inward, letting in a bright yellow light and a blast of warm air.

That was one problem solved, then. Now she had to figure out how to get the cargo, get off-planet, and get that thing off Leroy without hurting him. Hurting him more than she already had, anyway.

How could she possibly make this up to him later? She couldn't. She had really fucked up this time, and there was no coming back from it. Hopefully he would forgive her eventually, but if he didn't, she would understand.

I'm so sorry, she thought, staring numbly at the broad outline of his back. She scooped up her pistol and the EMP and followed Leroy through the door.

The room beyond was strangely clinical compared to the rest of the monastery. Low ceilings were lit by yellow orbs that hung in nets suspended at regular intervals. The floors and walls were the same reflective stone of the communion room, but less polished. At the far end, a giant lift platform hovered in a cylindrical hollow in the rock.

But what caught Eva's attention were the rows upon rows of beds on which people lay facedown, naked as they came.

Next to the beds, containers of some unknown material waited to be used, or had been filled and were waiting to be collected by the monks who walked the aisles, murmuring softly to the people. The liquid inside was an electric yellow that could have come from the light, or could have been the natural color of the stuff.

And it was coming from the back ends of the parasites clinging to the necks of all the people in the beds.

Please tell me that is not what I think it is, she thought. No answer from the parasite. Just as well, since it was a rhetorical question.

"Are you ready to be redeemed?" The ahirk monk who had led them there reappeared at her side, wiggling their tendrils drunkenly.

"I, uh . . ." She struggled to regain her composure. "We should deliver the cargo as promised, before the crew of this one's ship becomes suspicious and violent."

"Why would you not call them to inform them of your redemption, that they might be drawn to be redeemed themselves?" asked the monk.

"That is . . . a thought. But I—we do not think they would believe the redemption was voluntary, no matter what we told them."

Leroy stepped in. "This is logical. This one's memories suggest the one called Eva was volatile and not prone to reasonable choices."

Eva's mouth twitched but she said nothing.

"Very well. Deliveries must be made. I am sorry to see two newly Redeemed leave so quickly, before their first true redemption." The monk gestured for another to approach, and together they led Eva and Leroy to the back of the room.

The second monk began loading containers of butt juice onto a cargo pallet next to the lift, and Leroy joined him after a moment, which twisted a knife in Eva's guts. She had seen him do the same thing so many times on *La Sirena Negra,* but now the easy sway of his muscles was stiffened by the awkward control of the parasite. She wondered whether Pink would be able to get the thing off without hurting him. Whether he was too far gone to save.

{{If you remove the Redeemer on your ship, they will die.}}

Oh, welcome back, you little comemierda, she thought. I had hoped you'd given up.

{{Our failure to ensure communion will mark us as unworthy. We will be rebuked.}}

Not my problem, she thought. It's either you get off my neck before I get off this rock, or my medic figures out how to remove you, and you get to do the vacuum rhumba until you freeze and pop.

Silence replied. Should she ask the thing about getting a parasite off? Probably a waste of time. Why would it want to tell her such valuable information, even if it might save their lives?

Instead, she continued to watch Leroy and the monk load cargo. Her hands kept wanting to pick at the scab on her neck, but of course there was a giant thing in the way.

"This is sufficient to fulfill the contract," the monk said.

"Then let us return to the surface and load the ship." Leroy pushed the floating pallet onto the lift.

They all climbed on and it started to rise. There were a few windows here and there, but mostly the ride was smooth and boring, a straight shot up from the bowels of the monastery to the original room where they had entered.

The only one in the antechamber was the muk monk who had put the parasites on them, what felt like a million years before but had probably been a couple of hours. Now she should be in commlink range to reach the ship, with any luck.

((Pickup,)) she pinged at everyone on the ship. She didn't know what the monks' defensive capabilities were, and she didn't want to find out the hard way.

{{Our ideas are the only defense we need. Our arguments are impenetrable.}}

Eva's eyes rolled so hard she thought they would fall out. She hoped the monks didn't see it.

{{You are very cynical.}}

Eat a turd, she thought.

{{You are also very rude.}}

"And you're a parasite attached to my skull who can't seem to understand the meaning of the phrase 'Jódete, coño!'"

Eva took a deep breath and hung her head, peering up at Leroy through the hair that had fallen over her face. She hadn't meant to say that out loud, but here she was. No sense closing the barn door after the cows got out.

"So, hey," she said. "I guess my communion didn't work out after all. Why don't you take your little guy back and give them another shot with someone else?"

The ahirk monk waggled their tendrils. "When a communion fails, there can be no redemption. There is only the cleansing."

Eva began to back toward the entrance. "Cleansing, huh? Is that like a nice relaxing trip to the spa? Maybe a hot stone massage and a nutrient dip?"

"No," Leroy said, advancing on her with his meaty hands clenched into fists. "You will be given to the waters of flame, that your defective form may be purified and give rise to a new Redeemer without flaws."

"Fed to an underwater volcano, huh? Sounds hot."

Leroy paused, cocking his head to one side. "It is hot, yes."

"Maybe you should redeem yourselves a sense of humor. Here's a voucher." Eva pulled out the rigged EMP and flicked it on, tossing it at the door behind her.

She wasn't prepared for the entrance door to blow outward like it had been kicked by a giant. The impact sucked her back, onto the planet's cold surface, her isohelmet flickering on just in time to seal her suit against the thin atmosphere. The pressure coils activated to maintain internal pressure, but unfortunately did nothing to cushion her fall on the hard rocks outside. She bounced once, then slid to a painful stop.

Leroy's helmet also activated, but the monks apparently had not been prepared for a breach in their monastery. They fell to their knees, gasping, as the carefully regulated interior atmosphere began to equalize.

To her surprise, the parasites abandoned their hosts, scuttling down the backs of the people and toward the elevator to the redemption room. They moved slowly, like crabs with arthritis, dragging long, wet tails behind them.

Bet they won't be "cleansed," she thought bitterly. What a bunch of jerks.

{{And what of us?}}

Eva scrambled to her feet, eyeing the lumbering form of Leroy and his still-intact parasite. "I'll drop my helmet for a few seconds. You can make a break for it. Pretend to be my buddy's parasite, say you escaped just in time."

{{You would let us go free?}}

"I can still chuck you out the airlock if you want."

{{We would rather take our chances with our own kind. Though we are sorry not to see the great dark seas in the sky.}}

Eva feinted right and ducked under Leroy's outstretched arm, sprinting back to the monastery entrance.

"Get ready, bug. Move quickly or you'll get to see that dark after all."

{{We . . . appreciate being given a choice.}}

She skidded to a stop, opened her helmet, and counted to five as she held her breath. There was a feeling of lightness, then another like someone running a hand down her back, and then it was gone. The helmet closed again.

Eva didn't bother looking behind her. Up ahead, *La Sirena Negra* flew in, its landing gear engaged. But Leroy still advanced on her, his gait growing more sure as he moved.

((Leroy's compromised,)) Eva pinged at the crew. ((Stun him.))

A few seconds later, the cargo bay door opened. Vakar bounded out with his helmet already activated, while Pink hung on to a hook next to the door, behind the gravity curtain that kept the ship's atmosphere intact. Vakar landed, weapon raised, and with two quick shots he nailed Leroy in the back.

The big man didn't stop.

"Well, that's unfortunate," Eva murmured.

Vakar fired again while running toward them, but missed Leroy by a few centimeters. Pink, meanwhile, was preparing her sniper rifle, her hands moving with quick precision, eye patch flipped up to reveal her cybernetic eye.

Eva found herself backed into the monastery, and she bumped into the cargo pallet, which she'd forgotten in the confrontation. She kick-started the levitation device, and it rose into the air, hovering at hip level.

"Hey, Leroy, catch!" She grabbed it like a throwing disc and spun it toward him, wrenching her biceps and shoulder, hoping belatedly that the cargo wouldn't be damaged.

Leroy did catch it, grabbing it in both hands and staring at her over the top of the containers. "Why do you want us to catch this?" he asked. "It is very illogical."

Pink shouldered her rifle and peered through the scope.

"That's me," Eva said. "Highly volatile, unreasonable choices. Nighty-night."

"It is not time for the local star to be—"

Pink fired, the tranq disc attaching itself to Leroy's ample backside. His eyes rolled up into his head, and with a soft sigh he slid to the ground.

Vakar got an arm under him and lifted him up, starting to carry him back to the ship, smelling pained as he exacerbated his own still-healing injuries.

"Throw him on the pallet!" Eva shouted. Behind her, the lift returned, so she rolled and hid behind the containers in case the approaching monks were armed.

They were. One of their shots cracked open a container, which oozed yellow liquid.

Vakar hefted Leroy onto the pallet, and Eva yanked on it, running backward toward the ship. Pink caught it and angled it into the cargo bay, while Eva and Vakar leaped through the open door and lay flat on the floor, projectiles whizzing past them.

Pink closed the door as Eva pinged Min to get them gone. The doctor rested the butt of her rifle on the ground, pursing her lips and glaring at Eva like God's own mother catching her with a hand in the cookie jar.

"What happened this time?" Pink asked. The ship shook as their shields absorbed a hit, but she didn't lose her balance.

Eva scowled. What had happened? Shit had gone wrong again. She should never have agreed to let Leroy come with her in the first place. This was all her fault, and now all she could do was damage control.

"Leroy has a parasite on his neck," Eva replied. "Get it off him."

"Parasites are tricky, woman; they—"

"Get. It. Off him. Vakar?"

"I have not injured myself further." Vakar sat up slowly, checking himself for shrapnel. Underneath the pain, he smelled inexplicably of vanilla and almonds. The translator couldn't pin that one down, but suggested "savage delight."

"Bullshit. Secure the cargo while I help move Leroy to the med bay, then let Pink examine you, too."

"I'll get Leroy. I don't need you dicking around in my business." Pink put her rifle away in a locker and gestured to the pale redhead lying on the pallet. "That's two injuries in two cycles, hon."

"I know." Eva realized her hands were trembling, whether from anger or despair, she wasn't sure.

Por qué no los dos?

The cargo listed as the ship evaded more oncoming fire. Eva got to her feet and steadied the containers, grimacing at the pain in her arm and shoulder. Vakar grabbed some nearby straps and helped her secure them more carefully. They'd already lost one batch of that crap; it would probably be coming out of her pay for the job. The thought put a sour taste in her mouth.

"You were not injured?" Vakar asked.

"Probably won't want to wrestle you for a while, but I'll live."

"That is good."

She cocked a grin at him. "I know, you're tired of getting your ass kicked. Not my fault I'm more flexible."

He smelled slightly spicy. "I am sure I could submit to a handicap if necessary to place us on equal footing."

"You sassy little stinkbug, if you think—"

Min spoke through the intercom. "Cap, where are we delivering the cargo?"

Eva pinged her the coordinates, trying not to show her displeasure at the interruption.

"Plenty of time for wrestling," Min said in a teasing tone. "That's a few hours away."

"Nah," Eva said, wagging her head and giving Vakar a rueful smile. "It's going to take me at least that long to wash the memory of all that shit off."

More importantly, she wouldn't be able to focus on anything more complicated than standing in a hydrosonic shower until she knew Leroy was going to be okay.

Chapter 7

DAMAGES

The bug-juice cargo was handed off to another grumpy scientist, this time in a big mobile facility on Beskore, in the Gespora system. Unlike the last place, this one was well within BOFA territory; Eva wondered what cover story they were using for their activities here, especially since she had no trouble with the system or planetary authorities when she was filing the appropriate customs forms after coming through their Gate. While the majority of the planet's inhabitants lived in elaborate underwater bubble cities at subduction zones on the edges of the few large land masses, The Fridge's people had set up on the surface near the equator. The steady rain in the area matched Eva's mood perfectly, right down to the fact that it was composed of sulfuric acid.

"There were supposed to be twenty containers," Grumpy said, with a tone that suggested he'd be asking for Eva's manager.

"A container was damaged in transit," Eva replied. "You won't be charged for it."

"I don't care about the cost." He gestured at one of the heavily armed security guards flanking the entrance. "See that she doesn't leave until this is resolved."

Eva forced a smile and settled in to wait. By the time she was released, she'd cleared some of her q-mail backlog, sent a few late payment notices on old invoices, and even reposted ads for her various shell companies' services on the usual free boards and AR relays. She'd also plotted several ways to escape if things went from dull to dangerous in a hurry.

Anything to keep from thinking about Leroy.

She was surprised to find her handler just outside the entrance. Pholise wore a spacesuit like Eva's, only armless, and they had coverings for each of their three lower appendages but no visible shoes. The pattern was also different, nearly translucent, with a cloth wrapped around the outside like flexible glass.

"Nice to see you in person," Eva said. "You couldn't message me the next job instead of getting in my face?"

Pholise's head ruff rose slightly, then fell again. "The imperfection in the previous assignment was deemed sufficient to warrant more direct attention and oversight."

"I screwed up, so I have to talk to the real live instructor instead of finishing the q-net class by myself." So Grumpy had called her manager after all. Splendid.

"That assessment is not inaccurate." They rotated slightly. "The damaged container will be deducted from your compensation. Or it can be added to your debt, according to your preference."

Eva snorted. "What is it with people giving me a choice between two things that suck plutonium exhaust? You know I almost got turned into a glorified zombie, right? And one of my crew is still in the med bay getting a parasite disentangled from his brain stem and spine."

Pink wasn't sure Leroy would make it, but Eva didn't tell the tuann that, partly because she was avoiding telling it to herself.

"The Fridge cannot be held responsible for imperfect execution of a given task."

Once again, it took every ounce of willpower Eva possessed not to punch them. Lightning flashed in the distance, forking across the saffron-colored sky.

"What's my balance, then?" Eva asked.

Pholise told her.

"That can't be right. Who's coming up with these valuations? Because they're—"

"Criminal?" Pholise's ruff twitched, and this registered with Eva's translator as amusement.

"Yes, ha." At that rate, Eva would be working for The Fridge until this planet dissolved from the rain. And here she had thought this would all be over in a few dozen cycles.

"The amount owed was altered due to the increased risk associated with your performance metrics."

"So someone added a few points to a multiplier somewhere and now I'm double-fucked. Great." She wished she knew as much about this kind of math as her mother did, but there was a reason she hadn't gone into banking, namely that she found it more boring than piloting spaceships and punching fools. And yet being captain of her own ship meant doing loads of math every cycle; not the same as monitoring transactions or auditing thousands of accounts in multiple currencies, maybe, but close enough for hand grenades.

Don't think about Mom, she told herself. Focus. You don't want your next call to her to be bad news about Mari.

Pholise sighed. "If you are finished airing your grievances—"

"As if."

"—then your next assignment should be communicated." They did a strange, swaying dance for a few moments, then straightened. "You are to proceed to the planet Futis, to procure a shipment of a delicate nature."

"Is it alive?" Eva asked, thinking of the cats she still hadn't sold.

"It is inactive. Delivery coordinates will be provided once your cargo is secure and you have departed the system."

Inactive? Machine, then. Proarkhe, maybe, like the one on Suatera, though she'd be surprised if The Fridge would trust her with something so rare and valuable. Especially if they were worrying about her performance metrics.

"Aren't the Futisians a bunch of people-eaters?" She crossed her arms, trying not to think about the scab on her neck that she wanted to scratch until she bled.

"In a strictly legal sense, no, they are not."

That sounded bogus. "So then, yes, but they have really good lawyers. Come on, if you know something, tell me so I don't end up with a parasite in my cuca next time."

Pholise swayed again. "Your ill will toward me is notable, Captain Innocente, but my intent is not to make your job more difficult." They made a sound like a sigh. "On Futis, a card will be assigned to you that signifies you are a member of a sapient species."

"A card? Like, a physical card I have to carry around in my pocket?"

"Yes."

"That's pretty archaic," Eva said. "What's the point?"

"If you should lose your card, it would signify that you were not, in fact, sapient. In which case, you would be considered meat, and may be butchered as such indiscriminately."

It was Eva's turn to laugh. "Of course. They could just do a commlink registration or something, but then how would they keep up the gray market trade in exotic body parts?"

A couple of pings came in from Min. ((Bad news. Glorious.))

Eva darkened her helmet and stared up at the sky. Sure enough, there was that asshole's enormous ship, descending through the crimson clouds. It looked like one of the old-fashioned stars people used to put on Christmas trees, with four large points bisected by four smaller ones. She had only ever seen them in pictures; her grandparents favored angel tree toppers, and her mother had continued that tradition until she stopped putting up a tree at all. Still did presents in the shoes after the New Year, though, for the wise men following a star . . .

"I guess this is goodbye again, Pholise," she said. "Wish I could say it was a pleasure, but I kind of hope I'll get to shoot you once this is all over."

Pholise straightened until they were a half-meter taller than Eva. "Your selfishness and cynicism do you no credit, Captain Innocente. Did it never occur to you that a handler is also in control of me, and my assignment is you?"

It hadn't, of course. She'd been so wrapped up in keeping her lies straight, keeping her crew ignorant, keeping her face from showing how much this would be driving her to drink if she hadn't sworn it off. She was being selfish all right, and it stung to acknowledge it. Especially with what had happened to Leroy. If he didn't make it—

Eva flushed and looked away. "Mierda. How did things get so bad with these creeps? Why hasn't anyone stood up to them?"

"As was said before: they are not in the habit of meddling with anyone who has nothing to lose."

Futis. Damn it all. This was going to go over like a fart in church with her crew. Eva ran toward her ship as Glorious's ominous star descended, and the acid rain turned to a dusting of sulfide metal snow.

Eva returned to *La Sirena Negra* and sat through an extra decontamination cycle as Min evaded their fish-faced friend, telling herself it was for her safety and everyone else's. It had nothing to do with stalling before she had to face everyone, especially Leroy.

Once inside, she ignored the cats that curled around her legs as if trying to trip her and went straight for the med bay. The room was barely big enough to fit three people, lined with cabinets containing supplies, equipment or both. They weren't fully stocked—hadn't been for a while, with business being mediocre—but Pink had a knack for synthesizing what they needed in a pinch.

Leroy lay on the bed that took up the center of the room, curled up on his side with his eyes closed. He would have looked like he was sleeping peacefully, covered by a blanket from the waist down, except for the gas-and-nutrient mask covering his nose and mouth, and the parasite still latched to his neck. His tattoos flickered like a broken holovid.

I should never have let him come with me, Eva thought. She'd told herself that so many times now that it might as well have been a mantra. And yet she couldn't undo it, couldn't take it back; all she could do now was hope he didn't die because of her mistake.

Pink sat on a stool in one corner, eye patch flipped up so her cybernetic eye could watch Leroy. Her brown skin was a shade paler than usual, like someone had done her makeup with the wrong color foundation.

"He's stable," Pink said before Eva could ask. "Not many people have run into these things, so finding information has been like digging for coal in a cave at night."

"Has Min—"

"She's helping search the q-net, yeah."

"Is there anything else I can—"

"No, but if I think of something, I'll ping you." Pink rose to her feet and cracked her neck. "You delivered the cargo?"

Because of course what mattered right now was the cargo, the client, the job. "Yes, thankfully that was all over before the Glorious Shitface showed up. Got paid, less the busted container. I'll eat that one, don't worry." Eva swallowed, blinking rapidly to fight off tears. She sounded like her fucking father.

"Oh, I'm gonna worry," Pink said. "My head is a hive all buzzing with worries right now, my little Eva-Bee."

Pink stepped out of the corner to lean against the counter next to her. Where Eva was short and stocky, Pink was tall and lean, with the body of a swimmer. They both knew Eva could kick Pink's ass if it came to a fight, but they also both knew Eva wouldn't dream of doing something that stupid.

"Let me give you a taste of this worry honey, straight from the honeycomb," Pink continued. "I'm worried about Leroy, for obvious reasons. I'm worried about Vakar for different reasons. And I'm worried about you for one big, sticky reason."

"Yeah?"

"You're lying again."

On the side of the bed, a tube snaked out from under the covers, depositing urine into a container near the floor. Drip. Drip. Eva waited for Pink to say more, but the woman was silent. Patient. Expectant. She knew Eva would crack first.

She wasn't wrong. "The nondisclosure clause was—"

"Horseshit. Nobody is that paranoid. They'd just have all of us sign it." Pink paused. "Unless there's naughty shit going on. Which I know you would not be a party to, because you're not a skeezy prick like Tito and your dad are. Right?"

"Hell no." That was true enough, or so she thought. So far nothing had been illegal or unethical, just dangerous—or, in the case of Miles Erck, incredibly annoying. But she needed to smooth this over with Pink, or she might as well tell everyone to walk now. Hell, that's probably what she should do, if she didn't want anyone else to end up like Leroy.

She thought of what Pholise had said. Cynical and selfish. Every time she tried to find the strength to leave, her own feeble desire to stay with these people, her people, overpowered her.

Every damn time.

Oh, Mari, they'd better not do anything to you, she thought. Because if I fuck over my entire life and theirs to save yours, and it ends up being all for nothing . . . She couldn't bring herself to imagine that outcome, because it felt like a black hole waiting to suck her in.

"One job went wrong, that's all," Eva said. "They thought the parasites were an urban legend, too. It was nobody's fault."

"Yeah, well, tell that to Leroy. You keep secrets, people get hurt."

Eva watched the big man's chest rise and fall slowly, rhythmically, remembering how he felt about commanders who withheld information and straight-up lied. How he almost killed a comemierda paleotechnologist for that very reason, because he'd watched enough of his fellow soldiers end up exactly as he was now. Lying on some slab, machines breathing for them if they were lucky; the unlucky ones had their organs systematically removed for donation, because they didn't need them anymore.

If she kept thinking about it, she'd lose her damn mind. As it was, she was on the verge of locking herself in her cabin and screaming until her voice was gone.

Something else Pink had said tugged at her attention.

"You're worried about Vakar?" she asked.

Pink chuckled with her mouth closed, a low, deep sound like a handful of plucked bass notes. "You need to do something about him, girl."

"Really."

"He's a good engineer. Better than our last one, even."

"Connor, or Irann?"

"Irann. Connor was a worthless thief; of course he's better than Connor." She sighed. "Anyway, I'd hate to lose him. But . . ."

"But?"

Pink leaned her elbow on the counter, her expression softening. "These things never work out."

"These things?"

"You repeat one more word I say, I'm going to slap you. You know what I'm talking about."

Eva scrutinized her boots, cheeks coloring.

You learned the rules when you first started flying: Don't fuck people who aren't on your level. Above or below, it doesn't matter. Because at some point, one of you will have to give an order, and the other will have to take it.

Once that wedge is hammered in, the crack will only get bigger, not smaller. And then, no matter how much fucking you've done, you're both well and truly fucked.

"It's not like that," Eva said. "You're imagining things."

"Is that what your fancy smell translators tell you? The expensive ones you definitely didn't install for the sake of one particular crew member?"

Eva started to answer, but Pink waved her silent.

"Look, even if I didn't know him—and after two years, I know him well enough—I know you. Lying to us is one thing, but lying to yourself? Treat this before it spreads, before the cure is worse than the disease." She smirked and slapped Eva's shoulder. "Now buzz off, little Bee, and let me get back to work."

Pink's expression turned serious again as she moved to check one of the machines hooked up to Leroy. Eva left the woman to her thoughts, wishing she had a clever response in her back pocket to all the stuff Pink had laid on her, that she had a defense against the accusations.

Unfortunately, that would involve lying to herself, and she'd only be proving that Pink was completely right.

Eva found Min in the mess, the pilot staring at the food synthesizer like it was a mystery she had to solve.

"Hungry?" Eva asked.

Min nodded, her blue hair swaying gently. "I can't decide what to eat," she said with her human mouth.

Eva wasn't even hungry, but her body was, so she sent the synthesizer a command for a protein patty with her commlink, and the machine's timer started counting down. "That's when you need someone else to make the choice for you. My mom used to do that. I'd get too hangry to do anything but yell."

Min turned up her chin, confusion plain on her face.

"Hungry and angry." Funny that the colloquialism hadn't translated; it was an old one. A few words never did, though most eventually got added through use.

"I never had to feed myself until I started bot fighting," Min said. "I had too many aunties. They were always cooking something and making me eat it, then telling me I would never get married if I didn't lose weight."

"Sounds like my abuela," Eva said. "Except she always said I was too skinny, and no one wanted to marry a skinny person because that meant they couldn't cook."

Min giggled. "You still can't cook."

"Yeah, you can't win with abuelas and aunties." Eva picked at the scab on her neck, even as the voice of her abuela echoed in her head, reminding her that she was only making it worse. It would never heal unless she left it alone. She'd never been good at leaving things alone.

"Leroy's going to be okay, you know," she added.

"I know. He's tough." Min's eyes lost their present look, as if she'd retreated back into her ship body. "The cargo bay is just so quiet without him. Empty. Like someone took out my liver and there's a big hole where it used to be."

What could Eva say? It was her fault. An apology wasn't enough. One thing was for sure, though: she'd do the next mission herself, because if no one got off the ship, no one could quasi-legally be shot for meat.

She didn't want to think about that now, though. Eva grabbed a meal bar from the cabinet and handed it to Min, who tore it open and started to eat it mechanically. She was the only one who didn't mind the seaweed-and-lentil flavor.

"Did you get a chance to play your game?" Eva asked, leaning against the counter. "Before the station got, you know."

Min swallowed and smiled. "Yes! Though I couldn't finish because the station protocols locked everything down once the speakers were hacked."

"Hope your friends weren't too mad."

Min gave a dismissive wave with the remnants of the bar.

"They thought it was cool. All of them live on colonies doing boring stuff. They don't get why I still play when I'm out having real adventures."

Eva's protein patty dinged. "Why do you still play?" she asked. She blew on it while she waited for it to cool.

"It's a different kind of rush," Min said. "You know you're not really in any danger, so you can let loose more. And you get prizes!" She slid a hand across her mouth. "Not that getting paid isn't good, but it's not the same as getting cool armor and stuff."

Eva laughed. "Yeah, a bunch of credits in an account are definitely boring compared to swords and flying horses."

Her patty tasted like a sad attempt at chicken. At least it was edible when hot. Min finished her bar and tossed the wrapper in the recycler, then started making herself tea.

"Any new prospects for the cats?" Eva asked.

Min put her cup on the counter a little more forcefully than necessary. "Someone wanted to know if they were uniform in size and color, and someone else asked if they were sensitive to metal or radiation. I deleted those."

"And what happened to your little revolutionary buddy?" Eva took another bite of not-chicken.

Min swiveled her head, brows furrowing.

"The cat." She swallowed. "Little bastard is a troublemaker."

"It's a girl cat. Almost all calicos are girls."

Eva took another bite. "You gonna name her?"

"Maybe. I mostly call her Manjiji Mala."

Eva choked on her food, coughing it up into her mouth. "Come again?"

"Manjiji Mala," Min repeated. But this time Eva heard it in her head as "don't touch." She wondered if the pilot knew what the word "mala" meant in Spanish. The translator might pick it up, or it might not. Names could be weird.

"Mala it is," she said, taking another bite as she walked toward her room. "See you later, mija."

The food turned to mush in her mouth as she considered how she would deal with Vakar. Maybe Pink was wrong. Sure, he'd gotten her a present, saved her ass a couple of times, but some people were just nice. It didn't have to mean anything.

But you want it to, the voice in her head whispered.

Shut the fuck up, she thought back.

Eva gulped down the rest of her food, then flopped onto her bed without bothering to take off her spacesuit. She'd decontaminated enough to kill a small ecosystem, so she wasn't as worried about showering as she might normally be. And if Vakar could smell anything weird on her, well, that was his problem.

I'll figure it out after Futis, she told herself. Whatever other thoughts tried to plague her were quickly silenced by bone-deep exhaustion. She didn't even have the energy to dream.

Chapter 8

THE RACE CARD

From space, Futis looked like a blasted desert hellscape with occasional shiny metal domes. But on the surface, it looked like a junkyard overgrown with plants the color of sand. The metal domes were the spaceports, where local and off-world merchants mingled to make deals and trade wares and double-cross each other in traditional fringe-world style. Futis wasn't a part of any planetary federation, and that suited the native kartians and other nonindigenous species just fine; for all the lack of protection that came with being independent, they could also make up their own laws and compel strangers to follow them at their own risk.

The place was oxygen- and nitrogen-rich, which gave Eva a little giddy oomph until the nanites in her blood started compensating. As she left her ship, she was approached by a harried-looking kartian with a small metallic box hanging from a strap slung across his body. His eyestalks faced in different directions, only one of them at Eva.

"Name?" he asked in a singsongy whistle.

"Captain Eva Innocente."

He wrapped his hairy proboscis around the box and pointed it at her. A light flashed, momentarily blinding her. By the time she had blinked away the hazy spot, he was holding out a small metallic card.

"This is your identification card," he said. "If you lose it, you may obtain a replacement card at any spaceport on the planet for a small fee."

Huh. Maybe things had changed since Pholise got their intelligence about the place. Still, Eva didn't want to find out the hard way.

"Will any of your other crewmates need a card?" he asked.

"No," she said.

"Yes. Vakar Tremonis san Jaigodaris."

Eva scowled at Vakar. How had he snuck up on her like that? Normally she could smell him coming. "You're staying on the ship."

"I would prefer not to. Also, Pink told me to come, and then we engaged in the ritual handshake she created to reinforce our friendship." He paused. "She indicated that she was concerned for your well-being."

Or she's suspicious, or she wants to give me time and privacy to talk to Vakar about . . . things, Eva thought. "I'm ordering you to stay on the ship."

"After what happened last time? Captain, I cannot in good conscience allow you to venture out alone, especially not in a place like this. Do not compel me to do so. Please."

They stared at each other. Vakar didn't blink any of his eyelids, and he had the unmitigated gall to smell like licorice and worry. She should say no. Tell Pink to stop trying to start shit.

Selfishness won again.

"Me cago en ti," Eva said. "Fine. Stay behind me."

Vakar accepted his card from the kartian and tucked it away.

"Thank you for your visit. Please enjoy our many exciting tourist attractions with an approved guide." But before Eva could ask for directions, the kartian was gone.

Eva examined her card. Thin, metal, with relevant information—name, species composition, protein quantity, macro- and micronutrient proportions, allergen warnings, even a "best by" date—imprinted on the top along with a terrible picture that must have been taken when the light flashed. She looked like she was saying something, squinting with her lip curled up. Worse than her manual piloting license; at least in that one she just looked surprised.

She flipped it over to check out the back. A bunch of disclaimers about the government of Futis not being held responsible if she lost the damn thing, and also making no representations as to the accuracy of the card's contents.

Oh, this was rich: *Do not give your identification card to any third party. Retain control of your identification card at all times.* How many idiots had handed them over to hunters before they added these friendly reminders? And why bother at all, if they didn't actually care? Plausible deniability, maybe.

Eva slid the card into an inner pocket of her suit and sealed it, then pulled up her commlink. Her map said their contact should be about ten kilometers west of the port, at one of the many junkyards catering to both locals and off-planet folks like her trying to source spaceship parts on the cheap.

She led Vakar through the bustle of the station, where other boxes of cargo were being loaded onto pallets and floaters for local delivery ships as small as a shuttle or huge cargo transports that took up five docks in width, their lengths sprawling back into the dusty vegetation, which grew fast even though it was constantly trampled and burned by thrusters. A lot of people seemed to be hanging out with nothing to do, watching the traders and merchants with more than one set of eyes as if waiting for something to happen. Mercs, maybe. Or—

Someone came running into the station, a human by the looks of him, blood trailing from a wound on his thigh. A shot took apart his knee, and he collapsed to the ground, but still tried to crawl his way toward one of the kartians with the metal card-making box.

"Please," he gasped. "A card."

The official looked down at him impassively. "Name?"

Before the man could answer, another shot took him on the side of the head. The shooter was a kartian with a missing eye-stalk, which had been replaced by the lens of an optical laser weapon of some kind. She was also missing a leg, which had been swapped out for a metal one with perhaps more joints than it was meant to have. She moved quickly despite the prosthesis, or because of it, and she had to shoo off a few of those layabouts who had inched closer to the body while its blood pooled on the ground.

"My kill, slackers," she sang-whistled. "Go hunt your own meat."

"Aw, Grissy," someone whistled.

"Stick it in your snout," she replied.

Grissy's commlink was an older model, strapped to her wrist instead of implanted, so she ran her hairy arms together and wiggled them in the appropriate gestures to do whatever she was doing. Which seemed to be giving a bribe to the official, who maybe had been a shade slower than absolutely necessary. They touched proboscises lightly and the official moved away to let her stuff the dead guy into a bag with an antigrav ring around the mouth.

"That was abominable," Vakar said, smelling disgusted. "Did he not know the consequences of losing his card?"

Eva shrugged. "Maybe it wasn't his fault. Or maybe he thought no sapient species would be so gross about, you know." She gestured at the kartian hunter as they passed her, whistling softly to herself. "Some humans used to hunt dolphins before they took out a subduction power plant in Chile."

"Dolphins?"

"Aquatic Terran mammals, bigger than me and twice as charming."

"You have your charms. And penchant for destruction."

"Flatterer."

Eva resisted the urge to pat her pocket to be sure the ID card was still there. She had a feeling some of these kartians had a lot of practice at pickpocketing.

"Have you been here before?" Eva asked.

"Twice," Vakar said. "Once on a resupply mission, once to find a missing freighter."

"Did you find it?"

"Most of it. Not the crew."

She started to ask more, but his morose smell put her off. Vakar hated to talk about his past. Eva knew he was clean because she'd run a background check on him when he first joined up, and since then he'd never given her cause to worry. He did his job, grew scented crystals in delicate glass containers as a hobby, was social when he felt like it and scarce when he didn't.

Maybe it was a little weird how good a sparring partner he was for an engineer, but she wasn't one to pry.

She knew what it was like to want to forget. Not just Garilia, but all the shit leading up to it, all the ways in which she'd been the kind of person she would happily give a boot to the ass now. The lying, the cockiness, the easy violence . . . And worst of all, she'd been so sure she was a good person, even while she was doing bad things.

Denial was a hell of a drug.

They rented one of the cheap two-seater gas dashers people used to get around there, with their weird triple-balloon tank system in the rear. Eva climbed in first and Vakar took the back seat, standing and gripping the roll bar. She had the controls, which she used with practiced ease, despite the antiquated system not syncing properly with her commlink.

She leaned back, thinking about how she didn't often get to see Vakar from this upside-down angle. The pangolin-like scales on his neck were smaller than on the rest of his body, smoother; she resisted the urge to rub them, then mentally shouted at herself for even thinking it in the first place. Pink's plan to fix their little situation was going swimmingly already. Like a fucking dolphin on a murder mission.

"You ready?" she asked.

"Yes." Vakar smelled like a candy store, literally. Were her emotions that complicated? Probably.

They sped off, vegetation rippling in their wake. If there was a speed limit here, she was probably breaking it, whatever the punishment for that might be. She weaved in and out of the other traffic, which was mostly pedestrian until they passed beyond the immediate border of the spaceport area, and then it was a long, empty road except for the occasional pit stop or scrapper yard. In the distance, jagged rocks leaned against each other like enormous dominoes fallen sideways, and she could have sworn she saw someone ride a dasher off the edge of one and glide toward the ground.

Not her idea of fun at the moment, but maybe another time.

There was no sign in front of the place where they stopped, but it matched the coordinates. It was gated, with a shoulder-high fence overrun by vegetation. Tarps and metal sheets covered the merchandise, no doubt to keep the plants off. Just inside the gate, there was a sturdy building with a door made of razor wire, electrified, judging from the low hum emanating from it.

Chained next to it was a hard-shelled crehnisk, its carapace shimmering green in the golden light, grinding a piece of metal in its circular mouth. It paused and turned beady eyes toward them, fluttering hidden wings.

She couldn't identify half the stuff in the piles, even though she considered herself relatively savvy when it came to ship parts. She'd learned from her dad, after all, and he had bought and sold a few hundred different kinds of starships in the time she'd spent with him, before she took off with Tito's crew. So long ago, it seemed like forever, even if it had only been ten years.

That made her think of her mother, of course, and her sister. They had been so mad when she went to live with Pete. She hadn't cared at the time about his less legal dealings, had assumed the stories were either exaggerated or somehow justified, especially the ones that sounded dangerously interesting. She'd thought they just didn't want her to leave them, didn't want her light-years away in another star system instead of getting a boring job like monitoring credit transactions or cataloguing the dry data points of emerging species on planets no one would ever visit. Screw that. She wanted to visit them. She wanted to live, really live, instead of reading about life in books or experiencing it through other people's memvids. And look where that selfish urge had gotten her.

Oh, Mari, she thought. How did they even find you? Why did The Fridge decide you were a target? Was it because of Dad? Or me?

Or, she thought suddenly, was it something her sister was researching, something she had discovered—

"Who's there?" came a whistle-song from inside the building. "I got an alarm, so don't try nothing or you get the Chomper."

The Chomper? Must be the crehnisk, which ground its metal snack at her more vigorously. Eva inclined her head and shouted, "Jappy? Captain Innocente. I'm here to pick up some cargo."

The kartian appeared behind the door, eyestalks flicking his gaze between her and Vakar. "Cargo, yeah?" He opened the door and stepped out, one of his legs dragging a bit from what looked like an old injury. His carapace was shiny, almost iridescent, and he rubbed his tiny hairy arms over each other like a nervous tic. "Lemme see your card, so I knows it's you."

"Not a chance," she replied. "I'd like to keep my kidneys. I'm sure you have a scanner anyway, if you really want to check." She wasn't sure, but it stood to reason; if she were too paranoid to pull out her card, anyone who had lived here long enough would know better.

He grabbed a small device off a nearby shelf and pointed it at her. It gave a tinny whistle, and he whistled back, sounding almost disappointed.

"Wait here," he told her. "Don't want you touching anything."

Jappy wandered away, down a row of stuff like any of the other five rows that wound in no discernible order or arrangement. Eva squinted up at the cloud-diffused yellow sky. The urge to check for her ID card strengthened. She ignored it.

Vakar wandered a bit, not so far as to arouse suspicion, but far enough that she couldn't always keep an eye on him. Maybe there were some other parts for the ship they could grab while they were there? He'd know best what needed repairing or replacing. Plus he probably enjoyed seeing all the random stuff Jappy had on display, like a museum or a catalogue with treasures waiting to be discovered. Maybe she could get him a gift?

Eva-Benita, she screamed at herself. Feelings. Stop. Madre de dios.

"Here it is," Jappy said, limping back from his search. He towed over a cargo floater with a large metal box that steamed slightly—or rather, condensed. Refrigerated? Why refrigerate a machine? There had to be a way to ask what it was without seeming foolish, though the kartian might not have any more idea than she did.

"I was told it's inactive," Eva asked.

"S'right," he replied.

"Hasn't given you any trouble?"

All his eyestalks swiveled to face her. "No trouble," he said. "Can't figure out how to shut off the subspace beacon, but it's weak. Box dampens it."

"Right, of course." Subspace beacon? What the hell would it need a subspace beacon for? To send a distress signal? She remembered the strange rectangular metal thing at the lab where she'd left Miles Erck, and wondered again if this was more of the same. Could it really be Proarkhe stuff? Leroy probably would have been salivating at the thought. As would her sister.

But the Proarkhe had been gone for eons. Nobody even knew what they looked like; none of the remains that were found near their artifacts were old enough to be them, and everything else was more void than substance. Vast impressions in eroded landscapes that might once have been cities, the mysterious Gates scattered across the universe, fragments of machinery whose original purpose was usually impossible to guess. Unless you believed the rumors about BOFA hiding all the working tech somewhere so they could experiment on it. Which she didn't.

Where would it be transmitting to, anyway? And what? And why would The Fridge need the booze from Dalnulara, which had nothing to do with ancient tech? No, it didn't make sense. Not to her, at least.

She'd need more pieces to have any hope of putting that puzzle together.

Vakar came back around and his hand crept to one of his pockets. The one where he'd hidden his ID card? He patted it, a faint whiff of anxiety wafting from him. Had it fallen out on their ride over here? That was ridiculous; the suit was skintight and pressurized. But maybe something had happened.

She glanced at the metal-eating guard dog, then at Vakar, picturing his card tumbling end over end and getting gobbled up by the excited creature.

As if it could read her mind, Chomper fluttered its wings and bobbed gently in the air, pulling on its leash, then settled back down to chew on another hunk of metal. Could he have? No, Vakar wasn't that foolish.

So why did he smell like dismay and panic? He glanced at her, and the ping came in. ((Card gone.))

"You are shitting me," Eva said.

"Whatsit?" Jappy asked.

"Nothing." What had happened? It didn't matter. All she had to do was keep a straight face until they made it back to the ship. Stay away from card detectors, move quickly and quietly.

They were fucked.

"Floater should tether to your dasher, yeah," Jappy said. He gestured to a button on the side of the box, then resumed his hand-rubbing, eyestalks swiveling in multiple directions. "Drive careful."

"Pleasure doing business with you." Eva motioned for Vakar to follow and together they walked back out to their dasher, pushing the floater.

Eva waited for him to tether the cargo and climb onto the back, then she took her seat. "So. You've got, what, a stun grenade, an EMP, a flashbang, and two smoke bombs?"

"Also a pistol and a container of synthetic lubricant," Vakar said.

Eva raised her eyebrows at that. "I'm assuming there are sensors rigged along the roadway to alert people to fresh meat."

"That is likely. Are you able to drive and shoot at the same time?"

Eva snorted and didn't answer, summoning up a dark visor with a silent command. She wasn't sure why Vakar had bothered to ask, really.

"All right," Eva said. "Let's burn this candle."

"I am sorry," Vakar said. "It simply disappeared. I suspect sabotage."

"Wouldn't surprise me." Eva checked her own pocket. Her card was intact. Made a sick kind of sense; if someone was handing out self-destructing cards, or using some special device to destroy them from a distance, they wouldn't target every visitor. Might discourage repeat visits, and then where would the fresh meat come from?

"You could always leave me here," Vakar said.

"What?" The thought hadn't remotely occurred to her. "No way, macho. I'm not leaving you here to be someone's lunch. You may just be meat, but you're my meat."

He smelled embarrassed. And there was that licorice scent

again. It was driving her bananas. She thought of her talk with Pink and sighed.

Eva wasn't sure what the sensors would look like, or if they would even be visible along the side of the sand-colored road, but she tried to keep her eyes open anyway. They might be closer to the rest stops, to let hunters hide near them in comfort, or they might be in more isolated areas, to avoid any chance of poaching.

What a planet, she thought, where people could be hunted as meat. Then again, was it really worse than other awful treatment people suffered in places that pretended to be civilized?

The first sensor they hit was a shrieker, going off as they passed so fast that the sound faded behind them into a low moan. A short barrier appeared in front of them, manned by a handful of kartians whose eyestalks were whipped sideways when Eva dipped the nose of the dasher down and then yanked it up, jumping the barricade with only a mild jostling of the cargo. She didn't even have to waste a shot on that group.

The second sensor was silent, and instead of a barricade they hit a tunnel with no ceiling, sharpshooters crouched on the walls to target the travelers inside like fish in a barrel. Vakar tossed in a smoke bomb before they reached it, and luck kept them from being hit by any wild shots from the aliens above. There was a third sensor on the other end, presumably to catch people coming from the direction of the spaceport, and that one had the added bonus of a flashbang that would have blinded Eva if her eyes weren't shielded behind her dark visor.

By now, they'd attracted the attention of hunters with their own rides, ones who weren't content to sit around waiting for the fish to swim into the net. A set of dashers sped up to flank them, followed up by a lumbering tank of a vehicle that spewed smoke behind them.

"Take the shine!" one of them shouted, and the others hollered back, "Kaboom!"

Eva cranked their dasher, but it was carrying two plus cargo, and there was only so much it could handle. On the plus side, Vakar didn't have to worry about steering and aiming, so he was able to pick off one of the pursuing dashers with a trio of well-placed shots to the gas balloons in the back. The other evaded more deftly, its driver flaring the purple tendrils on the end of her proboscis like she was blowing a raspberry.

The tank behind them opened and closed a horizontal door in the front, like a great maw, drawing slowly closer. The pilot wasn't visible, presumably safe inside with monitors to guide them. Eva ducked a shot from the remaining dasher, squeezing off a few of her own at the driver, none hitting. The girl was good. Too bad she wanted to sell Eva off as a snack or they might have been best pals.

"Hang on," Eva shouted. Vakar grabbed on tight to the bar behind her head.

Eva swerved toward the other dasher, which sped ahead to avoid the collision and glanced back at them. With a rush of air and gut-churning momentum, Eva yanked the dasher's brakes, pulling it sideways just in time to drift off the road and avoid the chomping doors of the tank. The other dasher wasn't expecting the maneuver, and didn't get out of the way in time. Eva could barely hear the sickening crunch and boom over the howl of the wind and the roil of her breakfast trying to make an unwelcome return.

They made it back on the road within a few seconds, just in time for them to pass a rest stop with its own sensor mounted to the roof. It blasted a whistling alarm that made Eva's cuca clench.

More vehicles appeared behind them, others in front of

them heading in their direction. They were going to get crushed between two waves of kartians in no time. Vakar shot one of their balloons, then another, but that only slowed a few of them down.

The balloons, she thought. It was worth a try. But would it work with the cargo hooked to the back? Only one way to find out.

((On me,)) Eva pinged. ((Lap.))

Vakar fought against inertia to climb over the bar and straddle her. It slowed them down, but gave her time to squeeze off a few choice shots at the oncoming vehicles. Two of them collided; the rest swerved but kept coming. She didn't bother looking behind her.

"Come and get me, punks!" she shouted, crowing. Shots whizzed past her, including an energy weapon like the one the hunter in the spaceport had used. If this didn't work, they'd be fried chicken. Or pan con lechón.

Some of the vehicles peeled off the road, wary of an oncoming collision. They probably figured they would have easy pickings of the survivors, or the debris and corpses. But the rest revved up and came on faster.

((On mark,)) Eva pinged. ((Shoot balloons. Ours.))

She had to time it perfectly. Too early or too late and they'd be creamed, along with the cargo. She held her breath and allowed herself one glance over her shoulder, and immediately wished she hadn't. That was a lot of people. Que rayo, had they all been waiting around for the dinner bell?

More shots, more evasion. Nearly time. Steady, steady. Eva could almost see the kartians' little hands washing each other, they were so close.

((Now,)) she pinged.

She braked hard, yanking the nose of the dasher so it was

nearly vertical. At the same time, Vakar shot the gas balloons in the back, which blasted the dasher into the air like a rocket.

Below them, dashers and tanks smashed together or zipped sideways or leaped over each other, an orgy of metal and carapaces and thin, hairy legs. Balloons exploded into fires that burned yellow as sulfur, and the pained and frightened whistling of the kartians added to the cacophony. Above it all, Vakar and Eva flew like a glorious rooster about to land claws-first on their enemies. Except they didn't have any claws, and their enemies were burning like marshmallows.

They landed hard, skidding sideways, their dasher rendered useless by the maneuver, since it was gas-powered. Eva dragged a leg out from under the metal wreck, her arm singing with pain, back burning from the explosion of their balloons. Vakar had apparently fared better, tossed a few meters away but already on his feet.

The cargo was still tethered to the back of their dasher. She limped over and unhooked it, grateful that the floater it was on rendered it nearly weightless. The box still condensed, seemingly undamaged from her stunt, and she sent up thanks to the Virgin for the good luck.

The shimmering dome of the spaceport was within view. Eva pinged Min to be ready for them to take off in a hurry, hoping she was within range, hoping if they made a run for it they wouldn't end up like that nameless human who'd almost lived.

No response.

A huge blast blew a crater in the road next to her, knocking her sideways. Eva's injured arm hit the ground first, a bright pain that clenched her eyes shut for a moment.

In the distance, between them and escape, was the kartian hunter with the robot leg. Grissy.

Another blast chunked some plants in front of her, throwing grit into her face. Grissy wouldn't want to hit them directly, because the market likely paid less for ground beef. Plus, Eva still had her card, so theoretically killing her would be murder. Theoretically.

She pinged Min again.

((Where?)) Min asked.

Eva pinged her the coordinates, wondering whether the ship could possibly make it in time. At least if it didn't, she wouldn't have to worry about doing any more asinine Fridge jobs. And her crew would be able to sell *La Sirena Negra* and split the profits, as per her will. The idea of earning her freedom from debt with her own death was strangely unappealing, though.

Not to mention, it meant Mari would end up in an asteroid mine at best, or be flushed out an airlock because she was no longer valuable.

Grissy was clearer now, her dark shell smeared with plants to blend in with the sandy color of the road. She had a giant tripod-mounted blaster cannon anchored to the ground to absorb the recoil, and she took her shots carefully. Eva wondered if she'd also booby-trapped the road, and was rewarded for her speculation by the low boom of a hidden explosive nearby. Probably hitting poachers coming for Grissy's kill.

Not this cycle, Satan, she thought as she lay on her back. She had to get that cargo back to the ship.

With a groan, she rolled to her good side and struggled to her feet. Vakar had been farther from the blast and was approaching her with a concerned smell, saying something she couldn't hear over the ringing in her ears. She made what she hoped was a reassuring gesture, staggering in the direction of the cargo, which had been pushed a few meters away.

To her left, Grissy skittered toward them.

The kartian pulled a small gadget out of a pouch and

pointed it at Eva. It gave a brief whistle, and Grissy sang a note of disappointment. Then she pointed it at Vakar, and was rewarded with a tinny alarm.

"Not too meaty," she whistle-sang. "Maybe good for soup, though." She pulled out a smaller gun and aimed it at him.

"Hell no!" Eva shouted. With all her strength, she pushed the cargo toward Grissy, who fired a wild shot and dodged as the box sailed toward her. Vakar readied his own pistol, and the two stared each other down, weapons raised in a standoff.

Eva's pistol was nowhere in sight.

She had to move quickly, or the other kartians would be on them soon—the ones who had survived, and any more coming from the port for the promise of meat. But now the cargo was out of reach, and Vakar was in danger again, and there wasn't a damn thing she could do.

Well, there was one thing.

"How much?" Eva asked Grissy.

"Pardon?"

"How much would he sell for?"

Grissy scanned her with one eye, while the other watched Vakar. "Ten thousand or so. Why, you want to barter?"

Ño, qué barato, she thought sarcastically. "How about I take him and you take my cargo? It's worth ten thousand easily, and I can set you up with a buyer."

What was she thinking? The Fridge would have a fit when they found out. They might even hurt Mari to get back at her. But it was the only bargaining chip she had.

To Eva's dismay, Grissy hissed. "I only take cash, local currency."

"Twenty thousand, then. I don't have local cash."

Grissy whistle-laughed, but her pistol didn't move. "Who you tryna scam? No meat's worth that."

He is to me, she thought, surprised by the force of the feeling. Way to go, Pink, great plan to get me to figure my shit out.

"The cargo is," Eva said. "Twice that, easily, to be honest."

"Not worth the hassle, or the risk. I got redundant organs, at least. Quennian here doesn't."

"Eat shit, then." Eva pointed up.

The kartian followed her gaze, then threw herself on the ground as *La Sirena Negra* dropped from the sky like a giant missile.

Min brought it down to hover in front of Eva and Vakar, and the cargo bay door cracked open enough to allow them inside. Pink fired off warning shots at the other hunters who had started to arrive, scenting blood.

Eva limped over to Vakar, and together they raced to the ship and jumped in.

Through the slit of the closing door, Eva saw Grissy get to her feet and dust herself off, reaching for her blaster cannon.

"Jump, Min!" Eva shouted. And so she did, engines roaring. Within a minute, they were out in the black, the pale sepia mess of Futis shrinking behind them, along with The Fridge's cargo.

Vakar gently removed a mewling cat from his chest as he sprawled out on the floor of the cargo bay.

"Remember when we were contracted to deliver kittens to a peaceful café in a protected system?" he said to no one in particular.

"I do have that recollection," Pink replied, staring down at the pair of them.

Eva prodded her shoulder, wincing. "At least we're alive."

"Yes," Vakar agreed.

"That's a pretty low bar," Pink said.

Eva sighed and closed her eyes. She was fucked. If Grissy kept the cargo, at least Eva could tell The Fridge where to find it, but then they'd have to send someone to pick it up and pay the hunter off. Assuming they didn't just kill her and take it. And if someone else got to it first, it could be anywhere on the planet within a cycle.

Would The Fridge add this to her debt total as well, or do something more extreme? And when would she get the next job from them? After these last two, she didn't know how many more she could handle.

However many it takes, she thought sadly. Whatever she had to do to get Mari back.

It was time to let the crew go, though, to bury her selfishness before it hurt anyone else. This wasn't fair to these people, her people, not by a long shot. Pink's expression said much the same, lips pursed in disappointment.

"Your head's bleeding," Pink told Eva. "Get to the med bay so I can patch you up before you make a mess."

"I'll be fine. It will stop eventually."

"Sure, when you run out of blood. Vakar, talk to her. I'm getting back to Leroy." She walked briskly toward the med bay, shaking her head.

"Are you well?" Vakar asked, sitting up next to her.

"Airtight," Eva muttered. Vakar kept staring at her, and he smelled like cinnamon and licorice. It was distracting.

"You saved my life," he said.

"Smell more surprised. It makes me feel like an asshole."

"I did not mean . . . I am sorry."

"It's fine. You're fine. Everything is fine. Go have her check you for injuries, please."

Vakar's smell turned to green things. "She will be upset with me if I leave you here."

"I'll be upset if you don't. Pick your poison." When he didn't move, she added, "Go."

He stood, staring down at her. She closed her eyes, and his steps receded, along with his smell.

With impeccable timing, her scent translator finally processed that nagging licorice smell, and Eva suppressed a groan.

Pink was right about Vakar. About how he felt. Damn it.

Now Eva definitely had to figure out what to do about him, and none of the options were particularly appealing. Well, some were, but she shoved those away as fast as they presented themselves.

It's fine, she thought. You're going to ditch him, ditch all of them, so it doesn't matter. You'll both move on, problem solved, congratulations.

A quiet calm spread from her chest to the rest of her body, soothing her aches as much as her racing mind. She took a deep breath and slowly released it, then looked down.

"Get off my chest, please," she said to the calico cat Min had christened Mala.

Hazel eyes stared back at her, half-lidded. A rumbling purr started up in the feline's face, spreading quickly to her belly.

"I guess I can't get up now," Eva said. It was just as well; as long as she didn't move, she could almost pretend she wasn't going to be in a world of pain later.

She scratched Mala under the chin and bled on the floor of the cargo bay.

Chapter 9

WE'RE GONNA NEED
A BIGGER SHIP

Since Eva had no way to contact The Fridge, *La Sirena Negra* proceeded without the cargo to the drop point, a ship floating in the middle of the Cadrion system, which was attractively close to a Gate but had been essentially strip-mined of all useful elements thousands of years before any BOFA member race showed up. The science vessel was manned by a dozen humans wearing the same uniform as the ones back on that planet where she'd ditched Miles Erck. Just thinking of the little puke made her want to drink heavily. The scientists were mostly professional, but something about their demeanor made her twitchy—their eyes were a bit too bright, almost feverish, and they stood stiff as toy soldiers.

They also seemed strangely unconcerned about the lack of cargo, but at least this way she expected word would get back to whoever did care. And then she'd find out the price of her failure, and whether she could ever hope to pay it.

Glorious showed up again right when she climbed back onto her ship. How he kept finding them she didn't know, but it was one more aggravation she didn't need. Min had to fly evasively for hours, blowing through fuel they could ill afford, while Vakar and Eva struggled to keep the shields and medical equipment working without sacrificing engine power.

By the time they finally reached the system's Gate and escaped, they were running on fumes, their energy shields were flickering like nubby candles in a breeze, and Vakar was cursing almost as much as Eva. Her injured arm was bleeding again, and the burns on her back oozed through her bandages to stain her white shirt. Worse, Vakar smelled so much like a bonfire the entire time it gave her a headache, and Pink finally ordered him to stay in the engine compartment until he pulled himself together.

As Eva lay on her bed afterward, recovering from her wounds, a call from The Fridge came in on her private channel. She sat up carefully, one arm in a sling, and cultivated an air of professional remorse as the lights dimmed and the crackling holovid appeared.

"Failure is unacceptable," the modulated voice said.

Eva stifled the urge to launch into sarcastic niceties. "The cargo was last in possession of a bounty hunter named Grissy," she said calmly. "I'm sure someone can—"

"The cargo will be secured," the voice said. "If your next mission is also a failure, there will be consequences."

Before she could ask what they would be, the quality of the sound changed.

"Eva," Mari said, her voice trembling. "Eva, please, please do what they say. They put me in a tank, and they got me back out to tell you . . ." She sobbed, and Eva closed her eyes, fighting to maintain her composure.

"They told me to tell you," Mari repeated, "that if, if you mess up again, they're sending me to the asteroid mines. That I'll have to work there until you pay your debt."

Eva took a deep breath. "I won't let that happen," she said. "Don't worry. I've got this."

"Eva, please—" The sound cut out again, and the modulated voice returned.

"Your next assignment will be sent presently. Apply yourself to the task, or your sister will suffer."

The holovid went dead. Eva left the lights low, staring at her fish tank, the rush of bubbles along one side like a reminder to breathe.

Eva couldn't let that happen to Mari. Wouldn't. It was practically a death sentence, especially for her sweet, soft sister. Digging up Proarkhe bits was nothing like mining. Asteroid mines were hard labor. Long hours in spacesuits, rebreathing your own farts and drinking recycled piss. Handling dangerous equipment, including explosives. Digging deep into the sides of objects hurtling through space, hoping you didn't get thrown clear into the black, hoping tunnel walls didn't collapse and trap you until you died of dehydration or starvation.

Usually, the danger meant the job was done by robots, but there were always people desperate enough to work for less than the cost of a capable machine. And in The Fridge's case, people who had even less of a choice.

Whatever this next assignment was, she had to get it done.

The message came in as she lay back down on the bed, blinking away tears of frustration and shame that threatened to escape her eyes.

PICKUP AT ATTACHED COORDINATES. TARGET IS
DANGEROUS AND UNCOOPERATIVE. RECOMMEND
AVOIDING DIRECT ENGAGEMENT. NONLETHAL FORCE
REQUIRED.

That was ominous. But worse, it was exactly the kind of job
she had no desire to do, especially not with her crew. It was bad
enough she had put them in harm's way so many times already;
this was going after someone who was "dangerous and uncooperative." Not to mention that if she was nabbing a person,
she could guess what The Fridge wanted them for, and it wasn't
remotely good.

She had to figure out an alternate job for her crew at the
same location, something that would mean leaving them on
the ship. And then she'd have to take down this target herself,
get them on board, and deliver them to the drop point without
anyone noticing.

Yeah, that all sounded really stupid, even in her head. There
had to be a better way.

The attached coordinates made her groan. The holopic of
the target made her groan louder.

I'm going to need a bigger ship, she thought.

Eva and Vakar walked across the broad tarmac of her father's
used spaceship lot on New Nogales, a human settlement in the
Cruz System that had been established for long enough to lose
its charm along with many of its residents. The ships on display
were spread out so as not to crowd each other, and ranged from
little one-seater moon jumpers all the way up to a midsize merchant vessel for twenty crew. The bigger ones were in orbit, of
course; asteroid wranglers, deep space explorers complete with

miniature biospheres, maybe even a colony transport, depending on the current futures trade.

Eva remembered when she had last set foot here, stood in almost the same spot and seen *La Sirena Negra* for the first time. God, she'd loved it. Even the knowledge that it was her father's way of getting rid of her didn't dampen her enthusiasm. Hard to believe it had been seven years.

"Strange that we received two jobs that had to be completed at the same time," Vakar said.

"Yeah, shitty coincidence," Eva replied, glad her own body smells didn't give away her feelings the way Vakar's did. "But the retainer one has to get done, and you know, we can always use the extra creds." She scratched at the scab on her neck, wondering whether it would ever heal. Vakar smelled like the air just before heavy rain.

They passed through a pair of glass doors and a soft alarm began to sound. A trio of subtly armed and armored truateg guards appeared from different sides of the room, each looking relaxed but decidedly alert. No offense, they seemed to say with their bright eyes and wet noses, but we'll be on your ass in a heartbeat if you try anything.

The room was broad and high-ceilinged, intended to accommodate a wide range of sizes and tastes while attempting to offend none. The walls were painted with subtle shades that looked different depending on what range of visible light one's eyes could see. Scent patterns also shifted in the air, so delicate as to be hardly discernible, and Eva knew there were nullifiers hidden in strategic areas to account for the people with particularly sensitive olfactory organs. The light installation on the ceiling was meant to mimic being underwater, and it had always fascinated her while simultaneously making her slightly nauseated. Different kinds of tables and desks were arranged in apparently random configurations throughout the room, as were holographic displays of ships that changed based on input culled from commlinks. Not entirely legal, that, but difficult to prove.

A slick-suited annae hovered over to them, their branches curled delicately behind their trunk. "Welcome, valuable customers," they said, inclining their mawed head. "My name is Fjorsl and I am proud to serve you. You have no doubt heard of our excellent reputation, and may I congratulate you on your wisdom in patronizing our dealership."

Eva stepped forward, raising one shoulder in a nervous tic. "I'm here to see Pete."

Fjorsl's teeth flexed outward. "Mr. Larsen is with other customers at present, but he will no doubt be delighted to assist you in the culmination of your transaction without delay. Perhaps there is something I may—"

"Stand down, papo," she said. "I'm sure Pete will be out in a minute. He probably already knows I'm here." She began to walk toward the staircase to the second floor of the building.

"I'm dreadfully sorry, but you cannot go up there," Fjorsl said. They uncurled their branches from behind their back and gestured at the truateg, who began to close in casually.

Vakar backed up to Eva. "I thought you knew this person," he whispered over his shoulder.

"I do," she said. "Coño, take a chill pill and relax."

The annae planted their feet and began to grow. Within a few seconds, they were a head taller than Vakar. The truateg were almost on them.

"Of all the stupid—" Eva said. She put her fingers in her mouth and whistled, this time a trill like the call of a bird. The truateg froze, rocking backward on their haunches and letting their tongues loll out of their mouths.

Fjorsl grew another half meter. "This is all highly irregular."

A pair of double doors flew open upstairs and a man stepped out. He was tall by human standards, broad-shouldered, with salt-and-pepper hair and a build like a luchador. His brown eyes locked onto Eva's, but his smile didn't reach them.

"Bee Alvarez, great to see you," he said, all honey.

"Pete, always a pleasure," she said. "Sorry for the fuss, but we're in a bit of a rush."

"Anything for my most loyal customer." He turned away as two women in business suits stepped out of the room behind him, twitching as only adrenaline-enhanced humans did. "Ladies, thank you so much for coming, and I'm sure that ship will meet your needs perfectly. Fjorsl will escort you to the vessel and ensure that you depart safely."

At the mention of their name, the annae shrank a few centimeters, though their head remained the same size. "I would be delighted to attend to their every whim."

"You bet," Pete said. He bowed to the women, and they inclined their heads in return. "You take care, now. And don't hesitate to call me if you need anything else."

The women descended the stairs in unison, each with one hand on the banister. The look they gave Eva said suspicion, curiosity and maybe a hint of threat. They each had one cybernetic eye, pale blue where their other eyes were darker, and their skin was light as protein powder.

Eva coolly ignored them, waiting until they were leaving with Fjorsl before she began to ascend the staircase again. Vakar followed her up, taking measured steps while smelling of ozone and incense.

"Come in, please," Pete said with a gesture. "Will your associate be joining us?"

She sighed and turned to Vakar. "Wait out here. This shouldn't take long."

Vakar said nothing, but the incense smell strengthened. Such a worrier.

"Back to posts," Pete barked, and the truateg moved as if coming out of a haze, wandering back to the sides of the room.

The double doors closed behind Eva and she found herself in the antechamber to her father's main office. She briefly regretted not letting Vakar wait in here, but he was better off outside. He might get too comfortable in the plush couches and special form-fitting chairs that reshaped themselves for different body types. The food and drink dispensers would probably distract him as well.

Okay, she should have brought him in. Maybe she'd let him at it when they were getting ready to leave.

Pete's office, or at least this front office, was tastefully decorated in faux wood and stone, with more of the carefully selected art and decor that was meant to be taste-neutral so as not to offend as wide a variety of clientele as possible. Though as he had always said, people who were offended by stuff humans did tended to stay away from them anyway, so catering to them was an exercise in futility. At most, he had little touches that would catch the sensory organs of particular groups to make them feel at ease.

Pete took a seat behind his big desk, which Eva knew was outfitted with various alarm systems that activated on command or in reaction to certain conditions. She had always wondered if he left them on for her, too.

"What can I do for you, girlie?" he asked, leaning back in his big leather chair.

"I need a ship." She stared at a tiny tree on his desk, growing miniature oranges. She couldn't remember the last time she'd had a real orange.

"Right, I figured this wasn't a vacation." He gestured and a screen popped up between them, showing the rotating figure of a cargo ship. "What do you need? Fast? Sturdy?"

"Big. I'll get it back to you as soon as I'm finished with it."

He closed the catalogue. "Is this what I think it is?"

"Yes."

"And how big are we talking?"

"Todyk."

"No shit. Do you know what kind?"

"The kind no sane person should be trying to kidnap." She flicked at a metronome on his desk, which began to tick and tock, swaying back and forth.

"What do they even want with a todyk?" Pete asked.

"Me cago en diez, who cares!" she exclaimed, banging on his desk. A tiny red light shined in her eyes from somewhere, and she froze. Well, now she knew. Security systems on.

"I'm more worried about me and my crew," she said coldly.

Her father whistled and the light vanished. He ran a hand over his face and leaned forward.

"It's been hard for me, too," he said. "I've been trying to get intel, but people don't talk. They're too scared of being targeted, or retargeted. But I've been back on this since they got Mari."

He waved a hand, and another image popped up between them. This was a list of names, pictures next to them, all kinds of people from aahx to zyfin.

"I've attempted to gather as much data as possible on the victims and their families, to see if there are any connections, anything that makes them significant." He inclined his head, and the image vanished, replaced by a map of the galaxy with lines crisscrossing it. She could just make out numbers attached to the lines, and the names from the previous list.

"And?"

He shrugged. "Some are rich, some are well connected. Some have very specific skills, or access to restricted facilities. Some, I suspect, are . . . shall we say, working near the fringe and more amenable to engaging in activities that would normally require more expensive mercenaries and particular professionals."

"I suppose that's me," she said bitterly. "Not that I'm amenable. So we're the janitors, doing the cleanup jobs no one else wants to touch."

She wanted to believe the concern in his eyes was genuine. It probably was, or as genuine as he got. "If I could take it on instead, I would," he said. "They've bled me dry, but they've still called me twice to do my usual chop and swap. I don't know why they decided that wasn't enough."

"They told me they ran the numbers and you weren't as much of a cash comet as they had hoped." She watched him wince, and part of her enjoyed it.

"You're definitely more mobile, and you've got a good team," he said. "After that stunt you pulled on Garilia—"

"Don't." Eva struggled to keep her jaw from tightening. He knew full well how she felt about her part in that, for all that he had washed his hands clean of the whole thing. "After 'that stunt on Garilia,' as you call it, I decided some things were more important than money."

"Definitely harder to spend it when you're dead," he said amiably. "You were always the fearless one. Funny to see you like this now."

"I'm not ten anymore."

"You're not thirty anymore, either. But that's neither here nor there." He steepled his fingers. "I need you to give me the intel on your handler. Another piece for that big puzzle."

Another token on the Reversi board, she thought. This simple spaceship dealer, on a backwater human settlement, in a system that had been left alone for eons because it didn't have any resources to strip-mine or any worthwhile sentience to speak of. And here he was, playing at power, as if he had anything like the resources or contacts to do a fraction of what people like The Fridge were doing.

"Let's get back to this ship I need," she said.

"Eva-Bee, come on."

"You know I hate it when you call me that."

He raised his hands defensively. "All right, you're the boss. I'll trade you, then. Information, for a ship. A loaner, to be returned once the job's done."

It was the best offer she was going to get, but she didn't have to like it. "Fine. Show me yours, and I'll show you mine."

"That's my girl," he said, smiling.

Her stomach hurt at the pride she couldn't help but feel when he said that.

Twenty minutes later, she had the codes for a big junker her dad called the CS *Malcolm*. It was a kloshian ship, close enough to human physiology that it needed only a few quick control program swaps to make it run smoothly. It had a jack instead of wireless; Eva hated flying that way. It always put the taste of peaches in her mouth for cycles. Disgusting.

Her father opened the door and she strolled out to find Vakar pacing. He smelled like incense and mint.

"I haven't had the pleasure," Pete said. "Peter Larsen. And you are?"

"Vakar Tremonis san Jaigodaris," Vakar replied. "Engineer."

Eva sighed internally. Vakar must have heard Pete use Eva's alias earlier, but even so, he could never manage to come up with a good lie.

"Surely someone with your expertise should be on one of the Home Fleet battle cruisers?" Pete said. "How'd you end up with Bee here?"

Eva tensed, throwing a glance at Vakar that tried to tell him he didn't have to answer.

"It is a long story," Vakar said cautiously.

"I love stories," Pete said, smiling jovially.

Vakar's palps twitched, his gray-blue eyes darting between Pete and Eva. "She intervened in an argument between myself and a group of human supremacists. I needed a ride off-world, and she offered transport if I would fix a faulty rotor coupling."

Pete clapped a hand on Eva's shoulder, grinning. He was almost a third of a meter taller than her, and a fist taller than Vakar. "She's a good one, eh? What, did she tell them off? Shoot her way out? I taught her how to shoot, you know."

"She was very . . . persuasive." Vakar's smell took a turn toward fresh-cut grass.

"I licked his face and told them he was my boyfriend," she said. "Then I beat the shit out of them."

Pete stared at her for a moment, then let out a hearty laugh. "You would do that, wouldn't you? You're such a troublemaker."

She didn't mention the part about how she'd had an allergic reaction and hallucinated for three cycles while Pink pumped her full of drugs. Though he probably would have found that funny, too. Especially if she told him about the vivid purple owls she was sure were following her for weeks.

And now she was thinking about licking Vakar again, allergies be damned. Madre de dios, she told herself, get your shit together.

"She does sometimes make trouble," Vakar said cautiously. "But she is capable of handling it."

"Yes, I'm an excellent captain," Eva said. "Speaking of which, our clients are waiting for their deliveries. Thank you so much for the ship, and I'm sure I'll probably get it back to you in one piece."

Pete laughed, and she smiled, even though she hadn't been joking.

"See you then, Bee," he said. "Tremonis." He squeezed her shoulder and let go, walking back into his office and closing the door behind him without another word.

Eva avoided touching the banister as she walked down the stairs. She didn't want to get her hands dirtier than they already were.

Vakar sped up to walk next to her. "Who was that?"

"We'll talk later."

"Was that—"

"Later," she said sharply. Other customers had come in, a pair of humans who looked perfectly normal, like a young couple shopping around for their first ship. Ready to start a life of high adventure together in the glittering darkness of the uncharted seas of heaven. She remembered all that romantic nonsense from when she was younger. Not that she'd had anyone to share it with. Not that she'd wanted anyone. She wanted to explore the universe, no attachments, nothing to tether her to any one place like a space elevator to an orbiting station. Besides, she had seen what happened to her parents' marriage, and it looked like way more trouble than it ever could have been worth. No relationships meant no nasty breakups, which meant no bad memories trailing after her like the tail of a comet.

As if there weren't plenty of other kinds of bad memories to make, she thought bitterly. The scar across her cheek tightened for a moment, as if in sympathy. She could have had it removed, but she kept it as a reminder of how stupid she had once been, a reminder that failure happened and it sucked plutonium exhaust.

A reminder that she was alive, and a whole lot of Garilians weren't.

They made it back to *La Sirena Negra,* assembling in the mess to plan their routes. Eva briefed the rest of the crew on their assignment, an easy enough pickup on Kugawa with a drop-off on an asteroid mine near the Virgo Fringe. She'd already negotiated everything with the client, who would be meeting them on-site. It was perfect. Safe. Boring. Eva's head ached.

"Mine should be about as easy," she lied. "Wish I could take one of you with me, but the client is being finicky about that confidentiality clause."

If they didn't believe her, she couldn't tell. But the crew simply nodded assent, or in Vakar's case, tapped his fingers on the table and smelled like rain.

"So we'll rendezvous back here at the dealership after I deliver the cargo, then move along." They had split up before, she told herself. Everything would be fine. That feeling that she would never see them again was just a feeling, and it would pass, probably some time after she saw them again and they had been traveling for a while.

Feelings were such crap.

"All right, let's go."

Nobody seemed interested in moving. Vakar smelled . . . off. Like himself, but wrong somehow.

"You need something, Vakar?" Eva asked.

His palps twitched. "No, nothing," he said. Then he got up and left.

Eva shook her head. Pink leaned against the table with her arms crossed.

"How's Leroy?" Eva asked.

"Getting there," Pink said. "Coming back to himself. But it's taking time."

Eva sighed and rested her forehead on her hand. "Is he going to be okay?"

Pink pulled out a chair and scooted it over to Eva, sitting in front of her so they were at eye level. "You want me to tell you it's all gonna be fixed, like magic. Back to how it was. But you know I ain't got no crystal ball, and I'm sure not gonna lie to make you feel better."

"Do I at least get a maybe?" Eva asked.

"Girl, you got a handful of 'gimme' and a mouthful of 'much obliged.'" Pink's uncovered eye stared at Eva.

Eva swallowed a retort and nodded. "Fair enough. You take care of everyone while I'm gone."

Pink snorted. "I take care of everyone when you're here, too. You don't need to tell me my business."

A loud purr alerted her to the fact that Mala was already in her lap. Eva had no idea how long she'd been petting the cat, and she resented that immensely. Especially since it made her feel a little better.

She let her legs be kneaded for a few more minutes before rising to head toward her cabin. She wouldn't need to pack too much: a change of clothes, her usual complement of weapons, a few tools that might come in handy, and a first aid kit with some stims in case things went really badly. If anything happened to her, she figured it would be easier for the rest of her stuff to be sent to her mom if it was all here and not on some strange ship in another sector, with no one to collect it.

And it makes it less likely that your dad will end up with everything, a little voice whispered. A cruel voice. She didn't like that one.

Eva opened the door to her cabin, revealing Vakar sitting on the corner of her bed, staring at her fish. The whole place smelled like air freshener, vanilla cherry almond.

"I thought my door was locked," Eva said, stepping over to the cabinet that held her clothes.

"It was."

"Rude." She knelt and opened a drawer under her bed, pulling out a duffel bag. "What do you need? I have to shove off already."

"Take me with you."

Eva paused to look up at him. "I told you, I can't. Client's orders. Total privacy and secrecy. If it weren't good money, I would have told them to move along."

Vakar grabbed her arm and she shook it off, frowning. "Why are you lying?" he asked. His smell took on a strange sharpness, like licking an old battery terminal.

"Why would I be lying?" she said carefully, tucking her disassembled sniper rifle into her bag.

"I do not know," he said. "But I do not like it. You have lied to us before, but not like this."

"Oh, so I'm a habitual liar. Nice. Am I a thief, too? A killer?"

"Eva—"

"No, please, I want to hear all about it." She could feel the anger rising, but another part of her said, He's never called you that before. Always "Captain," never "Eva."

"No, you do not," he said softly. "And I do not want to tell you, because it does not matter."

"Get out of my room," she said. "I need to change."

"What are you so afraid of?" he asked. "You have been smelling strange for cycles now—"

"I'll take more baths."

"Stars above, can you take a single nanosecond to look around you and stop making jokes?"

Eva closed her bag and stood. "How's this for serious: I don't know what you thought the two of us had going, but you're an engineer on my ship. That's it. I'm the one in charge here, not you. If you don't like it, you know where the airlock is. So use it."

His inner eyelid closed as if she'd hit him. Quietly, slowly, he got to his feet and staggered to her door, opening it with a thought. It closed behind him, not with a bang but a whisper, and left her more alone than she'd ever felt.

There it was. Orders given, orders taken. The wedge was hammered in, and now it was only a matter of time before the crack split them entirely.

Pink will be proud, she thought, but that was a lie, too.

She shouldered her bag and took a deep breath, trying to stop her body from shaking. Her whole room smelled of licorice, so strong that she thought she would never be able to get the scent out of her hair, her clothes, her skin.

Chapter 10

EL ORGULLO Y EL PREJUICIO

A flock of brightly colored birds broke through the tree line and took off into the azure sky of Ayshurn as Eva crept through the underbrush, swatting at clouds of bugs with the hand that wasn't gripping the stock of her sniper rifle. Her quarry was nearby, as evidenced by the birds, but for a two-ton tower of muscle, he was surprisingly quiet.

Luckily, he left a trail of broken brush behind him that even she could follow, and her tracking goggles helped with chemical trails and other layers of visual marking, like heat sensing and minute motion detection. She kept having to tinker with that one, though, because of all the damn birds. Why the todyk seemed to like them so much, she wasn't sure. Maybe for the same reason humans liked monkeys; they reminded them of another branch of the family tree.

Eva clicked on her gravboots and climbed a tall tree, slowly so as not to attract attention. Once the tree started to bend under her weight, she stopped, flicking on the zoom function of her goggles to catch sight of the elusive Jardok. He should have been just over . . . there.

As tall as the trees were, and as well as his feathers blended in, Jardok could only partly shield his bulk from her array of sensors. She had trailed him out here, all the way from the main spaceport and the city that surrounded it, and she still had no idea what he was up to.

Another form appeared in her sights, almost as large as Jardok. Eva zoomed in to look at the other todyk's plumage, delicate browns and creams instead of the vibrant red and green that Jardok sported.

She climbed down from the tree and stalked the path of broken branches and flattened grasses and brush, trying to place her feet carefully to make as little noise as possible. Whenever she heard movement, she froze, even though her research assured her it was a myth that the todyk couldn't see you if you stood still.

Her sensors showed they had moved a bit southward, toward what appeared to be a body of water. Crap. If they crossed it, she might lose them on the other side. Eva sped up as much as she could, trying to stagger her movements so that they sounded more random, less like pursuit. As she neared their position, the sound of splashing grew louder, along with the vicious roars that haunted the dreams of many a child raised on images of enormous, ancient bones painstakingly unearthed from beneath dirt and rock. How foolish the scientists must have finally felt when confronted with the reality, in the flesh.

And yet, still afraid. Because seriously, some todyk were really big. And toothy.

Eva caught herself just before she would have stumbled over

the edge of a cliff—not too high up, but enough that something probably would have gotten broken on the way down, or at the bottom. The valley below was mostly clear of trees, replaced by a strangely manicured-looking grass. To her right was a gentle rise that led up to a stone pyramid that, were she more archaeologically inclined, she might have called a ziggurat.

To her left was the water, a lake as it turned out, in which the figures of the two todyk could be seen cavorting, splashing each other with their tails. At this distance, her translators kicked in, and she realized the two of them were laughing.

Could she have been so lucky that Jardok never noticed her following him? Stick that in the plus column. The minus column, unfortunately, was currently occupied by the giant problem of her only having enough tranquilizers for one todyk. She would have to wait until the other one left, or Jardok did and she could follow him elsewhere.

With an inward sigh, Eva sat on the ground and tried to make herself comfortable. If only she'd remembered to bring something to eat.

"Are you hungry, my love?" Jardok said, as if he could hear her thoughts. Eva's stomach rumbled in response.

"Famished, darling," said the other todyk. "Shall we dry ourselves and partake of a light lunch?"

Well, Eva thought. That is certainly not how I expected todyk to talk. Then she scolded herself for being judgmental.

"I shall ask Dardon to bring us food immediately," Jardok replied. He must have used a commlink, because he didn't say anything aloud. She wasn't entirely sure how words were being shaped at all, given his mouthful of huge, curved-dagger teeth.

Dardon turned out to be a smaller todyk, with giant toe claws and iridescent green and blue feathers. He carried a shallow box filled with an array of charcuterie that gave Eva the meat sweats from looking at it. Draped over his arm was a blanket, which he laid out on the ground before placing the box on top of it.

"Thank you," the female said, giving him a look that lingered a moment too long.

With a bob of his head, Dardon turned to go.

"A moment, Dardon," Jardok said. He had backed a few steps away from the other todyk. "I know I've been away on business, and left my dear Onaatan in your care. I wanted to thank you for being so diligent in your duties."

"Of course, sir," Dardon said. Eva didn't know much about todyk interactions, but the way this guy ruffled his feathers made her nervous.

"But then, perhaps you have been too diligent." Jardok turned his head to one side, staring Dardon down with one enormous black eye. "Altogether too attentive, in fact. Perhaps you have something you would like to confess to me, hmm?"

"Jardok, please, you can't be serious," Onaatan (presumably) said. "What you are suggesting is preposterous."

"Indeed," the smaller todyk echoed faintly.

"It is preposterous, isn't it?" Jardok clasped his tiny hands in front of his chest and paced back and forth, his tail swinging as he walked. "To imagine that someone of your station, Onaatan, with an asteroid mine and ranches in Pratania, would debase herself by consorting with a common butler."

Both Dardon and Onaatan flinched. Meanwhile, another todyk approached from near the pyramid.

"Quite preposterous," Onaatan said. "He is certainly beneath me."

"Is that so?" a new voice roared. "Because I am prepared to offer proof that within the last cycle, you were very much beneath him."

Onaatan gasped. Jardok growled. Dardon ruffled his feathers but otherwise remained stoic.

The newcomer was built like Onaatan, but her feathers were bright like Jardok's.

"What do you want, Nushmee?" Onaatan hissed. "You're always eager to stir up trouble."

"I only want what's best for Jardok," Nushmee replied coolly. "He deserves to know that his fianceé is a liar and a harlot."

Onaatan stepped forward, tail lashing. "You've always been jealous that he chose me over you. It burns your blood like lava boiling beneath a mountain."

Eva yawned and checked her watch. Rich people were so ridiculous.

"I may have been jealous once," Nushmee said. "But that time has passed. My only concern is for a friend, a dear friend, who should not commit himself to an unfaithful wench like you."

"Wench," really? Eva made a mental note to check her translator nanites. Maybe there was an update she hadn't installed.

Jardok bristled, his feathers sticking up on his neck. "I appreciate your concern, Nushmee, but this is between me, Onaatan and this concupiscent charlatan."

Dardon roared out a cough, flexing his toe claw. "I suppose, sir, that I should not address the matter of your illicit liaison with Nushmee, the very cycle before you left on business and put Onaatan in my care?"

Onaatan gasped. Jardok growled. Nushmee spun and struck the smaller todyk with her tail, baring her teeth.

Mierda, Eva thought. If this turned into a free-for-all, she might never be able to capture Jardok. Not alive, anyway.

"Is this true, Jardok?" Onaatan said. "That you would chastise me so ferociously when you yourself have been with another?"

To Eva's utter lack of surprise given how this was playing out, Jardok turned away, his feathers flattening to his head. "I was intoxicated," he admitted. "I hardly knew what I was doing."

"You took advantage of him!" Onaatan shrieked, leaping over to Nushmee's side and snapping at her face. The ground shook from the movement, and Eva had to flatten herself to the cliffside to keep from falling.

Unfortunately, her rifle didn't fare as well; it slid down to the bottom of the cliff, landing in a clump of bushes. Eva cursed silently but with relish.

"As if I would compel him to do anything against his will," Nushmee said as the two circled each other. The box of meats between them was long forgotten by everyone but Eva, whose stomach was still attentive. "He was quite willing. Eager, even. There is no pleasure to be found in an empty conquest."

Slowly, hand over hand, Eva crawled down the face of the cliff. It was sloped just enough to keep her from sliding, though she could have stopped the descent with her boots at the cost of revealing her position. The thick blades of grass bit at her face, which was the only exposed part of her, and she fought the urge to sneeze. More bugs had found her, too, because life was not fair.

"Ladies, please," Jardok said. "You will do yourselves harm!"

They ignored him and continued their dance, feinting and lunging and attempting to bite or swat each other with their tails. Onaatan got a good hit in with the side of her muzzle, knocking Nushmee down, but the other todyk lashed out with her claws, nearly drawing blood, then scrambled back to her feet. Eva glimpsed that last bit as a blur, because the impact had shaken the ground again and made her slip a few meters before catching herself.

"Enough," Jardok said. He waded into the fray and Dardon followed his lead, the two pushing the women apart with their bodies and heads.

"Slut!" Onaatan cried.

"Stale!" Nushmee replied.

"Enough, I say!" Jardok turned his head right and left to look at them in turn with his black eyes. "I must apologize to you both, for I have done you great ill. I have . . . my own confession to make."

Their frenzied pants and roars fell silent.

"What is it, my love?" Onaatan asked.

Jardok turned to face the lake, hands clasped in front of him. "The truth is, I do not love you."

"Ha!" said Nushmee triumphantly.

"I do not love either of you, though you have both brought me pleasure," Jardok said. "I proposed to wed Onaatan because of her holdings, and because it satisfied my family. But it was not my heart's desire."

Eva was almost to the bottom of the cliff. There were only a half dozen meters between her and her rifle.

"My tryst with Nushmee was born of despair, not passion," he continued. "For I harbored a painful secret, one that I could not reveal to anyone because it might cost me everything."

Three meters.

"The truth is . . ."

One meter.

"I'm in love with . . . Dardon!"

Onaatan gasped. Nushmee growled. Dardon fell to one knee.

Eva froze, hand hovering over her rifle, her face scrunched up in disbelief. Rich people, she thought again. They had no real problems, so they spent all their time making ones up.

Not like you, hmm? the voice in her head whispered. Eva was really starting to hate that voice.

"It's true," Jardok continued. "He has been my constant and faithful companion for so many years. Familiarity became affection, and as time passed, this turned to love." He stepped over to the smaller todyk and reached out a tiny arm. "Can you forgive me for deceiving you? For the cruel things I said about you and your station?"

They held that pose in silence for several long moments. Eva again suppressed a sneeze.

"Oh, sir," Dardon said. "Of course, sir."

"There's no more to be said, then." Jardok shook his head at Onaatan. "I am so sorry for all of this. I shall make my excuses to your family, my dear, and see that some measure of my estate is transferred to supplement your dowry."

"And me?" Nushmee said.

"I should be happy to remain your friend, if you would allow it," he said.

"And me, sir?" Dardon asked.

"I shall provide a generous stipend and references so you may find gainful employment with another household." Jardok walked once more to the shore of the lake. "Now, if you would all leave me in peace, I must contemplate the remains of my future."

The only sounds were the soft lapping of waves in the lake and the quiet hum of insects trying to eat Eva's face. But finally, finally she had some hope that she could finish this damn mission and go home. The other todyk would leave, she would hit Jardok with some night-night juice, and then—

Dardon leaped onto Jardok's back and did something violent-looking to his neck, though there wasn't any blood.

Jardok writhed in shock but didn't defend himself. Onaatan and Nushmee joined the butler, and soon they were all rolling around like a giant ball of feathery . . . lust? Yeah, that was what it looked like, all right. Those certainly appeared to be bits of anatomy that Eva was tangentially familiar with.

Well, she thought, that escalated quickly. She tried to avert her eyes while crawling backward toward the pyramid, rifle in hand. Broken blades of grass preceded her, and she very definitely did not think about Vakar at the smell of them.

His nonsense was well and truly done, at least.

Eva hung her head and sighed. She needed to apologize to him. Assuming he was even there when she got back. What if he'd left? What if she never saw him again, and the last thing she'd told him was to fuck off?

She suddenly didn't feel so hungry anymore.

Her gaze returned to the todyk. My goodness, but they were energetic. And more flexible than she would have expected. When was the last time she had . . . Being a spacer wasn't terribly conducive to maintaining a healthy relationship, but a body had needs. How long had it been since someone else had fulfilled them for her? A year? Two?

One of the todyk cried out, and Eva turned on her helmet so she wouldn't have to hear them anymore.

Damn it, she thought. I can't do this. I already put Leroy in a coma and nearly got Vakar turned into quennian soup, not to mention what happened with Glorious at Omicron. I can't undo the past, but I don't have to go through this Gate just because it's in front of me. I don't have to kidnap this guy and fly him a bazillion light-years away from his, um, whatever is going on here. Cargo is one thing, but these are people, with lives and families and love. If I cross this line, I'm well and truly fucked.

I'll be no better than The Fridge, and just as bad as Tito and my father, if not worse. I'll never be able to look my crew in the face again, or my mother.

Or Mari, assuming I ever get her back. Which at this rate is never going to happen anyway. They don't want me to earn my way out, they want me stuck until I'm no use to them anymore. They want to ride me into the ground like a secondhand space-ship, until all I'm good for is scrap.

Que se joden.

The thought of defying The Fridge made her feel simultane-ously terrified and liberated. Unless they were lying, they were going to send Mari to their asteroid mines if Eva left without the todyk. Everything she'd put her crew through so far would have been for nothing. All the lies, the danger, the pain . . . She'd still be indebted to The Fridge, still be doing whatever shitty jobs they threw at her. Her sister could die before Eva ever made a dent in the absurd amount they had decided she owed them, assuming they even wanted to keep her on. More likely, she'd be on the run from them for the rest of her probably short life. She might even be putting her mom directly in danger, if they thought Eva would run to her for help.

But at least she would know she'd refused to become like them. Her mother would respect that, and probably Pink. Mari herself might even prefer it to the alternative. If she survived . . .

No. This was how they worked. Fear. Paranoia. Never-ending spirals of guilt and hope and suspicion. Mierda. They weren't invincible, no matter how hard they tried to seem that way. There had to be something she could do, some way to get Mari back and keep her crew safe. She would figure this out, because the alternative was unacceptable. She needed to stop acting like she was a piece on The Fridge's Reversi board and start acting like a player. Maybe she'd never been the best at games, but she had to get good, and fast. She had to try flipping the board to white, or she'd be awash in darkness forever.

Dinosaur sex, she thought. That is a hell of a place to draw the line.

Eva landed the *Malcolm* on her father's lot and swallowed the acid that kept surging up her throat. There had been no transmission from The Fridge; either they didn't know she had failed, or they had some nasty surprise planned. She assumed it was the latter. Which, now that she thought about it, meant that it wouldn't be much of a surprise, since she was expecting it.

The lot was empty of customers. It wasn't usually bustling with activity, but this was utter silence. The buttery light of the local star made it look like high noon in a history memvid, set in Earth's cowboy times—or the flat film versions thereof. All she needed now was some gun-toting nemesis to wander out and stare her down.

As if on cue, Pholise Pravo emerged from the dealership building, their three legs giving them a rollicking gait that broke the mood like a baby at a wedding. They were tailed by Fjorsl, already tall and bristling with spines along their arms and back, their long maw of a head opening and closing as they spoke to the tuann too softly for Eva to hear—and she had every sensor channel open right now for that very purpose. One of these cycles she would invest in a lip-reading upgrade to her translators, but she was still paying off the smell one.

The rest of her scouting of the area didn't turn up anyone in hiding, though that didn't mean they weren't there. And *La Sirena Negra* was nowhere in sight, either, which was good or bad, depending on the reason.

Might as well get it over with, she thought.

Locking up the controls, Eva climbed out of the cockpit and down to the main airlock. Her bag was right by the door, untouched since she'd shoved her sniper rifle back in before leaving Ayshurn. Maybe she should change now? Her mother always told her to wear clean underwear at least. Ah, screw it. There'd be time later.

She threw her bag over her shoulder and opened the door. Pholise and Fjorsl waited outside, the annae with one of their limbs grown and woven into a thick mass that looked almost like a hammer.

"I see you got my message," Eva said, hopping to the ground.

Pholise hesitated. "No message was received from you."

"I figured showing up without a giant sedated todyk would be as good as putting an ad on Nuvestan commwalls." Then again, how *had* Pholise known to be there? Something else had to be going down.

"Ah, your meaning becomes clear." Pholise's head ruff was elevated, though not fully expanded. Their whispery breath was set to be amplified less than usual, so they were harder to hear.

"So what now?" Eva asked. "Mari gets sent off to hard labor and I keep shoveling your shit? Fine. But you can tell whoever your handler is that I'm not sorry. I'll do a lot, but kidnapping is over the line."

Even more quietly, Pholise whispered, "Run."

Eva's eyes widened. So that's how it was going to be.

"It has been determined that your use has reached its conclusion," the tuann said. "Your worth as an operative has been eclipsed by your worth as a commodity."

"A what?" She'd been expecting to get spaced, but this was something else.

"An extraordinarily large bid has been made for your retrieval, by the Gmaargitz Fedorach himself, and so I was sent to bring you in."

"Who the hell is—" Eva stopped and let her brain catch up to her mouth. "Glorious Asshole. Resingado hijo de mierda, that guy will not give up." Pholise's ruff rose and fell in time with their breathing. "So he put a bounty on me bigger than my debt? Coño carajo. Wait. Why are you telling me this? Why are you giving me a chance to get away?"

"Because it would be believable for you to escape," Pholise said. "And because you are not alone in growing tired of crossing lines that were once drawn."

They stood in silence under that yellow star as Eva calculated her next move. She could get back in the *Malcolm* and make a break for it, hoping Pholise didn't have backup fast enough to catch her before she could plot an FTL trajectory. The damn ship wasn't built for speed or maneuverability, so she was at a disadvantage. But she couldn't be sure she could reach her dad in time to get the codes for something faster.

And where the hell was her crew? She'd have to send them a message, a warning. Arrange a rendezvous point. Or maybe this was it, and it was finally time to cut them loose. They'd be safer without her. Running from The Fridge would be painting a giant target on her back, and in all likelihood, there would be a bounty on her big enough to make every mercenary scuttling through the fringe of BOFA space do a little cucaracha dance of joy. Glorious had made sure of that.

She thought of her last conversation with Vakar again and gritted her teeth. She could get all sentimental later, if she survived.

"Why did they let you bring Fjorsl out here?" Eva asked. "Why not your backup?"

"It was intended to seem less suspicious," Pholise said. "But when you are not apprehended, I will be distrusted regardless. So this must be made convincing."

"What must—"

Fjorsl lashed out at her with their club-hand, her reflexes throwing her backward in time to feel the wind of it on her face.

Hell, she was convinced.

She dodged a downward swipe at her head and clicked on her gravboots, jumping backward onto the side of the ship and stomping over to the airlock.

Shots pinged and sizzled off the exterior of the *Malcolm* as she settled into the pilot's chair.

Exterior sensors told her there were a half dozen shooters. Eva scanned the area for more action but couldn't identify which was their ship—none of them were starting up yet. Which meant either they were a hair slower than she was, or they'd come on a shuttle and their main ship was already in orbit waiting for her.

Bad odds. Plus she was losing time because it was taking too long for the controls to come online and go through all the automated system checks.

Ugh, I'm going to have to jack in, she thought. Gross.

Eva moved her hair out of the way and opened the hole at the nape of her neck with a terse thought, wishing the ship had more sophisticated controls, like the jackless implant Min used. Enough older boats still had obsolete tech like this, so her dad had insisted on the install when Eva was younger, and she was glad for it now even as she hated using it.

Settling into the pilot's seat, she folded her hands in her lap and sent the command to the tether. It slid into her with a soft, wet slurp and her consciousness flooded into the ship like water filling a glass.

Peaches, she thought. It always tastes like peaches. God, I hate peaches.

But now the ship was all hers, she was the ship, and her every thought was enacted more quickly than the processors would have managed alone. She could feel that everything was in order, ready to go, so she powered up the thrusters and sent the *Malcolm* into the sky so fast she could feel the tug of the air turn into a sonic boom behind her. She was free, giddy, soaring toward the violet horizon and up into the velvety black, to the stars, burning from within like a rocket, like a thousand tons of brilliant mass, a falling star in reverse, and—

Oh crap, there was the Fridge ship now.

The ship hailed her, and she ignored it, focusing on running through the calculations that would take her far away faster than the speed of light. But where could she go?

Home, said a whisper in the back of her mind. You want to go home.

And she did. Eva wanted to run to her mother and cry and eat real food and sleep in a real bed with a window that looked out on the same scrambled egg tree that had grown in their front yard since she was ten. But even though she hadn't been home in twelve years—had it really been twelve years?—she was sure the Fridge operatives would think to look for her there. She couldn't put her mother in danger like that. Not after what had happened to her sister.

Oh, Mari, she thought. Where are you? Will I ever see you again?

Now the other ship was firing on her, and her rear shields were holding up, but they wouldn't for much longer. She had to go.

Every evasive movement she made meant recalculating her jump, and every time she aimed the cargo ship's single defensive cannon and fired she was wasting time on fighting instead of fleeing. Scarlet lights dazzled her external sensors; she could feel the shields thinning, flickering. The few seconds she had remaining stretched out into the queer horizon that was shiptime. Everything seemed to slow down around her as she thought and thought.

Another weapon fired past her starboard side: *La Sirena Negra* had finally arrived. Her crew, her precious baby, flew to her side and put themselves between her and the guns of The Fridge.

Eva threw all her efforts into her trajectory. If she were gone, the Fridge ship would have no reason to keep up the fight, and *La Sirena Negra* could make its own escape.

If everything was already screwed, there was only one place in the galaxy where she might have a chance at safety. Maybe not freedom, maybe not revenge or justice, but probably safety. Probably. At least until she could figure out what to do next.

Just before she fired up the FTL drive, she sent a message over to her ship on the secure channel. She hoped it was working, but if it wasn't, then perhaps they weren't meant to meet again. Perhaps that really was for the best.

Eva sent them a single word, and then disappeared into hyperspace.

((Nuvesta.))

Chapter 11

GOING DOWN

Nuvesta was impressive from space. The seat of government for the Benevolent Organization of Federated Astrostates was a giant station that had been constructed over centuries by numerous alien races coming together to ostensibly govern the galaxy in peace and mutual respect.

That didn't always work out, of course. With great power came a great big plate of arroz con mango.

The various sectors of the station had grown out from each other like a wild, invasive plant, sometimes haphazardly and sometimes as part of a sporadic but focused campaign to help curb overpopulation in other sectors. Each sector operated on its own cycle, some matched to the roughly twenty-eight-hour cycle that was the average among the major species that inhabited the station, while others were geared toward specific species so they had somewhere comfortable to live and work.

The sectors closer to the hub, where the Assembly met, were cleaner and brighter, filled with exotic plants and artwork and all the cultural detritus that builds up over generations of people trying to suck up to other people. But farther out on the edges, where new sectors were being formed, things were simultaneously barer and busier, construction causing riots of metal and dirt and the smell of things being made, whether by fire or acid or concentrated biology.

It was easy to get lost in the crowds of the human quadrant. Near the embassy, the sidewalks were broad and lined with trees transplanted or engineered from biological data scraped from deep layers of soil, untouched by the pollution or radiation on Earth. Statues were erected to the human heroes who had made colonization and expansion possible, many of them the same kinds of people who had similar statues back on Earth, with all the baggage that implied. There were plans for a zoo, but animal rights groups from a variety of races, human and otherwise, had banded together to kill that effort. The annae hadn't been ecstatic about the trees, frankly, but at least those weren't sapient.

Eva didn't hang out near the embassy. She couldn't afford to. But between what passed for suburbs and the hub was the Bends, a vertical and horizontal maze of elevators and prefab buildings where working-class types lived in apartments smaller than her cabin on *La Sirena Negra,* usually four to a room, sleeping in shifts.

At first, she thought she would use her meager savings to get her own room there, lie low for however long it took for her crew to pick her up, then tell Pete where to collect his ship once she made it safely to the other side of the galaxy.

That was before she found out her accounts were frozen and Glorious's little bounty was common knowledge. The *Malcolm* was impounded when she couldn't pay the docking fees, so she couldn't even run to another planet. She was well and truly spaced. Or in this case, grounded.

The first cycle was spent wandering the Bends, riding up and down in elevators, trying not to attract attention while she figured out her options. She needed food, shelter and a disguise—just enough to last until her crew came for her, and not necessarily in that order.

Aside from the apartments, there were small stores that reminded her of the bodegas in the town where her abuelos lived, except these were sanitized corporate garbage, automated to the point of being glorified vending machines, and the prices were outrageously high. Vakar probably could have hacked them easily, but Eva didn't have his aptitude for software stuff. Someone else must have, though, because more than one person was covertly selling supplies for credit chits on random street corners.

There were also a handful of restaurants, with tables and counter space for maybe a dozen people at a time, several of which offered weekly meal services—no surprise given that most of the apartments didn't have kitchens. They might let her barter work for food if she asked, but no sense trying that until she was a little more desperate. Still, her stomach grumbled as the customers wandered in and out, carrying boxes that smelled way better than anything she'd eaten in months. One of the few benefits of being tethered to a station.

Most of the people who lived there worked low-pay jobs around the embassy—where there was an uncomfortable prestige associated with using human labor rather than bots—or at the docks, running the machines that loaded and unloaded ships, monitoring the cargo for contraband, servicing the mechs and bots, and doing whatever else wasn't automated. She was definitely more suited to that labor, but again, she told herself she didn't need to rush into it; she'd be off-station well before she needed a steady income.

What she did do, as a precaution, was pawn the stims from her med kit. That got her enough credit chits for bleach for her hair, and cheap face mods that caught her off guard whenever she saw her reflection: a too-wide nose, lighter skin, fuller lips, and eyes in a shade of purple that no one would mistake for real.

It was only for a cycle. She'd messaged Min that she was going to Nuvesta, so they'd pick her up soon. (Did the message go through? It must have.) Pink was sour at her for lying, and her last words to Vakar had been ugly, yes, but he wouldn't abandon her. None of them would. (Of course they would. Why wouldn't they? After what she had done?)

Only a cycle.

But then what? Eva had failed her sister, failed her mother even if she didn't know it. Failed Pete, but fuck him, he'd already been involved and he hadn't helped, either.

The Fridge had said they would force Mari into hard labor on an asteroid mine somewhere, but would they? Or would they just kill her? Either would be a waste, given Mari's skills and knowledge, but maybe they didn't care. People were hardly real to them, mere assets or liabilities, like on the balance sheets her mother dealt with. What was one human to them, more or less?

Eva didn't want to think about it, but she had nothing but time for thinking while she walked the streets of the Bends, head down, shoulders hunched, trying to make herself look as small as she felt.

One twenty-eight-hour cycle turned into two, which turned into ten. She pawned her tactical flashlight for enough chits to buy a week's worth of lunches, and did odd chores at the same restaurant for dinner whenever the proprietor—a middle-aged woman named Myriam with an easy laugh, who called everyone "my heart"—could find something for her to do. Eventually she started hanging around the docks, and after another worker was fired for showing up drunk and crashing his loader, she was hired as a temp for half pay under the table. A room was still out of the question with the few credits she was able to scrounge that way, but as tired as she got of sleeping in random ventilation shafts at odd hours, at least she was alive. As long as she was alive, there was hope.

But her crew was nowhere to be found.

She didn't want to contact them directly, in case the ship was being monitored. She checked prearranged places for messages whenever she could buy a few minutes at a q-net café or steal access from an unsecured network. Personal ads, job listings, even particular message boards Min used for her own amusement. Nothing.

Something must be wrong. They wouldn't abandon her. Had the message not transmitted? Had the ship been damaged? Or, heaven forbid, captured? No, she didn't want to imagine that. The Fridge couldn't have them and Mari, too. That was a nightmare she airlocked from her mind every time it resurfaced, and yet it kept coming back, like one of the free-floating corpses spacers kept accidentally finding in the horror vids.

Maybe if she held out long enough, The Fridge would move on. The Glorious Apotheosis would lose interest eventually and withdraw his bounty and she could move out to the fringe and get on with her life, such as it was.

Yeah, she didn't buy that line, either. But it kept her going.

Until the bounty hunters started showing up.

The first was a vroak with a vibroblade and an ugly acid tattoo on her face. She tried to corner Eva at the docks while Eva was loading cargo onto a big freighter, near the end of her shift. As tired as Eva was, years of hand-to-hand practice and actual combat experience under the guidance of Tito "Fair Fights Are Stupid" Santiago meant that within seconds, her body had taken care of the situation while her brain was still registering that there was a situation at all.

Eva panicked, as much as one could with a mechanical heart regulating itself. There were cameras everywhere, ostensibly for theft prevention, but they were monitored by a single foreman who spent most of his time working on his fantasy league team and gambling away the half of Eva's salary he didn't pay her. Had he seen? Would he say anything? She cleaned the vibro-blade, wondering how much she could pawn it for, whether it would be enough for a safe place to rest for a night or two. Whether she'd be able to go back to work the next cycle, or whether security would come for her. The cargo was one body heavier when it left, and Eva didn't sleep for a cycle, but nothing came of it after all.

The second bounty hunter was a buasyr, one of his four arms replaced with a laser chainsaw apparatus that stopped working when Eva cut it off him with her recently acquired vibroblade. He ran from her, swearing vengeance, and she was too tired to chase him down and finish the job. Besides, she was in the middle of delivering food to one of the apartment buildings, and she was fairly sure she'd taken a wrong elevator and would have to waste time doubling back to get her bearings. She hocked the chainsaw later for a fair amount of money, to a kloshian doctor who let her sleep in his operating room in exchange for a sample of her genetic material. She needed a haircut anyway, though the antiseptic smell of the room gave her a headache.

Things started to blur together after that. An annae with

petals around her head maw ambushing her in the bathroom
at the docks. A pair of pointy-eared truateg and their trained
crehnisk—was that outside the restaurant after a shift, or after
she'd bought a spare pair of pants off the kid with the perpetu-
ally runny nose, because hers were too baggy now? Even a small
todyk came for her, with an eye laser and special shoulder rifle,
his feathers blue and gold but dull from age or hard living. Some
hunters she fought, some she evaded, waiting for them to stop
coming, waiting for the universe to move on.

Money encouraged persistence.

After almost a month, Eva gave up.

It was easier than she expected. One cycle she was telling herself she might try calling her father, seeing what had happened
to him, whether he could come pick her up or wangle a ship for
her to escape on her own somehow. The next cycle she was milling around the docks like the rest of the laborers, arms folded
across her chest, her short dyed-blond hair falling into her eyes,
trying to look strong and capable but not lippy or willful, and
she realized she didn't have to pretend anymore. That was just
how she looked now.

She still worried about her ship, her crew. She wanted to believe The Fridge hadn't tracked them down and taken revenge
on them for what Eva had or hadn't done. Wanted to believe
they were okay, that at some point someone would show up with
a wild story about daring escapes and endless searching for poor
lost Eva. That there was a good reason they hadn't contacted her
already, and that it had nothing to do with giving her the collec-
tive finger and moving on with their lives. Even she wasn't buying her own bullshit, though. The sooner she accepted that, the
sooner she could stop pretending she had anything to live for.

And Mari. Poor Mari. She could hardly even remember Mari's face. And in the mirror, her own face was a stranger's, pale and thin and hollow-eyed behind the cheap mods.

What was the point? Why was she bothering anymore? Nobody gave a shit about her, and frankly, she didn't deserve one. It was like Pholise had said: she was selfish, and she'd put her crew in harm's way for the sake of her sister, who could be anywhere by now, living or dead. Had it been worth the price Eva had paid? The price she was still paying now?

Sometimes she wished she had kidnapped the damn todyk on Ayshurn after all, because at least then she would still have her people, still have a chance to get Mari back. Hadn't she let Glorious blow up half of Omicron because she refused to sacrifice herself to him? What was the difference? One stranger's life in exchange for hers. Would it really have been so bad?

The thought shamed her every time it snuck up on her, in the odd hours when she was trying to sleep. Because no matter how much she told herself Omicron wasn't her fault, she kept thinking of what she could have done differently. Ignored Glorious. Walked away. Let him do what he wanted. And then she got angry for blaming herself, when she hadn't been the one making unreasonable demands and firing the plasma cannons everywhere.

That was the difference: If she had loaded that todyk into her ship and turned him over to The Fridge, it would have been her choice, her actions, start to finish. Following orders, perhaps, acting under duress, with arguably pure intentions, but doing it nonetheless. On Omicron, she was one of many victims. On Ayshurn, she would have been the bad guy.

On Nuvesta, she was nobody at all.

A dytryrc came for her that cycle, wearing a hover belt with boosters and leaving a trail of slime splatters everywhere he went. He was slow for a bounty hunter, and she almost felt sorry for him.

"Hey, buddy," she said, climbing out of the access tunnel in the Bends where she'd been hiding. "Who are you looking for?"

He turned so fast he overspun and had to rotate backward. "Captain Eva Innocente, formerly of *La Sirena Negra*?" His voice was so perky, Eva wished she could bottle it and drink it for energy.

"That's my name, don't wear it out."

"Ha!" His robotic arms leveled a gun at her. "The bounty is mine! At long last!"

Eva leaned against the wall, her head swimming with fatigue. "So what am I worth now, anyway?" She yawned.

"Enough to feed my family for a year!"

"Wow," she said. "Wow. Does your family eat a lot, or—"

"Stop talking! We will go now and I will be paid!"

And she almost did. He trained his gun on her and she raised her hands and started to walk in the direction he indicated. Glorious was a disgusting asshole, but she was tired of hiding, tired of fighting. At least this way she'd finally have some closure.

As they moved, the people of the Bends avoided her gaze, stared when they thought she wouldn't notice, or gave her the barest glance before getting back to whatever they were doing. She almost laughed, thinking of how worried she'd been about that first bounty hunter that showed up weeks earlier. Nobody gave half a crap. She'd made no friends here; nobody even knew her real name. She wouldn't be missed.

They passed into a vendor area at the edge of the sector's docks and the crowd parted around them, humans and nonhumans alike sticking to the walls and the shop counters.

The smell of incense, and a hint of licorice, stopped her cold.

The dytryrc almost ran into her, eager as he was to move her along. "Do not delay our departure!" he exclaimed.

Eva couldn't find the source of the smell. Maybe she had imagined it. Maybe she had finally lost her mind. Or . . . maybe it was a sign. A wake-up ping. Madre de dios, what an enormous cabezón she had been. Waiting for her crew to find her like a damsel in distress? That was some high-grade ridiculousness.

Suddenly, she felt truly awake, and better: she was righteously pissed off.

No me busques, she thought. Porque me vas a encontrar.

She turned to face the bounty hunter. "Sorry, buddy. Looks like your big break isn't as broken as you hoped. I wanna live."

Diving sideways, she rolled into an alley that looped around to a larger loading area. It would be full of boxes big and small, barrels and bulky shipping containers waiting to fly off to other worlds. Her boss might wonder what was going on, but he tended to take a hands-off approach as long as cargo wasn't being damaged. He'd call the authorities eventually, if he felt like it. Probably he'd just watch, assuming he was paying attention at all.

Eva wove between the containers, searching for a nook she could slip into until the bounty hunter gave up. She dodged robots and power loaders and another human snatching some shut-eye in a narrow space between boxes. He'd get squished if he didn't watch out, she thought.

All her running was wasted because the bounty hunter simply flew above her, skimming the tops of the containers. "Halt or I will fire at you!" he shouted.

"Shoot me and you don't get paid!" she yelled back.

"Yes I will!" he said. "I still get half if you're dead!"

She'd been hoping he didn't know that. Certainly none of

the others had put forth much effort to take her alive. Well, it was worth a shot.

Eva reached into her gravboot and pulled out her vibroblade, lamenting the loss of her weapons stash in that access tunnel. She was making some exceptionally poor choices this cycle. Time for one more.

Sliding to a stop, Eva vaulted onto the top of a nearby container, keeping her eyes on the bounty hunter. He aimed and fired, but she was tracking the barrel's movement and making sure she wasn't in the path of the projectiles. Too late he realized she was charging, and he couldn't react quickly enough to keep her from crashing her full weight into his slippery bulk.

But Eva wasn't trying to pull him down. She grabbed at the hover belt around his waist and sliced it off with a flick of her wrist. The bounty hunter squealed and fell to the ground below, one of his robotic arms bent at an inappropriate angle under his own weight.

To his credit, he kept trying to shoot at her with the gun, even if it was pointed straight up.

"Knock it off," she said. "I'm not going to kill you."

"I will kill you first!"

She kicked the gun away and stepped on the metal hand that had held it. "Unless you're going to slime me to death, this is over." She leaned in. "Where I come from, there's a story. A miller shows up to a mill with this cat. Now, see, the cat is a real killer, and all the mice that had been living there are going bananas trying to stay away from it, but they never hear it coming. So one by one, the cat keeps picking them off."

"What is a cat?" the dytryrc asked.

"Cute fuzzy thing that kills stuff. Stay with me." Was anyone else listening? No, they were alone. "So the mice have a meeting, to decide what to do about the cat. And one old mouse stands up and he says, 'What we need to do is put a bell on the cat, so we'll hear it coming.' And all the other little mice love this idea. They start talking about what kind of bell it's going to be, what color ribbon, that kind of crap, until finally one teeny-tiny mouse stands up and says, 'But who is going to put the bell on the cat?'" She leaned closer. "And they're all too scared to do it, so they up and leave the mill."

"What's a mill?"

"Damn it, mijo, you're ruining my story." She sighed. "The point is, all the mice are too scared to bell the cat. It's a metaphor. But me? I'm done being scared. I'm not going to bell the cat. I'm going to blow its goddamn head off."

The bounty hunter stared at her with his twitching eyestalks. Slowly, quietly, he whispered, "What is a bell?"

Eva stood up and left. She didn't know why she bothered sometimes.

Eva's bag was miraculously still in the access tunnel where she'd left it, so she sent up a prayer to the Virgin in thanks.

She felt like she was thinking clearly for the first time in weeks. The bounty hunters obviously knew where she was, so there was no point in hiding. They'd keep trying to tag her until she was good and tagged. This wasn't hide-and-seek, it was dodgeball, and it was time to start throwing shit back at the other team.

Eva cleaned herself up in a public bathroom, splashing water on her face and scrubbing her armpits, then slipping on the spacesuit she hadn't touched since she landed. The patrons who wandered in and out gave her pitying looks, but none of them said anything to the manager, so she finished her business and moved on. Next stop, q-net café.

She chose one closer to the hub, despite the higher rates, because the authorities were more visible there, so a bounty hunter was less likely to try something overt. The place was run by an yf who moved among their customers slowly, like a column of water flowing through a crack. She ignored them and slid into a seat, pulling up the comm network and sending out a call to her ship on the private channel.

No answer. Mierda. Eva rifled through various search engines looking for any reports, any mention of something happening to her crew, her ship. Nothing. Finally she went to the failsafe channels, combing through personal ads on specific dating sites looking for messages from Pink. Her paid time was almost up when she finally found something.

LTM SPICY LATINA LOVER. IF YOU LIKE PIÑA COLADAS AND GETTIN CAUGHT IN THE RAINS OF CASIMIR IX, IF YOU'RE INTO PASTELITOS AND DUNE CAPERS AT MIDNIGHT, PING ME AND ESCAPE.

Subtle as a hammer on a mirror, but she didn't recognize the commlink code. Maybe it was being rerouted? Or it wasn't her people at all. Eva glanced at the timer on the net access and winced. Almost out. She couldn't afford a refill, not yet. Holding her breath, she made the call.

There was no answer, just a strange hum that started to set her teeth on edge after a few seconds. When she thought she was wasting her time, there was finally a click and a sound like breathing.

"Pink?" she asked.

All she heard was "Eva—" before her time ran out and the call disconnected.

Not Pink. Vakar.

Her hands curled into fists and she banged them on the table in front of her, three staccato strikes, then stood up and grabbed her bag. The yf must have heard her because they were drifting over to see what the noise was about. She brushed past and out onto the sidewalk, where the rich and important and wannabe rich and important were going about their lives, which at the moment included giving her confused or dirty looks because her grimy hair and spacesuit didn't fit in.

Inventory time. She had a sniper rifle, a pistol, a vibroblade, a spare set of clothes, and a burning ball of anger that was getting bigger by the minute. She needed to get some more credits so she could try that commlink code again and let her crew know where she was. Whether they would come get her was another story. Clearly they were looking for her or there wouldn't have been that ad. Maybe they just wanted to know if she was dead so they could claim her ship free and clear.

No, that was a shitty thing to think, even after all this time. She'd reserve judgment until she talked to them.

So, short term, get another job and make enough money to call again. Get picked up. Apologize profusely to everyone. Then fire them so she could find her sister, no matter how long it took.

And if Mari couldn't be found, or if something had happened to her—if she's dead, Eva told herself, don't sugarcoat it—she'd go on a rage-fueled revenge binge against the comemierdas who had kidnapped her.

The idea appealed to her way more than working off her debt to The Fridge, she had to admit, even if it was utterly outrageous.

The worst part about the Bends was the elevators. Waiting for elevators. Waiting inside elevators. The sheer number of elevators in this place had always astonished her, especially since no one ever seemed to be using them. At least she'd be able to catch up on news reports, since some well-meaning person had decided piping them through the elevator speakers was a great way to entertain a captive audience. Unfortunately, the reports weren't updated frequently, so the news wasn't exactly new anymore by the time anyone heard it.

Eva stepped into the first elevator and briefly considered taking a nap inside. It was brief because about a second later, she was sharing the elevator with a human wearing a suit that was slightly too shabby to be appropriate for the hub. The person had blue hair, purple eyes, and a pair of wrist knives that looked really sharp when they swung past Eva's face.

"I do not have time for this," Eva said. She aimed her knee at their groin but they blocked it, pushing her into the back of the car, and she countered with a kick to their stomach that they all but walked into. She ducked and dodged as they tried to slice at her eyes, her neck, her stomach.

A mellow female voice began the news brief, oblivious to the fight. "Repairs are ongoing following the Gmaarg Empire's apparently unprovoked attack on a space station near the edge of federated space, an attack that resulted in a number of casualties—"

The doors opened behind the bounty hunter just as Eva managed to grab their forearms and lean in for a swift headbutt that knocked them onto the floor outside the elevator, their nose broken.

Unfortunately, another two bounty hunters were waiting, as if some signal had been sent out that now was the time to push. Maybe the dytryrc had squealed.

Eva smacked the switch to close the doors and dropped to the ground to avoid their pistol fire, rolling sideways and wedging herself into the tiny space next to a door.

They vaulted over the prone human, who grabbed at one of

them, tripping him while the other, a kloshian, made it into the elevator.

Eva grappled the woman into a choke hold, but the bounty hunter was wearing a spacesuit underneath and it went rigid in her grip. Eva released her and lunged at the woman's gun, which they fought for as the elevator moved down to the next floor.

"After years of closely monitored trade restrictions and a veil of secrecy, new leadership within the ranks of the Dalnularan order has announced the relaxing of visitation requirements as it launches a new line of specialty liquors—"

The doors opened again, and this time they were greeted by a gaggle of children and what might have been their teacher, who stared at the fighting women and didn't move.

A ragged cheer started, cries from the kids of "Punch her in the face!" and "Kick her butt!" shushed by the flustered human in the prim blue uniform. Eva winked at a small boy off to one side, getting her leg in between the bounty hunter's and dragging her to the ground, an arm locked behind her back. Finally, Eva got her leg untangled and kicked the woman in the back of her head with her gravboot, once, twice, and that fight was over.

Eva rolled the limp kloshian off at the next stop and stood, retrieving her pistol and vibroblade from her duffel bag and slinging its strap across her body like a bandolier. At the next level, she would be ready. She spat a rusty-tasting gob of blood into the corner and stared at the doors.

Someone thumped onto the top of the elevator car, and a moment later, a laser saw began cutting through the insulated metal.

Eva felt like a protein slab in a can, waiting to be eaten. But she couldn't fire at the person yet, because her shot wouldn't penetrate the ceiling. She had to wait until the can was open.

The hole they were carving would be too small for them to fit through, though; they were probably planning to snipe her through it, or drop in a gas canister.

"After the recent high-profile disappearance of the Futisian ambassador's broodmate, government representatives were once again compelled to publicly dismiss rumors of an organized crime syndicate allegedly manipulating people into engaging in illicit activities—"

Clucking her tongue, Eva turned on her gravboots and jumped to the ceiling, next to where the hole would be, and crouched there with her short blond hair sticking straight up. Or falling, depending on your perspective.

A chunk of ceiling dropped out. Eva caught a glimpse of an eye peering down into the elevator, which she promptly greeted with a vibroblade. The eye's owner retreated with a shriek. She followed that by shoving her own pistol to the hole and firing in what she hoped was the person's direction. None of the shots seemed to hit, but there was a sound like gravboots powering on, and then a thunk against the wall of the elevator shaft.

Then, because nothing could ever be easy, the elevator doors opened again and Eva found herself face-to-upside-down-faces with about a dozen tiny pizkee. They smiled in unison like a squad of needle-toothed blue fairies and ran into the box, screaming profanities.

But they soon found they couldn't reach her with their knives because she was still stuck to the ceiling, holding herself about a meter and a half off the floor.

A human couple passed the elevator and looked inside to see the band of aliens trying to form a pyramid to reach Eva. She shrugged at them as the doors closed.

Blood was starting to pool in her head, and she spat again,

then fired a warning shot at the pizkee. They apparently decided she wasn't worth their trouble, because at the next stop they all got off, grumbling to themselves about big jobs.

Again, Eva was alone. And mercifully, the news reports had stopped. They were so distracting.

She turned off her gravboots and twisted to land on her feet, standing up straight and readying her weapons again. Enough was enough. She was getting off this damn joy ride to hell.

The doors opened, and she didn't wait to see who was on the other side. Eva launched herself out, crashing into someone taller than her, slightly wider, and definitely not human.

They both fell to the ground, Eva winding up on top, her hand already raising her vibroblade to sink it into their chest. But her eyes were slower than her other sensory organs, and she dropped her knife before the conscious part of her brain had registered whose chest she was sitting on.

Fire. Cigarettes. A dash of cooking oil, a whiff of fart. Not the slightest hint of licorice.

"Sorry, I thought you were someone else," she muttered, grabbing her knife and getting to her feet. She held out a hand to help Vakar up, but he stayed on the floor, facing the ceiling with his eyes closed. Around them, a few people stared, but most on this level tended to ignore violence unless it was directed at them.

"More bounty hunters might be on their way," she said. "We have to go."

He still didn't move. She started to wonder if she'd really hurt him, but his smell hadn't gone bad.

"Vakar?" She nudged him with her boot.

He opened his eyes. "So you do know who I am."

"Of course I do, what the hell?"

"You said you thought I was someone else."

"A bounty hunter. Trying to kill me. Hence the aggressive hello, for which I apologized."

"Is that all you are sorry for?"

That was a hell of a question. "No," she said. "It certainly is not."

The cooking-oil smell diminished but didn't fade entirely; he was still suspicious. Despite that, she grinned as if she hadn't just fought her way down the elevator of death.

"We can talk more when we're not out in the open. Did I mention the bounty hunters?" She held out her hand to him again.

This time he took it, and she helped him up.

"Now," she said, "where the hell is my ship?"

Chapter 12

EL QUE LA HACE LA PAGA

That is not what I wanted to hear," Eva said, scowling.

Pink, sitting across from her, shrugged. "If we'd brought *La Sirena Negra* here, she'd be impounded. We had no choice. You're lucky she even made it out in one piece, after what happened to—"

"Did we have to meet here?" Vakar interjected. "It is somewhat distracting."

"Music's loud so no one can hear us," Pink said. "And the drinks are good."

"I think he means—" Eva gestured with her chin at the stripper hanging from a cage above their table, gyrating in time with the music.

Vakar smelled briefly of grass.

"I'm enjoying the view," Pink said, swirling her drink and watching the dancer with a tiny smile.

Eva had to admit, the man was very limber. "Okay, so first we have to get me off Nuvesta, then go to New Nogales to get the ship back, and then—"

"Slow down, sunshine," Pink said. "What's this 'we' business?"

Eva paused, looking back and forth between her two crewmates, apparently former rather than current.

"You lied out your ass and almost got us all killed," Pink continued. "More than once, I might add. You sold us out and disappeared. And then Min finds your message in a cached memory, so we haul ass over here only to find you're wanted for—" She snapped her fingers at Vakar. "What was it again?"

"Petty larceny, assault, possession of unlawful weaponry, contempt of court and disturbing the peace."

Pink steepled her fingers. "I agree, my peace is quite disturbed."

Eva had given a lot of thought to this conversation: how she would handle it, what she would say and how she would say it. She had imagined their reactions, from anger to disgust to indifference. If she had managed to find well-paying work, she had intended to offer them money by way of apology, to fire them properly and send them on their way.

Until this cycle. Until this moment. Now she knew how much she needed them, and she had no idea where to begin begging for their forgiveness.

"Well?" Pink asked. She and Vakar stared at Eva.

The dancer in the cage above them was human, though other dancers above other tables were kloshian, or tuann, or buasyr. There was even a quennian off in one corner, not moving very much but probably exuding a range of interesting smells for his audience. All of them doing what they did for money. Mercenary. Disconnected. Few of them bothered to make eye contact with their viewers, though of course some of them didn't have eyes in the first place. They weren't people so much as products, interchangeable and replaceable. Like furniture or artwork.

But many businesses were more like family, or what a family should be, watching out for each other and taking care of each other and sharing in the pain and profit of the establishment equally.

She hadn't seen her ship and crew that way at first. Pink was around from before she even had a ship of her own. Eva had pulled Min out of the bot fights for an unrelated mission and kept her on because the girl was frankly a much better pilot than she was. Bigger cargo opportunities had arisen, so she'd scouted out Leroy as extra muscle.

And then there was Vakar. An accident, really. A whim. She remembered him standing there, facing down a trio of skinheads with their stupid bar code tattoos, to signify they were made on Earth. His hands up, palms out in front of him as he backed away. The ringleader, grinning, hefting a rock and throwing it. Vakar dodging, quick as a snake, which made them angrier. He'd had a gun, she remembered, but hadn't drawn it, and that had made her curious. Interested.

She had wandered over, extra swagger in her step, extra sway in her hips. By this point Vakar was bleeding from a crack on his face, and she could smell him even though she didn't know what it meant yet. Vinegar, but also vanilla, a combination that had brought her back to her abuela's house in a flash.

It had gone basically as he'd told her father. Eva stood between him and the skinheads, one hand on her hip. They sneered and called her names, and she turned to Vakar, stood on her toes and licked the blood from the side of his face.

The ringleader had drawn a vibroblade, and Eva had broken the woman's arm in two places before smashing her face with the same rock that had hit Vakar. The other skinheads had flanked her and attacked, but they weren't fighters, just angry kids with grievances bigger than one quennian. Eva broke them both quickly, efficiently. She enjoyed doing it. She felt righteous.

Vakar had watched it all with his gray-blue eyes, but when she was finished, he hadn't thanked her. He had said, "Why did you do that?"

And she hadn't known how to answer him. Because she thought he was in trouble and she wanted to help? Because he was clearly trying not to hurt anyone and they were bothering him anyway? But really, she thought, she had been in a terrible mood and was looking for a reason to hurt someone else. He was a convenient excuse.

She had shrugged, smiled. "Does it matter?" she had said.

Then things blurred a bit, because of her reaction to his blood, but they made it back to *La Sirena Negra* and Pink took care of her and Vakar was there when she woke up. He'd been there ever since.

"Ship to Eva, come in, girl," Pink said, snapping her fingers. "Do you need a script or something? Because this little show's about to end with us walking away because you can't remember your lines."

Eva shook her head. "I'm sorry. I did a lot of stupid things. I'm going to tell you why, but only because you deserve to know. If you want to forgive me, that's up to you."

She told them everything. About her father, her sister, The Fridge. The mission gone wrong and the aftermath. They listened, and stared at her, and didn't interrupt except to ask about specific things that had happened.

By the time she finished, the cage where the dancer had been was empty; presumably he'd gone on break. She hadn't even seen him leave.

"Eva-Benita," Pink said. "You are the biggest pile of crehnisk shit I have ever seen."

Eva shrugged and nodded.

"Why did you not tell us?" Vakar asked.

"Does it matter?" she said softly.

Pink leaned back. "You dragged us into a bunch of sketchy-ass situations. And you did it knowing full well they were sketchy."

"I thought I could handle it," she said.

"Things got handled, all right. You remember when we left Tito because he was pulling this kind of shit with us? And what did you say?"

Eva closed her eyes. "I said I'd never be able to follow a captain I couldn't trust."

"And yet, here we are."

"I'm not Tito." Eva spat each word like a curse.

"Tito probably wasn't Tito at some point," Pink said.

She was right. Once you started lying to yourself, everyone else was easy. The road to hell wasn't a road, it was a slide greased with good intentions and a whole lot of bullshit.

"I promise I'll do better," Eva said. "It's not like I can do any fucking worse."

Pink rolled her eye. Vakar smelled like a perfume store after a fire. Eva couldn't look at him.

"Your sister remains in cryostasis?" he asked.

"I don't know," Eva said. "She could be. Or she could have been moved to an asteroid mine already, like they said she would be. Or they could have shot her into a star for all I know." My fault, she thought, her stomach twisting with guilt.

"What's your plan, then?" Pink scratched the eye under the patch. "You stewed here for a few weeks, let people shoot at your fool ass, busted a few heads. You wanna get your ship back and go do that somewhere else instead?"

"No," Eva said. "I want to find my sister, and if I'm too late, I want to fuck up these sinvergüenzas and shut them down for good."

Pink barked out a laugh. "And then you're gonna find the lost colony of New Venus? And convince the rogue AI on He-nope to live in peace with organic life? Maybe reverse-engineer a Gate and make your own and retire to a tropical paradise?"

"I guess, if I don't have anything better to do. Everyone needs a hobby."

"Damn it, girl." But Pink hadn't stopped grinning. "You're ten kilos of crazy in a five-kilo bag. Have I mentioned your hair looks like shit?"

"I didn't do it up like this for you, mija."

"You certainly didn't do it for Vakar, unless it's got a special perfume I can't smell."

Vakar's aroma took on a greenish edge but was still muddled, laced with fiery anger.

Pink settled their tab with a gesture. "I'm not promising anything, mind. But we got a rigged box to hide you in, get you on board our borrowed tub. We'll see where it goes from there."

"Thank you," Eva said. "It's more than I deserve."

Pink stared at her as if waiting for more, but Eva was all out of sarcasm.

"Leroy's gonna be happy to see you," Pink said finally. "These chumps took bets on which part of you I'd stab first, and he won thirty creds."

"First?"

"Yeah, first. Min had your right arm. Leroy said I wouldn't do it because then I'd have to fix you after."

"And you?" she asked Vakar.

The cut-grass smell intensified. "Your posterior. It seems meaty enough to absorb damage."

Taking bets on scalpel injuries. Maybe things would be okay after all.

Min sat in the bridge of the borrowed ship, staring at the control screen. "Welcome back, Cap," was all Min said. It was enough.

Leroy rested in his bunk, his facial hair long and a bit scraggly. His muscles sagged under his pale flesh, like he was a spacesuit without a person inside. But he looked better awake than he had in a coma. That seemed a million years ago now.

"How's your brain?" she asked.

"It's mine," he said.

She wasn't sure what else to say. She settled for "I'm sorry."

He scratched the tattoo on his left arm. Right now, it showed a Dragon-class starship on a field of blue, lasers firing in the front. "Shit happens. Better than being off in some corporate war fighting for stupid stuff nobody cares about."

How would he feel fighting for something he did care about? "Is it really?"

He considered this, then nodded, cracking a smile. "Not everyone can say they survived a brain parasite, right? Loads of people get shot. That ain't no story."

She smacked his shoulder and walked to the door, stopping on the way out. "What happened to that thing, anyway?"

"I think Pink has it in cryo somewhere. I told her you said it was supposed to get flushed out the airlock, but she said you didn't get a vote when you had stupid opinions."

"Fair enough," Eva said, closing the door behind her.

Min's voice came over the loudspeaker. "Cap, we're ready to go if you are."

Eva stalked up to the bridge, where the pilot was fully immersed, her face tranquil. On her lap sat Mala, her hazel eyes blinking sleepily. The cat yawned and put her face down on her paws, purring louder than the FTL drive.

"Didn't want to get left behind, huh?" Eva said. The purring intensified, and she grinned despite herself.

"All right, Min," she said. "Punch it."

Silence fell for a moment. "Did you forget something, Cap?" Min asked.

"Oh, right." Eva walked back to the hallway between bunks and yanked up the floor, exposing a crawl space underneath. She climbed in, tucking her knees against her chest, and pulled it closed above her.

She hoped they could get out of Nuvesta quickly. Hiding always made her want to pee. But within minutes, curled up as she was, out of the reach of bounty hunters at long last, she quickly fell fast asleep.

The trip was quick and quiet, with Eva feeling as if she were a passenger instead of the captain. She tried to help, but Min was busy flying, Pink was busy taking care of Leroy, Leroy was busy resting and doing PT, and Vakar was busy hiding in the bowels of the ship. So she kept mostly to her bunk, doing push-ups and ruminating on how much of a jerk she was. She had no idea how she was going to make all of this up to her crew, but she'd be damned if she didn't earn their trust back somehow.

She'd rather take a naked spacewalk than end up like Tito and her dad.

But she was also planning. Finding her sister and taking down an enormous galaxy-spanning organization wasn't as easy as picking up shady cargo. She was tired of running, tired of defending herself against one bounty hunter after another, tired of constantly looking over her shoulder until she was spinning around in circles like a dog chasing its tail. As long as The Fridge existed, she would never be free. If they were so ready to screw her over for a hefty fee from Glorious, then she was ready to make herself an incredibly expensive nuisance to them until they regretted ever hearing her true, full name.

And once she found out what had happened to Mari, well, she would decide how to handle that situation, whether it ended up being a rescue mission or a funeral. If it was the latter, what happened at Garilia would look like a statistical anomaly compared to what she would do to these fuckers.

So she plotted, and she schemed, and she brainstormed. She thought up and rejected a hundred different ideas. It all came back to a single problem: information. She didn't know where The Fridge kept their cryo storage, and she didn't know who might know where it was kept, so before she did anything, she had to figure that part out.

Her father, at least, might have someplace to start, some stray thread they could pull so the whole tapestry would start to unravel. It was just as well they'd left *La Sirena Negra* with him, because she could take the opportunity to shake him down for everything he knew. Assuming he would help her at all, if he thought she was going to run off on a fool's errand.

Assuming The Fridge wasn't watching him, waiting for her to resurface so they could scoop her up like a wayward toddler.

They arrived at New Nogales to find the dealership reduced to a handful of ships, scruffy dust runners and secondhand speeders and a conspicuous lack of Eva's own starship. She jumped out of the borrowed boat and half jogged over to the building. Vakar came with her, while Pink stood in the doorway with her sniper rifle ready.

Inside the showroom, all the displays were turned off, most of the artwork was gone and half the lights were dark. No security greeted them, and no salespeople, either.

Upstairs, the door to her father's office was open. Eva tiptoed up, drawing her pistol. She told herself this wasn't a trap, because they would have grabbed her outside. She told herself that her father couldn't be dead, because he was worth more alive than dead. She told herself a lot of things so she wouldn't stop taking one step at a time into the unknown.

To her surprise, she found Pete standing behind his desk, facing away from her. The room was otherwise empty.

"You got extra valuable all of a sudden," Pete said.

"To some people," she replied.

He turned around, looking older. Exhausted. His forehead was lined with worry and his lips were wrinkled from frowning.

"They took it all, and they told me it still wasn't enough," he said. "I'm supposed to get a crew together and pick up where you left off. Work for them until my vital organs decay."

"So forever, then," she said.

He didn't crack a smile. Instead, he sat down, folding his hands together and resting them on the top of the desk.

Vakar stood behind her, and she considered sending him out. No, she thought. Not anymore. No secrets.

"I need the information you were collecting," she said. "I'm finding Mari, wherever they've stowed her. Whatever it takes."

Now Pete did laugh. "Of course you are. You made up your mind. I know how you operate, little girl." He rubbed his face with both hands, leaning back in his chair. "I remember once when you and your sister were kids, and you found where your mother had hidden a stash of candy. You ate that stuff until you were about ready to barf, but as soon as your sister took one, you ran to tell me all about it."

"I don't remember that."

"You must have been six or seven. My point is, you grow morals when the mood strikes you, and then you prune them back like a wild rosebush when they get too thorny."

And like a rosebush, that stung her. Was she really that bad?

She'd always thought she had a code, even if it wasn't as strict as other people's. But then, who was he to talk about morals?

"Are you going to help me or not?" she asked.

"I should send you to bed without dinner, is what I should do," he said. "But then you'll just climb out onto the roof like you always did and be gone before the moons rise."

She waited, eyes locked with his. Brown, like hers, so dark the pupils were hard to see. She hoped hers were less bloodshot, but after weeks of stunted sleep, she wouldn't be surprised if they were the same.

"Think about it," she said. "This is your only chance to get in on the ground floor of an exciting new venture. Otherwise you get to read about my exploits in the *Freenet News* like every other pirate and scavenger in the 'verse."

He snorted. "You mean this is my only chance to be part of the plan instead of watching you get yourself killed from afar."

"I don't die easy."

"It hasn't occurred to you for a second that maybe I don't want to lose both my girls, huh?"

It hadn't. Partly because she refused to admit she might lose. Partly because she'd convinced herself a long time ago that he didn't give more than half a shit.

"You won't," she said.

He gestured and the files he'd shown her before appeared. With a flick he sent them to her commlink; the information arrived with a soft ping. "That's everything I have. Names, places, amounts of money. Anything I could scrounge up, be it half-truth or rumor."

Her dad stood, walking around the desk to stand in front of her. Still a big man, he wrapped his arms around her like he had when she was little, when she felt like he could do anything and no one could hurt her because his arms were too strong.

Now this felt like goodbye, and she hated it, but did it anyway, trying to reclaim that lost piece of her young self.

It didn't work.

Then, to her surprise, he let her go and turned to Vakar. "Shoot her first if she does anything stupid," he said. "Don't let them get her."

Vakar's palps twitched. "Sorry, sir. I only take orders from the captain."

Pete smiled, elbowing Eva in the side. "Good answer."

Vakar must have been doing a self-control exercise, because all she could smell of him was a hint of lavender. The hell did he have to feel smug about?

"Not to shoot the elephant in the room, but where's my ship?" Eva asked. "You didn't sell it, did you?"

"Come on, Bee," her father said. "Do you really think that little of me?"

She pursed her lips.

"It's at my private dock. Even you don't know where it is, and I'm not about to tell you." He walked back to his desk and opened a drawer, pulling out a pair of gloves and slipping them on. "Wait here and I'll bring her around."

"Yeah, yeah." She walked back out to the antechamber and took a seat, crossing her legs primly. "I'll raid your pantry while you're gone."

"The expensive stuff is in the back," he said with a wink. She watched his head bob down the stairs and disappear.

When he had left, Vakar said, "You know he probably hid a tracker program in with all that information he gave you."

Eva smiled. "Of course he did. He's slippery as a starwhale in liquid methane."

"Taught you everything he knows, did he?"

"Not by a long shot."

La Sirena Negra floated in as gracefully as her namesake, the battle damage to her dark metal exterior making Eva wince. Pete stepped out of the airlock, pulling off his gloves and tucking them into a zippered jacket pocket.

"She's still got a leak in the tail, but she'll run," he said. "You'll have to double up on coolant until you patch it."

"Vakar can handle that," she said, resisting the urge to hug her ship. She'd get a wicked burn if she tried it, judging by the ticking of the hull and the heat radiating off it. The secret dock must not have been planetside.

"Stay safe now, Eva-Bee," he said. "I'll see you when I see you."

With a quick wave, Pete walked back down the landing strip to his building. He favored his left leg, as if his med kits had run out and all the old wounds of the past were catching up with him. Which was probably what was happening. She had to get this whole mess sorted before he ended up wherever they were trying to send him.

Her family was busted enough already.

Her crew had come up behind her, their minimal baggage in hand. Min practically salivated, her eyes watering. Pink stood with an arm around Leroy to keep him steady. Vakar, well. He smelled like vanilla and ozone.

"Come on, then," she said. "You waiting for an invitation from the president?"

Eva went in first, carrying her bag to her cabin and dropping it on the floor. She could almost feel everyone taking up their posts, slipping into old habits like hands filling gloves. ((Mess,)) she pinged, and got a chorus of acknowledgments.

Family.

Chapter 13

DAME PAN Y DIME TONTO

They sat around the table in the mess, as if they hadn't been apart for almost a month and running from trouble. Eva explained her intentions with her mouth half-full of food.

"So you're saying you're loopy as a bug in a window," Pink said.

Eva shook her head. "We can do this. All we need is a plan, a solid plan. But flexible enough to survive contact."

"And our incentive for helping is?" Pink asked, pursing her lips.

"Not much, so if you want out now, I understand," Eva said. "Absolute best-case scenario, we save my sister and take down a bunch of terrible people who've been preying on others for years. Worst case, we die or end up on some asteroid mine wishing we were dead." She shoveled more food into her mouth.

"I think I liked it better when she was lying to us," Leroy muttered.

"There's probably money to be made, one way or another." Eva swallowed, then chased it down with a sip of coffee. "They have their own bank accounts, assets, caches of weapons and other stuff we could steal and resell."

"That sounds like piracy," Vakar said, smelling minty. Anxious.

"I prefer to think of it as vigilante justice."

"Or war," Pink said. "Sorry, Leroy." She cast a glance up at the big man next to her.

Eva nodded. "Leroy, you especially don't have to be any part of this. It's . . . a lot."

He stared down at the table, his right eye twitching as he reached up to tug at his beard.

"Where else am I gonna go?" he said quietly.

"There are plenty of—"

"Yeah, I know. I could be a stevedore on Nuvesta, or Boulea, or Stabanov. Maybe sling crates on some merchant freighter." He closed his eyes. "Nobody's gonna want me around after the first time I lose my shit. If it ain't the nightmares, it's the temper."

"You haven't had a nightmare in a while, thanks to your meds. And anyway, people would understand."

"They'd tranq me up or fire me. I know it would happen, because it happened before."

Pink put a hand on his arm. "You're doing better than you think."

"Am I?" His voice cracked. "Look at our last passenger."

Vakar said nothing, but his smell had gone from mint to incense. Eva was pretty concerned herself.

You could go back to your moms, she almost said, not for

the first time. But there was a reason he mostly chatted with them by holovid instead of visiting: he was more afraid of hurting them than he was of nearly anything else.

"If you stay, you stay on the ship," Eva said instead. "I don't want you out there in the middle of a firefight getting ideas."

Leroy nodded, then grinned. "Someone has to watch out for Min, right?"

"Assuming Min wants to stay."

"Of course I do," Min said. "I don't want to go back to the pits. Robot fights are awesome, but not as awesome as space. And I definitely don't want to be a solar farmer."

That left Pink and Vakar.

Eva considered Pink's expression over the rim of her coffee cup.

"Don't give me those puppy eyes," Pink said. "My brother would let me sleep in his basement if I asked, and I'd get to hug my niblings before bed every night. Hell, I could get a job on any ship or station or planet in the fringe if I wanted."

"If you wanted?"

Pink smirked. "I don't, but I could. Anyway, my brother's basement is cold and I like stealing from assholes. It helps me sleep at night, almost as good as hugs."

I don't deserve you, Eva thought, not for the first time. Pink inclined her head as if she knew exactly what Eva was thinking and agreed.

Vakar, on the other hand, was pumping his uncertainty right into the air, the sharp tang of ozone nearly burning her nostrils.

"Vakar?" she asked.

"I require more time to think," he replied.

"Fair enough."

Eva stood and gathered her waste, tossing it in the recycler, then knocked back the last of her coffee. More time to think.

What did that mean? Was he still angry at her? He should be; she was terrible, and she'd been a huge jerk to him specifically.

She felt queasy about everyone else opting to stay, like she was more responsible for them than ever. If she let them down again, shit was going to go straight-up Humpty Dumpty.

"I assume you've got some grand plan you're cooking up," Pink said. "Spill."

"Shouldn't be too tough," she said, shaking out of her funk. "We retrace our steps from the deliveries and make some trouble, see if we can't hack their terminals and find other locations to hassle while we figure out which asteroid mine has my sister. The ship may have moved on, but the bases are at least likely to be on the same planets."

"What kind of trouble do you intend to make?" Vakar asked.

Eva's lips curled into a snarl. "The kind I used to be really good at: persuasion with a side of punching. These assholes came looking for me, and they have most certainly found me."

What Eva found, unfortunately, was a whole lot of nothing.

La Sirena Negra flew to Suatera first, where they had disposed of the delightful Miles Erck. The lab was in the same place, but scans revealed that not only was its security inactive, there were no signs of life inside. Eva and Pink took a quick look around to confirm the readings; sure enough, the place was completely empty, like a corpse picked clean by razor ants. Not even the computer terminals had been left.

Vakar stayed on the ship, performing never-ending system checks and minute repairs. Eva saw him only at the late cycle meal, and he didn't look at her, just sat around smelling morose and uncertain.

Beskore was no better than Suatera, its acid rain replaced by radiation that strained Eva's suit to the limit. It took them some time to locate the mobile facility, which had moved since the bug-juice delivery, but it was equally bare inside. Scorch marks from blaster fire and the occasional larger explosive residue suggested a fight, but against whom? BOFA? Pirates? The locals had no answers, or weren't interested in sharing them with her.

The ship in the Cadrion system was both easier and harder to find; it was very near where they'd last seen it, but it was apparently blown to pieces. Most of the fragments were too small to offer any clues, and the rest hurtled through the frictionless void toward unknown destinations.

Eva could relate.

La Sirena Negra lazily drifted toward the nearest Gate, waiting for a destination.

Everyone once again sat in the mess room, staring at Eva, who herself was staring down at her hands as if they would tell her the right place to begin.

"I've been reviewing what information I have," Eva said. "There are definite patterns. Some of this is guesses based on reports from the Freenet—"

Pink made a scoffing noise and rolled her eye.

"—and the coverage in more mainstream news channels," Eva finished. "Which are run by rich people with their own agendas."

"What's wrong with the Freenet?" Leroy asked. A chorus of groans answered.

"Man, don't get me started," Pink said. "Ain't nobody got time for that."

Eva leaned forward, her hands moving as she talked. "It's possible to draw some lines between random crap and people dropping into or out of the spotlight. Or deals getting done that

came out of nowhere. Pete did a lot of research over the years, off
and on, and more in the past few months, but it seems like The
Fridge moves fast to plug any leaks."

"So what do we have to work with?" Pink asked. "Names,
places?"

Eva shrugged. "Mostly, we know the victims and not the
perps. Sometimes there's overlap, of course, because of how The
Fridge operates. That makes it harder to separate valuable targets from useless ones."

Vakar drummed his gloved fingers on the table. "It's a shame
you can't contact your handler. They were a victim, too, assuming they weren't lying."

"That's the good news," Eva said, grinning. "Min found my
handler."

Min made a scoffing noise through the speakers. "I would
have found them faster if I hadn't had to keep running that
noob through the same dungeon until the boss dropped the
stupid epic helmet he wanted," she said.

"Lord save us from noobs," said Pink. "And the bad news?"

"They're being held as collateral by quennian military right
now, under cover of a pleasure cruise in Crux Zagreus, while negotiations are ongoing over a trade embargo with a tuann faction in the quadrant."

"Why would they be collateral?" Leroy asked.

"They are a high-level diplomat," Vakar said. "Or related to
one. It is not uncommon for a prisoner exchange to occur, to
encourage civility among negotiating parties."

Eva eyed Vakar, leaning back in her chair. He sure knew a
lot more about this than she expected from an engineer. Then
again, not many engineers knew how to fight and shoot, either.

"I don't suppose you know any specifics, quennians being
involved?" she asked.

"It is not as if all quennians are allied, any more than all humans are." His palps twitched and his smell soured.

"I wasn't assuming anything, just asking. According to what I found, House Remilin is the prime negotiator. That ring any bells?"

"I know of them, but am not acquainted with any of their members directly. Their commander was Veltus Nazaril, last I heard, but that may have changed. I apologize for my ignorance."

Eva rolled her eyes. "Please. I couldn't tell you the name of the president of my home planet if you put a gun to my head."

Vakar wagged his head and raised a hand diffidently.

"It's not Veltus anymore, anyway," Eva said, scanning her notes. "Now it's someone named Galenia Farinus san Bellitan."

Vakar froze, and Eva held her breath.

"That," he said, "is interesting."

"Someone you know?"

"I know of her."

That sounded like a story for another time. Eva filed the thought away for future reference, because it really didn't make a whole lot of difference for her plan.

"So. We need to bust in on this pleasure cruise somehow and talk to Pholise, without starting an intergalactic incident," she said. "Normally that would be up to me, but I don't suppose they're likely to have any humans hanging around?"

"You would be like a firebat at an yf funeral," Vakar said.

Leroy perked up. "Why not take Vakar with you?"

"No way," Eva said.

"That is a bad idea," Vakar said at the same time.

"You can smell him from a mile away," Eva said. "He's a terrible liar."

Vakar smelled embarrassed, and a touch confused. "I . . . Yes. The captain is correct."

Shit. Eva hadn't told Vakar about getting the scent translators installed. Well, that cat was out of the habitat.

As if in response, Mala leaped onto the table and settled down into a furry loaf position.

"Then again," Eva said slowly, "a good lie should be almost true anyway. It would just take some careful phrasing and a solid cover story." Plans percolated in her head like coffee. Plans, and more plans. Could she? No, it was a terrible idea. Disrespectful. Arrogant. Presumptuous. And yet—

Pink snorted and stood. "Y'all fool asses come and get me if you need something. I'll be in my room talking to my ancestors."

Eva nodded. To Leroy, she said, "You can go, too, if you want."

"I'll check on the cats," he said. "And our supplies, so we can restock before we leave."

"Min," Eva said.

"Yeah, Cap?"

"Take us over to Crux Zagreus. Any recommendations on a place to park, Vakar?"

He made a pensive clicking noise. "Antrade has a decent port. It is BOFA space, but far from Nuvesta."

"Out of sight, out of mind, then. Take us there, Min." Eva stepped over to the food synthesizer to prep another meal. "I'll get back to you in a few, Vakar. I need to see if I can pull any strings. Unless—" She swallowed. "We could drop you off somewhere along the way, or at Antrade, when we get there."

"I will consider the offer." He looked like he wanted to say something more, but got up and left, trailing a smell like ozone and cigarettes.

Eva had plans, all right. They were crystallizing as she walked to her cabin. But first she needed to talk to Pink.

"Are you serious?" Pink asked.

Eva nodded. She sat on the bed in the med bay, kicking her right leg nervously.

"First of all, you're ridiculous. Second, you're so full of shit, your eyes are brown. Third, this is the worst plan you've ever had."

"Come on, I've definitely had worse."

Pink choked on a laugh. "Name one."

"Okay, what about . . ." Eva snickered. "The zenorach."

"That wasn't a plan. That was self-defense. And you were laughing the whole time like a teenager."

"Please, it was a giant plant with tentacles that looked like penises."

Pink snorted. "It was a protected species."

"And I protected us from getting eaten alive. You're welcome." Eva tapped her pursed lips. "Remember that time on Drazania, when we were trying to sneak through that blockade to pick up those weird pets—"

"The ones that wheezed toxic gas?" Pink wrinkled her nose. "They smelled like a corpse ate another corpse and then had diarrhea."

"Yeah, those." Eva shook her head. "I swear, rich people will buy anything just because it's rare. Anyway. We made it in, got the critters, then realized our exit had been cut off."

"And you had the bright idea to take us through a gas mine instead of waiting for Tito to find another way to extract us."

"It would have been perfect if Cook hadn't taken a potshot at that floating gas bag."

Pink slapped Eva's arm and smiled. "That's how you're going to play that? You were the one egging him on. We had a half dozen military boats chasing us for miles once they saw the fire.

I had to shoot at them out the open back of our transport, with Wolf and Dyer holding on to me so I wouldn't fall."

"Yeah, it was pretty great." Eva grinned. "Dillin threw up twice and swore she'd never work with me again."

"And she never did, bless her." Pink's smile faded. "This plan, though. This plan has layers of foolish. It's like a big birthdate cake of foolishness with a lot of damn fool frosting on top."

Eva shrugged. "If it doesn't work, you'll have one less thing to worry about."

"If it does, I'll have one more thing. And you think Tito will help?"

"He owes me a favor."

Pink shook her head, mouth half-open in disbelief. "I said you're ridiculous, right?"

Eva nodded.

"Fine. Bend over."

Eva found Vakar down in the tail of the ship, trying to patch that leak her father had warned her about. He muttered to himself softly as he worked, her translator catching only a few words while the rest were a deep, rhythmic hum like a bass guitar being strummed. He wore thick gloves and a mask to protect his face from the chemicals he mixed, which were strong and acrid enough to disguise his smell, whatever it might be.

That made her nervous. She had gotten used to being able to read him like a feed, thanks to her translators.

"Vakar," she said, ducking into the narrow space. "Do you have a minute to talk?"

"Can it wait? I am occupied."

"Let me rephrase that. It's talk time."

He carefully closed the containers of chemicals but left the mask in place. "That sounds very official."

"Don't sass me." She knelt, keeping a respectful distance, if only because of the chemicals. "I've looked into the cruise, pulled a few strings, called in some favors, and I think we can make this work."

"'We'?"

"I have a plan, but a lot will depend on you being able to hold your own. If you come."

"I believe I would be savvy enough to follow your lead," Vakar said. "If I went. You are already accustomed to doing most of the talking. And your skills at prevarication are excellent."

Sarcasm. Very nice. "Are all quennians as terrible at lying as you are?"

"Are all humans as rude and insensitive as you are?"

"I didn't mean it like that."

"Your intent does not change your words."

"Sorry." She sighed and picked at the scab on her neck. It was an old friend at this point. "You know, I thought getting the smell translators would help me understand you better, but you—"

"So you do have them."

"What?"

"Smell translator nanites. When did you obtain them?"

Eva flushed. "A few months ago, I guess? I thought the upgrade might come in handy."

"For your many dealings with quennians."

"Right. And ualans." She'd never even seen an ualan.

"I do not have a human tonal translator, but that did not sound entirely truthful."

This conversation is getting away from you, mija, Eva told herself. But she found she couldn't figure out how to say . . . anything.

Vakar turned back to the part he was fixing, laying a sheet of metal on top and adjusting it. "To answer your earlier question, no, not everyone is as bad at lying as I am."

Eva laughed nervously. "Why is that?"

"It is what you might term a disability, though of a milder nature than most." He reopened the chemical container and poured some of the liquid carefully on the metal, where it hissed and steamed. "I struggle to control my scents in ways that others do not. While people may claim to value forthrightness, a certain level of polite dishonesty is typically expected."

Eva's legs started to cramp from crouching for so long, so she sat on the floor and hugged her knees. "What does a lie even smell like?"

He laid down another sheet of metal. "Guilt. Anxiety. Fear. Discomfort. What does a lie feel like when you tell it?"

"Like that, I guess. Like bugs squirming in my chest and spreading everywhere else. But I'm the one who put the bugs there."

"And yet you do it despite that."

She watched the metal melt and warp, then solidify, merging into the part as if it had always been there. "Maybe you would, too, if you could get away with it."

"Perhaps. Certainly other quennians evolved to be adept at hiding undesirable scents, as well as finding ways to circumvent the matter entirely."

"Weird that quennians didn't evolve to be really truthful instead of learning how to lie better."

"Weird that you did not evolve to be excessively hairy instead of wearing clothing."

"Remind me to take you to a nudist colony sometime. Naked humans as far as the eye can see."

Vakar didn't respond, instead pouring out more of that chemical. Hiss. Steam.

Eva coughed and ran a hand through her short blond hair. She couldn't wait to go black again. Maybe later. Did she have any hair dye? She'd never needed it before. Maybe Pink had something. Okay, now she was stalling. Or letting herself be stalled. Maybe Vakar was stalling, too?

Pinga. The problem with telling the truth was that sometimes it felt as bug-creepy as telling a lie.

"So the plan."

"The plan," he echoed.

"You and me."

"Right."

"We could go on the cruise as a couple."

His hand shook, spilling one of the chemicals onto his glove. He swore, which was translated into something like "spawn of a waste shoveler," and pulled the glove off, tossing it against the plating.

"You okay?" Eva asked, trying to get a look at the hand.

"No," he said.

"Pink can—"

"My hand is fine, Captain."

"Ah. So we're back to 'Captain,'" she said. "That's fair." And it was, after all that had happened. It wasn't what she had hoped to hear, but it was just as well. "I wasn't sure about it either, that's why I came down here. I'll make a new plan. Don't worry about it."

She stood, as much as she could stand in the cramped space, and immediately felt dizzy. From the fumes, she told herself. It would pass. These things always did.

"You want to know about quennian emotions?" Vakar yanked

the mask off, throwing it next to the glove. His gray-blue eyes were dark as stormy water. "Here is what a translator will not tell you. When we desire a mate, it is obvious, because our smells begin to synchronize."

She leaned against a bulkhead as the room listed sideways. "Huh."

"That is how we are able to indicate interest. It is like . . . like how one human will smile, and then another will smile in response. Then you know the interest is mutual." The acrid scent of the chemicals was starting to dissipate, or he was getting worked up, but either way she was starting to get a whiff of him. Tar and cigarettes. Dude was a bundle of bother.

"Smiling is a little more complicated than that." She hunkered down in front of him again, a few steps closer. He avoided her eyes.

"As is this." He covered his face with his bare claw. "It does not matter, because it does not mean anything. Because your body does not function the same way mine does."

Eva knelt, leaning forward, one hand on the floor. "So what do I smell like, exactly?"

His palps twitched, the barest hint of licorice creeping in. "It is difficult to explain."

"Is it." She crawled closer, a smile touching her lips. "So. The plan."

"The plan?" His blue-gray eyes searched hers.

"I thought, hey, we could take care of the most glaring lie. To make things easier."

He sighed, closing his eyes. More cigarettes. "Easier to lie about? No, thank you."

"It's only a lie if you want it to be."

"What does that mean?"

"You smell like candy," she said. "Delicious goddamn candy."

"Delicious?" The licorice level crept up slightly. "I do not understand. You said we were not . . . You told me to leave."

"I was lying."

"And now?"

Eva sat back on her knees, centimeters from his leg. "What if I told you I would never leave you or lie to you again?"

"Eva." He reached out a trembling claw to touch her hair.

She grabbed his hand and licked it. Vakar snatched it back, staring at her.

"You will hallucinate," he said.

"I already got a shot from Pink. In my meaty backside, in fact. I've also been doing other kinds of research. Very scientific."

"Research? What, like—"

She ran a finger along the inside of his left palp. His inner eyelids slammed shut and he made a low twanging sound.

"So that memvid was accurate." Eva grinned and straddled Vakar's lap. "Let's run some more tests, hmm? There was one position especially that looked— Well. It's probably easier to show you. If you want."

He grabbed her and pulled her closer, which she took as a yes. Especially since it smelled like someone had set off a licorice bomb in the tiny space.

Delicious.

Eva never knew what to do with herself after sex. Clean up, maybe. Sneak back to her bunk. Grab something to eat. Whatever would get her away from the other person quickly, so she wouldn't have to engage in any awkward small talk.

Because before, she'd only ever knocked gravboots with strangers and fellow crewmates—on other ships, of course. So either she wasn't likely to see them again and she didn't feel like pretending otherwise, or she'd definitely have to see them again and didn't want to make a big deal out of it. People had needs, like eating or peeing. Simple.

It was all fun and games until someone got serious. She had never wanted to be that someone, and she didn't want anyone else getting the wrong idea.

This, though. It crossed all kinds of lines, then looped back around and crossed them again. Not to mention she had lied to herself about her feelings for so long that now she didn't know what to do about them. She was like a dog chasing its own tail; catching it wasn't a victory, it was biting herself in the ass.

Pink was right. This was a mistake. What was she thinking?

Vakar stirred under her, smelling content, like cinnamon or nutmeg or some other kind of spice that made her think of winter holidays. But it was laced with anxiety, concern, even a hint of fear and guilt.

Eva thought about what he'd said about lying, and wondered.

"I should go," she said, sitting up.

"Should you?" he asked.

She hesitated, then nodded. "I need to . . . you know."

"What?"

Clean up. Eat. Cry? Punch things? Damn it, Eva, say something. "I need to figure out a cover story to get on that ship." Fucking brilliant.

"Of course." Now he smelled disappointed. "I will not keep you."

Eva lay back down. "It's really not fair that I can smell every damn thing you're feeling, is it."

"I am accustomed to that inequity." He ran the back of a claw along her arm. "Though until now, I had not realized you had the requisite translator nanites."

"Yeah, well. You probably figured out I didn't get them for shits and giggles."

"They are not inexpensive."

"That's what Pink said when she found out." Eva chuckled. "If I'd known someone was going to blackmail me for an assload of credits . . . Actually, I probably would have gotten them anyway. And a bunch of other stuff. Blown my whole savings so at least I'd have something to show for it."

"What is an 'assload'?"

She told him, and he sat up so fast he knocked his head on a pipe.

"You cannot be serious," he said, rubbing his injury.

"Serious as a heart attack." She pulled on her underwear, which wouldn't stay up due to apparent battle damage. She gave up and tossed them, reaching for her pants instead.

"Maybe I should thank Glorious for putting that hit out," she said bitterly. "Gave me a reason to fight instead of rolling over and showing my belly for the rest of my life, however short it will be either way."

"I will help you." Vakar's smell had charred at the edges in anger.

"No, that's— No. I didn't come down here for that. I mean, I did, but . . . Ay, mierda." She stared at the ceiling. "I said things, before. And then everything happened, and I thought I'd never see you again."

"I thought the same."

"I have fucked up a lot of things in my life," Eva said. "I can count on one hand how many will stay with me until the end. Maybe this wouldn't have been one of them. But I did not want to find out the hard way."

And just like that, she felt hollow, like she'd been carrying a giant rock in her stomach and she'd finally dug it out and tossed it out the airlock. But she wanted to cry, too, and scream, and punch things. She'd never been so desperate in her life, not even when she was staring down the barrel of a blaster.

Get your shit together, Eva, she told herself sternly. You do not have time for this.

"I should go," she said again, grabbing her shirt.

"Your plan," Vakar said. "What was it?"

She told him, and he smelled amused.

"I was expecting something more dangerous."

"It's not all gunfights and dasher chases with me," she said. "But you see how I couldn't have you smelling weird all over the place."

"You realize that could have been accomplished in myriad ways that did not involve the pretense of being my mate."

"I may have had ulterior motives. Or primary motives." She pulled her shirt over her head. "Christ, are you going to be a pain about this? You smell smug as hell."

"Eva, I have spent longer than I care to admit wishing I knew how you felt about me. I am most certainly going to revel in the present situation for at least an equal amount of time."

She made a disgusted noise. "I'm going to have to find a new engineer, aren't I?"

"You are not." His gray-blue eyes met hers. "And moreover, I will help you with this plan of yours. Make the necessary preparations, and tell me what I must do."

Eva wasn't sure whether she felt relieved or guilty, and finally decided it was perfectly possible to feel both at once.

"It'll be fun," she said. But she couldn't help but think she was due for another kick in the head.

One thing was absolutely true, though: she intended to get out of this mess alive and free, and if this was the first step, she was sure as hell going to make it work.

Chapter 14

A NIGHT AT THE OPERA

Eva stood on the deck of the interstellar cruise ship *Justified Confidence* and thanked the Blessed Virgin that catsuits were in this season, because it meant she didn't have to slink around in a dress and high heels while pretending to be someone important. Unfortunately, leopard print was also in this season, as were aggressively sloping necklines. Either that, or Pink was playing a cruel trick on her because she knew Eva would trust her on affairs of fashion.

At least her hair was black again, even if it was still extra short.

On her arm, Vakar looked as dashing as all the other quennians milling around. His outfit was worse, if that was possible, mostly because it was nearly identical to hers but in a strange geometric pattern with a sash across his chest, so he had what might be termed a boob window, except without boobs. They'd had a good laugh at each other when they first emerged from their respective cabins back on *La Sirena Negra,* but now that they were in the thick of the undercover operation, they were less amused.

"Pholise is on deck sixteen, near the theater," Eva said, calling up the map again on her commlink.

"They will in all likelihood be guarded," Vakar said. "But they would not be here if the intent was to sequester them in their cabin for the whole trip. So there is certain to be an event they will be expected to appear at."

"Right, show everyone it's all happy fun times so the treaty gets signed and no one gets shot." She would definitely have to ask him how he knew so much about this kind of thing. Later.

Eva watched the stars crawl past at sub–light speed. "Can you believe there was a time when people traveled this slowly because they had no other choice?"

He wrapped an arm around her shoulders. "It is good they discovered how to hurry."

"If they hadn't, I'd probably be living a comfortable life on Mars, with a hydroponic farm and a swarm of babies."

"You give birth to swarms?" he asked.

She punched him. "Do you?"

"Perhaps."

She punched him again, then wrapped her arm around his waist. She wasn't one for displays of affection, but she was determined to make this look legit. It felt nice, but that quiet voice in the back of her head whispered: Don't get used to it.

"You know I only have the one sister," Vakar said. "Did you think the rest of my swarm vanished mysteriously?"

"My research into your mating habits wasn't particularly scientific." Vakar didn't talk about his family much, either, any more than she did. "What's your sister's name, anyway?"

"Pollea." He smelled pensive. "Have I never said so?"

"Nope. You said she's a scientist, lives in a space station some-where. That's it. I figured it was, I mean, that you had reasons—"

His smell shifted to discomfort, with an edge of shame. They'd wandered into bad space, she thought. Time to reroute.

"If there's a big event planned, it's probably on the ship cal-endar," Eva said. "Unless it's private, in which case we'd have to figure out what rooms are reserved when. Try to narrow down the options."

Vakar stared out the window, his smell shifting from relieved back to pensive. "The main activity for the evening appears to be a show in the Grand Amphitheatre. A famous ualan opera performer, Raya'il of the Radiant Blessings."

"Ugh, operas. Not my cup of coffee."

"That is because your human operas do not engage all your senses." He smelled spicy for a moment. "Also, they are terrible."

"What, you don't like a little sex and violence buried under a lot of singing?"

"I do not know, perhaps you can try singing next time we—"

"No way, you don't want to hear that." Eva pulled up the event listing and read through it. "We might as well go, if only to hang around the entrance to try to catch Pholise."

He leaned down to brush his palps against her face. "What-ever should we do until then?"

"What any sane person does on an enormous luxury star-ship cruising through exotic star clusters," Eva said. "I'm going to eat free food until I look like I'm pregnant with a swarm of babies."

The foyer of the Grand Amphitheatre was so crowded, Eva briefly considered flicking on her gravboots and seeking out emptier real estate on a wall, or next to one of the grandiose light sculptures on the ceiling. Instead, she stuck as close to Vakar as was physically possible, breathing in the sweet licorice that had become his nearly constant scent. With all the quennians running around, the place was an orgy of aromas, most of them pleasant but all of them competing for attention. People were excited, nervous, and in a few cases valiantly trying to hide more carnal intentions.

The walls were crafted from crystals, which Eva had heard were grown from tiny seeds by expert craftsmen on one of their homeworlds. These were a lush purple, clustered in places to mask equipment or provide additional structural support. It was almost like being inside an amethyst geode, but the floor was safely smoothed out instead of sharp and pointy.

"Can you see a single damn thing in here?" Eva asked. Being short had its downsides.

"Too many people. Once they are all sitting down, we should have a better chance."

The doors finally opened, and people began to pour into the other room. Eva let herself be carried along by the movement, trying not to stomp anyone with her gravboots, since she probably shouldn't have been wearing them in the first place and didn't want to call extra attention to herself. She also kept a hand near her belt, in which she had secreted a few toys in case of emergency.

The Grand Amphitheatre was, as promised, grand. The roof was easily twenty meters up, with rows of seats extending almost the full height of the room along the back and sides. More crystals graced the walls but were less conspicuous since they were so far away. Not that anyone was likely to be looking at them; the main attraction was the enormous window behind the stage, granting a spectacular view of the swirling black hole at the center of this particular star system. They were nowhere near it, of course. No cruise ship would be so foolish.

"Our seats are in this direction," Vakar said.

"Nosebleeds, I'm sure." Eva took his hand and stomped up the ramp, which moved slowly upward so she didn't have to walk. They climbed and climbed, other passengers stepping off as they reached their own rows. She scanned the crowd, trying to find Pholise amid the thousands of faces, as if a single green ruff would be visible from there.

What she did see was an awful lot of security. Except the more she examined them, the less professional they seemed. They wore uniforms, certainly, and some of them were big enough to be bouncers, but none of them had any weapons beyond stun batons. Then again, between shields and the gun battery the ship no doubt possessed, maybe internal security was less of a priority.

Or the real deal was out of sight.

Eva and Vakar finally reached their seats, which were some billion rows up, almost near the ceiling. For the size of the favor Tito claimed she was calling in to get them on the damn ship, she had expected a bit better. The stage was set back from even the closest rows, and she wondered how the full sensory experience was going to be broadcast to everyone else, if at all.

Pulling a scope off her belt, Eva began a more careful perusal of the audience. Mostly quennian, with some tuann as part of the diplomatic or press corps, and a few others sprinkled throughout for reasons of their own.

"Oh my, a human, is it?" said a voice at her elbow. "We so rarely see your kind so far out here."

The voice belonged to a quennian, an older lady if her smell was any indication, but Eva didn't want to assume.

"Human, yes," Eva said, smiling. "Guilty as charged. Beni Alvarez, and you are?"

"Ania Ditaris san Tantius. And what brings you to this prestigious company?"

"We were invited, of course. What was that lovely man's name, mi amor, the one who gave you the tickets? Kinsey?" She ran a hand down Vakar's arm.

"Kaesna Poslin san Renotis," he replied. His smell took on a slightly tinny edge but was otherwise normal.

Ania cocked her head to the side. "I am not acquainted with him. Which ship is he assigned to?"

"*Valiant Strike*," Eva replied. "He's first director of the Disaster Retaliation Division." She said this proudly, as if his merits were shared by association, even though she had no clue what the actual post meant. It was true enough, though, thanks to Tito.

"How noble," Ania said. "And he gifted the tickets to you? He must be an excellent friend."

"We hardly know him," Vakar said.

"Oh?"

"It's a long story," Eva said quickly. "Very boring. How did you come to be here?"

"My mate is the second director of the Situational Relief Division on *Victory Covenant*. She is resting in our cabin, poor thing, with a nasty acid imbalance. The first director gave us her tickets since the anniversary of our union ceremony was this cycle."

"That was very kind of her," Eva said. "We're on something of a honeymoon ourselves." She smiled at Vakar and rubbed her leg against his, reveling in the licorice reaction.

"How nice."

"I have to say, I feel so shy here." Eva rested her chin on her hand and considered the woman's icy green eyes. "I simply don't know anyone, and Vakar is terrible at introductions. Are there many famous people here? There must be."

"Oh, goodness, yes. Just over there, the tan fellow in the purple suit, he has been in a number of very popular memory productions—"

The woman was happy to drone on about the various people in attendance, actors and athletes and especially high-ranking members of the military and political establishment. Eva tried to keep up, but at some point she had to acknowledge she was swimming in a sea of names and ranks that meant little to her, so she made appreciative noises and asked the occasional follow-up question. All the while, of course, trying to find Pholise in the crowd.

The conversation was finally cut short by the lights in the amphitheatre dimming. Those who were still standing or milling about sat or drifted off to their seats. A hush fell over the crowd as sound dampeners were turned on to stop any lingering chatter.

"Honored citizens and guests," an unseen announcer said, "it is our great pleasure here on the luxury starship *Justified Confidence* to present to you the unparalleled talents of Star-Singer Raya'il of the Radiant Blessings."

The floor opened and a platform drifted up, the performer occupying the center of the transparent circle. Their feathers were dark and covered most of their body, the only exposed parts consisting of shining golden eyes that winked in no discernible pattern as their many wings moved. It was vaguely hypnotic, and there was a rush of smell like gingerbread cookies. Eva wondered whether there would be music starting, like in a human opera, but instead the ualan took a whispery breath and began to sing.

As they did, the color of their feathers changed, glowing softly at first, then brightening as the song rose in pitch and intensity. The hue shifted from gold to white to a brilliant crimson, as if they were on fire, the feathers like tongues of flame. Eva found herself leaning forward with her mouth half-open.

The song itself was a current of joy that went straight to her nervous system, liquid notes that seemed to harmonize with themselves so that the one voice sounded like a whole chorus. She almost wanted to sing along, as if she were being infected by some memetic virus that could incite echolalia. Her translator struggled to resolve the words, if indeed there were any. There were more accompanying aromas, dissonant ones that somehow resolved into distinct and pleasurable sensations— sunscreen, churros, night-blooming jasmine—

A hand covered hers, breaking the spell. Vakar was interested but nowhere near as transfixed as she had been. He held a scope, to better see the stage, and smelled like cinnamon and anise. Relaxed. Content.

I could get used to that, Eva thought. The force of the accompanying feeling surprised her.

In the window behind the Radiant Raya'il, a ship appeared, floating into view leisurely, as if it just happened to be in the area. It was black with gold trim, pointed in the front but otherwise long and cylindrical as an oxygen canister, with a large protrusion on the bottom that Eva knew was the actual ship quarters; the rest was the drive core.

But what made her arm hairs stand up was that the ship didn't have a name on the side, which meant it wasn't registered, which meant it wasn't supposed to be in BOFA space.

Muted as his voice was, Eva could barely hear Vakar mutter something about a Gabbiani-class starship before the viewing window blew outward in a glittering cloud.

The cruise ship immediately slammed down a gravity curtain to keep the air from escaping, through which leaped a kloshian in an isofield. He landed on the stage with a flourish of his long coat, white hairlike tendrils gleaming from the rapidly fading light of the ualan singer's feathers. Far away as he was, his features were a blur to Eva until she grabbed the scope from Vakar and trained it on him.

"Raya'il of the Radiant Blessings," he said, voice amplified by his own tech. "You're coming with me for a little private show." He grinned, stretching the patchwork of scars on his pale cheeks.

Raya'il said something in reply that Eva's translators finally managed to decipher midsentence. "—great and terrible hosts will destroy all flesh in which there is the breath of life, will rain fire out of heaven to consume the enemies of—" The sound cut out as the newcomer used the isosphere on the ualan, much to Eva's relief.

((Do something?)) Vakar pinged at her.

((No,)) Eva replied. ((Blow cover.)) Let security handle this, she told herself.

Except the security guards weren't doing anything but looking at each other in confusion. A few of them were muttering to themselves or gesturing at the stage, but they didn't make any moves to stop the stranger.

What are they waiting for? Eva wondered. Somebody shows up to kidnap the main event, and they're standing around comiendo mierda instead of stopping him.

And then a hatch opened in the ceiling, and a group of people began dropping through it one by one, wearing antigrav belts and brandishing weapons that varied from long vibroblades to pistols to laser rifles. These were a mix, with a human, a robot, a kartian, a truateg and two buasyr. And, harder to see, a tiny pizkee with a gun half her size. They fell to the floor and took up positions around the stage, posing aggressively.

"Ahoy, you witless layabouts!" the human said. Their hair was pink as cloud candy and they wore a black coat over a mini-dress, and a three-cornered hat pinned at a jaunty angle. "I'm Captain Sakai. The crew of the LC *Pleasure Cruise* is honored to rob you on this fine cycle. Render up your valuables and no one will be harmed."

Now the security sprang into action, rushing up to the stage en masse brandishing stun batons in an expertly ineffective fashion. The strange kidnapper on the stage watched in what appeared to be a combination of amusement and confusion.

They aren't together, Eva realized. *The space pirates and shitty guards must be part of the show? Not the kidnapper, though . . .*

"Oh my, space pirates!" Ania said, her palps atwitter. "How exciting!"

Eva stared at her incredulously. "'Exciting'? They're threatening to steal your stuff!" If this were all staged, though, maybe the security guards were going to defeat them, or they were going to return their ill-gotten goods afterward.

"It is such an adventure," Ania said, already removing her elaborate shoulder jewelry, even though the pirates were nowhere nearby. "My friend told me this might happen. On her last cruise, she was robbed, and she said the thieves were absolutely riotous. I made sure to wear nothing of value, naturally, only a few of my less well-cultured crystals."

Or maybe they really were space pirates and they wouldn't return anything. Rich people were so damn weird. What kind of cruise allowed their guests to be robbed for entertainment?

Meanwhile, the pirates sparred with the not-really-security-guards, flinging their weapons at each other in a flurry of strikes and ripostes that would be convincing only to someone who had never used a weapon in their life. The kidnapper apparently had enough, because he began to tow the captive ualan singer toward the gravity curtain, where his ship waited on the other side.

"Pretty sure that's not part of the show, at least," Eva muttered. To Vakar, she said, "Maybe we can get out of here and hide in Pholise's room, snag them when they get back. Come on." They stood to leave.

The pirate captain must have decided they didn't like the extra unanticipated cast member, because they knocked down the guard they were fighting and turned their attention to the stranger. "Where you going with that prize, my son?" they asked. "I'm thinking that be rightfully part of my booty."

"You should think again," the kloshian replied. "Take your baubles, but the star-singer is mine."

Captain Sakai grinned. "Say that to the smart end of my sword, love." And they swung at him with more speed and precision than any of their previous attacks had exhibited.

So that pirate does know how to fight, Eva thought, even if the bits with security are fake. Kidnapper is definitely real, too.

Some of the other people in the audience had gotten up to leave as well, but they were being stopped at the doors by what looked like real security guards finally arriving; their uniforms were different, and they were armed with pistols instead of stun batons. A couple of them were also sneaking onto the stage, flanking the pair of fighters with the helpless ualan still muttering creepy threats beside them.

The stranger must have seen them, because he reached into a pocket, pulled out a handful of golden discs and flung them at the guards. They spun in the air as they flew, making impact with a series of tiny explosions that blinded and stung, judging from the way the guards flinched and covered their eyes. The security guards retreated, but both drew their pistols.

"No snipers, seriously?" Eva asked. "They've got a ship full of VIPs and their security is a joke."

The lights flickered, and the ship listed sideways about twenty degrees, sending people stumbling into one another or to the ground, some sliding down the aisle until they hit a wall. The fake guards onstage mostly lost their balance and slid off, but the pirates and real guards kept their feet, Captain Sakai and the stranger continuing their fight, both physical and verbal.

"Perhaps the ship security has other problems," Vakar said, gripping a seat to stay upright.

The ship straightened out just as the exit doors slid open. The guards in front of them were gunned down as lines of tru-ateg mercenaries marched in, armed with assault rifles and wearing military-grade body armor. Black Moon company, by their markings.

Qué coño? Eva thought. First a kidnapper, then pirates and fake security, then real security, and now mercs? And the blood leaking out of those guards they shot was definitely not fake.

One of the mercs aimed his weapon at the ceiling and fired a quick volley as the others spread throughout the amphitheatre. Shards of crystal rained down.

"Sit and don't move or we shoot you and blow up the ship!" he shouted.

This caused a lot of screaming, but miraculously no one disobeyed and suffered the consequence. People, including Eva and Vakar, took their assigned seats as the mercs walked up to the stage, where Captain Sakai and the stranger had separated to examine this new enemy.

"Drop your weapons," the merc leader growled, and they obeyed. Eva doubted, however, that they were fully disarmed.

"We demand the return of the one known as Pholise Pravo," he continued. "If they are not turned over to us immediately, we will begin executing passengers."

Eva sank lower into the seat and cursed. She had hoped she'd be able to wait out this silly farce, but now she had to get involved. No way was she letting these resingados get Pholise.

((Screw cover,)) she pinged at Vakar. ((Party time.))

Chapter 15

THE MAD SCENE

The other people in the audience muttered to each other, looking around as if they would be able to spot Pholise themselves
in the crowd of quennians. But no movement occurred.

"Okay, step one," Eva said to Vakar. "We get to a better position without being seen. Step two—"

"What are you intending?" Ania asked, leaning over the arm
of her seat.

Eva smiled. "Nothing, nothing at all. Why do you ask?"

She pointed at Vakar. "His smell."

Eva sniffed the air. Vakar did indeed smell apprehensive but
alert, eager even. She gave him a sour look.

"Are you two secret security?" Ania asked. "Is this all part of
the show?"

This was the woman who was excited about being robbed,

Eva reminded herself. "Yes, it's all for show," she whispered. "But you can't tell anyone. We don't want to spoil it."

Ania covered her mouth and winked her inner eyelid.

"Our first execution will be in two minutes," the merc said. "Bring Pravo to us now."

Pholise must not be in their cabin, Eva realized; these guys would have checked there first. If she were security, she would have shoved Pholise off into an escape shuttle as quickly as possible. But then again, there was probably a ship out there watching for that, so maybe not.

Think, Eva, think, she told herself. Pholise must be hiding in some prearranged safe spot, waiting for backup to come take the ship back. And the mercs probably had control of the bridge, or at least the bridge access. The ship captain would be radioing for help, assuming they were still in command and communications hadn't been cut off. Which any smart merc squad would do, so assume they were.

The mercs spread out, grabbing every tuann they found and dragging them down the aisles to the stage. They'd only gotten three so far, but there were more, and some were likely hiding out of fear. The various pirates stood where they were, gazes flicking back and forth between the mercs and their captain on the stage.

Eva checked for escape routes. The only one that wasn't being blocked was the opening in the ceiling that the pirates had come through. She could walk up there using her gravboots, but it would take so long she'd probably be shot down before she got halfway. She needed a diversion, and not the kind that would get foolish people killed.

"Vakar, do you think you can get control over the audio-visual equipment from here?" Eva asked.

"Not from here," he said. "But if I can get to one of the tech nodes in the columns in the back, then probably."

"I need you to kill the lights," she said.

"What are you going to do?"

"Climb through the ceiling and scout out the situation outside. We don't know where Pholise is, but I'm hoping they're nowhere near this mess."

"They could be in here somewhere."

She nodded. "If they don't come forward, it will take time for the mercs to find them. Time I can use to plot an escape route once I find out how much of the ship the mercs have taken."

Ania leaned over again, her emerald eyes glistening. "Is there nothing I can do? I would love to be able to tell my partner I participated in the show."

Possible plans bifurcated in Eva's mind like a map of branching possibilities. The woman could be a distraction to let Vakar reach the back unimpeded.

Someone in the audience made a break for the door and was immediately shot by a merc. Eva cringed and looked away.

"No, it's best if you stay here," Eva said. "Leave the stunt work to the professionals."

As it was, only one merc was covering the wing where they were seated. He paced back and forth along the row at the bottom of the section, black eyes scanning the crowd for signs of movement—and any tuann, no doubt. Eva waited for him to reach the farthest point from where they sat, then ducked below their seats and crawled toward the exit aisle.

Down on the stage, the merc leader shouted, "The first hostage will be killed in one minute if Pholise is not brought forward!" Despite herself, Eva began to count down.

"What are you doing?" someone hissed as she passed. "You will get us shot, foolish human!"

"We're security," she said. "Stay seated. Act casual." But the murmur had already gone up along the row, and now the merc's doglike ears had perked up and he was facing their direction.

Eva cursed under her breath, and Vakar smelled like incense. The merc stepped into the aisle and climbed toward them.

"New plan; follow my lead," Eva whispered.

"That is not really a plan, by definition," Vakar said.

"No jodas tanto."

The merc was almost to their row. The people around her clutched the arms of their chairs, leaning away from his gun as if it weren't a projectile weapon that could hit them anyway.

Eva pulled out her vibroblade and handed it to Vakar, then leaned backward, one leg crossed over the other knee so her foot was elevated.

"What are you—" The merc was interrupted by Eva clicking on her gravboot, which yanked his gun away from him, then Vakar leaping over her to bury the knife in his chest, knocking him down. In the time it took the truateg to grab the handle with one hand and Vakar with the other, Eva had retrieved the gun and shot him in the head.

Ania clapped. "Well done! Good show!"

Eva resisted the urge to bow, because killing wasn't a cause for celebration, and because other mercs had heard the shot and were rushing up to their area.

"Everybody down," Eva shouted at her fellow audience members. She ran down the aisle to the bottom row, Vakar in a crouch behind her, vibroblade in hand. A merc appeared at the foot of the ramp and she shot at him, ducking behind the wall for cover when he returned fire.

So much for sneaking out, she thought.

A few more shots and the merc was down, just as another was coming up the ramp on the other side of the wing.

Vakar retrieved the dead merc's gun, tucking the vibroblade into his belt. "So is this the violence part of opera?"

"I guess so. Hopefully we'll get to the sex later."

She got a good view of the stage, where apparently the pirate captain and the kloshian kidnapper had also gotten tired of standing around. The one had pulled an anchor line from their belt and was holding it like a garrote, sneaking up on the merc leader, who was distracted by the other taunting him from behind the ualan in the isosphere.

The rest of the pirate crew drew their secondary weapons— they hadn't disarmed—and went after the closest mercs, alone or in pairs. Only the security guards in that fight must have been actors, Eva thought, because these guys certainly knew what they were doing.

The exit was one level down. The mercs were split now, with some heading for the stage and others still circling toward her up the ramps. She sent a few cover shots in their direction, trying to plot the quickest route down. But then what? She'd have to make it past the ones guarding the doors, and then through whatever lay beyond. And then find Pholise.

And to think this cycle had started so nicely.

"Shortest distance between two points," she muttered. "Vakar, cover me."

"What are you—"

She vaulted over the edge of the balcony, trailing the smell of licorice with a spicy edge. She was surprised she could identify it within the cloud of other scents coming from the assembled quennians. Most of them smelled scared, or excited, or confused.

An eternity later, she hit the ground and rolled, coming to a stop at the base of a fight between merc and pirate. They paused

in confusion and she fired at the merc, earning her a ragged sa-
lute from the buasyr. She got to her feet and edged past the lip
of the balcony, pinging Vakar with a terse ((Come.))

Only one merc was watching them, so she fired at him until
Vakar got down. His legs were built to absorb shocks better, so
he landed with a thud and they both ducked behind a row of
seats. Now all they had to do was make it to the door.

Which was being guarded by three guys in full body armor.

"Me cago en la hora que yo nací," she muttered. "Vakar, did
you bring your isosphere?"

He pulled it out. "It will only work on one person, though."

"Can you get the door open behind them?"

With a low hum of frustration, he took out the vibroblade
and dug it into the wall, tearing off chunks of crystal to reveal
circuitry behind. With a few deft moves, he had the door opening and closing at regular intervals.

"That's the best I can do," he said, smelling apologetic.

"Good enough. Use the isosphere on me when I say go, then
come after me."

"What?"

She watched the timing of the door. Open. Shut. Open.
Shut. Open . . .

"Go!" She leaped around the corner, dropped onto her back
and clicked on her gravboots, shooting like a missile toward
the three guards. For a long moment, she thought Vakar was
frozen. The guards raised their weapons and took aim at her.

Then she was surrounded by a shimmering field of force and
rammed into them like a snowball with a rock in it.

The one in the middle went down as the others flanking him
slid sideways, away from the door. And because she had timed
it right, the one she hit fell straight back into the doorway, the

panels sliding open and closed around him, leaving a gap big enough to squeeze through.

Unless you were surrounded by a big isofield, which she was.

Until she wasn't, because it disappeared as Vakar slammed into her from behind and knocked her outside.

They landed in a heap, each rolling sideways quickly, but unfortunately in the same direction, so they got even more tangled up as they struggled to stand.

A small contingent of security guards pointed guns at them.

Eva immediately dropped her weapon and raised her hands. So did Vakar.

"Get down!" someone shouted.

She hit the floor, taking Vakar with her, in time to avoid being blown apart as the guards fired at the open door.

"Someone fix that dung heap!" said the same voice. Immediately there was a flurry of movement and the door closed with a sigh.

The owner of the voice stomped over, leaning down to glare at Eva and Vakar. A heavily armored quennian lady with a rank insignia on her chest. "Nice stunt. Who the stench are you?"

"Beni Alvarez," Eva said, putting a nervous tremor into her voice. "Thank goodness you're here! There are men inside with—"

"Cut the nonsense." Icy blue eyes bored into hers. "I am not talking to you." She turned the gaze to Vakar, who smelled downright steely.

"I am Vakar," he said.

"Vakar what?"

"Tremonis san Jaigodaris."

She hunkered down in front of him. "Do I know you?"

He paused. "Were we in basic training together?" he asked finally. "Meulia?"

"No, I trained on *Boundless Progress*. I am Second Squad

Leader Laetia Proculus san Aridonis." She stood. "Now, if you will excuse us, we were about to take back that room."

Eva got to her feet, nudging the gun with her toe. "It seemed like the pirates were gaining the upper hand. Maybe you should let them all fight it out until they've culled some of the mercs."

"We cannot risk it. There is a sensitive target in that room and we need to get them out."

Eva's lip curled. Probably Pholise. Mierda.

Laetia gestured at her squad, who took up their previous positions around the door. "Stay here, and we will deal with you when we return."

"Yeah, right," Eva muttered.

Either the quennian didn't register the sarcasm, or she didn't care.

As soon as Laetia's team busted through the door, Eva stuck a toe under the now-unattended assault rifle and kicked it up into her hands. "Come on, Vakar, we need to get back in there and get to Pholise first. We may never get the chance again."

Vakar smelled uncertain. "What makes you think we will be able to find them now, when we could not before?"

"Now we can watch the guards and see where they're going. Cover me."

Screams ensued as the audience finally got the memo that things were rotten in the state of the *Justified Confidence*. The guards by the door had been electrocuted, it looked like, and lay twitching on the floor. Other mercs were using guests as human shields, firing at Laetia's team, who were hiding behind walls and trying to limit the collateral damage.

Laetia had charged up the aisle and was exchanging shots with the merc leader, who had at some point retreated behind a pillar on the stage. The pirate captain and the kloshian wannabe-kidnapper were behind the matching pillar on the opposite side of the stage, with the kloshian nursing a wound to his stomach and the pirate clutching their left arm, pink hair streaked with blood.

Eva watched the placement of the guards, the ebb and flow of their movements, and especially the attention of the second squad leader. Pholise had to be in the bottom tier, obviously not the front few rows or they would have been found already by the mercs. Two of the guards were circling around the back of the rear right quadrant, one more providing cover fire as another backed toward the wall . . .

Middle right quadrant, had to be. Eva darted behind a merc, diving into a roll that took her to the second row from the back of that section. She slid into the row, which had been vacated for the most part as the audience members had crawled toward the wall or hidden under their floating chairs. No Pholise.

Under the seats, a few faces stared back at her, unreadable. But their smells told a whole other story, and spoiler alert, it was utter terror. She caught a glimpse of tuann legs and grabbed the seat, sliding underneath, pushing herself along as the sound of gunfire cracked and pew-pewed around her.

It wasn't Pholise, it was some other tuann. "Where's Pravo?" she asked the person.

"The honored guest?"

"Yes!"

The tuann inclined their head toward the wings of the stage, just as two of the security guards arrived and grabbed them, dragging them to relative safety. Either they didn't realize they had the wrong person, or this one had been in Pholise's party, too.

A merc raced up and opened fire, so Eva fired back, then slid to the next row down. More quennian faces peered at her in surprise and fear. She tried to ignore their smells.

Vakar jumped into the row at her back, firing at another merc she couldn't see. His posture was near-perfect military reg, which looked pretty absurd with his tight suit and boob window.

"Pholise is over there," she told him, pointing. "Still got that sphere?"

"It was damaged after your last exciting maneuver."

"Then we do it the fun way." She fired a few rounds at the merc, who had finally found them, then scanned the undersides of the seats for a clear path. Not this set of seats, but the next. She crawled over, lay on her back, and turned on her gravboots.

Eva shot down toward the stage, clutching the assault rifle to her chest. She slammed to a stop at the bottom of the stage, where Laetia was still crouched down and taking potshots at the merc leader. The squad leader glanced over her shoulder, pointing two fingers at her eyes and then at Eva before returning her attention to the mercs.

Good enough for me, Eva thought. She turned off her boots and crouch-walked to the wings, where Pholise was decidedly not visible.

"Pholise?" she called out in a stage whisper. "It's Eva. I'm here to rescue you." That was mostly true, if not for entirely altruistic reasons.

No answer. She listened for any hint of a noise, but the sound of gunfire rang in her ears. Why did tuann have to be so damn quiet?

"Pholise?" she called again. This time there was a rustling under the stage. If this were a human theater, there would be some kind of trapdoor, some way to get down there for future grand entrances, but this wasn't a human stage. And now that she thought about it, Pholise probably had bodyguards or handlers of their own.

Eva jumped out of the way just in time to avoid a flurry of shots from an eye laser. "Are your translators damaged?" she hissed. "I said 'rescue,' comemierda."

A smell like hot cooking oil answered her. Quennian guard, of course. Between the scent and the angle of that laser shot, she now had a decent idea of where exactly they were located.

Unfortunately, that was the moment a pair of mercs found her.

She had just enough time to drop one with a head shot while thinking, This blaze is insufficiently glorious for me to go out in, when the dead one crashed into the other and fell, because Vakar had thrown himself at the pair.

Eva stopped shooting so she wouldn't hit him. In one swift stroke, he slit the remaining truateg's neck with his vibroblade.

His smell was a heady mix that her translators struggled to interpret, but rage was in there along with licorice. The rage dissolved into dismay as he watched a bleeding merc become a corpse.

"You okay?" she asked.

He didn't respond. As far as she knew, he'd never killed anyone in close quarters like this. If they hadn't spent so much time sparring back on the ship, she wouldn't have expected him to know how.

"Pholise is in here. How do things look now?"

Still nothing.

"Vakar? Status report!"

He shook himself out of his reverie. "Reinforcements have arrived. The mercenaries are cornered, surrendering or dying. The second squad leader will be along in a moment, I am sure."

Eva knocked on the wall. "Pholise, I said it's Eva. Captain Eva Innocente. I really need to speak with you in a hurry. Please?"

A panel slid open, and a quennian poked his head out. He wore an eye laser and a scowl. "The honored guest is unconscious, you dung pit. And I am not moving until my superior officer tells me to."

"Good," said a voice behind Eva. "Next time do not open the door to say so, either."

Laetia stomped grimly forward, flanked by guards with their weapons aimed at Eva. Vakar was already being held by another guard, who slipped a manacle belt around his waist and locked it.

Eva dropped her weapon for the second time and slowly got to her feet. For this, she earned her own set of manacles and a rough shove in Vakar's direction.

"Secure the honored guest," Laetia said. "And get these two to the brig with the others. I will be down to question them after we have finished cleaning up this mess."

Eva let herself be guided out of the wings and up the aisle, toward the door. Some audience members had left; others were still paralyzed with fear or were being carefully herded by the guards back to their rooms.

Just outside the door, Ania was being nuzzled by someone who must have been her partner. "Look," she said, pointing at Eva. "That is the one who—" She noticed the manacles and stopped. "Wait," she said slowly. "So this was not all part of the . . ."

Eva laughed, the kind of laughter that bubbles up from the inside and won't stop coming, all the way down to the brig.

Chapter 16

NO HAY PEOR CUÑA QUE LA DEL MISMO PALO

Behold, the brig of the luxury cruise starship *Justified Confidence*. Its walls were soft but impermeable, the color of nutrient paste. Its floors were more of the same, as was its ceiling. But because it was a luxury ship, it featured hard, light furniture that conformed to a variety of body types while being effectively useless as tools for escape. Guards were posted outside the transparent entry wall, which was designed to lightly shock anyone who touched it without proper protective gear, and strongly shock anyone who continued to touch it after the initial warning zap.

The pirates had been thrown in there, along with Eva, Vakar and the kloshian who had tried to kidnap the ualan singer. She was surprised he hadn't escaped, even with all his injuries, which had been treated by a sour-smelling medic who'd only recently released him into the guards' custody.

"What's your name, anyway?" Captain Sakai asked him. Now that they weren't performing, the heavy pirate slang had subsided.

He bowed with a flourish and a wince. "Captain Orlando Baldessare of the *Leporidae*, at your service."

"Ha, I knew it." They held out a hand, and with a grumble, one of the buasyr in their crew forked over a credit chit.

"I think I've heard of you," Eva said. "Didn't you try to kidnap the leader of the White Falcons?"

"Oh, I kidnapped her," he said, smiling. His teeth were sharp as daggers. "We had a lovely picnic on the third moon of Ocliri and then I returned her. In my defense, I thought she was someone else."

"I heard you played cards with the first and second lieutenants of the Charguard and they had to drink poisoned Dokloot Horrors when they lost," Captain Sakai said.

He rolled his head. "That was embarrassing. The second lieutenant tried to back out and the first lieutenant shot him. Raised her glass to me and took it in one gulp. Hell of a woman."

The stories continued, each more far-fetched than the last, but Captain Baldessare kept confirming them with an easy grin, the scars on his face almost winking. Finally, he demurred.

"You must have your own stories, Captain Sakai," he said. "How long have you been robbing pleasure ships with your crew here?"

"Ah, me, a few years now, I'd say," they said, scratching their inner thigh. "Got the commission from my mum when she retired. Staari and Jaraari were already on the crew"—they gestured at the buasyr, who were apparently twins—"and I picked up Natsis on a station over in Ophiuchi." The kartian rubbed her small front arms together as she lay on a couch, one eyestalk scrunched down into her head while the other two scanned different sides of the room.

"Where'd you get a bot?" Eva asked.

"Gotto? Now that's a tale. We had docked on NS-386 for emergency repairs—"

Eva let herself be lulled into relaxing by the rhythmic voice of the human captain. Vakar sat on the ground next to her, and she put a hand on his head and idly rubbed his ridges. She was rewarded with the smell of licorice, and smiled even as she wondered how the ever-loving fuck they were going to get out of there.

The other two crew members were the truateg, Tubs, and the tiny blue pizkee, who apparently didn't have a name but whom everyone called Zaza.

"What about you two?" Captain Baldessare said, pale hair tendrils haloed in gold in the buttery light.

Eva contemplated lying, because she assumed their conversation was being recorded, but the quennians already knew who she was, so there was no point. "Captain Eva Innocente," she said. "Legendary smuggler."

Vakar made an amused rumbling sound as the rest of the assembled prisoners stared at Eva.

"Huh," Captain Sakai said. "Never heard of you, mate."

"Doesn't ring a bell," Captain Baldessare said.

"I don't like to brag," Eva said.

"No one's bragging here." Captain Sakai hugged one knee, the other leg dangling. "Not bragging if it's true."

"You're the one calling herself legendary," Captain Baldessare added.

"It was a joke," Eva muttered.

Captain Sakai pointed at Vakar. "This your pet, then? How'd you two end up together, like?"

"He's not a pet," Eva said. "He's my engineer."

"You're certainly stroking him like a pet." Captain Baldessare grinned again.

Eva's hand froze. Keeping her face neutral, she leaned backward and crossed her arms, much as she wanted to break a few of the kloshian's pointed teeth.

"How'd you even get dragged into the big show upstairs?" Captain Sakai asked. "You're dressed like a posh, but they've got you snuggled up here with us?"

"I don't want to bore you." Eva ignored their polite but decidedly half-hearted protests, and soon enough they were swapping more stories of their many misadventures.

Vakar stood and stretched. "So, how are we getting out of here?"

"I'm thinking some kind of elaborate plan involving a sharpened candle and a body bag." She pinged him, ((Escape pod.))

He pinged back, ((How?))

((Careful timing.)) But before she could continue, Second Squad Leader Laetia Proculus san Aridonis marched up to the transparent wall and gave them all the stink eye.

"Captain Sakai," she said. "You and your crew are free to go, with our thanks for your efforts in repelling the kidnapping and the mercenary attack."

The captain bounced to their feet and stretched, their miniskirt inching up to give a generous view of their thighs. "Come on, mates, we got us a schedule to keep. Them ships aren't gonna rob themselves."

Laetia shook her head in annoyance. "Captain Orlando Baldessare, despite your initial actions, we have determined that you ultimately saved the life of Raya'il of the Radiant Blessings, for which they are exceedingly grateful. You may visit them in their cabin if you desire, where they have agreed to grant you a private concert."

Captain Baldessare shrugged, scars twisting into a smile. "Alas, it's no fun that way. Perhaps some other time."

What a cabrón creeper, Eva thought.

Captain Sakai strolled up to Baldessare and gave him a punch in the shoulder. "Look me up sometime, like. Or maybe I'll be the one kidnapping you."

Baldessare pulled a coin out of their ear and slipped it into the pocket of their coat. "I'd love to see you try."

Eva smelled Vakar's silent laughter. What a goddamn pair those two were.

"Captain Eva Innocente," Laetia said. "And Vakar Tremonis san Jaigodaris. Come with me."

The other captains and crew eyed them incredulously.

"What you want them for?" Captain Sakai asked.

"That's classified," Laetia replied. The wall opened and she jerked her head in the direction of the exit.

"Wait, did you say your name was Innocente?" Baldessare said. "Don't the gmaarg have a bounty on you?"

"Isn't Innocente the one who got Omicron blown up?" Captain Sakai added. "Armida said she'd kill you if—"

"She made it? Good for her." Vakar stood first and helped her up. "I hope she still smells like burned fart."

"My cousin Grissy tried to roast you on Futis," Natsis hissed, rubbing her front hands together. "She lost another leg when you blasted off right over her head."

"In fairness, your cousin was attempting to kill me," Vakar said.

"It was her principal leg." The kartian raised and lowered her eyestalks. "I thought you'd be taller."

"I thought you'd be prettier," Captain Baldessare said.

"I thought you'd be smarter," Captain Sakai said.

"Being legendary is fucking garbage," Eva said as she followed the squad leader out.

The furniture in the conference room was real, as was the food placed just out of Eva's reach on the table. The buffet selection for humans was as small as the list of human passengers, and apparently none of those items had made it down here to the brig. Vakar politely abstained, though she could smell that he wanted to dig in. She was about to tell him to go ahead when another door opened and Pholise stepped in, the door sliding shut behind them. Laetia glared at everyone equally.

"This is an awkward position you have put me in, Captain," Pholise said in their whispery voice, taking a seat.

"Yeah, well," Eva replied. "I was trying to be sneaky, but then the fun started."

Laetia leaned on the table. "We reviewed the security footage and took testimony from a few witnesses. You clearly instigated the initial counterattack—"

"Not on purpose—"

"—which gave us the time we needed to get into position before more hostages were killed, even if it did force our hand. And you eliminated a number of the mercenaries personally."

Eva paused. "Yes, I did do that." Maybe they weren't as screwed as she thought.

Laetia began to pace. "The question is, why? You were attempting to reach our honored guest, but your motivations elude us. You told their guard you wanted to rescue them. From the mercenaries or someone else? How did you know there would be an attack?"

"That's a lot of questions," Eva said. "Wanna run them by me again? Maybe in order of importance?"

The second squad leader stopped pacing and stood behind Vakar, gripping the back of his chair. "You. Tremonis. Why aren't you with your unit?"

His smell sharpened in a way Eva found vaguely nauseating, and one aroma overrode a riot of others.

Shame.

Eva assumed whatever it was, Laetia would find out eventually. She'd done enough digging to know Vakar wasn't a criminal, but quennian archives weren't wide open to any old human with a pilot who was also an accomplished hacker. He had never wanted to talk about his past, and now didn't feel like the time to start. Not here, at least, and not like this.

"I didn't know there would be an attack," Eva interjected. "I was just trying to talk to Pholise about something personal. Nothing to do with your embargo stuff."

Laetia released Vakar's chair and he couldn't stop himself from smelling relieved. She stepped over to Eva and spun her chair around. "Keep talking," she said.

"That's it, really." Eva pursed her lips. "We scrounged up tickets to get on board, figured we might run into them at the opera, and bam. Arroz con mango. I was trying to sneak out when the merc got frisky, so I defended myself and now here we are."

"Here you are indeed." Laetia's palps twitched. "I am not permitted to interrogate the honored guest, who has diplomatic immunity. But you were quite keen to reach them, so here they are. Your reward, for your assistance."

Eva raised her eyebrows. "What, just like that? Talk to them right now, in front of you?"

Laetia shook her head in that weird quennian approximation of a shrug. "I can continue to question your crewmate instead. I am quite interested to know why some of his records are sealed, for one thing."

Maybe Min should have dug a little deeper. But now wasn't the time to worry about that. She glanced at Vakar, who continued to smell like a secret blend of unpleasant herbs and spices.

Okay, she was worried.

She forced herself to turn her attention to the tuann. This was going to be fun. How to ask questions and get usable answers without incriminating Pholise somehow?

"So," Eva said.

Pholise said nothing.

"Are you okay? You were unconscious."

"All injuries to my person have been adequately addressed."

"Good, good." She stared at all the food she couldn't eat. This plan was supposed to be easy. Safe. Stupid mercs.

"I'm trying to locate a mutual acquaintance," Eva said finally. She didn't mention that Pholise was her only lead.

"That is curious," said Pholise.

"You know the one I mean?"

"Not many of our acquaintances are shared, Captain."

"Any information you can provide would be very much appreciated."

Pholise's head ruff flared slightly. "Assistance in this matter cannot reasonably be offered, Captain."

"You're sure? You can't tell me anything?"

"My certainty is absolute." They seemed to wilt a little into the chair, as if sorry, or ashamed.

"Great," Eva muttered, her hands balling into fists. That was a lot of work for not a cabrón thing. "I guess that's it, then."

Laetia's palps twitched. "You have nothing else to ask? You risked your lives for this audience and this is the result?"

Thanks for rubbing it in, Eva thought. "I could ask them about the weather, but we're in space. What are you going to do with us now?"

Laetia's smell barely concealed disappointment. "I could detain you and turn you in to the authorities when we reach our destination. Your criminal record on Nuvesta is a compelling argument for this. However, given the delicate nature of negotiations, your very presence on this ship could constitute a treaty breach."

"You could let me hail my ship and I'll be out of your hair in a few hours," Eva said.

"I hardly think releasing a criminal on their own recognizance would be considered reasonable by any metric."

"Can't blame a girl for trying."

"My other option, while arguably less salient, is—"

"I'll take that one, whatever it is."

Laetia's palps twitched, and Eva immediately regretted her decision. Laetia's smell said "too old for this shit" in a language that Eva probably would have recognized even without translators.

"Take these two back to the brig," Laetia said. "Someone will be along to collect them shortly."

"Who?" Eva asked. The only people who should have known she was here were her crew and . . .

Tito. Mierda, mojón y porquería. She had a bad feeling about this.

Neither she nor Vakar said a word as they walked back to their cell. Her instincts screamed at her to run, to hijack an escape pod, to do anything but march meekly back to whatever—or whoever—awaited them.

As soon as the containment wall shimmered back into place, footsteps signaled the answer to her most pressing question. She took a seat and stared at the floor, as if ignoring the problem might make it go away.

"Beni, Beni, long time no see," said a faintly accented voice.

Enter the white teeth and perfect tan of one Tito Santiago, alias too many names for her to remember. The ones she knew were probably aliases, too, but this was the most popular one.

"Tito," she said. A tiny bud of hope sprouted in her chest, but she stomped on it. "I don't suppose you're here to escort us back to *La Sirena Negra*?"

"Ay, mija, you know I don't run a skycab service," he replied, clasping his hands behind his back. "You've become quite the hot commodity."

"And you're a giant comemierda," Eva replied through gritted teeth. "Was this a setup from the start, or did you get lucky?"

"That will have to be one of life's little mysteries, won't it?" He practically sashayed forward, grinning like a cat in a dairy. "You and me, we have a date with some very wealthy people."

"I didn't know you'd gone merc."

"I didn't know you went vigilante." He wagged a finger at her. "There's rules, and then there's rules, Benita. You break the wrong ones, and they break you back."

"I can think of a few things I would enjoy breaking," Vakar muttered.

"Sexy," Tito said. "Your smart mouth is rubbing off on your boyfriend here, Beni."

"How's your boyfriend, Tito?" she retorted. "He know you're into kidnapping now?"

"Nope, and he never will. Now get up, and let's go."

She had to get away from him before he brought her to his ship, or she'd be screwed. Escaping planetside was one thing;

space had fewer places to hide, and a lot less air to breathe. Then again, Vakar did have his isosphere . . .

"Where we going, hmm?" she asked. "You can tell me that much."

"Nope."

"Come on, just tell me if you're unloading me here or somewhere else."

He laughed, the kind of laugh he always had when he knew something she didn't. Eva hated that laugh. "Okay, fine, you win. Bring it in, boys."

A pair of humans walked in, guiding a large floating container about three meters long by one meter wide. It took some maneuvering to move it over to the cell, by which time Eva had figured out what it was. Her skin went hot and cold all at once, but she didn't flinch. She wasn't going to give him the satisfaction.

"Ta-da!" Tito said, gesturing at the stasis pod like it was a present just for her. "Now get in, or I'll have one of my people knock you out first. Then you'll wake up from cryo with quite the headache, which, mira, I can tell you from experience, no vale la pena."

She stared at him, then back at the pod, then let out a long breath, slowly. This was it, then. She wouldn't be able to rescue Mari, and she certainly wasn't going to wage some epic campaign against The Fridge. When she woke up, she'd be part of a fish-faced asshole's fuck squad, whatever that entailed. With any luck, she would eventually escape and make her way back to her people again. Otherwise, she could look forward to a shitty life or a quick death.

"What about Vakar?" she said. "And the rest of my crew?"

Tito pursed his lips. "Don't care. I'm assuming they get *La*

Sirena Negra if anything happens to you, and I heard this guy is getting shipped off somewhere else."

"Where?" Eva asked sharply.

Vakar smelled ashamed again. "I believe I know."

"What the fuck does that mean?" Eva was standing now, hands clenched at her sides. The harder she stared at Vakar, the worse he smelled, and he wouldn't meet her gaze. "Will you be okay?"

"I am not entirely certain." He smelled afraid, tired, but also strangely relieved. She knew that feeling from her time on Nuvesta, and the idea that he might be reconciling himself to something terrible—

"As much as I'd love to hear all about it, I've got a schedule to keep," Tito said. He gestured at one of the quennian guards, who opened the cell even as she kept a weapon trained on Eva and Vakar. The other crew member grabbed Eva by the arm and hauled her over to the pod.

"No," Vakar said, stepping forward. The guard's weapon hummed a warning as her finger moved to the trigger.

"Don't get shot, idiot," Eva said. "We can't fight our way out of here. Not this time." Not against Tito, who had taught her everything she knew about fighting, and no doubt knew more he kept in reserve.

Tito tapped at the console, keeping one eye on her. "I have to admit, I expected you to try. Fighting, I mean. After that locura on Garilia—"

"I am," she said, "so fucking tired of hearing about that."

"Should have thought about that before you did what you did. You ever hear how it all turned out?"

"Yes." A tendon in her neck twitched.

The pod hissed open, revealing an interior as pink as a womb but cool and dry. She took a step toward it, stopping as a scent flooded the room. It was like a bonfire made of licorice, smoke and aniseed, rage and love, so potent it burned to breathe.

"I will find you," Vakar said, his voice so deep it was practically a growl.

Eva couldn't think of a damn thing to say. Goodbye was pathetic. Adiós? Which god would that be? See you later? That was a promise she might not keep. I love you? She did, didn't she, for fuck's sake. What a time to stop lying to herself about that. Her throat was tight as an aahx's cloaca.

She nodded and quietly got into the pod, making herself as comfortable as she could with her stomach full of stones. Sorry, Mari, she thought. The pod door slid shut, and with a smell like blood, everything went away.

Chapter 17

WAKE UP AND SMELL THE COLADA

The first thing Eva heard when she woke up was a soft whir-click, followed very quickly by a hiss, a warm whiff of air, and a blaring klaxon that might as well have been inside her skull for how loud it was. It took her a few seconds to realize her eyes were open, because everything was dim and vaguely pink.

"Eva, get up," a voice said, barely audible over the klaxon. It sounded familiar . . .

"Whuh," she mumbled, her mouth tasting like acid and blood.

"I said get up. You need to leave now, before the guards get you."

That sounded serious. She willed her limbs to move, and they grudgingly obeyed, so slowly she wondered whether she was dreaming.

She climbed out of a stasis pod, where she had been put

by . . . someone. Tito. That cabrón resingado comemierda. How long had she been asleep?

"Stay low but move quickly," the voice said. Where was it coming from? It floated around her, like the source was moving. "Get outside and make a left, then a right at the first junction. Second door on the left has a locker room where you can probably grab a weapon."

"That," Eva mumbled, "is a lot to 'member."

She limped at first, the room careening around her like her ship in a bad plasma storm. Her eyes gradually focused on bare metal walls and a few computer stations, security cameras up in the corners. No people. Weird. The door opened at her touch, revealing a T-junction.

Left, she thought, okay.

Letting one hand trail along the wall for stability, Eva staggered forward, toward another T-junction up ahead. Right here. Or was it left? And why did it smell like—

Whatever was to the left exploded, the blast hitting Eva like a fiery linebacker and knocking her backward. She hoped that wasn't the right direction, because it looked very wrong now. Staggering to her feet, she headed the other way.

Windows, and through them low walls and banks of desks. Q-net stations? Still no people, though. A pair of doors at the far end opened and closed over and over, but didn't shut all the way, a limp form on the ground between them. Ah, well, that was a person. Past tense.

"Second door on the left," the voice said. "Take whatever you can find."

Finders, keepers, Eva thought. She opened the door to the locker room and found rows of neat bunks with storage lockers between them. First set was locked, as was the second. Third was also locked but she got impatient and threw a chair at it.

Repeatedly. Inside she found a blaster with a spare magazine and an empty tin of chewing gum.

She slid the magazine into a slot on her belt—still wearing that awful leopard-print jumpsuit, of course—and headed back outside. Still no people.

"What's going on?" she asked, assuming the voice could hear her.

No response.

She followed the hallway to another door, which opened onto an atrium with benches and large planters. At the far end of the room were a pair of guards, who exchanged fire with a pair of . . . mercs, maybe? They were in a uniform she didn't recognize. And they were all heavily armed and armored. She slid behind one of the planters and wondered where she was supposed to go next.

"Who the fuck is that?" someone shouted, and now she was under fire. Who was on her side? Anyone? Her head was a mess of fog clearing way more slowly than she might like, and she still had no idea where she was going.

Guards across and mercs to the right, so left it was. She waited for a break in the volley and raced for the door, diving behind the wall inside. Unfortunately, she found she wasn't alone, but the guard was so shocked he didn't so much as flinch before she knocked his face sideways with her gun. One more smack and a swift kick later and now she had two guns and extra magazines. Much better.

"This area is locked down," the voice said. "Head right and let me reroute power to the doors or you'll be trapped."

Yeah, that would suck, Eva thought. But given how much of a vacuum things were at present, she figured they were reaching deep-space suck levels already.

To the right was a bare white room with another door on the

end—locked—and scanning equipment in the center. No, that was a memvid recorder. A studio?

"Where the actual fuck am I?" Eva muttered. Was this a Fridge facility? Some kind of waystation? How long had she been out, and what was happening now?

And who kept giving her instructions?

The door beeped and slid open, revealing the other side of the recording facility, whatever equipment they needed to manipulate and play back the memvids. Had Mari been dragged through here when she was first taken? Eva gripped her weapons more tightly.

"Left out of this door, and then—mierda," the voice said. "Cargo bay. Quick. I have to go."

There was a muffled sound like shots being fired, then Eva was left to the klaxons again. At least they might have a ship in the cargo bay for her to steal. It was as good a plan as any.

She exited and followed the hallway left to a door, through which she found herself at the end of what did indeed appear to be a cargo bay full of shipping containers.

The roof was about ten meters up, and there were big double doors in the far wall for ships to enter and leave through. A few short-range shuttles sat around, so this facility probably couldn't support bigger boats. That made her nervous; if there wasn't an FTL-capable exit strategy then she'd just be orbiting shit central station until she could raise someone on a comm buoy. Assuming there was one, and that she didn't get shot down while she was comiendo mierda.

There was a booth to the left, likely where the traffic controller sat, or the foreman. It was empty, unless there was a body on the floor Eva couldn't see. Should she pick a shuttle and jump? Or wait for mystery voice to show up and bring the mystery plan together?

"Over there!" someone shouted, and now she was taking fire from guards pouring in through the cargo doors. She returned the favor, darting from cover to cover as the ones she didn't take down moved closer to her position. She wouldn't be able to reach the shuttles at this rate, let alone entertain the hope of getting off whatever rock they were on.

There was a muffled scream, and she peeked out of cover just long enough to see a guard drop, convulsing. From what? Another cry, another guard gone. Either the person was fast as light, hiding really well, or they were cloaked. Which would be expensive. Annoying, too, but apparently on her side, so she'd take it.

"My shuttle is outside," the voice said, right next to her again. Eva jumped, swinging her gun in the direction of the sound. It connected and the person yelped, then cursed thoroughly in Spanish that trailed off as they moved.

Not they: she. Eva knew that yelp, and that string of foul language. But it couldn't be, could it?

Questions later. She dodged fire from two more guards, ducking behind one container after another until she reached the shuttles. The door she had come through opened and the mercs arrived, communicating in hand signals as they spread out through the cargo bay. The guards hesitated, then turned their attention away from Eva to the bigger threat.

Sucking in a breath, she hustled out the bay doors and found herself under a red sun on a red rock that was mostly, well, rock. She was relieved the atmo bubble extended to the escape route, since she wasn't wearing a proper spacesuit.

At least she had her grav boots, for whatever that was worth.

"Over here," the voice called, and she raced after it, almost running into a shuttle, which wasn't cloaked but did have a decent camouflage mod that made it look like more red rocks.

The door lifted open and she dove inside, rolling to her feet and throwing herself into a seat facing the rear of the craft.

"Are they going to shoot us down?" Eva asked.

"I sabotaged their cannons," the voice said from the pilot's chair. "Cállate, I need to concentrate."

Eva closed her eyes as they lifted off, savoring the way her stomach fell into her crotch. She was alive. Within minutes they were free of atmo, the curve of the planet lit by a star that was more orange than red. They banked toward a small moon, where they landed next to a long-range ship—an Albatross, of all things, a human vessel that was out of production but still common as a cold because it was reliable and easy to customize with whatever wild tech you picked up. This one had been modded with a cargo bay door, an FTL supercharger with the requisite extra cooling tanks, and most importantly, a big fuck-off cannon.

Eva swallowed questions like nasty medicine as she exited the transport and made her way to the Albatross's bridge.

Her rescuer was already there, still invisible. "This is Agent Virgo," the voice said. "The package has been retrieved. The merc assault was ongoing when I disembarked."

"Well done, Virgo," a husky female voice responded through the comm. "What about your secondary objective?"

Virgo was silent for a moment. "That package was also retrieved," she finally said.

The mystery woman laughed. "Glad to hear it. We're less than seven cycles out from the priority mission and we need your head in the game now more than ever."

"Yes, ma'am. Virgo out."

The link died, and Eva cleared her throat.

"So," she said. "Qué pinga, Mari?"

Whether she decloaked on purpose or her power supply

went dry, Mari was suddenly visible in the pilot's chair. Eva's sister looked enough like her to mark them as related—brown hair, tan skin, same resting bitch face. But everything about Mari was a shade lighter, like she was slightly better lit, and she was about ten kilos thinner. She'd always beaten Eva at hide-and-seek, but Eva could knock her out with a solid punch.

And here she was. After all Eva had done, after all the worrying and danger, after nearly a month on Nuvesta and beyond, thinking Mari was dead or worse. Relief fought with confusion and anger in the pit of her stomach, which was otherwise as empty as it had been when they'd thrown her in the brig on that starship. When Tito had dragged her away from Vakar . . . But she didn't want to think about him yet. Not yet.

"Well?" Eva asked.

"Well what?" Mari said.

"You didn't answer my question."

Mari rolled her eyes. "'Qué pinga?' is not much of a question."

"No jodas tanto."

"No es lo que jode sino lo seguido."

Eva got up and moved to the copilot seat next to her sister. "Where are we going?"

"A safe house, for now, until I decide what to do with you." Mari's hands flowed quickly through the motions of setting the ship aloft and programming in their destination.

Her sister was so calm, so collected. Same as she always had been. And like before, it drove Eva right into a supernova.

"What to do with me?" Eva asked. "What is this? What's going on? Merc assaults, secret missions . . . You're a historian, a scientist, not a—" Eva gestured at the whole bridge, as if that could encompass the galaxy of shit that didn't make sense. "How about you fill me in on, I don't know, fucking everything?"

Mari stiffened, then slowly seemed to relax, muscle by

muscle. "There are some things I can't tell you for security reasons, but I'll do my best."

"Were you ever actually kidnapped by The Fridge? What happened?"

"It was a necessary deception, to secure their cooperation."

Eva slammed a hand on the console. "You're talking like a weird spy. Get over it and use normal words, Agent Virgo."

Mari threw her a hard side eye. "My bosses wanted me to get in and steal their stuff, basically," she said. "Information, resources, whatever I could manage, with the ultimate goal being a hostile takeover. But The Fridge has a lot of layers, little scattered cells that needed to be found. So the plan was for me to offer myself to them as an agent, and offer you as an asset to prove my loyalty."

The skin on Eva's neck went hot. "So you sold me out by pretending to be in trouble? I thought you were . . . that whole act you put on when you called me was fake? Coño carajo, my crew almost died! *I* almost died! Repeatedly!" Eva's right hand clenched into a fist tight enough to choke a sentient gas, even as her eyes filled with traitorous tears. She'd be damned if she cried now, no matter how much this hurt.

"I didn't expect them to send you to such dangerous places," Mari said. "I thought it would be standard supply runs." Her face twitched like she was suppressing a bunch of expressions. "You always acted like the work you did for Dad was boring and safe, like Mom had exaggerated when she said he was a criminal. You never told me about Garilia."

"Fuck you," Eva snarled. "Like that's a big fucking excuse. 'Sorry, Eva, if I'd known you had a reputation for doing wild shit, maybe I wouldn't have used you like a credit chit.' You could have done anything else, but this? You got me involved, you didn't warn me—"

"Your reactions had to be realistic," Mari said. "You're not nearly as good a liar as you think you are."

"Tu madre."

"La tuya."

"Same thing." Eva ran her hand over her face. Whatever fog she'd been in before had definitely lifted, because now she was starving and furious. "So when the gmaarg put out the bounty on me, what did you do?"

Mari took a deep breath, exhaling it slowly. "I had posed as a mercenary, pretending I didn't care what happened to you. I couldn't start caring because the situation had changed. It would have blown my cover."

"Right, of course. I'm sure it was a real challenge."

"I'm not a robot, comemierda. As soon as I found out, I started making plans. It took some time, but thankfully there were . . . mitigating circumstances that worked in my favor."

For some reason, this yanked a laugh out of Eva. Maybe because she had spent so long thinking she was the one helping Mari. Which was apparently true, if not how she had expected.

"What's so funny?" Mari asked.

"What isn't?" Mari had been the one playing Reversi all along. Eva didn't want to play anymore. She wanted to flip the fucking board and set it on fire.

"I know this is a lot to take in at once, but—"

"What did you tell Mom?" Eva interrupted.

"About what?"

"Anything. Everything. Pete knew you were missing because The Fridge contacted him, but you and Mom have always been closer. She would have freaked out looking for you if you hadn't told her something."

Mari looked at a point past Eva's shoulder. "I said I was starting a new project in a remote place and I wouldn't be able to call her for a while, but I'd write when I could. The Fridge was careful enough about loose ends like that to ensure their operations wouldn't be compromised."

Loose ends. Mitigating circumstances. Assets. Missions. For all that Mari sounded like a spy, she also sounded a lot like their dad. She was certainly as good a liar as he was, better than Eva had ever realized.

Eva stared at the bridge screen, the stars streaming past them in wavering lines. "Where is my crew?" she asked coldly.

Mari fidgeted with the controls, but an Albatross mostly flew itself, so there wasn't much for her to do. "They're scattered. Min stayed with the ship, working for Dad."

"Dad has my ship?" Me cago en diez. And poor Min. If Pete did anything to her—

"Yes. He's been shuttling people around, delivering stuff. Nothing serious or dangerous. Mostly."

Asshole. Of course he'd taken advantage of Eva's temporary absence; she just couldn't believe how quickly he'd moved. And how had he managed to get *La Sirena Negra* away from Pink? Her skin flushed hot and cold all at once. "Leroy?"

"He's on Brodevis."

"'Planet of a Thousand Paradises'? The hell is he doing there?"

Mari smirked. "Let me show you." She gestured at the bridge screen.

At first, Eva wasn't sure what they were watching, but suddenly Leroy's face took up the whole screen—well, most of his face, since his eyes and forehead were covered by a green mask. His hair had been cut and spiked up, even dyed a little more extremely orange. The shot pulled back to show him wearing a yellow jumpsuit that looked strangely reptilian, like it was made of snakeskin, along with metal spiked bands on his wrists and biceps.

"What a ridiculous costume," Eva said. "Is that . . . is he on *Crash Sisters?*"

"Yes." Mari rolled her eyes. "They call him The King. Have you ever watched this show? It's absurd."

On the screen, Leroy threw back his head and roared, his eyes wide with apparent rage. But Eva knew how he looked mad, and this wasn't it. This was wild, unmitigated glee.

"He's the big villain this season," Mari continued. "But my sources suggest he's secretly dating another actress, who plays a character named Momoko. His ratings are excellent, for the moment. Fame can be fickle."

That probably didn't matter to him. He was living his best life just being on the show, his favorite show. Eva could only imagine how excited he and Min had been about the whole thing when it went down. And she had missed it . . .

Eva's stomach rumbled, bringing her back to the present and the rest of her questions. "How about Pink, then?"

Mari waved her hand and Leroy's face turned back into stars. "Pink is on Sceilara. She's working at a clinic for all the classy types who party there and need to clean themselves up before they leave."

"Gross. Hope she's making bank, at least."

"I haven't checked. I've been a bit busy."

"I'm sure." Pink had always threatened to get a cushy gig in the fringe, but it was weird that she'd jumped right to that after whatever happened with Pete. Hopefully it wouldn't be too hard to tear her away from it once Eva got her ship back.

Because Eva was absolutely, positively going to get it back.

Eva's hand went to the scab on her neck. "What about the cats?"

"Eva."

"Well?"

"They're still on your ship. Min was adamant about that, for whatever reason." Mari turned to look at her now, an eyebrow raised. "You haven't asked me about Vakar."

"Fuck do you know about him?" Eva gritted her teeth. Her sister's tone was gentle, not teasing, which did not bode well. "Yeah. Well?"

"He's gone."

All the breath went out of her at once, and her mind blanked like a booted datapad. Don't cry, she told herself. Crying is bullshit. You knew what you were getting into and you knew what would happen. Life's a bitch, then you die.

"Dios mío, you look like you swallowed a turd." Mari put a hand on Eva's knee. "He's not dead, he's just gone. Somewhere in quennian space. Last seen boarding *Silent Vigil* after visiting his sister on DS Nor."

Eva sagged with relief, then shook Mari's hand away. She didn't want her sister to touch her right now, the fucking snake, much less feel her trembling. What the hell was Vakar doing? Never mind; she'd find out soon enough.

"Well. I guess that's it," Eva said. "Dump me at Dad's and I'll get my ship, get the gang back together, and figure out the best way to help you nuke The Fridge from orbit."

"Not a chance. I'm taking you somewhere safe to lie low until my mission is complete."

Eva remembered the conversation Mari had been having before she uncloaked. "Right, your important priority mission. In a week? Maybe that doesn't seem so long to you, but I'd rather claw my own face off than sit around for a whole week waiting for you to come back and get me."

Mari smiled with her mouth closed. "Think of it as a vacation. You haven't taken one of those in a while, I'm guessing."

"Nope, I'm good. I want my ship, I want my crew, and I want revenge, in that order." Eva reclined her seat and closed her eyes as Mari fumed, and it gave her a savage glee.

"Would it kill you to think about someone other than yourself for a change?" Mari said.

That wasn't the bite she expected, but she was more than happy to bare her own teeth. "Oh, it's on," Eva said. "Mira, resingada comemierda, you saved my life, and I'm pretty happy about that right now. But my life wouldn't have needed saving if you hadn't fucked me over in the first place."

Mari opened her mouth to say something, but Eva shoved her hand in her sister's face.

"Cómetelo, I'm not done yet." She leaned forward, staring into light brown eyes that she would gladly punch at the slightest provocation. "I don't know what kind of batshit fucking loco comemierdería you're playing with, but you're not in charge of me. You're not my boss, you're not Mom, and you can go swim in a waste collector like the piece of shit you are."

Mari took a deep breath and closed her eyes. Eva could almost hear her counting to ten in her head. "The Fridge's resources have the potential to be extremely dangerous in the wrong hands. They've found things that— Look, this is bigger than you and your crew, and I don't want you in the middle now that I've finally got you away from them."

"I'm already in the middle," Eva snapped. "Or near the bottom, maybe, since shit flows downhill and they had me shoveling it."

"Yes, but—"

"I'm not stupid." This was more of a long shot, but she went for it. "A paleotechnologist specializing in the Proarkhe? Mystery tech sending out a subspace signal? What did they find, and how are they hiding it from BOFA?" She still wasn't sure about the todyk and the booze run on Dalnulara, but maybe this would bait Mari into explaining.

It didn't. "Not your problem," Mari said. "Olvídalo. Worry about yourself."

"First I'm selfish, now you want me to worry about myself?"

"That's all you have left to worry about." She leaned closer, eyes narrowing. "Dad has your ship and you can't afford another. And even if you could, your crew have all moved on."

Eva stood and stretched. "I'll ask them. Maybe they're not as in love with their new lives as you think. It's not like I've been gone that long, right?"

Her sister smiled again. It was not a happy smile.

Everything Mari had said replayed in Eva's head, dread climbing in her chest despite the mechanically controlled rhythm of her heart. Because the thing about cryo was, you went right to sleep, and then you woke up, and in between there weren't even dreams to give you a bridge between moments. It was like a Gate, where she'd gone in one end and come out somewhere entirely different, and there was one question she hadn't asked yet, one very, very important question that hadn't occurred to her until now.

"Mari," Eva said quietly, "how long have I been gone?"

No answer. Eva pulled up the chronometer on her commlink.

"Me cago en diez," she whispered.

Chapter 18

THE EMPIRE STRIKES FORTH

Eva looked like shit. Being in cryo hadn't done much to deteriorate her muscle mass, but she still felt weaker. Brittle. Every line on her face seemed new to her, like she was really looking at herself for the first time.

A year gone. A whole damn year.

Eva felt slightly worse about giving Mari shit after hearing what had gone down in that year. She'd already be dancing for the Glorious Turd if her sister hadn't tampered with the delivery in a lot of minute ways, from message disruption to outright sabotage. The final fabrication that had kept her safe until Mari could free her was completely overriding shipping manifests to make it look like Eva was a random container bound for storage, where she had sat, quietly, for more than nine months.

Considering it was pretty much Mari's fault Eva had been on Omicron in the first place, she didn't want to give her sister too much credit. Nothing to be done about it now. Onward and upward, off this ship and back to her own.

And then? Justice. Revenge. And, of course, there was the little matter of finding her crew. Finding Vakar.

Her skin prickled with nerves. He had said he'd find her, and he hadn't. Not that she was surprised; hadn't she failed to find any Fridge facilities herself? And Mari had been actively hiding her the whole time.

It had been a year, though. He might have given up. Moved on. Or whatever trouble he'd been running from when she met him might have caught up.

But back to the task at hand: getting her ship. The Fridge had come down hard on her dad before they took her, throttling back once they got what they wanted, but he'd still been pretty much ruined. And after she went missing, they'd assumed he had something to do with it and conscripted his ass the same as they'd done to Eva, according to Mari. Getting *La Sirena Negra* back had been a godsend for him, however he had managed it, but that didn't mean she was going to let him keep it.

Eva took one last look at her reflection—at the gray spacesuit Mari had given her to replace that awful leopard-print thing she'd slept in, at the scar that hadn't disappeared from her cheek by magic—then snarled and gave herself the finger. People didn't hire her because she was pretty, they hired her because she could fly, fight and fake civility. And because she did her fucking job.

Back in the bridge, Mari was prepping for landing. "You're sure it's here?" Eva asked her, dropping into her seat.

"If you ask me one more time, I'm spacing you. And no, I'm still not going to tell you how I'm tracking it. Now shut up so I can concentrate."

"You could let me fly," Eva muttered, but she settled back to watch their approach. It had been hard enough convincing Mari to bring her here at all; she didn't want her sister to change her mind now, not when she was so close to her ship.

The planet of Conelia in the Talyl system was a garden world, full of diverse intelligent life that bore a sometimes-uncanny resemblance to certain Earth animals. A lot of truateg lived there, along with a few toad-like vroak and delicate eac, which had razor-sharp beaks but skin more like a snake's. The biggest groups were the rani and neho, whose fuzzy fox- and rabbit-like forms were the delight of humans with corresponding preferences. The military training facilities were top-notch, and their labs had a penchant for coming up with interesting new tech and slapping it onto spaceships. They needed both, given how often they ended up fighting someone or other.

Which was why her dad was there, presumably. While the Conelians weren't ones to keep most of their inventions to themselves, they were in the middle of a civil war. According to Mari, the planet had been blockaded for a month, with the rebel faction attacking anyone who was coming or going. This made Conelian tech a bit harder to come by, as not only were the Conelians hesitant to sell things they could use to blow stuff up, but planetary defenses got trigger-happy with outsiders because of the near-constant surface raids.

But they also needed money to fund war efforts, so trade still happened with those daring enough to brave what could turn into a combat zone at any time. Assuming her dad was still working for The Fridge, Eva had no doubt that "daring" translated to "unwilling but able."

They dropped through fluffy white clouds onto a brown, green and blue surface whose cities were hard to spot because of how they'd been built, in harmony with the plant life instead of bulldozing through it. But most people lived in the mountains during wartime, hunkering down in cave networks, which made landing more of a challenge if you wanted to be anywhere near the stuff you were picking up.

Mari maneuvered them through a series of canyons, soaring rock formations arching overhead or forming natural bridges farther down. Eva remembered flying through here a long time ago, during a different war, back when Tito was her boss and attitude was her copilot.

"You ever get the urge to do a barrel roll in here?" Eva asked.

Mari didn't roll a damn thing, not even her eyes.

They touched down at a narrow landing platform that held a squad of ships, none of which was hers—all Conelian fighters, guarded by a squad of truateg wearing uniforms a darker shade of blue than the sky. Eva's skin prickled with anxiety. Had *La Sirena Negra* already left? Or had something else happened? She tried to ping Min, but there was no response.

"I thought you said they were here," Eva said, narrowing her eyes at Mari.

"They are," Mari said. "I'm getting too much interference to pinpoint their location. Try to pull them up on comms."

Eva gestured and a display popped up. "HSS *La Sirena Negra,* open line, are you receiving?"

No response.

"*La Sirena Negra,* are you receiving?" Eva repeated.

Still nothing. Her stomach twisted.

"Strange," Mari said. "I wonder if—"

An alarm cut in from the platform outside, quiet but insistent. A queer buzzing in Eva's teeth told her the rest of the sound was likely at a frequency higher than she could hear, and after a moment her translators pinged her as much.

"The Conelians are under attack," Mari said, gesturing at a message that had popped up on a holoscreen. "Probably the rebels again. They're scrambling ships for defense."

"Coño carajo," Eva said. "Great timing."

Outside, pilots began to pour out of a reddish-brown building and race toward their ships, lean pieces of work with too many sharp angles for her taste, or triangular, with wings that seemed too small to keep them airborne or maneuver. Nothing like her sleek black mermaid; more like angry birds and warty toads.

The holoscreen translated the Conelian comm chatter, mostly a list of names and ship orders, a few of which Eva recognized from the bad old days. Vixen Nimbus, *Awing 2,* Conelia City. Slippery Croke, *Aggressive Badaba,* Conelia City. Caracara Carlo, *Heaven Talon,* Conelia City. Lively Hea, *Zorr Twice,* Conelia City . . . Pretty much everyone was converging on the same location, the planet's capital.

Mari took a deep breath through her nose and exhaled slowly through her mouth. "Looks like we're stuck here for now. We'll jump if this location comes under fire."

"We're not leaving until I get my ship back," Eva said.

"We won't get your ship back if we get blown up first, cabezona."

Eva slumped down into the copilot chair, lips pursed. So far, this ship recovery operation was not going well. Where the hell were Min and her dad?

There was a sudden pop on comms. "This is *La Sirena Negra,* line open, we are receiving. This location is under attack." It was Min, sounding panicked. "We're stuck under debris and can't evacuate. Requesting immediate assistance."

"No me diga," Eva said. "Mari, I have to find them!"

Mari shook her head. "It's not safe. We wait for this wave to be over and then we go look for them."

"They could be vaporized by then." Eva grabbed her sister's shoulder. "Please, Mari, I have to get to my ship."

"Absolutely not. What could you even do to help?"

Min cut in again. "Repeat, requesting immediate assistance to Conelia City. It's the gmaarg, they've found us again, we—" With a squeal of static, the line went silent. Then, another voice cut in.

"Insipid breathers of oxygenated gases! We have come to recover Eva the Innocent, captain of the Black Mermaid vessel. Give her to us or we will destroy your planet and defile its ashes!"

Eva closed her mouth, which had fallen open at some point. It couldn't be.

"Glorious?" she asked. "He's here? Why? How?"

"He's been tracking your ship, too," Mari said. "I haven't figured it out myself yet, but every few months he chases them around in his fathership for a couple of cycles and then gets bored and goes home again." She steepled her fingers and tapped them against her lips. "The gmaargit social structure really is fascinating, when you consider no one seems to care about the time and resources he's wasting to chase one random human."

"Yes, fascinating," Eva said. "You should write a book about it."

"Please, with everything on my plate, I don't have time to—"

"I was joking, comemierda!" Eva shouted. "Fucking move!" She had to get to Min before this turned into another Omicron.

Mari closed her eyes and breathed, then opened them again. "I said no. It's too dangerous."

Eva stood and loomed over her sister, leaning against the back of the pilot's chair. "Hey," she said quietly. "You want to find out what's really dangerous?"

Mari stiffened. "Are you threatening me?"

"Nope." Eva smiled. "I'm making you an offer. You let me fly over there, and I won't airlock myself right now and hitch a ride with someone else."

"You can't hitch a ride on a Conelian ship; they're single-seaters."

"Shit, you're right." Eva pulled out one of the pistols she'd nabbed at the Fridge base. "Guess I am threatening you, then."

Mari stared at the gun, lips twisting like she'd bitten into a sour orange. "Don't be ridiculous. How would you fly while holding me at gunpoint?"

"I wouldn't." Eva gestured at the airlock. "Get out, and I'll come back and get you once this is over."

"After all this, you're seriously ready to shoot me? Because I'm not moving."

Eva was tempted. Very, very tempted. But she sighed, deflating slightly. "No. Asshole. But . . . I will definitely shoot myself. I'm assuming there are medical facilities at the capital. I'm betting you can reach them before I bleed out." She aimed the gun at her own leg.

"How will being stuck in a hospital help your crew?" Mari shook her head. "That's like five bad plans you've had in two minutes. How are you still alive?"

"I move fast." The blinking comms alert on the control panel caught her attention. "Okay, final offer: you let me fly there, or I tell Glorious exactly where I am right now and we see what happens."

Mari rubbed her eyes with one hand, pinching the bridge of her nose. "This is seriously that important to you? You would shoot yourself or risk being captured by the Gmaargitz Fedorach?"

"Yes, and the longer we argue, the more desperate I get." Eva stared her sister down, wishing she could exude the smell of her earnestness like Vakar.

"Alabao, fine." Mari got up and sat in the passenger seat. "There. Go. Show me your fancy pilot skills."

"You're coming with me?" Eva asked. "No, it's too danger-ous. Get out."

Mari raised her eyebrows and cocked her head to one side, pursing her lips as she slow-blinked at Eva.

"Right, point taken." Eva sighed. "Let's go."

The comms crackled again. "Your prevarications emphasize your ineptitude! My empire will unmake your pathetic planet, you—"

Eva flicked the comms off. "Seriously, that guy. How has no one strangled him with their own bra?"

The ship's controls were as simplistic as Eva remembered, and a single flick of the wrist turned everything on. Most of the work of flying an Albatross was done by the computer systems, with only the actual maneuvering controlled by the pilot. There was a trigger for the laser cannon, a red button she didn't im-mediately recognize, and—

Eva raised an eyebrow. "You have a gravity disperser? Fancy."

"And a spinner shield," Mari said. "That's the green button. Please don't use it unless you have to. It makes me queasy."

Spinner shields were nearly invincible, if you remembered to trigger them in time. The gravity disperser let the ship stop al-most instantly and make turns that would break necks in most other cases. Vakar knew how it worked, and he'd explained it to Eva once, but that was back when she still spent her downtime between jobs drinking away her spare creds.

Vakar. The thought of him burned her blood faster than booze. Suck it up, girl, she told herself. No time for piss breaks. You have a ship to find.

"What's the red button for?" Eva asked.

"Escape bubble," Mari replied. "Don't touch it."

Eva rolled her eyes. "Do I look like someone who randomly presses buttons for no good reason?"

"Te conozco, mascarita." Mari sat with her hands folded in her lap, her legs primly crossed at the ankles, like she had since they were kids in school. "This is still a terrible plan, for the record," she said.

"You could have stayed behind," Eva said.

"And you could make better life choices," Mari replied. "Maybe that's how Glorious keeps finding you, he just follows the trail of bad decisions."

Eva ignored that comment and flew off after the bulk of the fighters, who she assumed were all heading for the city where *La Sirena Negra* was stuck. Within a few moments, a pair of gmaar-git ships dropped in front of her, flanking another Conelian fighter and promptly shooting it down. They were almost pretty, their rear assemblies like flowers just beginning to bloom. If flower petals were made of metal, that is.

"All right, cannon, let's see what you've got," Eva muttered. The trigger was a simple button on the front of the control stick, so she aimed the ship and fired.

The giant laser was . . . slow. She resisted the urge to count how long it took before the damn thing finally loosed a bolt of sizzling green light that completely failed to hit the enemy. It did tear a huge chunk out of a mountain, which Eva hoped hadn't been occupied, and the debris at least managed to hit one of the ships and send it careening into the ground.

"This thing is useless," Eva muttered.

"I prefer to run than fight," Mari said. "But if I have to fight, I want to hit hard."

Eva resisted the urge to roll her eyes at that logic. If it was going to take that long for every single shot, she'd need to make them count. She tracked the other ship, watching its movements for a few seconds, then aimed at where she thought it would end up, given how it was dodging. She nicked the edge of one of its tail fins, which had the unfortunate side effect of making it spin toward her like a sawblade.

Eva yanked the controls back and the gravity disperser kicked in, the ship shooting up at nearly a right angle straight into the sky. Mari shrieked. Collision avoided, but now she was heading for the clouds, which were currently dropping more of Glorious's fighters like glittering snowflakes of death.

She fired at them as often as she could, each time holding her breath as the huge cannon recharged. Their blasts were more frequent, but thankfully the ship dodged well enough, even if it was limping along at what felt like the speed of sound.

"What are you doing?" Mari yelped. "They're going to blast us to pieces. Get down into the canyons."

"I don't know them well enough," Eva retorted. "I'm as likely to hit a wall as I am to avoid fire."

Mari cringed. "Fine. Use the spinner shield, then."

Spinning sounded good to her. Not. But given how slow this ship was, it was probably the safest option. Taking a deep breath, she pushed the button.

Sure enough, the ship spun in a tight circle, with the gravity disperser somehow making it feel like her stomach was in the same place the whole time. Eva got an incredibly strong urge to pee. Mari gagged.

But outside the ship, a shimmering green shield sprang up, deflecting fire from a few of the enemies who had broken off from the main force to go after her. By the time the cannon was primed to spit lasers again, the shield had vanished.

Eva yanked the ship to a stop to let two enemies crash into each other, exploding in a shower of purple fire. Then she hit the spinner button again and accelerated once the shield was up.

"This is worse than I remember," Mari muttered.

Eva risked a glance back at her sister. Mari was gripping the sides of the seat, her eyes scrunched closed.

The Conelian defenders continued their hit-and-run maneuvers, popping out of the canyons long enough to take down a couple of fighters before hiding again. Some enemy ships followed them in, whether that did them any good or just made for a lot of shiny debris. For her part, Eva stuck close to the ground, moving inexorably closer to Conelia City in the wake of the faster fleet.

And she spun. Over and over again. Each time, the disperser compensated to make her feel like she wasn't moving at all, but she could still track the motion through the front display. Gradually, a queasiness grew as the disconnect between her body and her eyes was repeated. She fired another shot, clenching her teeth as it connected, trying to let the savage glee drive away the nausea.

"I take it back," Mari said, her voice strained.

"Take what back?" Eva asked.

"The spinner shield is terrible and I hate it. Don't ever use it again."

Eva burped with her mouth closed. "We can do this. Remember our first time in zero G?"

Mari groaned. "Dad thought it would be hilarious to surprise us. He acted like it was going to be the most fun thing ever."

"He even made us clean up our own barf afterward. But the point is . . ." Eva sucked in a breath, exhaling slowly. "The point is, we both agree that he was an asshole."

"And you're sure you want to save him?" Mari asked.

"No," Eva said. "But I definitely want to kick him off my ship. Picture the look on his face when I show up and tell him to pack his shit and leave."

Mari gave a dry laugh. "Make him clean up first."

Eva hit the green button, swallowing spit as they spun again.

The outskirts of Conelia City appeared beneath them, blending into the environment so seamlessly that she almost missed the transition. Unlike the rocky area where they'd landed before, this was fertile farmland, buildings nestled among rows of crops or even underneath them.

At least they would have been, if most of them weren't on fire.

"Mierda de mono," she muttered. "This is Omicron all over again."

The fires sent up screens of smoke that interfered with visuals, ironically helping ease some of the nausea from all the spinning. Debris flew into the air with every enemy crash or stray shot, sometimes settling onto the kinetic barrier for a few moments before the shield dropped again and it fell to the ground.

Space was so much cleaner. Mostly. She couldn't wait to get back.

They arrived at a clearing that used to be the center of the city and was now a series of charred craters. Above them, enemy ships swarmed like angry wasps wearing sharp metal skirts and shooting red lasers. And at the apex, Glorious's fathership, at least five stories tall, hovering in the air above the wreckage like an eight-pointed star with a red core, which Eva realized was a huge cannon when it blasted them head-on.

If the shields hadn't been up, they would have been deep-fried. As it was, the force of the hit knocked them to the ground, their ship skipping along the surface like a rock on a pond. Eva banged the shield button like a bongo, spin-hopping until she finally regained control and brought the flight to an abrupt halt. More gmaargit fighters poured out, and she considered that maybe, just maybe, Mari had been right, that they should have stayed where they were in the first place and waited for this to blow over.

She also considered that Glorious was on that ship, and with that thought came a beautiful, terrible idea.

Eva flew them to a spot behind one of the remaining intact buildings. "Hey, Mari, you okay?" she asked.

"I almost died, so no?" Mari replied. Her face was red as a ripe pitanga. "We need to get away from that fathership before it fires on us again."

"Or, hear me out . . . Maybe it has a weakness? An exhaust port we could bomb or something? So the whole thing would go boom?"

"Que rayo . . . No! We are not attacking that monstrosity!"

Eva grinned at Mari over her shoulder. "Come on, think about it. This is our chance to—"

"No. Absolutely not. You're insane."

"I'm being totally rational. We take down Glorious, we not only save my ship and Min and Dad, we save a whole city. No more bounty on me, no more gmaarg chasing me all over the universe. It's perfect."

Mari started to unhook her restraints. "That's it. Salpica. I'm getting us out of here."

Before she could move, a gmaargit fighter found them and chased them out of hiding. Eva spun again, and Mari stumbled back into the seat with her hands covering her mouth. The fathership's enormous eye of a laser opened, the iris glowing like the core of a star. This time Eva got them out of the way before it fired, but that meant bouncing off the smaller fighter behind them and careening hard in the opposite direction.

Eva cursed silently, then cursed again out loud because what the hell, she didn't care if Mari heard her. "I don't suppose you have any weapons besides the cannon?"

"Eva, come the fuck on," Mari said. "I didn't pull you out of that freezer to have you get us both vaporized."

"Like the poem says, mija, it ends in fire or ice," Eva said. "And fire's looking like good odds right now."

She angled to the left, and the fathership followed her movement, as if it knew she was the one Glorious wanted. Ships flung themselves at her like flies at a windshield, and she had to stop so often she thought she'd never make it anywhere.

"Please, Eva," Mari said, voice strained. "We're not equipped for this. We don't have a plan. How about you let the Conelians handle it; they have the appropriate weapons and training to—"

"Or how about I fly inside and pop that thing open like a giant piñata?" Eva snapped.

There was no reply for a moment.

"I should have left you in cryo," Mari finally said. "At least when you were frozen in a box, you couldn't get anyone killed."

"We're still alive," Eva said.

"Qué suerte."

Eva zipped sideways, then back down, spinning for good measure and firing off a shot with her cannon. "Those ships are coming from somewhere, which means there's at least one opening, which means we can get in. Worst case, we do limited recon and fly right back out. Best case, we can hit something that brings Glorious down for good."

"Worst case, we get blown to pieces before we get inside!"

The huge laser eye rotated toward her again, and Eva barely dragged the ship out of the way by shooting straight up. She hit the spin button as she did, more debris landing on the shield like a curtain of dust.

"Come on, Mari," Eva said. "Help me find the hangar bay door."

"I'm afraid I can't do that," Mari replied.

"Why not?"

"Because if I open my eyes, I'm going to throw up."

Some fucking spy, Eva thought. She must do all the ground missions.

Her last maneuver had put them high in the sky, looking down at the mess below. Conelian fighters chased gmaarg around destroyed buildings as the fathership drifted serenely through, its giant laser tearing through stone and metal like they were paper. But the door, where was the door . . .

She saw it—or them, because two of the points on the massive star shape had doors, one with gmaargit ships flying in and the other sending new ones out.

"Gotcha, cabrón," Eva said. Now, how to get in?

Stop flying like this is *La Sirena Negra*, she told herself sternly. Drop it like it's hot, woman.

She pushed the ship into a nosedive. Just before hitting the ground, she yanked it to a stop and shot forward between the lower spokes of the fathership. It tried to fire but the angle was all wrong, and she was out the back side before it could turn to track her.

With a twitch of the joystick, she flipped the ship upside down, her hair hanging normally instead of falling up because of the gravity disperser. Behind her, Mari gave a long, low moan punctuated by the muffled burp of her suppressing vomit.

Eva came in at an angle from above, skimming the surface of the ship's pointed arm. She'd have to time it carefully.

"Come on," she muttered. "Few more seconds . . ."

The door appeared below her and she braked, her stomach heaving, then dropped down inside.

She wasn't sure what she had expected to find, but it turned out to be a vast, nearly empty space like a creepy bubble nest. Each bubble was a gmaargit fighter waiting to be deployed, and she took some comfort in the fact that there were only a few hundred more left. A thousand at most. Maybe two.

Yeah, okay, that wasn't comforting at all.

Up through the center ran a giant pylon, channeling the energy to the big fuck-off laser that was ruining everyone's cycle. It thrummed like the galaxy's biggest bass speaker about to drop the beat.

"That looks like a good thing to shoot," Eva said.

"Eva, oh my god," Mari whispered. "You hit that, you're going to trigger an explosive wave that will tear this ship to pieces, shield or no shield."

"I can get us out in time."

"Can you?"

Eva squinted and wagged her head. "Yeah?"

Mari hissed out a breath. At least she didn't sound nauseated anymore.

The gmaarg had noticed them and were deploying fighters, which she ignored with a final gut-wrenching, shield-raising spin. She waited for the fathership's laser to charge, a bolt of energy racing up the pylon like lightning.

"Pew-pew," she said, and fired.

The bright green laser scored a direct hit on the pylon with a noise like water hitting a hot pan. Eva didn't wait to see what happened; the cannon would take too long to recharge for another shot anyway. She flipped the ship around, spinning as she did for extra torque, and raced for the exit. "Race" being a relative term, slow as her ship was.

"Come on, you tub of—"

Eva couldn't finish her thought, because it was drowned out by a massive boom behind her, and then they were riding concussive force like a surfer on a tsunami. She spun continuously, because if the shields dropped, they were toast. She had one chance to get out, her mechanical heartbeat seeming to slow as she aimed the ship's nose at the exit, that tiny exit, how had she even gotten through such a small door in the first place—

And then she was out, but she had nicked the edge, so the ship was twirling around, the controls all but useless in her hands, an alarm informing her calmly that something was on fire. She tried to spin her shields up but it wasn't working, so all she could do was whirl sideways toward the ground like a badly aimed chakram, her stomach in her throat.

"Eject!" Mari shouted.

Eva pressed her eject button, waiting to be launched into the sky by whatever mechanism this particular ship used.

Nothing happened. To her, anyway.

The ship's ceiling opened and Mari flew up and out, a shimmering bubble of force surrounding her. She disappeared almost instantly, and Eva had just enough time to hope Mari landed safely before she herself hit the ground.

The impact slammed Eva's head into the seat so hard her teeth cracked and her vision blurred. Almost worse was the crunching and grinding as the ship slid along atop a sea of rubble. Bits of control system and interior paneling sheared off and bounced around the cockpit, hitting her face and arms and chest. With a sickening metal groan, part of the floor beneath her peeled back and more debris kicked up into the mess.

It felt like forever, but was probably only a few seconds, and then the ship finally stopped moving. An eerie silence rang in Eva's ears, the fire alarm having given up on the obviously unconcerned pilot. The fire itself, however, was burning merrily, smoke filling the room and suggesting that maybe she should get out before she got blown up like the gmaargit fathership.

Eva fought with her restraints, ultimately pulling out her vibroblade to cut herself free. She crawled over the side of her chair to avoid the jagged metal that had once been floor and staggered to the escape hatch, which ignored her commlink-sent orders to open. Coughing and sputtering, she hit the manual release button and hissed in frustration as the small door opened barely wide enough for her to squeeze through.

The ship was far enough off the ground that she had an unpleasant drop, poorly gauged because her vision was still slightly blurred. Her gravboots took some of the impact, but her knees and hips would be angry at her later.

Still, any crash you could walk away from . . .

Or limp, in this case, away from the ship in case it decided to explode. She had no idea where she was, or where Mari was, or where her own ship was, but she did know one thing: Glorious was gone. Finally.

The part of her mind that registered danger gave a brief, belated scream at the realization of what she'd done. She'd have nightmares later, but as usual, she couldn't focus on that now. A chill passed through her, despite the relative warmth of the air. The trail of bodies left in her wake had grown a little longer. It had felt like victory when she was younger, like proof of her superiority and righteousness. Now it felt like ablation damage, like pieces of her were being chipped off and cast into the void of space, and all she could do was try to fix it and keep going and hope there wasn't a hull breach.

A ping interrupted her sour thoughts. Mari. ((Location?))

Eva considered not answering, letting her sister think she was gone for at least a little while, but that would be cruel. She sent a location ping in reply.

((Stay put.))

Given that she was lost in an unfamiliar city, and a casual swipe at her forehead came away bloody, and the places her restraints had been were starting to ache and burn, sitting down sounded pretty good. Eva leaned back against part of a former building and summoned up her spacesuit's isohelmet to filter out the smoke and dust. Above her, gmaargit ships fell from the sky like sparking cherry blossoms, lost without the fathership to guide them, and in the distance an alarm squealed at a register above her hearing until her teeth ached even more.

She must have blacked out briefly, because one second she was alone, and the next Mari was shaking her like a bottle of protein drink.

"Ow, what?" Eva asked.

"Seriously?" Mari replied. "I thought Schafer was bad, but you're a whole new level."

"Who?" Eva asked, but Mari fell stubbornly silent. She pulled something out of her belt pouch and handed it to Eva: a nanite dose, which Eva obediently pinched a nostril and inhaled. It was a small tube, more to stabilize her injuries than repair them, but it was a lot better than nothing.

"This way," Mari said, hauling Eva to her feet and guiding her with a hand on her forearm. Everything felt like it was still spinning, like the horizon kept trying to move in the distance, and the nanites made her insides itch.

They came to a landing strip not far away, other Conelians already there and shouting and hugging and crying over their victory. Did they know who made it happen? Probably not. Didn't matter, especially since they were still at war with someone else entirely. That was war for you, like a game of musical chairs where seats kept disappearing until only one was left, and people rarely stopped to ask who the hell was in charge of the music.

Mari released Eva and crossed her arms. "I'm going to find a place where I can make some calls, then I'll see if I can salvage any of my stuff."

Eva winced. "I know you think I don't care, but I am sorry about your ship," she said. "I'll give you a ride to wherever you need to go once I get *La Sirena Negra* back."

"No, no," Mari said quickly. "Dad doesn't know about me. He can't know, or my mission will be compromised. Bringing you here was already a risk. I'll find a way off-planet, don't worry."

"Okay, fine, if you say so."

They stood in silence for a few moments, Eva scratching the scab on her neck, Mari with her eyes closed, taking slow breaths.

"I guess I'll see you around," Eva said.

"I hope not," Mari replied quietly. "What I'm doing is . . . Please, just stay out of trouble. Please."

Eva smiled with her mouth closed. "You know I can't promise that."

"Then at least try to be more careful."

"You're the one with some big mystery mission coming up in a week. You be careful."

Mari leaned forward like she was going to reach for Eva, then stepped back, putting her hands on her hips instead. "I hope you find your crew. And good luck with Dad."

"I don't need luck for that," Eva replied. "Just patience, so I don't kick his ass." As if she were in any shape to kick anything bigger than a gasket.

Mari laughed, raising her hand in a final wave as she turned and walked away. Within moments she had disappeared into the smoke and rubble, either hidden by the celebrating Conelians or cloaked by whatever invisibility tech she'd used before.

Eva was still angry at Mari, and hurt, and she didn't know if she would ever really forgive her sister for what she'd done. But love, that was there, too, nestled in the bottom of her mechanical heart like a battery that wouldn't run out of juice. Funny how that worked.

She'd deal with those feelings later, when she wasn't standing in a burning city on a strange planet in the middle of a civil war. And if she could manage, she might even get in on whatever major action Mari and her bosses were planning against The Fridge within the week.

Eva pinged Min. ((Location?))

At first, there was no answer from her. Then a stream of coordinates popped in, and Eva mapped them with her commlink. Not too far.

Maybe luck was on her side after all. Eva blinked back tears—caused by the smoke and dust, naturally, it couldn't be anything else, even if she was wearing a helmet—and started to limp toward her stolen home.

Chapter 19

RETURN OF THE JODIENDA

Eva received no further transmission from her ship as she walked to the remains of the cargo port in the western quadrant of Conelia City. She could only imagine what Min was thinking, getting a ping from a ghost in the middle of a war zone. A year was a long time for people to rage, and grieve, and ultimately move on with their lives.

She'd certainly had her share of doing just that over the years.

The destruction of the fathership had cut control to all the gmaargit fighters, but some gmaarg had survived and were engaging the Conelians on foot, occasionally wasting their ammo on the ships that crisscrossed the pale blue sky above them.

She arrived at a small clear space surrounded by blown-out buildings and impact craters. Most of the civilians had been evacuated well before the fighting began, so the remains of the city were already empty of life. It was like walking through the bones of a huge creature who was still on fire. Soldiers emerged like furry ants to sort through the wreckage for survivors and supplies, and to prepare for the next wave, whenever that might come.

Eva climbed gingerly over debris, favoring her left leg and avoiding areas her sensors noted were more unstable. How she was going to get *La Sirena Negra* out of wherever it was, she didn't know; it all depended on how badly it was damaged, buried, or otherwise inoperable.

She found what had once been a landing platform but was now a hole in the ground with half a building on top of it. At the bottom of the hole, about four meters down, was the top of her ship, its exterior shielding shimmering as bits of debris were dislodged by Eva's footsteps. Intact shields were a good sign; it meant the hull hadn't been breached. She eyed the obstruction pinning the ship down and sighed, but another part of her was downright giddy with hope.

After everything she'd been through, moving a pile of rocks was a simple logistical challenge.

Climbing down took a few minutes of scouting for a good spot, picking handholds carefully and then cursing when she chose poorly and slid halfway down on her already-tender stomach. She landed near the airlock, but it was blocked by a thick column that had cracked in the middle, so she clambered back toward the emergency airlock and tried to open it with her commlink. It was locked down, which probably meant all power was directed at the shields and life support. With a sigh, she opened a gap in the shields and pulled out the metal key that would let her open the airlock manually.

It took a few minutes of wrenching, but she finally got the damn thing open and climbed the ladder inside, closing the hatch behind her. The transition area was just large enough for two people; the last time she'd been in there was with Vakar, she remembered, and she scowled at herself for remembering. She stood in the cramped quarters while she waited for pressurization and decontamination to finish. It finally did, with a ding like a meal done prepping, and the door opened with a hiss. Four guns and a pair of knives greeted her on the other side.

"Honey, I'm home," she said.

"Who are you and why do you have Eva's commlink?" asked one of the gun holders.

"I have it because it's mine, which should answer both questions." She squinted down the various sets of arms holding the weapons, at the faces staring into hers. With a start, she realized one of the faces belonged to her dad. He had lost at least twenty kilos, his cheeks thin and ragged as an old rug that had been beaten too many times.

"You look like shit, Pete," she said. "No es lo que jode . . ."

"Sino lo seguido," he finished. But he didn't drop the weapon. "What's your favorite food, Bee?"

Second countersign. Okay. "Arroz con mango. How's the weather up your own ass?"

Now he did lower his arm, eyes shiny with a bit of extra fluid. "It's a shitstorm as usual. Where the holy hell have you been, girlie?"

She was so startled by his apparent emotion that she almost told him the truth. The lie she had rehearsed while she walked felt like sand in her mouth, but she spat it out anyway. "I don't know, exactly, what with me being in cryo the whole time. The facility I was in got jumped by mercs, one of them let me out, and when they left I hitched a ride. Took me a while to track you down, but here I am."

His face went blank, like he could smell the crap but didn't know which shoe it was under, but he knew better than to call her on it in front of other people.

"How did you get to us?" he asked. "There was quite a debacle outside last time I checked."

Eva smirked. "I might have aggressively borrowed a ship. I also might have blown up the Glorious Assbiter, since he was in my way."

Pete's eyebrows shot up so high, his forehead turned into a mass of wrinkles.

"You did what?" he asked, his tone mild by comparison.

She ignored his question and gestured at the people in front of her. "So who are these friendly folks waiting to put something deadly in my skull?" she asked.

Pete inclined his head, and the weapons disappeared. "My crew. Let's do introductions in the mess. And maybe you can explain yourself a little more thoroughly." He gestured at her head. "You've got blood on you, by the way."

Eva shrugged and kept her expression neutral. He had slid in like a hermit crab and taken over as soon as she was away, and now she had to play nice until she could take her shell back. She couldn't show weakness, though, or the game was already over.

"Min, you coming?" she asked.

"I've been here the whole time, Cap," came the response through the speakers. Min sounded strangely subdued. Eva didn't like it.

They practically marched her into the mess like an armed guard. Eva fell into her seat at the head of the table, half out of habit and half to make her intentions clear. Whether Pete picked that up she wasn't sure, but he sat at the other end of the table with that same poker face. One of his crew stood behind him and the other two flanked him, and she began to feel like maybe she was at the foot of the table despite her intentions.

As if she had been waiting for her cue, Mala leaped onto the table and sat down in the middle, tail curling around her feet as she settled into loaf position. She cast one glance at Eva before closing her eyes and starting a low, rhythmic purr.

"Right, so, can I get you anything?" Pete said, breaking out his best salesman smile.

"I'm fine," Eva replied. "If I want anything, I know where to get it."

"Could be some stuff moved, but fine. Introductions, then." He leaned back, gesturing first to his right. "This is Jaedum Caliso, from here on Conelia originally. Worked for me as an engineer back in the day and now here he is again."

"Engineer, weapons upkeep, building spare parts out of spit and scraps," Jaedum said, voice raspy like he had a cold. He was a kyatto, with velvety fur the gray of an oncoming storm and big eyes as blue as Earth's oceans. "Don't know how you kept this heap in the sky so long without a major overhaul."

"My engineer was the best," she replied, half grinning, and his ears flattened against his skull. Prick. He could go fry ice when she got Vakar back.

"Where is your engineer, by the way?" Pete asked. "You two seemed . . . tight."

Eva's grin evaporated. "Why don't you finish the introductions?"

"This is Sanannia T'vetari," Pete continued, and the woman on his left inclined her head. "She's pulling triple duty as our resident historian, appraiser and occasional medic."

Kloshian, almost human-looking except for her brilliant green skin and black eyes. As Eva watched, the color transitioned to a pale teal and the eyes lightened, mimicking iris and pupil even though the alien had neither. Thin tentacles that passed for hair were tied back in an approximation of a pony-tail, and the smile she gave Eva was thin-lipped to hide her jagged teeth.

"A pleasure, Ms. Innocente," she said. "I have heard much about you, all good."

"That's nice," Eva said. "And it's Captain Innocente." Appraiser could be useful. And she was clearly a pro liar, dropping a line like that without batting an eye. Hearing good about Eva? Please.

"Last but not least," Pete said, turning in his chair. "You might remember Nara Sumas, inventory control and customer service."

Eva snorted to hide her disgust. "Is that what they're calling bounty hunters now."

Nara stood behind Pete, arms crossed, face obscured by a smooth black helmet. "Stood" was the wrong word; "loomed" was better. Decked out in a suit of armor that would make a merc jealous, Nara was more than two meters tall and wide as a buasyr. Shorter outside of the suit, but not by much, and human.

And the last time Eva had seen the woman was on Garilia, from the wrong end of Nara's miniature plasma cannon. In Nara's defense, it was richly deserved, but Eva hadn't known that at the time.

Eva wondered how Pete could afford that kind of muscle. Knowing him, probably blackmail.

"Right, so." Eva leaned back in her chair. She had questions, sure, but she found her curiosity outweighed by a more powerful desire. "Now that we're all on friendly terms, let's talk about how we're going to get you off my ship."

Her father laughed. "Easy, my little bumblebee. We both know it's not as simple as all that. I've got my bosses to worry about, and you've been gone a long time. Long enough to be declared dead on most worlds."

Careful words, those. This was going to be fun. "Long enough, sure, but you and I both know how bureaucrats like to drag ass on that stuff. Otherwise every Fulano de Tal would be faking his own death to settle debts. So, *La Sirena Negra* is mine."

"El que fue a Sevilla perdió la silla, as your mother used to say," he said, folding his hands on the table. "The same lawyers will be happy to drag their asses about getting me evicted. Not to mention my bosses might have something to say about it, and your criminal record is still muddying the waters."

Damn it. To even take him to court, she'd have to settle whatever charges The Fridge had fabricated back when she was hiding on Nuvesta. Plus they might very well come after her again once they found out she was alive and obstructing their operations. Not good odds.

Eva let her gaze wander the room, as if she weren't interested. "Even if the ship isn't mine, by law it belongs to my crew. I left it to them in my will."

"And yet they are unfortunately absent, except for Min. So right now, one of us has a crew and a job, and the other is sadly short on either."

That was it, then. Forget checkmate—kick the board over and fuck off. His people might be mercs, one way or another, but she couldn't risk what amounted to mutiny all by herself, with injuries besides. Min might stand by her, but the pilot wasn't a fighter—could only do so much to make flying the ship hazardous enough that enemies would abandon it—and Eva had a hard time picturing herself putting a gun to her own father's head after what happened with Mari.

Not that he seemed too troubled by the reverse. He always did look out for number one first.

Eva let her gaze linger on each of his crew members. Jaedum's ears were still angled back, but otherwise he studiously ignored her. Sanannia met her eyes and smiled that same toothless smile. Nara stood there like a statue, black helmet glinting in the dim light.

Mala stretched her furry cat legs forward, arching her back with her butt in the air. Then, with the nonchalance only a cat can manage, she sauntered over to Eva and dropped into her lap, looking up at her with big hazel eyes and purring profusely.

"I stand corrected," Pete said. "No one is friendless if they have a cat. Though I suspect you'd have trouble maintaining a ship with just her."

Eva scratched Mala's chin. "So I suppose I'm the one who has to hitch a ride."

"Don't worry about that." Pete slapped the table and got to his feet, all sunshine and lollipops now. So pleased with himself, sinvergüenza. "I'll be happy to drop you wherever you like. Within reason, of course."

"Of course," she said sourly. He knew damn well she had nowhere to go. *La Sirena Negra* was her home, and he had taken it from her. She'd lost her old life to The Fridge, lost her crew, and now her hopes of clawing her way back out of this hole were sublimating.

But if she could get her crew back together, Pete would have to give up the ship or face a serious fight. Maybe even lawyers, god forbid; Pink's brother, for one, or if he was too busy he might have some recommendations. It was a deep hole, but the ace was in there. Somewhere.

"I don't suppose you have a spare ship lying around," she said tartly. "What with you taking mine and leaving me homeless and unemployed."

"You know, I might," Pete said, rubbing his chin as if he were only just thinking of it. Eva hated his bullshit mannerisms.

"Really," she said.

"It's not on my way, but I might be able to detour. As a favor."

Favors were currency. Favors had to be repaid. Not only had he screwed her over, now she was going to owe him. This cycle kept getting better. With family like this, who needed enemies?

Eva looked down at the cat. "You coming, or you staying here to keep an eye on these comemierdas?"

Mala meowed and dug her claws into Eva's lap.

"All right, I'll get you a case. Or are we bringing all your buddies, too?"

"The cats belong to Min," Pete said.

"Of course," Eva replied.

"Cap? I want to come, too. With you." Min spoke with her human mouth as she edged into the mess, hugging herself. She looked older, sadder, like she'd come down with a case of intestinal parasites she couldn't clear out. Which wasn't that far off, really.

Eva's jaw dropped. Speaking of hermit crabs leaving their shells, this was more like a soul leaving its body. She couldn't imagine anyone else piloting *La Sirena Negra*.

"Are you sure, Min?" she asked. "You don't have to."

"I know. I just . . . We can bring the cats, right?"

Eva nodded, swallowing a lump in her throat. It was more than she rightly deserved, after all she'd done. And she hoped Min wouldn't regret this later. Hoped the last year hadn't been so intolerable that this was preferable to staying.

It did wipe the smile off Pete's face, which was a plus.

Eva's stomach tensed. "Is any of my stuff still here, or did you throw it out the airlock at light speed?"

Pete rubbed the stubble on his chin. "I think we put some

things in the cargo bay. We did hope you'd make it back at some point, but we needed the room."

"What about my fish?"

His brow furrowed. "What fish?"

What fish, she thought. Fuck everything. When she finally got *La Sirena Negra* back, she was going to enjoy watching the airlock close behind him.

"Don't worry about it," Eva said. "Tell me about this new ship you're going to give me."

"This," Eva said, "is a giant piece of shit."

She, Min and Pete stood on the rocky ground of a small asteroid mining station, in front of a Yusari-class small cargo ship, a retrofitted buasyr craft that resembled a pair of lovebugs in midfuck. From where she stood, she could already tell it needed at least one aft thruster repaired and a grav clamp replaced, so she could only imagine what the guts looked like. Guts, no doubt.

"I thought you liked a challenge," Pete said, opening the remote cargo locks with his commlink.

"This isn't a challenge, it's a death sentence." Eva examined the metallic surface, which was reflective in an oily kind of way. Like a dark rainbow. "This thing breaks, I'm going to have to get out and push."

"Keep complaining about the free ship I'm giving you."

Eva shut up, but only because she didn't want to bite his head off. The starboard cargo bay door opened and Eva climbed inside, her left hip twinging in protest.

"Min, you coming?" she called back.

Min was still staring at the ship in dismay. It wouldn't have surprised Eva if Min was seriously considering going back to Pete. She might as well have been trading a spaceship for a bicycle.

Eva's initial prediction was unpleasantly accurate. All the pipes and cables that were neatly tucked away on *La Sirena Negra* were exposed here, as if some scrapper had come in and yanked out every panel that could be sold for more than a credit. Even the floor was gone, except for a single narrow path to the other side of the hold. An antigrav booster led up to the main deck through a gap in the ceiling. She called up lights with her commlink, and was relieved to see the power worked, even if it flickered and spat sparks.

"How am I even supposed to transport anything with this?" she asked.

"I'm sure you'll figure something out," Pete said. "You always do."

Annoyingly true. Eva was already analyzing the setup: variable low-grav, so she could string nets up to keep cargo away from the tender bits. If she calibrated it right, everything would just hover in the center of the room anyway . . .

She sniffed the air, which smelled like ozone and farts. "There's a gas leak," she said. "Gotta patch that before we go boom."

"I wasn't planning on smoking," Pete said.

Eva barely heard him. She was worlds away now, running mental system checks and sniffing her way to the source of the problem. There were probably tools somewhere on this station. Hell, maybe someone had left a few behind here. She'd also have to scavenge among the other busted ships and junk piles for parts, and if Pete wanted to give her shit about that, he could go fry ice.

She climbed up to the crew deck and poked around. It was pretty much a single long room with a galley on the port side and bunks welded to the starboard floor. The last owner hadn't even yanked out all the buasyr sleep pods, and the ones that were gone had left behind ugly metal stumps that apparently doubled as storage cubbies now.

The aft bridge, by contrast, was practically a palace. Some of the instrumentation still appeared functional, but most had been moved out for the installation of a bed big enough for a family, a desk, a couch, and even a private head with its own sanitizer unit and hydrosonic shower.

"What a waste of space," Eva muttered, looking out the open viewport at the stars spinning gently overhead. Then again, she'd never understood the whole double-pilot thing either, so who was she to judge.

She stalked to the fore bridge, passing Pete with hardly a thought. This was more what she was expecting, though it was strange to see the captain's seat right next to the pilot's chair in the middle of the room. That wasn't a buasyr setup either; this had been modded for some reason.

Eva sat in the captain's chair and synced her commlink to the ship's computer, holding her breath until that tiny mental nudge came, when the systems did the usual fist bump and hug. Something about that simple act felt like giving up, like *La Sirena Negra* was already gone and she was moving on. But that was what she did, wasn't it? Keep going. Move on. Don't linger too long in any one place, or the present would start to drag and the past would catch up.

She called up the diagnostics, reading through a laundry list of minor issues alongside the few major ones she'd already noted. Working long cycles, it would take at least a week to—

"Comfy?" Pete said, startling Eva out of her thoughts.

"Don't sneak," Eva said. "Beggars can't be choosers, right?"

"You always have a choice," Pete said quietly. "Don't ever let anyone tell you otherwise."

Eva opened her mouth to argue, then shut it, thinking of

Pholise suddenly. "She'll need some work before she's safe to fly," she said. "Some of it I can put off, but—"

"I'll leave you to it, then. Take any parts you want from the station." Pete crossed his arms like he was hugging himself, staring at Eva from across the room. Like maybe he had more to say but couldn't work up the testicular fortitude to spit it out.

"Salpica," Eva said. "I'll be fine. I'm a big girl."

"I noticed."

"No jodas tanto."

"No es lo que jode . . ."

The rest of the dicho hung in the air between them with everything else they weren't saying. Without another word, Pete waved and walked out. Eva watched him go, out onto the asteroid surface, back to her ship, and wondered where the fuck everything had gone so wrong.

The tears threatened to come again, the shakes, the inner scream that wanted to get out but wouldn't make her feel any better if she let it. She had fucked her crew over for a sister who never needed saving in the first place, and now here she was, trying to put Humpty Dumpty back together after he fell off a damn space elevator and hit the ground like a meteorite. Pink was gone, Leroy was gone, and Vakar . . .

Vakar. She had no idea where he was. One minute they're on a cruise, the next he's missing, and now what the fuck was she going to do?

Échale tierra y dale pisón, Eva told herself. One thing at a time. You've got Min, and you've got a ship to fix, before the fart smell gets any worse.

The new ship—which Eva christened *El Cucullo*—needed more of a crew than just her and Min, but she wasn't going to get the

band back together without making the damn thing space-
worthy, so that was step one. She started with the problems that
were easiest to fix, feeling a twinge of pleasure when some red
or yellow system diagnostic message flicked to green. But it was
still slower going than she had hoped, and every time she cut or
burned or zapped herself, she cursed the hour she was born that
no one was there to give her a hand.

Mala and the other cats were there, of course, but only as
moral support. They had no hands. And Min was busy integrat-
ing herself fully into the systems, getting comfy in her new shell.

Toward the end of the second cycle of work, Eva was deep in
the belly of the craft, trying to manually recalibrate the cargo
bay's grav core, when something crawled up her leg and perched
on her knee. Not knowing what it was, she went very still,
counted to three, then bashed the hell out of it with a wrench.

"Aw, sockets!" said a tinny, garbled voice.

Eva opened a panel in the bottom of the ship and peeked
out, upside down, at a human in a pink flight suit examining
a tiny clump of yellow metal. Her black hair was spiked out at
odd angles, and her face was smooth as a baby's butt and just
as dimpled and chubby. She hardly looked old enough to drink,
much less show up alone at a random secret shipyard by herself.

"The hell are you?" Eva said.

The girl frowned. "You hit Forty."

"I'm gonna hit your face if you don't talk fast."

"Agent Virgo told me you were tough," the girl said. "She
didn't say you were Cranky McCrankerson. I'm your new engineer, Susan Zafone. You can call me Sue."

Eva forced her face into neutral before her emotions took
off with it. "Hey, Sue," she said. "Sorry about the, ah . . ." She
waved her wrench at the yellow thing, which winced and let out
a squeal. "I didn't know you were coming."

"Really?" Sue's brow furrowed. "I've been signaling you for hours."

Eva had turned off comm notifications after an incident with the firewalls. Whoops. "I've been busy," she said. "Give me a minute."

She slid back inside and turned the ship's comm back on, then pinged Min. ((Messages?))

((Wow, yes.))

The pilot sent them over. There were several from Sue, and one from Mari. Audio only. Eva pulled that one up and closed her eyes.

"Congratulations on finagling yourself a new ship," Mari's message said. "I was hoping you would end up somewhere out of trouble, but at this point it's enough if you at least stay away from The Fridge."

"Not fucking likely," Eva muttered.

The message continued. "I've got another person who—well, it's a long story and not really your business, but she needs to lie low, too. So she comes with you, and you pretend like you're not babysitting."

"Not happening, mija," Eva said. She'd drop this girl off the first chance she got.

"She's an excellent engineer, so she should be able to pull her own weight. Or Vakar's, I suppose, unless you can find him. Meanwhile, I have to get back to The Fridge before they realize I'm off-mission. Cuídate." The message ended.

"Carajo. I do need an engineer." Eva frowned.

"Everything okay?" Sue called from outside.

"Solid as a hull." Eva slid back out, still upside down. "I haven't listened to all the messages, so why don't you fill me in on what they said?"

Sue's already-pale skin went a shade lighter, even as her cheeks turned as pink as her shirt.

"Well, okay," she said meekly. "The most recent ones were mostly me saying I was on my way. I only got lost once!"

"That's . . . good." Eva idly tapped her wrench against the ship's plating. "What else?"

"I, uh . . . oh, Agent Virgo had me tell you about my background."

"Which is?"

The engineer squirmed. "I'm originally from Nakkai—that's a settlement in the Ryship system—but we had to leave when I was little."

"Why?"

"There was a huge Proarkhe discovery!" Eva mentally groaned at the mention of the aliens, but Sue's discomfort was replaced by excitement, and she began talking faster and faster. "My big brother Josh was there, and he said it was this huge cave, and in the middle there was a weird pink lake with these ancient pumps that no one could figure out how to turn on, and—" She must have realized she was rambling, because she stopped and cleared her throat. "Anyway, some BOFA people showed up and kicked us all out."

Eva stopped tapping her wrench. "The whole planet?"

"Yeah. So we had to move to Katoru."

"That's near Nuvesta, isn't it?"

"Yeah." Sue's expression darkened. "It was a pretty quiet place. All my friends left for Nuvesta when they got old enough, but I stayed behind to work at my family's shipyard. Mostly repairs."

"Mostly?"

Her cheeks pinked again, and she gave Eva a shy smile. "I also designed and built mech prototypes. When I had time."

"Interesting." Especially given how young she was. If the engineer was old enough for her class-D pilot's license, Eva would eat her gravboots. "Well, welcome aboard, Sue. I'll introduce you to Min, and then we can—"

"Captain Innocente," Sue interrupted, standing straighter, her mouth set in a determined line. "There's something Agent Virgo didn't want me to tell you."

Eva raised an eyebrow. "And that is?"

"I . . . I'm kind of a criminal."

"A criminal?" This she had to hear.

"I figure you'd find out eventually, so I wanted to tell you first. Some bad people kidnapped Josh, and my family has been trying to pay the ransom for months. I got . . . impatient, so I started doing things I shouldn't have." A pause. "I may have robbed a few banks. And an asteroid mine. And a vet clinic, but that was an accident."

Bad people and kidnapping? Odds were she meant The Fridge, especially if Mari was involved. And that explained why Sue needed to lie low, as Mari had put it—Fridge problems plus a criminal record likely meant someone was after her. BOFA? Some planetary or system authority? People Eva was eager to avoid herself, no doubt.

"I understand if you don't want me on your crew," Sue continued, voice trembling as if she was holding back tears. "I promised Agent Virgo I'd stay out of trouble, though. She said you could help. I'd really appreciate that."

Oh, Eva was going to help, all right. Mari was trying to saddle her with this girl to keep her from going to certain places, or doing something reckless, out of a sense of responsibility. But Sue was old enough to make her own choices, and if the girl wanted to go after The Fridge and find her brother, Eva was more than happy to facilitate.

Eva grinned. "I think we're going to get along just fine. Would have been great to have you sooner, but there's still plenty to do."

Sue's expression brightened. "You bet! I'm great with repairs. What's left?"

Wiping sweat off her forehead, Eva gestured with her other hand at the grav core. "Trying to calibrate this, and then I wanted to see if I could fix some of the ablation damage to the secondary landing thruster before I—"

"I can do that," Sue said. She put two fingers in her mouth and whistled sharply. "Line up, everybody!" she shouted.

As if by magic, dozens of tiny yellow robots appeared, swarming over each other as they formed up in three single-file lines and turned in unison to face Sue.

"All right, troops, we've got an assignment." Sue marched in front of them like a drill sergeant, hands behind her back. "Ablation damage to the secondary landing thruster. Patch it up, smooth it out, and get back here on the double." She whistled again, and off they went in a rush, like a hungry mob at a buffet.

Eva watched it all with a raised eyebrow, unsure whether to be worried or impressed. "Did you make those?"

"Yeah." Sue practically preened. "They're best suited for repairs, cleaning, that kind of stuff." Her eyes widened as she leaned closer to Eva. "Just don't let them get any curry," she murmured. "Wreaks havoc on their little systems. Flaming burps for cycles."

"All right, as long as they don't muck up my ship." Eva climbed back up into the grav core, thought for a moment, then swung back out. "Get on board, pick a bunk. And make sure your yellow buddies don't mess with my pilot's cats, okay?"

Sue's face went white. "You have— Oh no." She ran up the cargo ramp.

Girl couldn't have been much out of her teens. A criminal already, thanks to The Fridge. But as long as she was a better engineer than Eva—

"Cap," Min said through the speakers.

"Yeah?"

"Are there any problems with my systems? Because I suddenly feel . . . tickled."

For the first time since Mari found her, Eva laughed, loud and long.

Maybe she would be able to make this work after all. Now that she had Min, it was just a matter of finding Pink, who would hopefully know what happened to Vakar.

And once Eva pulled her crew back together, she was going to give Pete a little visit. They'd see who was friendless then.

Chapter 20

ME SUBE LA BILIRRUBINA

Two cycles and countless repairs later, Min brought *El Cucullo* in for a gentle landing on Sceilara, one of Kepra's twelve moons. Kepra was a gas giant, and most of its moons were settled by miners, except Sceilara. What had started as a cozy spot for smugglers to hide in had been gentrified over time into a part-trendy, part-tacky destination for people who believed night-time was the right time to party. Sex, drugs, gambling . . . all manners of entertainment were available for a price, and all species with negotiable currency were welcome. There were still smugglers, of course; gentrification didn't stop them, but it did give them handy targets, if they were suave and subtle enough.

Pink's place was on the cusp of a seedier area, within a quick hop of the high-class spots but catering to folks who worked for a living, often underneath the people who played for a living. Like every other building on that street, its dark walls were outlined with brightly colored lights, the flashing sign out front simply reading CLINIC in alternating green, orange and, of course, pink.

Eva cursed under her breath about docking fees and the price of skycabs as she walked into a crowded waiting room. A dozen pairs of eyes took her in, along with a couple of probosci (proboscises? proboscodes? Eva could never remember) and a scandalously long purple tongue. She ignored them and ambled up to the receptionist, a kloshian who offered her a close-mouthed smile before returning his attention to whatever was streaming on his commlink.

"I'm here to see Dr. Jones," Eva said.

"Please provide an accepted form of identification and fill this out." He slid a datapad to Eva without losing his glassy-eyed commlink stare.

"I'm not a patient, I'm a friend. I need to see her."

"The doctor is engaged in a delicate examination at present and cannot be disturbed."

Right, and Eva was the queen of Spain. "How long is it going to take?"

"I am not at liberty to estimate, but if you'll provide an accepted form of—"

"Come on," Eva said. "Just tell her Eva is here. She'll want to see me." That was probably not entirely untrue.

"With respect, the doctor's friends don't visit her at her place of work during business hours."

One of the waiting humans spoke up. "We were here first, lady. Get in line." The others muttered agreement.

Normally she wouldn't have minded waiting—or at least, she would have pretended she didn't mind while being enormously grumpy about it. Okay, fine, she hated waiting with the passion of a million white-hot stars. But in her defense this time, docking fees were charged by the hour on this resingado chunk of vice, so she needed to leave as quickly as possible.

"How about I show myself in and she'll forgive you later?" Eva said.

"How about the door is locked and I've just armed the security lasers?" the receptionist replied.

Eva threw up her hands. "Fine, me cago en diez, I'll just ping her."

"No, I told you, she's in—"

((Pink,)) Eva pinged. ((Waiting room.))

From the back, a low hum was followed by a wet thud. Silence dropped like the kind of bass note you feel rather than hear, and a full minute later a door opened.

Pink stepped into the reception area, her nose and mouth obscured by an air filter, her mint-green biosuit covered in bright red blood. One of the humans in the waiting room squealed, and the alien with the long tongue let out a low moan.

"Well, that was not good, but he'll live," Pink said. "Welcome back from the dead, Eva. You look like something a cat puked up."

Eva had cleaned up the worst of her injuries, but she still had a few choice cuts on her face along with a split lip and a bruise under her right eye.

"You're the one with blood all over you," she replied.

"It's not mine. The other doctor on duty is handling the situation." Pink's cybernetic iris widened and contracted as she stared at Eva. "This had better be an epic story, and you've got about five minutes to tell it. I have to get back to my patients."

Eva reached out a hand for their usual handshake, but Pink ignored it. Not an auspicious start to the conversation.

"Not much to tell," Eva said, following Pink to an exam room. The walls were a soothing pale blue lined with cabinets, and a long chair floated in midair, facing a small vidscreen meant to look like a window onto the bright lights outside. There was also blood on several surfaces, not including the chair, which Eva sat on.

"A year is a long time for nothing to happen." Pink began carefully removing her bloody scrubs, glancing at Eva as she did.

The chair reclined gently as Eva leaned back into it. "I took an ice nap, woke up in the middle of a shitstorm, and now I'm trying to pull my life back together. The usual."

"You get *La Sirena Negra* back?"

"Nah, Pete's still got it. I did take down Glorious, though, so that's something."

"You took down— No, don't tell me, that's going to be a lot." Pink dropped her scrubs into a yellow box marked with a hazard symbol, followed by her gloves. "If you don't have a ship, how did you get here?"

"Got another ship from Pete. A real piece of shit, but I made it work. How did he end up with *La Sirena Negra* anyway?"

"I made the mistake of asking him for help finding you. By the time I figured out he was working for The Fridge, he'd already brought his whole squad on board and I didn't feel like using my medical powers for evil."

Eva scowled. "Did you leave, or did he kick you out?"

"I left." Pink jammed her hands into a sanitizer pod. "Went to live with my brother and his family for a while, which was nice, but I couldn't stay there waiting on you forever."

"At least something good came of this shit. Sceilara, though? Why here?"

"Turns out, working as a medic on a small cargo freighter doesn't get you the kind of experience a cushy doctor's office wants to see."

"Mierda, Pink, I'm sorry."

Pink pulled her hands out and moved to a nearby counter to fiddle with equipment Eva didn't recognize. "So you've got some grand plan to go after The Fridge again, and you want me to help?"

"I'm trying to get my ship back first. Revenge later." Eva sucked in a breath, staring at the fake window. "I don't suppose you know where Vakar is?"

"Not a clue. You both disappeared at the same time."

Eva released her grip on the hope she'd been clinging to. It had been a silly idea in the first place, trying to gather up the frayed ends of her old life. For her, it had been only a few moments, but for everyone else? A year was a long time; people moved on, and asking them to come back was as stupid as asking her dad to turn over a ship he'd made into his home and livelihood.

Still, Eva's abuela had always told her she was stubborn as a goat. Or was it crazy?

Pink pulled on a fresh set of gloves and set to wiping blood off the counter. "I'm sure you have a diplomatic and peaceable plan for getting our ship away from Pete."

"It's complicated. I was hoping if I could find all of you, get back to *La Sirena Negra,* maybe he would—"

"Roll over and play dead? This is the same Pete we're talking about, yeah?"

Eva resisted the urge to dunk her head into the sterilizer unit.

"And then?" Pink continued. "Duck and run for as long as it takes? Let me know when I get to the complicated part, by the way." She made a final brisk swipe, leaving the counter white as bone.

Pink had always liked to help people, even ones who needed the help because they'd screwed themselves over. Eva wanted to give her that: the righteous cause. The good fight.

But Eva knew all too well that no good deed went unpunished.

A thought occurred to her. "How's the lawsuit coming?" she asked.

"The habitat one?" Pink grinned. "They settled. My brother got us enough media attention that their sweet little honeypot turned into a beehive. We weren't the only group they'd pulled the same tricks on, and once everyone started comparing data, they couldn't shut us up fast enough."

"No shit." Any win against a big corporation was huge, beyond David and Goliath. More like ant versus elephant. But if you got enough ants together, if the ants were angry enough and careful enough . . .

"You know what?" Eva said. "You're right. It's not complicated. I want my ship back, and I want my crew back, and I want The Fridge blasted to a smoking crater so I can piss on the ashes. If someone else doesn't do it, I will. And I think I know someone who's planning on doing it in the next few cycles."

To her surprise, Pink laughed. "For a minute, I thought you were getting introspective on me. Nothing worse than being cooped up on a ship with a philosopher."

"So you're coming?" Eva tried to keep her tone neutral instead of eager-puppy.

"What's in it for me?" Pink asked, arms crossed.

"You get off this tired-ass rock, for one. Back to the black, wandering the galaxy instead of being stuck here."

"I didn't realize I was a sweet young moisture farmer with dreams of space travel." Pink tossed her soiled cleaning cloth into the yellow hazard box and grabbed a fresh one. "Maybe I'm old and I like solid ground under me now."

"You're not even forty."

"Y'all make me tired enough to be a hundred."

"Revenge, then," Eva said. "Against Pete, at least. And The Fridge, though that's more my target than yours."

"I would enjoy giving Pete a severe case of heartburn," Pink said, scrubbing at a stubborn bit of sticky blood. "Messing with The Fridge is more justice than revenge, but it would still be sweet. Not sweet enough, though. What else you got?"

Eva sank into the chair, squinting. "I'll be your best friend?" she offered tentatively.

Pink snorted. "You damn toddler, I'm already your best friend. What next, pretty please with sugar on top?"

"You want sugar? I'll get you sugar. All the sugar you can eat."

Pink pretended to throw the bottle of cleaning solution at Eva, who shielded her face with her arms.

"I'll make you co-captain," Eva said. "Big pay raise. You can even have my cabin."

"I don't want your cabin, and I know you pay yourself less than the rest of us, fool." Pink threw out her other cloth and stripped off her gloves, tossing those in the yellow bin as well. "I might take that co-captain title, though. Captain Rebecca Jones, hmm. Sounds sexy."

"It wouldn't just be a title." Eva sat up, leaning toward Pink and gripping the side of the chair. "I mean it. Equal partners, you and me."

"You definitely need someone around to keep an eye on you."

"What'll you do with the other eye?"

Pink threw her a glance that would melt rebar.

"Let me take care of my patients," Pink said. "Which includes you, fool. Coming in here looking like you got jumped in a back alley." She flipped up her eye patch and appraised Eva more critically. "You've got multiple broken ribs and some ugly lacerations on your chest. Did you crash a ship or something?"

"That's your first guess? Do I crash a lot of ships, is that a thing I do?"

Pink raised an eyebrow.

"Okay, fine," Eva said. "I crashed a ship. You happy?"

Pink shook her head, but she was smiling.

Yeah, things are gonna be all right, Eva thought. Or at least not quite so wrong.

They took a cab back to the spaceport. Min was delighted to see Pink, and Sue was aggressively cheerful, which Eva decided was either her natural state or an elaborate defense mechanism. Maybe both. Mala was Mala, and purred prodigiously, along with the rest of the cats.

"So what's our next stop, fearless coleader?" Pink asked after settling into her new med bay.

Eva flopped into the captain's chair next to Min, staring out the viewport at the stars.

Once upon a time, she had thought she was giving these people, her people, a good life. Room and board, a job, eventually something like a family. They'd finally climbed past the bottom rung of the ladder and she'd pulled them all back down again with her stupid Fridge problem. And now she was scouring the galaxy to find them all so she could get her ship back and lead everyone on a wild crusade, because . . . Why?

Revenge, sure, but that wasn't all. The Fridge was doing grotesque crap, and they'd keep doing it unless someone stopped them. She was only one person, but one person doing something was better than a whole lot of people doing nothing. Change had to start somewhere, with someone, and it might as well be her. Maybe it was like her dad had said: flip the right Reversi piece, and next thing you knew, the board would look a whole lot less dark.

But maybe more importantly, she just wanted her life back. Her family back.

Vakar back.

Eva pursed her lips. "What do you think, Captain Jones?"

Pink chuckled. "You know, I do like how that sounds, especially coming from you." Her expression softened. "I'm guessing you want to try finding Vakar?"

"I do." Eva rubbed her neck, her face burning. "But if my intel is right, some big Fridge arroz con mango will be happening in about two or three cycles. That doesn't leave us a lot of time."

"I had thought about trying to find his sister, to see if she knew where you two were, but you know. Things got busy."

Vakar's sister, of course. What was her name? Paula? Pollea!

"That's it," Eva said. "We start with her and see where it takes us." It was something, at least. More than she'd had a minute ago.

"Cap," Min said. "You've got a call on the emergency channel."

"Yeah? Let's have it." Eva crossed her arms and scowled.

Min hesitated. "You don't want it in your room?"

Eva shook her head. "No more secrets. Bring it up."

Her sister's face appeared in the comm projection. Tiny lines between her eyebrows betrayed more feeling than she typically allowed.

"Eva, you comemierda, I cannot believe you," Mari said.

Pink whispered in Eva's ear, "Isn't that your sister?"

"I'll tell you in a minute," Eva muttered back. To Mari, she said. "How may I assist you, Agent Virgo?"

"The Fridge has been monitoring your aliases since you went missing, including the one you just used on Sceilara. That means now they know you're alive and free."

Eva winced, recovering quickly. "I didn't have time to put together a new identity in a hurry. What's done is done. I've got Pink, Leroy is doing his own thing, and now I'm going after Vakar."

"How? The quennians aren't going to cooperate, you know. His records are sealed." Mari's smug face was so punchable, Eva briefly regretted not having taken a swing while she had the chance.

"I'm going to check with his sister," Eva retorted. "I'm sure you were too busy to stop in and chat with her, what with all your spying and shit, but maybe she'll talk to me."

"I was too busy, yes. I know you think this is all some elaborate game, but—" Mari froze, leaning away from the vidcam for a few moments before straightening again, her expression flat. "They bugged my comms. I have to go."

Mari vanished. Eva stared at the place where her sister's face had been, her mind pulled in a dozen directions. Presumably Mari meant The Fridge had bugged her comms, which meant they had heard the whole conversation, which meant Mari's cover was blown. Mierda, mojón y porquería.

"What on god's good green earth just happened?" Pink asked, one hand on Eva's chair.

"Mari was a double agent for The Fridge the whole time," Eva said, massaging her temple with one hand. "She's the one who pulled me out of cryo, but also she sold me out in the first place to get in good with them. Sorry I didn't tell you earlier."

Pink fell silent for so long that Eva finally twisted around to look up at her.

"Eva," Pink said. "That is real messed up. That is ten kilos of wrong in a five-kilo bag."

"Yeah."

"I'm serious." Pink knelt down and put both hands on Eva's shoulders. "Look at me, Eva Innocente."

Eva stared into Pink's eye, fighting the urge to look away.

"You didn't deserve that," Pink said. "You've made a lot of stupid choices, and I know you'll never forgive yourself for what happened on Garilia, but you're half an asshole trying to do better. Your family are whole entire assholes. You hear me?"

"My mom isn't so bad," Eva muttered.

Pink gave a short laugh and stood. "I'm starting you on therapy again as soon as we have a minute to breathe, woman. Don't you let me forget."

Eva nodded, finding herself unable to speak past the tightness in her throat.

"So what now, Cap?" Min asked.

Eva swallowed, flexing her hands. "We find Vakar's sister," she said. "She's on, fuck, what was the place called . . ." Mari had told her, just after she woke up. Last place Vakar was seen. Come on, Eva, think. "He was on a ship, and his sister was on some station in Crux Hemithea."

"DS Nor?" Min asked.

"DS Nor, that's it, of course. Big hub. Move it." Eva paused. "Assuming that's okay with my co-captain."

Pink grinned and patted Eva's head. "Next time, ask me before you start barking orders, 'kay?"

The FTL drives whined on, and Eva sent up yet another prayer to the Virgin for luck. Because if The Fridge had been listening to that conversation, they were probably on their way to Vakar's sister as well, and all Eva could do was hope she got there first.

Forty-seven minutes later, they were docking at DS Nor, a space station primarily for personnel involved in resource mining in the Crux Hemithea system. It was also a popular waystation for travelers, plopped as it was right next to not one but two Gates. Security was no tighter than most places with a high turnover; whatever credentials Pete had set up for *El Cucullo* seemed to be solid, and Eva's alias hadn't been burned by The Fridge for some reason, so they docked without incident.

Probably walking into a trap, Eva thought. At least weapons were outlawed, so all she had to worry about were the million other ways someone might come after her.

"You think we can manage this without violence?" Pink asked.

"We can try," Eva said.

"Eva, come on," Pink said. "I'd like to walk out of here calmly, without someone chasing me down or trying to kill me."

"I can't control what other people do."

Pink rolled her eye. "Can you at least promise me not to start any unnecessary fights?"

"Sure, I promise."

Getting to Vakar's sister meant walking down an endless circular corridor leading to the station's living quarters, past what seemed like a million identical doors. Pink had wrapped Eva's chest in stiff bandages and told her not to cough, or sneeze, or laugh. Her bones were still a work in progress, her skin was raw and itchy where the Albatross's restraints had dug into her chest and stomach, and her bruises were fresh as a country road. Which was to say, shitty.

"Hey, remember the last time you did something like this, on that cruise ship?" Pink asked.

"Yeah," Eva replied.

"Remember how you ended up a meat popsicle?"

"I do remember that."

"Just making sure."

They finally stopped in front of a nondescript door labeled

D-12, its only differentiating feature a tiny crystal stuck to the top of the doorframe. Eva raised her hand to knock, but hesitated. She was so close to finding Vakar, and all she could think was that something was about to go terribly wrong. It always did.

She knocked. Nothing. She knocked again.

"Maybe she's out," Pink said. "You think people just wait around in case you want to see them?"

Eva shrugged, then banged on the door more loudly, a booming staccato rhythm. On the third knock, an unseen intercom crackled.

"What do you require?" said a trembling voice.

"Station security," Eva said. "We need to speak to Pollea Tremonis san Jaigodaris."

"You are not in uniform."

"Undercover, ma'am. Please open the door or we'll use our priority access key to force entry."

Eva had no access key, but she assumed they existed. Cops on these kinds of stations gave zero craps about things like privacy rights and the violation thereof. When there was no immediate response, she assumed the worst and tensed up, leaning on the balls of her feet.

As soon as the door began to iris open, she dodged to the side of the doorway, expecting to get jumped. Instead, a quennian in a blue coverall poked her head out, staring at Eva. She smelled confused, suspicious, and enough like Vakar that it hurt.

Eva grabbed her by the arms and pulled her into the hallway, depositing the woman next to her and then glancing into the room. It looked perfectly ordinary, and empty of other people.

"Pollea Tremonis san Jaigodaris?" she asked.

"What is the meaning of this?" Her coloring was similar to Vakar's, too, eyes almost the same blue. Eva froze for a moment, lost in memory, then shook it off.

"Has anyone contacted you within the last hour?" Eva asked.

"I was told a station plumber would come to fix a leak in the wall tank. He should arrive any minute."

Probably The Fridge. Had she really beaten them here? She felt positively giddy. Unless this wasn't really Vakar's sister . . . But no, she smelled like him. Unless that was just Eva projecting.

Paranoia was a hell of a drug.

"We don't have much time," Eva said. "You're in danger, and we're here to keep you safe. Pink, search the room."

((For what?)) Pink pinged at her.

((Anything weird.)) Eva pinged. ((Struggle signs.))

"You cannot simply force entry and ransack my quarters!" Pollea exclaimed.

"Keep it down," Eva said. "We can talk inside. The plumber isn't a plumber, and more people may be on the way to kidnap you."

That got Pollea's attention. She stiffened, palps twitching. Eva gestured at the doorway and Pollea entered, followed by Eva, who closed the door.

Pollea stood in the living room while Pink gently poked around in the bedroom. There was also a bathroom and a kitchen. Cozy. Standard decor in the putty color of recycled materials, but with vibrant pops of purple, green and blue in a few places. Eva stepped over to examine the nearest one.

"Who are you and what do you want from me?" Pollea asked.

"I need information. It's about your brother." The colors turned out to be arrangements of plantlike crystals, like Vakar used to grow. The pieces fused together seamlessly, some of them small clusters of saltlike cubes, others larger hexagonal pieces that tapered to a point. They sat in delicate glass containers with necks no wider than her pinkie, and she remembered how carefully he would place the seeds inside, coaxing them to splice and nurturing them with different blends of chemicals only he understood.

"Has something happened? He was missing for so long, and then—" Pollea shut up, as if realizing she was about to say something she shouldn't.

Eva leaned in closer to examine one of the purple crystals. A wisp of smell drifted up and she stumbled back a step.

"Where did you get that?" she asked.

"A gift from my brother." Pollea smelled slightly less anxious. "His little hobby, growing these. Well, not anymore, I suppose, since he left that ship he was on."

It smelled like Vakar when he was melancholy, with an undercurrent of . . . loneliness? Yearning?

"All clear," Pink said, leaning against a kitchen cabinet. "You realize you can't just leave her here, right?"

Pollea stared at Eva, smelling concerned.

"Right," Eva replied hoarsely. "If anything happened to her, Vakar would never forgive me."

"Who did you say you were?" Pollea asked.

"I didn't," Eva said. "I was—" She swallowed. What was she? She thought she knew, but so many things had changed.

"I was captain on the ship Vakar left," she said finally. "*La Sirena Negra*. We were close, and things went bad—nothing to do with him. But I need to find him." I want to find him, she didn't say. I miss him so much it hurts to breathe in here.

"He never said where he was, not since he . . . He said it was easier that way. Is he in danger? His last message was infuriatingly cryptic, and—"

"So he has contacted you," Eva said. "There has to be something, some way to trace the messages back to their point of origin." She stepped over to the cluster of blue crystals and smelled the opening. Like cut grass. Bashful, shy. Eva's eyes watered. She'd come too far, gotten too close for this to be another dead end.

"There are some parts that are memlocked," Pollea said. "But they aren't for me. He said it was probably a waste of time, but he always included them just in case. Something to do with the fish." Her palps twitched.

"Fish?" Pink asked.

Pollea gestured, and a panel in the wall slid back.

There, floating peaceful as you please, were Eva's missing fish.

"Alabao," Eva whispered. How had that sly bastard . . . Never mind. "Those are my fish. Give me the last message. Please."

She opened her commlink to receive and Pollea, after a moment's hesitation, sent it over.

It was audio only, but her chest tightened at the sound of Vakar's voice. It had been a few cycles since she'd last seen him, from her perspective, but everyone else's time difference had tainted her perceptions, making it feel much longer. Or so she told herself.

"Pol, hope you're well," he began. "Apologies for the delay between communications. Work has been challenging, as usual. Give my love to everyone, and pray for me. I believe I'll need it this time." The recording stopped there.

Eva let out the breath she hadn't realized she was holding. The memlock loomed in her mind like the wall of a safe, waiting for the code to unlock it.

Only for me, she thought. She let the memlock rifle through her mind, looking for the right key. Memories rose unbidden: the taste of his face. Showing him how to make real coffee. Crawling into the guts of the ship to tell him something instead of just pinging him. She thought she might burst before the thing was through with her.

The two of them grappling in the cargo hold. Pastelitos. Another kind of grappling.

The smell of licorice.

Another recording began to play. "Eva, if you are hearing this . . . Many things have happened since you were taken, but we can share stories later, with any luck. I assume this means you finally came looking for me for . . . whatever reason." He paused.

"Finally"? she thought. "For whatever reason"? The hell did that mean?

"I am involved in some work I think you might be interested in. It is a breach of security to tell you this, so please be discreet. I am not sure how long I will be at the attached coordinates. Not very long, if all goes well. If not . . ." He paused again, and she swallowed a scream. "If not, I would consider it a personal favor if you could return my remains to my family. Assuming anything is left. Otherwise, please tell them I am sorry. Again."

Eva stood still as a post until Pink put a hand on her shoulder.

"Well?" Pink asked.

"When did you get this message?" Eva asked.

"Last cycle," Pollea said.

"Last cycle," Eva repeated. "If he got himself killed, I'm going to kill him."

Pink grinned. "And if not?"

"I'm going to get my ship back, and then I'm going to kill him."

There was a knock at the door.

"Answer it," Eva said.

Pollea, who had been as still as Eva, jerked her head sideways. "Yes, who is it?"

The intercom beeped. "Plumber. Here to fix the leak."

"Good." Eva cracked her knuckles. "I want to have a word with him."

"You promised, no fighting." Pink glared at her.

"You think this is going to be a real fight? Please. Don't make me laugh. You told me not to laugh, either."

The door opened, and Eva pulled the man inside.

"How was I supposed to know he was an actual plumber?" Eva said, opening the cargo bay doors.

"You could have asked before you got him in that sleeper hold," Pink said.

"Oh sure. 'Hi, are you a plumber or a secret ag—'" Eva froze, staring at the strange tableau before her.

Four people lay motionless on the floor of the cargo bay. On one side, two humans were buried in small, furry creatures that purred in unison like a giant living engine. On the other, a human and a kloshian were covered in smoking burn marks that smelled like lechón and crema catalana, respectively. A horde of robots stood guard over them.

Pollea stepped closer to Eva, luggage clutched to her chest like a shield. "Is that your crew?"

"I don't know if I'd call them crew, per se, but they certainly seem to be responsible for— Oh, you mean the other guys. Nope, not mine. They're the reason we came to get you." Eva approached the cats, whose expressions were a touch more smug than usual. "Pink, shall we take out the trash?"

"I can help," Sue said, climbing down the rear access ladder. "You're supposed to be resting, remember?"

Eva scrunched her lips into a frown. "I can rest on our way to Vela Perileos. Min, set a course. You." She pointed at Pollea. "Follow me."

She gave Vakar's sister the grand tour of *El Cucullo*, which wasn't long, and set her up with a bunk. It occurred to Eva that this was a potentially scary situation, being spirited away from home by a stranger to go rushing into unknown danger. She tried to think of something comforting to tell the woman.

"We probably won't die," she said.

"Excuse me?" Pollea stared at her, blinking her inner eyelids rapidly.

"I mean, *you* probably won't die," she amended. "And I haven't died yet, so my track record is pretty good. And I've saved Vakar's life a few times, so I figure I can do it again if I have to."

"You are attempting to give me courage, Captain?"

Or me, Eva thought. For all she knew, she was flying into a hot mess to pick up a cold corpse.

"You hungry?" she asked instead. "Sue is pretty good at making rations taste almost like food."

Pollea cocked her head to one side, a gesture so like Vakar's that Eva's breath snagged. "I am confused, and worried, and brimming with questions about all this. Hungry, I am not."

The ship's engines whined to life, and the bottom dropped out of Eva's stomach as *El Cucullo* took off. She leaned one hand against a bulkhead, wincing at the way her outstretched arm pulled at her bandages.

"You're as straightforward as your brother," she said quietly. "What do you want to know?"

"Everything."

"That narrows it down." She sank to the floor, resting her forehead on one hand. Where to even start? The Fridge? Cryo? Garilia?

"Once upon a time," Eva said, "a really cocky idiot thought it would be funny to lick a quennian."

Chapter 21

IT'S DANGEROUS TO GO ALONE

Vela Perileos didn't get a lot of attention because it was hours from the nearest Gate, its resources had been strip-mined long ago, and its planets bore the scars of some ancient battles that frankly gave most people the heebie-jeebies. Periodically, archaeology professors would trek out to a moon or something and spend a few weeks digging around in the dirt, find tiny pieces of stuff, write books about how the stuff was probably an ancient hair dryer, and force their students to buy the books so they could eat off the royalties.

It was, for all practical purposes, a dead system, and Eva had the bad feeling she was about to kick over some headstones.

Vakar's coordinates put him on Cavus, the fourth planet from the star. The place was technically under quennian jurisdiction, and they'd designated it as off-limits. Mysterious. That usually meant military shenanigans, or something really embarrassing to someone with enough power to build walls of bullshit.

El Cucullo touched down on a surface pockmarked with impact craters, its atmosphere thin as a whistle. Off to one side was a gentle slope into a valley dotted with squat, scrubby plants, while in all other directions the ground was level and bare as rock. Two other ships waited nearby: a stocky little Javelin-class beauty with no identifying marks, and a quennian vessel called *Persistent Ingenuity,* the dimness of its ruby hull suggesting it was empty, inert. Not a good sign.

Also not a good sign: Eva tried to ping Vakar, but there was no reply. He could be outside of ping range, or, well. Way outside of ping range, permanently.

"I want to come with you," Pollea said.

"Nope." Eva checked her weapons, and her backup weapons, and her emergency backup weapons. Then she scowled because she had to pee.

"He is my brother. I cannot simply sit here while you—"

"Listen, I can give you a long lecture about how bringing you would be the"—Eva counted on her fingers—"third-stupidest thing I've ever done. But I won't. I know how you feel, and I respect it, and I wouldn't take you along if you paid me double the bounty I used to have on my head."

"Why not?"

"Because I won't." Eva stared up at Pollea, gritting her teeth. Because, you dumbass, if anything happened to you, I could never speak to Vakar again as long as I lived. "Just sit tight. Help Sue with repairs if you need something useful to do. Pink, you're co-captain, so—"

"I'm coming with you?" Pink checked the sidearm she carried when sniping wasn't practical. "And don't even try to argue. Vakar is my friend, too, and you're still recovering."

Eva hesitated. "I don't want you to get hurt is all."

"Then you should have left me on Sceilara." Pink activated her isohelmet and gestured at the door. "After you."

Eva nodded, then activated her own helmet and slipped into the airlock before Pollea could renew her protests. Her suit's sensors told her the air was chilly in the pale blue light of dawn, and the gravity was a little lower than Earth standard, so she and Pink took big bouncy steps toward the quennian ship.

The door had a piezoelectric interface, which she'd never gotten the knack of hacking. After a few failed tries, she pinged Min to do it for her.

((Sure, Cap.)) A few moments later the rear hatch slid open, and she and Pink crawled inside.

The interior was a typical mishmash of retrofitted universal parts and carefully shaped crystalline structures of varying colors, mostly red. She activated the console to see whether there were any logs to give her a hint as to what the ship was here for.

"Access restricted," she said.

"Big surprise," Pink replied. "At least we haven't triggered any nasty security traps."

"Not yet," Eva replied. "Let's keep looking around."

Crew quarters, feeding-tube stations, lounge area. Normal stuff. Boring. And more importantly, there was no sign of Vakar.

"Smells like the crew has been gone for a while," Eva said. "You see anything interesting with your magic eye?"

"Not especially," Pink said, then paused. "Well, that's something. I'm getting strange business from behind that door."

Eva checked the door. Locked. "What kind of strange?" she asked.

"Like a quennian, but not. It's hard to describe."

"Be bold, be bold, but not too bold," Eva muttered to herself, and pinged Min again. To her surprise, this took longer to hack, causing Min to use a word Eva hadn't realized she knew. But the door finally slid open, and Eva gestured at Pink to wait while she looked around.

Pink gave her the finger, but she didn't move except to draw her weapon.

Inside was a bunch of random equipment, the kind of stuff you'd see on a mining operation, and a lot of gaps where Eva imagined other equipment had been stored. But suspended in a glass tank at the end of the room was a sleeping quennian.

She stepped over to it, wondering why they'd leave one of their own crew behind and go . . . wherever the rest of them had gone. There were no visible injuries, but the quennian's scales were strangely dark, and the closer she got, the more the rest of the body seemed like a blurred mess. Like a painting that looked okay from far away, but up close—

The quennian's head swiveled toward her, and it emitted a shriek that jolted through her body like lightning, stunning her so that she froze in place, unable to do more than whimper. As she watched, it unfolded its limbs and placed a mangled hand against the glass, palps writhing unnaturally. Its fingers rippled, the edges feathering like ink on wet paper, and she wondered what the hell the thing was, because it definitely wasn't a quennian.

Not only was she frozen, but the shrieking was giving her a bitch of a headache. Her heart, being inorganic, didn't falter in its beatless blood-pumping habit, which made it marginally easier to calm herself down. With a thought, she set her helmet to block out exterior sounds, and slowly, like she was uncramping every muscle one by one, she regained control over her own body.

The creature didn't move, just kept staring at her even though it didn't actually have eyes. It was like an artist's quick rendering of a quennian, all outlines and no definition. And thankfully, it seemed to be trapped inside the container.

Eva edged backward, maintaining eye contact with the creature until she was out of the room. She closed the door and locked it up again, forcing slow breaths in and out of her nose. Pink was just as frozen as she had been, eyes wide in terror, mouth half-open as if she were about to scream.

"Go to quiet mode," Eva told Pink through her helmet comm. Then she waited, rolling her shoulders and stretching her kinks out while still being mindful of her ribs and other injuries.

"What the sweet holy fuck was that?" Pink finally asked, also through comms.

"You're the doctor," Eva replied. "You tell me."

"It's not in any of my databases." Pink shuddered, shaking herself like a wet dog. "I'm not even sure if it's organic. Some kind of assimilating imitator, maybe."

It was Eva's turn to shudder. Creepy body stealers came in a lot of forms, from liquor-peeing parasites to brain worms to these gross little puffballs with teeth like razor wire. Few people were willing to tolerate a critter that would climb up your ass and wear you like a Halloween costume, so most of them were extinct. Any surviving species were, by nature, disturbingly good at not getting caught or isolated enough as to be undisturbed by sapient species in possession of tactical nukes. Or, you know, they made really good booze.

"No sign of Vakar anywhere on the ship, at least," Eva said. "Either he and the rest of the crew are somewhere else, or—" She swallowed the rest of that sentence. Despite the voice of pessimism breathing in her ear, she suspected it was the former; after all, someone had to have locked that thing up in there and taken all the gear.

"We'll find him, Eva," Pink said quietly.

"I know," Eva replied, with more bravado than she felt. The question was, where had they gone, and when were they coming back? Okay, that was two questions, but still.

"Maybe they left some tracks," Pink said. "Or maybe they were on the other ship?"

"Time to check that baby out," Eva said.

They slipped out the same way they'd come in, Eva briefly pinging Min with ((Nothing yet)) in case it helped keep Pollea placated. No way was she saying anything about the tank monster until she had more info.

She approached the Javelin-class ship more warily than the quennian one. It was smaller, bulky; her dad only sold these to grease monkeys who liked to work on their own rides, and—

Something tapped her on the shoulder. She barely managed to turn her head before she saw the gun pointed at it.

"Cops," she muttered, putting her hands up. She looked to her other side, where Pink was also raising her hands in the universal biped gesture of submission.

The gun holder circled around to the front. A quennian, in reflective gray armor that reminded her inexplicably of an old-school knight. It even had a helmet, same gray material, with a black bar where the eyes should go. This wasn't standard pig attire, though; she'd been arrested by quennians before, and they tended toward bright reds and isospheres instead of gunmetals and, well, guns.

This person was fast, and quiet as a cat. Impressive. What were they going to do with her?

Their posture shifted; the gun didn't. The silent standoff continued. Eva's bladder reminded her of that pee business from earlier.

How long were they going to stand there like this?

"Eva, your sound dampener," Pink said over comms, exasperated.

"Oh, for fuck's sake," Eva said, and turned it off. She'd forgotten the damn thing was on.

"—make me ask you again," the quennian said. His voice was gravelly and deep, distorted by the helmet.

"Sorry, my sound was off," Eva said. "What did you say?"

The quennian paused as if confused. Or exasperated, maybe, if he'd been talking at Eva the whole time with no response. She was surprised her head was still intact.

"Why did you turn your sound off?" he asked.

"That thing on the ship. Its scream paralyzed us, so I cut it off. I assume you checked it out already . . . It didn't do the same to you?"

"The logs told me what I needed to know, and it seemed imprudent to disturb the creature, given the description." His gun hadn't moved a centimeter. "This is a restricted area. Relocate your ship immediately or you will be detained indefinitely."

"Sorry, no can do," she replied. "I'm here on a mission, top secret, need-to-know basis. Probably above your pay grade."

"Nothing is above my pay grade. I am a Wraith. State your name and your business here."

Pink whistled long and low. Eva's face spasmed involuntarily. A Wraith? Coño carajo. What the hell had Vakar gotten himself into that quennian black ops were digging around in this shit, too? They were worse than cops. At least cops pretended to have rules. Wraiths had license to do whatever they wanted, wherever, whenever, and not even BOFA gave them shit about it.

Best cooperate, then, if she wanted to keep from becoming a statistic.

"My name is Captain Beni Alvarez, this is my co-captain

Dr. Rebecca Jones, and we're . . . looking for someone." She tried to keep her face neutral, inoffensive.

"For what purpose? Piracy?"

"What? No!"

"You unlawfully entered the vehicle of an absent party after trespassing on a restricted planet," the Wraith said. "Then you attempted to willfully mislead an agent of the law. State your business before my patience sublimates."

She opened her mouth to answer, but realized anything she said was going to sound incredibly stupid.

((Truth, fool,)) Pink pinged at her.

Probably safest. So Eva went with the truth, or one truth at least.

"A crew member of mine—former crew member—said he was going to be here, and asked me to come as a favor to him."

"Why?"

"I don't know. He said it would be dangerous, and he was worried he—"

"So you flew all the way to a restricted planet to meet with a former crew member for no known purpose?"

Eva scowled. "It sounds really unreasonable when you put it like that. But I do need to find him. I . . . need him to help me get my ship back. My other ship. It's complicated." That didn't sound any less foolish, now that she'd said it out loud. She already had a new ship, and a crew, which contained an engineer who was almost as good as Vakar. Sue even had robots.

Did other people actually buy the crap she was selling, because apparently she'd sold herself quite the pile. Pink sighed next to her, shaking her head as if disappointed.

And yet, after a moment, the gun was lowered and attached to a back holster. "Tell me, Captain Alvarez, what is the extent of your knowledge of the Proarkhe?"

"The Proarkhe?" Those fucking guys again. Eva lowered her arms slowly. "My cargo—former cargo handler was obsessed with them." Also The Fridge, especially her asshole sister and a shithead by the name of Miles Erck, but that seemed like more detail than necessary.

"What if I told you someone had found a Proarkhe artifact here?"

She crossed her arms. "Is that why this planet is off-limits?"

"No, it is restricted because a very dangerous creature lives here, a kind of giant lizard that bores through rock." He turned away, slowly scanning the terrain to the west. "A distress signal was intercepted by planetary monitoring sensors, and was eventually traced back to a group known as The Fridge."

"What? You're joking."

He glanced back at her. "Am I?"

"Hope springs eternal." The Fridge. Fuck a duck. She glanced at Pink, who flared her nostrils like the air had started to stink.

"Unfortunately, they did not survive their encounter with the indigenous life—"

"Good," Pink interjected.

"—but their interest in this planet did not go unnoticed, and a team was called in to determine what that interest might be."

Vakar. And other people, apparently. "So why are you here?" she asked.

"Because we received a distress call from that group two cycles ago, and shortly thereafter we lost contact."

And there was the sound of the other shoe dropping.

Eva closed her eyes, listening to the far-off cry of some creature that was less bloodcurdling than the one locked up on that quennian ship. The air smelled like a desert, like dryness with a hint of blood, cold because the local star was still just poking its head over the horizon. She couldn't smell the quennian in front of her, even though her helmet's sensors were working normally; part of the whole Wraith package, presumably. Creepy, though. Explained why he had been able to sneak up on her, apart from the whole no audio thing.

"So you're going to find them, right?" Eva asked. "That's why you're here?"

He cocked his head at her. "My orders were to conduct preliminary reconnaissance, await further instructions, and defend the site as needed from any Fridge incursion."

"What about the missing team?" Pink asked.

He didn't respond.

"You're going to leave them wherever they are," Eva said. "Dead, dying, whatever." She punted a rock into the valley to her left, and it clattered down the sloping side of the cliff face. "This is why following orders is bullshit."

"Even your own orders, Captain Alvarez?"

Eva ignored that dig. "Fine. I'm assuming you told us this exciting and highly confidential story because you want us to save these people? Because yes, we will. Damn it. Pink, let's tell the others we—"

"I was, in fact, extending an invitation for you to accompany me," the Wraith interjected. "I recommend that your associate remain here to guard the ships, as there is potential that The Fridge's agents will return in greater number."

Eva and Pink shared another look. "What about your orders?" Eva asked.

"I was preparing to violate them anyway. Wraiths have some latitude in such matters."

Well. Wraiths were supposed to be their own brand of elite badass among the quennians, so he probably wouldn't slow her down. And it would be good for Pink to keep an eye on the ship in case things went sideways. Again. Though apparently cats and tiny robots were enough to handle some boarding parties.

"What makes you think you can trust me?" Eva asked. "I could be a Fridge agent, for all you know."

"In my experience, they do not outfit their operatives with such . . . seasoned ships."

Pink snorted a laugh, and Eva tended to agree. That was one way to describe *El Cucullo*. Made it sound like a well-used cast iron pan instead of a dump.

"Let me confer with my co-captain privately for a moment," Eva said.

The Wraith wagged his head in the quennian equivalent of a shrug. Eva darkened her helmet to avoid lip-reading translator nanites and spoke to Pink through her helmet comm.

"What do you think?" she asked.

Pink pursed her lips. "I think you've got multiple fractures, lacerations and contusions, but you've also got a head harder than a rock. And my mama always said the good Lord protects fools from themselves."

"Hasn't exactly worked out so far," Eva said.

"You're still alive, aren't you?" Pink held out her hand for their usual handshake. "Go get Vakar back, ass. I don't need you moping around my ship for the rest of eternity."

Eva swallowed and blinked until her eyes stopped stinging, then took Pink's hand. Once they finished bumping hips, she turned back to the Wraith and made her helmet translucent.

"All right," Eva said. "We find the team, pull their asses out of whatever fire they're in, and if The Fridge comes we hit them until they stop moving. Right?"

"Agreed." He pointed down the slope, toward a wall of earth

that was steeper than the rest. "Come, Captain Alvarez. The entrance to the temple should be over there."

"A temple, huh? Fancy. Lead the way."

The sun rose slowly, heating the air with impressive speed, though Eva's suit regulated her own temperature. A light wind kicked up, pelting her helmet with dust, almost like a fine mist but less refreshing. And here she was, wandering around with a fucking Wraith like it was normal.

It was probably worth turning on a little charm to keep things friendly, instead of spending the whole time worrying that he might shoot her in the back.

"What's your name, anyway?" she asked.

The Wraith stopped, and she almost bounced into his back.

"I am called—" The translators fumbled the word, taking a full two seconds to finally supply "Memitim."

"Wraith Memitim? Or is Memitim a title?"

"It is a designation. Wraiths do not have names."

That was interesting. "Stop me if I'm being rude, but would you mind if I call you something shorter? Tim, maybe? Only because it's faster to yell in an emergency." Nicknames were a chancy thing; sometimes they brought strangers together, and sometimes they drove in a permanent wedge. She all but held her breath trying to gauge his reaction, which was nearly impossible given his helmet and lack of scent.

"Tim is fine, Captain Alvarez." He started to walk again, and she bounced after him.

"You can call me Beni," she offered. He didn't respond, and she winced. Wedge, then. Well, it had been worth a shot.

You never were as charming as Tito and your dad, she told herself.

They reached the entrance to what looked like a mine in the side of the valley, except it had a giant metal door—easily ten meters tall—covered in writing, or pictographs. None of them made sense to her, which meant they weren't in any language known to her translators. Ominous.

"Did The Fridge find this or was it here forever and no one noticed?" she asked.

"Their corpses were not forthcoming."

"Look at Tim with the sense of humor." She ran her fingers over the markings, her suit telling her the door was cold. "I assume your people got it open. How forthcoming were they?"

"Enough. Give me a moment." He scanned the door, then stepped forward and gestured at three places about four meters overhead. With a rumble, the door slid sideways, jerking to a halt twice before sticking about halfway open.

"They don't make ancient mystery doors like they used to," Eva murmured. "After you?"

The entry room was as cavernous as the door suggested it would be, sloping downward toward a hallway in the back. The walls were mostly flat carved rock, with pillars made of the same metal as the door placed at regular intervals, perhaps to shore up the ceiling.

In the center of the room was a box, its top open almost like a flower, if flower petals were triangular and metal. Next to the box was a broken lantern and a single quennian boot.

The planet's low gravity made it extra easy to jump to conclusions. "Way to go, Pandora," Eva said. This must have been where the body-stealing creatures or nanobots or whatever had come from. That poor quennian.

"None of the crew was called Pandora," Tim replied.

"I know, it's a story. Human thing. Guy tells girl not to open a box, girl gets curious and opens it anyway, everything goes to shit."

"Ah," he said. "A cautionary tale. Is it effective?"

She gestured at the shoe. "What do you think?"

The massive door closed behind them, plunging the room into darkness.

Eva flicked on the dim red light attached to her suit's collar, letting her eyes adjust. Now everything looked like it was bathed in flames, like they were about to head into the underworld with nothing but the guns on their backs.

Step up from a lyre, she thought.

The Wraith turned on his own light, blue instead of red, and slightly brighter. Her light reflected off his armor-suit and bounced into her eyes, so she tried not to face him directly. His no-face mask thing was creepy anyway. He made it easier by turning away from her and walking toward the room's only other exit.

"Do you have some way to track the crew?" Eva asked, loping after him.

"Their suits have tracking systems attached, yes. But that tells me only the direction, not the most efficient way to reach them."

Even so, that was a bit of hope; if there was still a signal, they might be alive. So they needed a map. She pulled up her own tracking system and pinned the room as their starting point. They'd at least be able to see where they'd gone and double back if needed.

"Ariadne," she said smugly.

"What?"

"Nothing." She had a brief pang, wishing she could tell her mother about remembering all the crazy myths they'd loved together when she was little. But as far as her mom was concerned, Eva was a boring old courier delivering boring stuff across the boring galaxy. She wondered if any ancient heroes had moms who didn't know what they really did with their lives, then chuckled at the thought of comparing herself to an ancient hero.

For one thing, she was way less naked. For another, she wasn't super keen on running into any minotaurs.

The hallway was actually a T-junction, and the quennian went left. The ceiling was still massively high, the walls four meters apart, but Eva turned her gravboots on at a low setting so she could walk normally instead of bouncing. An occasional flicker of a reflection seemed to indicate there were lights above them somewhere, no longer functioning, or maybe the on switch was unreachable.

Eva sent another ping to Vakar. ((Location?)) Still no response. Maybe he was too far away to receive it. Maybe he was weirded out, getting a ping from her after a year. Maybe he didn't feel like talking to her. Maybe—

Tim paused, turning to the right. "The signal is in that direction."

"Through the wall?"

"Yes."

Eva shrugged. "Might as well keep going. There must be a door or another hallway coming up." Unless they'd gone the wrong way.

They continued. The hallway sloped down as the other room had, the air around them growing warmer the deeper they went. The walls had cracked and bowed in places, or even fallen, bringing parts of the roof down with them. But they were able to walk around, or climb over, and continue on into the strange not-cave system.

"You said this was a temple?" she asked.

"That is what the scientists called it, yes."

"How do they know? Couldn't it be something else?"

"It could. You can ask them when we find them."

Not if, when. Good attitude. So far, this guy seemed hard to fluster. She wondered whether that was a requirement for Wraith training, or whether they beat it into him.

What kind of training did they get, anyway? Probably nothing he could talk about, or wanted to. Her walks down memory lane didn't usually include all the time spent having various skills pummeled into her by Tito and others.

The hallway abruptly opened into a long, narrow room that extended to the right and left, with a system of tracks running the length of it and posts at regular intervals on either side of them. An assembly line, maybe, but there was no indication of what had been assembled or for whom. Nothing, she supposed, if it had been a temple. Maybe the religious leaders held processions along the tracks, or their victims were carted in and then led off to slaughter, or this was some elaborate buffet where people grabbed one plate at a time from passing tables.

She resisted the urge to shout "Hello!" to hear her own voice call back. As it was, their footsteps echoed enough to turn into creepy shambling noises.

Her sensors told her it smelled dry, dusty, but with a lingering undertone of something warm. Something alive.

"They must have passed through here," she said.

Tim didn't respond, busy scanning the length of the tracks. She wandered to the right, toward where he'd said the signal was coming from. She didn't get far before finding a tall, thin wall made of metal. It had some kind of platform a few meters up—controls?

Farther down, a smaller version of the same wall was nestled underneath, and it did indeed look like a control panel. Runes like the ones on the outside door were inscribed on the surface. She leaned in to get a closer look, wondering what it said.

The panel lit up, projections of the pictographs hovering in the air above the console. Somewhere off to the left, a strange clunky sound turned into grinding, then a brisk whir. Lights in the ceiling slowly came to life, casting a blue-white glow on the huge room. The ground shook.

Faster than she thought possible, Tim was at her side. "What did you do?"

"Looked at it."

"You did not touch anything?"

"No, because I didn't want to end up like Pandora out there."

The posts on either side of the tracks began to glow, and shimmering walls of force sprang up between them. Tim examined one, apparently taking readings with whatever sensors his own suit had; hers were more geared toward environmental data, and informed her that a cool breeze emanated from somewhere to the left.

Without warning, a strange glowing pink cube appeared at the far-right end of the room, hovering in the air above the tracks. It moved deliberately toward them, then past them, then through one of two openings in the far-left wall. It receded into the distance and was gone.

"What was that?" Eva asked.

"An energy storage device," Tim replied. "Incredibly densely compacted. Likely very volatile." Another pink cube traveled toward them as he spoke.

"Volatile as in explosive?"

"Yes. We should determine where they are coming from, and where they are being taken."

"After we find the missing crew," she said, turning her attention back to the console. "Help me turn this thing off, if that stuff is so dangerous."

He stepped closer to examine the controls. Above them, the

larger version of the console was also active. Interesting. Had there been two different-sized groups here at the same time?

Her suit's sensors showed a slight temperature increase to the left, where the cool air had been coming from a moment earlier. She stared at the doorway and the gap where the tracks went, wondering which of those was the culprit. There were lights beyond, probably turned on when the console was activated, but she couldn't see very far. Strange that it should be so dark. Almost like something was smothering . . . With a thought, she switched on her helmet's infrared display.

The passage beyond lit up like a Christmas tree, almost literally; a mass of twinkling lights moving in their direction. The ground shook again.

"We need to go," she said.

"One moment. I have almost deciphered the controls."

"Very impressive. Look to the left."

"What do you— Ah. I see."

They ran. Eva turned off her infrared because the quennian was blowing it out at the sensitivity required to see the things piling into the room. Without infrared, there was only a mass of feathery blackness, like ink with a purpose.

Like that quennian in the tank back on the ship.

At the end of the room was a giant door, closed. Eva banged on it, which yielded no results.

"Tim!" she shouted.

"I have it," he replied, doing whatever he had done with the door outside.

Nothing happened. "Hmm," he said.

"Don't 'hmm' me, make it work." Eva turned to the roiling smear of creatures, drawing a flash bomb from her belt. She threw it and hid her eyes, counting to three. When she looked back, the morass had paused briefly, swirling around the area where she assumed the grenade had landed. More of the things clustered around as if drawn to it. Then, like a river encountering a rock, they surged around it and continued.

"Tim?"

"I am working on it."

The things eddied and swirled, as if they were flying instead of walking or crawling. They seemed to be attracted to the lights, lingering as they reached each of them. She squinted and drew her gun, firing off a shot at one of the farther lights.

Whatever it was made of, it burst when struck, and that section of the room and ceiling fell into darkness. The mass of things behind the shadow stopped as if they had hit a dam, then streamed down the sides of the wall toward a spot where the next light overlapped with the previous one. What happened to the ones that had been inside the cone that was now dark?

"Turn off your light," Eva said, flicking off the red one on her neck.

"I turned it off when the ceiling lights were activated," Tim said.

"Good." She shot at the next light, which also burst. Some of the things had already passed beyond it and were still coming, so she shot the light after that as well.

"What are you doing?" Tim asked.

"Plan B." Cubes of energy were still appearing regularly along the tracks, and the things were as attracted to those as they were to the lights. "How volatile are the cubes?" she asked.

"Very."

She shot at the second-to-last light, leaving them standing in a bright rectangle, then pulled out another flash bomb and threw it. This time, she darkened her helmet to see what happened.

Sure enough, the light drew the things like flies. She switched to infrared briefly; the ones within the darkness milled aimlessly, as if stuck in tide pools, gradually gravitating toward the glowing tracks and the now-blindingly bright cubes trundling along on them.

She turned the infrared back off, blinking away the spots that had formed in front of her eyes.

"Door?"

"Almost."

"Almost" wasn't good enough. She shot the light above them, plunging the whole room into darkness save for the glowing tracks and the periodically appearing cubes. Tim flicked his light on and she covered it with her hand.

"No, off."

"I cannot open the door in the dark."

She flicked her infrared on. Some of the tide pools had slid over to the tracks and were now flowing toward them again. There wasn't time for him to fumble around anymore.

"Well," she said. "I guess we need a different key. Get down." She raised her gun, took a deep breath and held it, aiming at one of the cubes being carried along in its strange invisible way. As soon as it was parallel to the control console, she fired.

As she lay on the floor several long moments later, Eva had to admit she hadn't expected the cube to be quite so volatile.

She had neglected to dampen the sound in her helmet, so her ears rang from the explosion, and her head and back hurt from where she'd impacted the door. On top of her already busted ribs and other various bruises, the new injuries left her with a strong desire to stay very still for a long time. Instead, she slowly sat up, taking careful, shallow breaths until she could manage deeper ones with only minimal pain. Her infrared flickered and wouldn't calibrate properly, rendering the Wraith in front of her as a painfully bright blob of white. If he was saying something, she couldn't hear it.

"I'm okay," she shouted. She wasn't, obviously, but he didn't need to know that.

He hunkered down right in front of her face, his helmet barely visible in the strange afterglow of the explosion. She wished he would take off the damn mask so she could at least see if he was talking, or smell him.

"I can't hear you," she said. "I can't see much, either."

In response, he grabbed both her hands to support her as she stood up, then led her toward the tracks. The room smelled like ozone and flame, tiny spurts of electricity shooting up from where the console had been. The entire track was in disarray, deactivated, and no more cubes were coming in.

With the posts off, they could now step onto the tracks. Tim towed her along them into the next room, which wasn't a room at all but a narrow tunnel, pitch-black except for stray wisps of light. She wondered if any of those strange black things had survived, and if so, what they were up to.

No sense waiting around to find out.

She let Tim pull her farther into the tunnel, stumbling every few steps until he slowed down in what she imagined was exasperation. Her lack of speed was driving her nuts, too, but if those things were attracted to light then they couldn't afford to risk it. At least he was the one with the sensors to figure out where they were going.

She consulted her map, realizing she had no idea how they would get back out if that room was awash with creepy critters. Too late to worry about it now.

As they went, she began to feel self-conscious about him holding her hand. She briefly considered offering to attach herself to him with her belt cord, but decided that would be too much like someone leading a puppy on a leash. Maybe she could grab him by the arm instead? That was weird, too. Put a hand on his shoulder? Nah, he was too tall, and she didn't think her ribs would appreciate it.

Why was this bothering her, anyway? It had to be done.

Because you don't want Vakar to see you holding hands with someone else, a little voice said.

Cállate, comemierda, she told the voice sternly. What were they, teenagers?

She thought back to his message, the one that had led her here. The tone was strange, stiff, almost formal. He said a lot had happened—like what? Scenarios raced through her head, and she didn't like any of them. If she wanted to go mythological on this, too, she felt like Odysseus coming back to Penelope, and wondered whether Vakar was going to be palp-deep in horny quennians.

There you go again, comparing yourself to heroes, she thought. Don't give yourself something to live up to.

Still, her vision was recovered enough that she let go of Tim's hand. He looked back at her and she gave him a thumbs-up, hoping it translated, then continued.

She suddenly wished she'd asked Tim if he knew anything about the crew beyond the bare minimum for the mission. Then she might have known what to expect, at least a little.

Jaw tight with tension, she sent another ping to Vakar. Still no response. Coño carajo.

Tremors came harder and more frequently now, probably a remnant of whatever mechanism had turned on in the other room. And yet, that was broken, so why was this still happening?

A dim pink glow ahead showed her they were finally reaching the end of the line. The proverbial light at the end of the tunnel. She hoped it wouldn't turn out to be a train.

It was worse.

Chapter 22

TAKE THIS

The room they entered was a huge cavern, apparently naturally occurring rather than shaped by whoever had crafted the rest of the temple—or whatever it was, because Eva decided it didn't feel very religious to her after the whole conveyor-belt-energy thing. Maybe a mine, or a factory?

The ground was rock, smooth but uneven in a few places, most notably the giant trench running the length of the area. Jutting out of the trench was a strange machine, made of the same materials as the doors and the consoles, its purpose inscrutable.

To their right was a door, which was likely the usual entrance instead of the back way they had taken through the tunnels. On the far side of the room was another door, glowing as if it had been recently activated, and a whisper of hope told her that maybe Vakar was on the other side.

Unfortunately, the dim light she had seen before came from stacks of the highly volatile pink energy cubes. Big stacks, all over the room. If they weren't careful, the whole place would be blown to kingdom come.

And to put the sprinkles on the sundae, they appeared to have found the source of the tremors. On the far side of the trench, milling about in front of the door, was the giant burrowing lizard Tim had mentioned earlier. It was about four meters tall and twice that long, with a single horn jutting backward from its head, and a tail tipped with a blunt weapon.

She had a feeling, however, that it wasn't supposed to be inky black and blurry at the edges, like that no-longer-quite-quennian thing back on the ship.

"Tim, you need to plug your sound holes," she said quietly, or so she hoped; her hearing was still shoddy. She muted outside sound anyway, to be safe. "If that thing screams—"

It opened its maw, and a chill ran down her spine, whether from a subsonic effect or just from being creeped out, she didn't know. Tim must have gotten her memo, because he pulled out his gun and fired a single shot at where the creature's eyes should have been. Not surprisingly, it bounced off.

And also attracted the thing's attention. Bad news. With another inaudible roar, it charged at them.

Tim ran left and Eva ran right, turning off her gravboots so she could bounce farther with each step even as she winced from each minor impact on her ribs. She pulled her last flash bomb off her belt; distracting it was one thing, but she also needed to get rid of it or they'd never get to that door, much less whatever was behind it. Part of her coolly suggested that maybe the creature had come from that room, that the crew was already gone and this was a waste of a perfectly good life.

She told that part of her to eat nails and shit blood.

Not that the dying part would take too long, at this rate. She threw the bomb at the creature and darkened her helmet, counting to three. She needn't have bothered; it reared on its hind legs and caught the bomb in its mouth, swallowing it as if she'd thrown a treat. Which she might have, considering the black things' attraction to light.

And energy. The cubes were mostly taller than her, but a few here and there had been compressed down into half a meter on a side. Maybe if she could—

The thing charged at her, leaping over the trench as if the gap weren't at least three meters wide. She dodged to the right as it swiped at her, bouncing awkwardly up to her feet after her shoulder roll because of the low gravity and landing almost at the edge. Her ribs screamed in protest, an involuntary grunt escaping her. A quick glance told her the pit was about five meters deep, but she didn't have time for a closer look.

She leaped forward, avoiding snapping jaws and the trail of black things that sloughed off the lizard like water off a duck. She loped, and dodged, and kept moving.

Tim fired at the thing from the other side of the room, but it had apparently decided Eva looked more delicious, so it ignored him. Go figure.

Eva ran toward the trench, skidding to a halt and twisting as she dropped over the edge, clinging to it by her fingertips even as her chest erupted in lances of fiery pain from her ribs and other wounds. She prayed the thing would leap over to the other side, or even better, fall in. Instead, it managed to claw its way to a stop and snap at her hands, forcing her to let go. Down she went, her boots taking the brunt of the impact when she hit bottom and bounced.

Okay, puppy, come on down here, she thought. You stay in

here long enough, maybe we can get that door open. C'mere, you rabioso pedazo de—

Mierda. It turned away.

Maybe she should let Tim handle it. He was a Wraith, after all, and she was injured to hell and back. He would have come in here alone if she hadn't shown up. She could get out of the pit with her gravboots after this was over, find Vakar, save his crew, live happily ever after.

Assuming the critter didn't eat Tim, or the parasite-whatevers didn't wear his body like a puppet. Then she'd have to fight her way past two monsters to get out of here.

Eva, she told herself, you are full of terrible ideas, as usual.

She flipped into a handstand and turned on her boots, shooting toward the ceiling. As she passed the edge of the trench, she turned off the boots and let the momentum carry her out, tucking her legs and leaning forward into a roll. She hit the ground with a cry and bounced to her feet, pulling out her gun.

"Over here, comemierda," she shouted, firing at the creature's back.

Now it was her turn to be ignored. What was Tim up to?

He stood in the middle of some piles of the glowing pink cubes, which shifted as the creature stomped around. In horror Eva watched one of them slide off its stack and hit the ground. To her surprise, it didn't explode; instead, it fizzled out, leaving behind only a heat shimmer in the air.

So either they weren't all volatile, or they needed some kind of catalyst. Eva grinned. She could work with that. She wished she could tell Tim about her developing plan, but they hadn't synced comms. For all she knew, he had a better idea.

Or great minds thought alike. He picked up one of the

smaller cubes and, with a spin for momentum, threw it into the creature's mouth.

The lizard swallowed the cube whole with one quick snap of its huge, inky jaws. Like the black things in the other room, this slowed it down as it—digested? Absorbed? Processed?

Whatever it was doing, Tim used the opportunity to dart around it and make straight for Eva. She gestured at him to go to the trench instead.

Meanwhile, she looked for a cube small enough that she'd have a prayer of lifting it. Finding one, she bent at the knees and hoisted it onto her hip. It was lighter than she expected, but still a solid ten kilos, and her various injuries were now bad enough that breathing was a constant source of agony. She was about to pull a sticky mine off her belt and attach it when suddenly Tim was there, trying to grab the cube from her.

The creature threw its head back and roared again, turning to find its prey. Again, it charged.

Eva struggled with Tim for a few moments before he finally released the cube, but it was too late; the creature was almost on top of them. She threw the cube and pulled Tim toward the trench, not stopping to be sure the creature swallowed.

The rumbling ground told her it hadn't taken the bait.

Eva immediately dropped backward to the ground, wincing at the impact to Tim and herself, then locked her arms tightly around him as she flipped on her gravboots. They slid toward the trench together, more slowly than if she'd been alone but still faster than they could have run. Together they fell into the pit, landing painfully in a pile at the bottom.

"This is nice," Eva said between shallow breaths, even though he couldn't hear her. "We could live in this hole. Maybe start a commune. Give tours to bored rich people." Surely the creature would wander off eventually.

Or it would start dribbling inky bits of itself all over the place. She imagined getting hollowed out like a blown egg. Not good.

Eva gestured frantically at Tim to hold his position, then turned on her gravboots again, this time to walk up the far wall. She was almost to the top when the creature leaned in to snap at her, falling just short, then backing up and leaping over the gap to the side with the door.

Well, shit.

She crouched and cut power to her boots, somersaulting in midair and turning them back on. As quickly as she could, she clambered over the edge of the trench. It dogged her as she ran, bounding almost parallel but on a slight diagonal that brought it closer to the pit. She pulled a sticky mine off her belt, reaching one of the small cubes and slapping it to the side.

The creature leaped back to her side of the cavern.

With just enough time to think "Hail Mary, full of grace," she tossed the cube at the monster and ran for the trench.

The thing reared on its hind legs again, maw widening—unhinging like a snake's—and snapped up the energy cube with the mine.

Eva wasn't going to make it to safety, but this was their only chance to kill it. She triggered the detonator as she leaped the last few meters.

Sorry, Vakar, she thought. Hope you get my remains home, if there's anything left.

The creature exploded in a flash that expanded to the other cubes in the room, causing a chain reaction as they all released their stored energy. It was kind of beautiful, actually, like drowning in light, the waves of white heat bursting into miniature supernovas that flowed around her like—wait, around her?

Eva closed her eyes, but the damage was already done; she

was blind again, this time from staring at a bunch of close-up explosions. Stupid. But why wasn't she dead?

She groped around, feeling a floor below her, curved rather than flat. Holy Mary, mother of God, she was in an isosphere.

A laugh fountained up inside her and spilled out, and she pumped her fist in the air and whooped for joy. For a moment, she wondered if Vakar had somehow found her, but she immediately realized how foolish that was.

"Tim?" she asked. "I can't see anything. Tell me you didn't bubble me and then get crushed by rubble or something."

She waited. No response. Shit, if she was stuck in an isosphere, this would be a very short-lived victory party. And she still couldn't see, either.

Come on, Tim, wake up, she thought. Then she smacked herself in the head.

"Aw, fuck me to tears, my sound was off again," she said, and turned it back on. "You okay, Tim?"

Still no response. Then, the low, rasping quennian equivalent of a laugh, sounding like it was coming from the bottom of a well.

"Yes," the Wraith said. "I am injured, but not gravely, and I am alive."

"Good. Great." She paused, feeling suddenly awkward. "Thanks for, you know, saving my ass."

"You have my thanks as well. Our posteriors were mutually saved."

The isosphere vanished, and she dropped a couple of centimeters to the ground, stumbling into Tim. She immediately stepped away, clutching her aching chest.

"Sorry." She coughed, and if she weren't already blind she would have seen stars from the agony. "So. Let's get back to finding your people. And my person. Former crew person."

"My sensors indicate the missing persons should be behind that door on the far side of the cavern."

Eva grinned. "I was hoping you'd say that."

She sent one last ping to Vakar, and her smile faded when he still didn't respond. Well, she'd find out what had happened to him soon enough.

Everything smelled like ozone and burning. The explosion had apparently blown out a wall and part of the ceiling, sending rocks sliding down to form a rough ramp they were able to climb without incident. Eva's vision was still a big black splotch, but colors were starting to slowly fade in at the edges. Once again, she had to let Tim lead her. Still annoying.

They reached the door, she assumed, because he stopped and released her hand. It took him a minute to get it open, but they at least had the luxury of not being chased to give him the time he needed. Soon enough, it made a grinding sound and her suit registered a gust of cooler air rushing out in front of her.

"Anybody home?" she called out.

"Citizens, are you safe?" Tim added. "I have been sent to recover you."

Smells flooded out, which Eva's translators registered as relief. "Bless us, they sent a Wraith," someone said. "We are here. I am First Scientist Orana Pulean. Lumus is injured, but the rest of us are merely fatigued."

"Do not forget Seiana," someone else said.

"I had not forgotten her, Volucia," Orana said coldly, smell tinged with anger and sorrow. "Her . . . remains are back on the ship."

That must have been the quennian in the tank. Eva felt a twinge of sadness for their loss, but she had more immediate concerns.

"Where is Vakar?" she asked.

A pregnant pause gave birth to a litter of uncomfortable silences. She felt the shape of a question in the air, punctuated by the scent of confusion.

"Who?" said the one called Volucia.

"Vakar. Vakar Tremonis san Jaigodaris. He's an engineer, he—" She stopped. A feeling crept up Eva's spine, tingling at the base of her skull, as the smell of confusion strengthened.

Tim had never said Vakar was one of the missing crew, had he? He'd just let her think that. He needed help to get to them, because he wasn't sure what he'd find. And he had trusted her, a perfect stranger, a human with a story that even she thought sounded ridiculous.

Eva ignored her protesting ribs and reached for the armored shape of Tim's shoulder. She had to reach up, of course, because he was taller than her.

She balled her other hand into a fist and punched him hard in the gut.

"You sneaky, stupid, lying little stinkbug!" she shouted, shaking her injured knuckles.

"Eva—"

"It *is* you! Me cago en ti! You didn't answer any of my pings! You let me think . . . You . . ." She sat down hard on the floor, staring into the fading gray that still obscured her vision, every ache in every injury vying for her attention even as all she wanted to do was scream in frustration.

Vakar crouched down next to her. "I could not have done this alone," he said. "I was going to. I was coming back from scouting the area, attempting to convince myself to disobey orders, and there was your ship. Except it was not *La Sirena Negra*. And you and Pink came bouncing out of *Ingenuity* like you had not been gone for a year. I chose to be prudent."

"You put a gun to my head."

"I did not know why you came, after all this time, in a strange ship, just as this Fridge-connected situation had become problematic. It was highly suspicious, though Pink being with you gave me pause. And when you said you needed me to get your ship back, I was concerned that if I revealed myself, you would attempt to convince me to leave immediately."

"Stop being so, ugh!" She pounded the ground with her fists. "You could have asked me to help."

"Would you have helped?"

"Probably. Maybe." She genuinely wasn't sure. With all her injuries, maybe not. She might have tried to convince him to leave instead, like he said. "Whatever. Let's get out of here. You can finish baffling me with your bullshit later."

"Yes, please," said one of the quennians, smelling relieved. Eva realized the air was thick with embarrassment, disdain and curiosity. She still couldn't smell Vakar, though, in his stupid suit.

"We cannot leave without the Proarkhe artifact," said Orana. "If it fell into the wrong hands, the results could be disastrous."

"Removing it could pose a challenge," Vakar said. "The room beyond has been substantially damaged, but the cave-in created a hole we might be able to use to climb out."

"Unless it is as large as the doorway, the artifact is unlikely to fit."

"I can see that. It is . . . quite large."

"I can't see it," Eva muttered. No one seemed to care.

They went back and forth about it for a few minutes, and Eva didn't bother trying to help. This wasn't how she had expected the rescue to go. Despite everything, she'd built up some ridiculous notion of busting in and saving the day.

In a way, that had happened, but she wasn't the hero; she was a tool.

Vakar had lied to her. He'd let her fill in the blanks all by herself. He'd manipulated her. Maybe it was her own fault for trusting a stranger in the first place, except he wasn't a stranger. And no, it wasn't her fault, because she wasn't the one who made the choice; he was.

You've lied to him, too, she thought. Yeah, and that was just as wrong as this. He'd forgiven her, but could she forgive him?

Also, he was a Wraith? Or was that a lie, too? What the hell had happened in the last year?

She tuned back in to the conversation when Vakar said, "You and I will get the other door open while the rest of your team prepares it for transport. I will scout ahead for the—" Her translator stuttered, then supplied "hungry darkscreamers."

"What about me?" Eva asked.

"Are you still blind?"

She squinted, trying to blink away the gray clouding her vision. "Yeah," she finally said, and the word tasted bitter as a banana peel.

"Then stay here for now. You can bring up the rear once we start moving."

The quennians called instructions to each other, setting up an antigrav harness system to move the artifact. They smelled excited now, eager. Eva considered shutting off her scent receptors but decided that would be childish.

Instead, she got up and groped her way back to the door, which wasn't far, edging around the corner to lean her back against the outside wall. It wasn't as if she could even see whatever magical wonders lay inside the precious room.

The sound landscape was different in the cavern, with more ticking echoes of shifting rocks, and the voices of the people in the room drifting out, along with Vakar and the lead scientist working to get the other door open. They succeeded, and soon enough the artifact was being towed into the cavern amid much grumbling and terse accusations of insufficient care. There was something else, though. A hum, far away, and a low bass note thrumming just beyond the edge of her hearing. Sounded almost like . . .

"Ship incoming," she shouted.

"Is it yours?" Vakar asked.

"You wanna wait to find out?"

"Get the artifact out of here as quickly as you can," he said. From their dismayed smells, Eva assumed that was going to be easier said than done.

The approaching ship's engines grew louder and louder, until finally Vakar grabbed her hand and tugged her forward. They climbed over rubble from the cave-in, which formed a bridge over the trench. He guided her in a strange arc, presumably to avoid the artifact, then bolted diagonally to the door.

"Wait inside," he said, leaving her with a hand against a wall. She was starting to be able to make out more shapes within the grayness, splotches of color and outlines of things, and movement. Peering out through the doorway, she saw something coming toward her, but it looked too huge to believe.

And then the explosions started.

The ship had arrived and was firing on them, which answered the question of whether it was *El Cucullo*. The ground shook as each boom caused tremors to spread like ripples in a pond.

"Get through the door!" Vakar shouted.

"But the artifact!" someone replied.

"They can take it now or take it from your corpse," he said coldly. "It is your choice."

No one else argued. Flickers of movement came through a spot in the ceiling that was brighter than the rest of the cavern—

a hole, she assumed, made bigger by whatever the attackers were throwing at them. Then the small-arms fire started, and she ducked behind the wall. She didn't bother to arm herself since she couldn't hit the broad side of a battlecruiser in her condition.

Just as quickly as it had started, it all stopped when Vakar closed the giant door behind them. Eva nearly gagged on the cloud of fear emanating from two of the quennians. As for the other two . . .

"Our superiors will not be pleased," Orana said, smelling like cold rage.

"With respect, First Scientist," Vakar said, "our superiors can lick my cloaca." He still smelled like nothing at all.

Chapter 23

SAVE POINT

By the time everyone got out of the temple and back to where the ships were parked, they found two piles of wreckage and a conspicuously absent *El Cucullo*. No sign of the quennian in the isolation chamber, but no sign of creepy-crawlies, either.

Not wanting to attract unwanted attention by signaling her ship, Eva assured them Min would circle back around at least twice before giving up on Eva as lost. So they sat, or stood, or paced in the musky dirt, which looked extra silly with the jaunty bounce in each step caused by the lower gravity.

The sun was still high because of the planet's relatively long cycle. Eva found this cruelly appropriate.

She refused to look at Vakar, except when he wasn't looking in her direction. Being angry at him made it easier to avoid asking him questions and having to hear answers she wouldn't like. It also helped that her vision was still hazy.

Sitting cross-legged on the ground, aching in every bone and muscle, she listened to him extract the scientists' story piece by piece. Research mission, everything fine until someone opened the mystery box and reached a hand in. Goodbye hand, goodbye person, hello creepy flesh-eating body snatcher. Apparently it was a machine, lots of machines, something like nanobots but vastly more complicated and possibly Proarkhe in origin.

So, they captured the former quennian with an isosphere and stuck her in the isolation unit, then went back to exploring. Ultimately they found their Proarkhe artifact—sounded like a big rectangular container, the way they described it, with in-scrutable controls—but couldn't figure out how to get past the lizard thing, so they waited for it to leave. At some point it got eaten by the nanobots and then they were really stuck.

One of the quennians, Volucia, bounded over to where Eva sat. "You came here looking for the Wraith?"

Eva scowled and didn't answer.

Volucia smelled embarrassed. "I meant no offense. I was simply curious."

"Yeah, scientist, professional nose-poker. I get it."

"We were puzzled as to why he would bring a blind person on a sensitive mission," Volucia continued. "You must have been very frightened when he battled the odogong."

"He—" Eva stopped herself. Sure, why not. One lie was as good as another, wasn't it? It was that kind of cycle. "Yeah, I was petrified. Couldn't move a muscle. He had to carry me out of there like a defenseless baby."

"Really?" The quennian looked at Vakar, who was sifting through his ship's pieces.

"Oh yes. And that was after he saved me from the, what did you call it? The hungry darkscreamers?"

"He did that as well? Fascinating." Her smell shifted from

curiosity to something subtler; Eva's translators vacillated between interest and amusement.

Eva leaned forward, resting her elbows on her knees and her chin on her hands. "You should go ask him about it." She lowered her voice. "You know what they say about Wraiths?"

Volucia tore her eyes from Vakar to look down at Eva. "That they are noble warriors who take vows of celibacy in pursuit of righteous causes?"

"They what now?" She'd never heard that before. Eva sniffed. The woman was . . . teasing her?

"You are a very strange woman, Captain Alvarez. I wish you the best of luck in whatever errand brought you here." Wagging her head, the quennian trotted over to talk to Vakar.

Eva wondered whether he would tell the truth or not, if Volucia asked. She didn't know why she cared; clearly the woman had already pegged her for a liar.

And she was, wasn't she? Not all the time, not to everyone, but enough that she could hardly take the high ground when it came to honesty. She'd even used an alias with Vakar, easy as breathing. And yet.

Her thoughts were interrupted by the arrival of *El Cucullo,* which touched down in a cloud of dust.

"All right," Eva said, slowly rising to her feet. "All aboard."

Vakar watched the scientists move, maintaining his position.

Is that how it's going to be? Eva thought. Is he going to wait for me to ask him to come?

He stood still, and Eva couldn't tell what he was looking at behind his mask. Still couldn't smell him. Was that how he'd felt all those years, watching her on *La Sirena Negra,* not knowing what was going on in her head?

Jerk. Liar. Selfish idiot.

When Eva was finished insulting herself, she sighed and waved him over.

Eva made sure everyone was as comfortable as possible, given the limited space, and the one called Lumus was being treated by Pink. They'd reach the Gate in a few hours, and from there it would be another few to meet up with *Patient Destiny*, the quennian vessel from which the scientists hailed.

Pollea had been surprisingly stiff and shy with Vakar, Eva thought, but her own family was such an arroz con mango that anything else seemed strange by comparison. And being a Wraith carried its own baggage, though of a less shit-covered variety than Mari being in The Fridge. Eva had left them talking quietly in the galley, Vakar still wearing his shiny-ass armor suit.

Eva got her own visit from Pink, including painkillers and a high-dose injection of a secret stash of healing nanites and accompanying body-building batter. And, of course, a lecture about necessary rest and taking foolish risks. Afterward, she locked herself in her cabin and lay on her bed, staring out her viewport at the light-speckled blackness. Eventually, the ache in her broken ribs had receded to a dull internal itch, and she took a seat at the secondary control panel and rested her forehead on it with a sigh. She then slowly, gently, banged her head on the metal surface repeatedly.

Behind her, Vakar coughed politely.

She started, wincing at the pain of the sudden movement. "Did you forget how to knock?" she asked.

"I did knock," he replied.

She leaned back in her chair, staring at a point past his left shoulder. "What do you need?"

"What are your intentions after divesting yourself of your passengers?"

Eva wished she could smell him. "I want my ship back. *La Sirena Negra,* I mean. Pete has more guns than I do, so I want you to come help me persuade him to relocate."

"You want me to abandon my mission to help you intimidate your father in the hopes that the situation will not devolve into violence?"

"You're right, it's a stupid plan," she said. "Not sure what I was thinking." Liar, she thought. Lying again. Just tell him.

He stood there like a statue, all silent and looming, as if waiting for her to say something else. Her gut churned.

"I'm sure you have stuff to do. Important Wraith stuff." She waved a hand dismissively. "I'll figure something else out, don't worry."

"And once you have *La Sirena Negra* back?"

"I'm—" She stopped. She had told Pink she wanted to kill The Fridge with pinches, but was that enough? Was it even wise, given how they were likely to swat her like a mosquito? But what else, then? Go back to delivering cargo for whatever random asshole paid half up front?

Sometimes you ended up right where you started only to find that everything had changed and there was no place there for you anymore. Like how she'd gone to visit her mom once, after leaving to live with Pete, and her bedroom had been repainted and turned into a sewing room. She'd managed one night of restless sleep on a leaky air mattress before leaving it behind for good.

"Cap, transmission for you," Min said over the intercom.

"Patch it through." Only one person it could be, anyway.

Mari's face popped up in the holo display. "Eva, what have you done?"

"Something incredible, I'm sure," Eva said.

"The Fridge has obtained an astonishing Proarkhe artifact my team had been desperately trying to recover first, and imagine my surprise when I checked your flight history and saw a very interesting correlation."

"No yeah, I'm fine, thanks for asking. Definitely did not get eaten by giant lizards or darkscreamers." You can eat me, though, she added silently.

Mari's forehead wrinkled. "We were looking everywhere for that artifact. It's believed to be extremely valuable and extremely dangerous. And now they have it."

"So you want me to help you get it back?"

"No, comemierda, I want you to crawl into a hole for at least the next cycle while I try to fix this problem. If our mission fails, it could mean disaster for the entire galaxy. And don't ask me why, because I'm not going to tell you, because clearly you have the self-control of an infant."

Eva resisted the urge to roll her eyes. Her sister was dead serious, but also still an asshole. "All I wanted was my ship back. You're the one who didn't feel like helping me get Dad to—"

"He's with me," Mari interjected. "His team is running a secondary mission to grab as much data and tech as they can get their hands on, in case we can't take control of the facility."

"You're taking Dad? With my ship?" Eva's mouth hung open. She couldn't even put words together. After everything they had both been through—

"Dad may be a lot of things, but he's reliable when it counts." Mari leaned forward, staring down at Eva. "His team is experienced, loyal, and ready to die for this mission. Can you say the same about your crew?"

"My crew is the best goddamn crew in the galaxy, you self-centered sinvergüenza. They have something you and Dad will never have."

"Really? And what's that?"

"You'll find out soon enough. Adios, Marisleysis." Eva cut the call, leaning back in her chair and steepling her fingers. She had to find them before her ship got blown to pieces in some crazy suicide mission. The next cycle, Mari had said? That meshed with what Eva already knew. Eva's injuries wouldn't be fully healed in time, which would make Pink angry, but it couldn't be helped. No, Pink was co-captain now; Eva couldn't unilaterally decide what they would do. But if they couldn't agree on a plan . . .

Eva was so lost in thought, she forgot Vakar was standing right next to her until he spoke.

"What is it?" Vakar asked.

"Hmm?"

"What does your crew have that she and Pete do not?"

"Oh." Eva shrugged. "I don't know, but she was pissing me off. Super condescending, talking about you guys like that. Pink is the best field doctor I've ever met and she can shoot a flea from a hundred meters, Min can literally fly this ship in her sleep, Sue has her crazy robot army, and you—" His mask was still inscrutable. "Well, you're a damn Wraith. They don't hand that shit out on crackers."

"That is why I left home, you know," Vakar said, leaning against the console. "I never wanted to be a Wraith. I wanted to be an engineer."

"Well. You never told me. I figured it was a family thing."

"It was. My mother was so proud when she heard of my acceptance into the program. Except I had not applied. There was an incident during my mandatory military service, and I distinguished myself. The commanding officer recommended me without asking my opinion on the matter."

"You couldn't just say no?" Eva had certainly said no to her own mother plenty of times, most firmly when she left to work for her dad. Her neck started to cramp from the angle she was looking up at him from, so she pushed her chair farther away.

"I did, but my mother is very opinionated. I wanted to please her. I left after my first field mission."

"And they let you?"

"My commanding officers were not pleased, but they were also not interested in wasting time on an unwilling recruit."

"So what happened to you on the cruise ship?" she asked. "Someone was there to get you. Who?"

"The Wraith who trained me. I was tracked after I left the service, and as your activities became more erratic—"

"They sent him to spy on you?"

"She was curious. Perhaps somewhat personally concerned."

Ah. Personally concerned. So that's how it was. Eva could pick up what he was putting down. It was heavy, though, and she hated how it felt.

"I'm surprised you left the Wraiths in the first place," she said.

Vakar fell silent. "Their goals were not aligned with mine," he finally said.

"Yeah, you seem really keen on goals right now," Eva muttered. "Guess they're really goal-oriented in the Wraith squad."

Vakar slammed a hand down on the console next to her, making her jump. "Where have you been for the past year, Eva? Nuvesta? A station in the fringe, far from a Gate?"

She pushed his hand away and scrambled to her feet, jabbing a finger at his chest. "You know where I've been, while you've been playing secret soldiers? In cryo. Meat popsicle. I woke up in the middle of a shit show, found out my own sister is the one who sold me out to The Fridge—"

"That person was your sister?"

"Found out a whole fucking year had passed and my life was gone, poof, like blowing out a candle. I try to find you, nobody knows where you are, and you, you . . . Fuck! Fucking, shove your attitude right up your cloaca, mister high-and-mighty tool of the state. My life is shit-flavored ice cream and I'm all out of spoons."

Turning her back on him, she stared out at the stars again, her stomach gnarled and knotted. "You won't even let me look at you," she muttered. "Or smell you. Vakar. Memitim. Whatever they call you now. Get back to your important mission already and leave me alone."

Everyone had missions except her. She just had pieces of a broken life and nowhere near enough glue.

A few seconds later, the door opened and closed.

Eva stepped toward the viewport and rested her forehead against it, looking down, down into the black, willing it to fill her mind as if it could push out all the memories and feelings cluttering up the place like so much space debris.

Fuck *La Sirena Negra*. Fuck everything. She'd told Pink she would go after The Fridge? Fuck that, too. Pink and Min and Sue could have this ship, and Eva would go to the farthest port she could find and take whatever job someone wanted to give her. She'd live a long and boring life, a quiet life, with only the ghosts of the dead to keep her company.

No, you won't, that voice in her head told her. That nagging voice she knew was her own, her second thoughts, the part of her that couldn't lie even if it wanted to.

You're not a quitter, that voice said. You're a captain and you're going to act like one.

Okay, she thought. In a minute, though. In a minute.

Eva wasn't sure how long she watched the stars go by, but the door opened and closed again and a hand touched her shoulder.

"What?" she muttered. Vakar held an injector. "What is—"

His helmet retracted into the collar of his suit, and his smell hit her like a sack of bricks. If bricks were made of licorice.

"I spent the last year looking for you," he said. "The Wraiths had resources and a grudge against The Fridge, so they gave me some flexibility with my assignments. But every time I thought I had found you, it was a dead end."

"Mari kept moving me," she murmured.

"Perhaps you can tell me about it later."

"Later, huh." Her lips curled into a grin. "You have more important priorities?"

He offered her the injector. "Pink said it will take about ten minutes to begin blocking your allergy. And to be cautious because you are recovering from serious injuries."

"Did they teach you to be this forward in your Wraith training?"

"No." His palps twitched. "But as you said, they did teach me to be goal-oriented."

She stared at the injector, doing a quick mental inventory of the parts of her that still ached. "I'm still pissed at you for playing me back there."

"I am sorry. I will not do it again." His smell was laced with contrition and regret.

"Yeah, well, it's not like I'm an angel, either." She took the injector and rammed it into her thigh, wincing at the pain. "There. In ten minutes you can make it up to me."

His smell turned a delightful kind of toasty. "I have had an entire year to consider how to proceed in this situation. I hope you'll allow me to demonstrate."

Eva hadn't realized ten minutes could feel like forever, but all things considered, Vakar made good use of the time.

Eva lay on her side, staring out the window. Sex was nice while it lasted, but sometimes you were delaying the inevitable. The harder Eva tried to push away all the nasty realistic thoughts crowding into her brain, the more of them showed up like un-invited relatives at a family party.

She had a ship, but it wasn't her baby. She had a criminal record, so she couldn't travel in BOFA space without risking arrest. She had gotten Vakar back, but he was going to have to leave again, probably sooner rather than later.

He had the gall to be asleep. Presumably another thing he'd learned in his time as a Wraith: how to pass out at the slightest opportunity. She remembered what it was like to be on a big ship, with multiple crews working in shifts, where only an emergency would interrupt your free time. On little rigs, everyone was always half-alert por si las moscas. And if you ran with Tito, well, sleep was something that happened to other people, and as with most things, if you wanted any you had to steal it.

Eva wasn't feeling particularly larcenous at the moment.

Her mind furiously turned over the problem of how to find her ship, or Mari, or both. Even a lead on the system would get her close enough to conceivably sniff out La Sirena Negra's energy signature in the dark matter.

But then she found herself thinking about Mari, and how

she was bringing Pete, of all people, on some grand expedition to take down the main Fridge base.

Más sabe el diablo por viejo que por diablo, Eva thought bitterly. She'd been through a lot, but Pete had more experience. Still. After everything she'd been through, everything Mari had put her through, knowing full well how much Eva wanted to stomp some Fridge faces—to deliberately exclude her, well.

Why would Mari even call to tell her that? The smart thing would have been to leave Eva alone until everything was over, which was apparently going to be within the next cycle. The odds of Eva finding her were slim to none, so it would be pretty hard for her to mess up the super-secret master plans. Or she could have lied and sent Eva on some wild goose chase to another corner of the galaxy. Even worse, Mari admitted she had been tracking them the whole damn—wait.

Mari was tracking them. She'd put a tracer on the ship.

Eva sat up in bed. If she'd had a heartbeat, it would have been racing.

"What?" Vakar asked, zero to alert in no seconds flat. He rested his claw on the small of her back.

"Tell me you know how to trace a tracer signal," she said.

"Doing so has a high probability of unintended consequences."

"And?"

"Yes. I can do it."

She sighed happily and snuggled up against him. After a few seconds, she scooted to the edge of the bed and grabbed her clothes. She always had been impatient.

"Come on," she said. "Let's get this party started."

Eva stood in front of the door to her cabin and frowned at the assembled crew.

"But, like, maybe I should explain it again more clearly," she said.

"We understand, Captain," said First Scientist Orana. "We wish to be involved in any potential recovery of Proarkhe technology."

The team of scientists stood, or sat, on the floor or seats of the crew deck. Vakar sat on a bar stool in the galley area, back in his armor. Pink leaned against the doorway of the med bay. Sue sat on the floor, elbows on her knees, cupping her chin in her hands. Min was, as usual, omnipresent.

"I don't want any of their tech," Eva said. "I want my ship back, and I want to bust some heads."

"The goals are not mutually exclusive."

"Maybe not, but they certainly aren't equally feasible." She paused and rolled her eyes. That sounded like something her sister would say. "To get *La Sirena Negra* back, I have to land near her—possibly in the middle of a firefight, depending on our timing—incapacitate anyone guarding her, get my whole crew aboard safely, disable any additional security precautions and then take off, still possibly in the middle of a firefight. That doesn't leave a ton of time for also sneaking into a facility that may be under attack by multiple forces on multiple fronts and trying to steal stuff from under their noses. And that all assumes we don't get there too early or too late."

"Do you not wish to assist your family, at least?" Pollea asked. "You cannot mean to leave them to their fate."

Eva glared at Vakar. "Who said anything about my family?"

He wagged his head.

"I'm sorry." Pollea smelled so embarrassed that Eva immediately regretted her tone.

"Yes, fine, my family is doing the attacking. But they're also the ones who got me into this mess and stole my ship in the first place."

"They're still your family," Sue said solemnly. "My brothers aren't perfect, but I'd never let them do something so dangerous alone."

A retort died in her throat. Mari and Pete were her family, it was true, but so was this crew. Pink, and Min, and Vakar, and even Sue now.

Suddenly, she wondered why she was still so keen on getting her ship back at all. This one was fine, and here they all were, ready to fly into danger because she couldn't let go of that piece of herself. Well, that wasn't the only reason; revenge was definitely still a priority, and removing the cancer that was The Fridge would leave the universe that much healthier. Kind of a stupid goal if it ended up getting everyone she cared about killed, though. And the quennians and their precious artifact were hardly her concern.

Her hand snaked up to her neck, the old reflex to pick at the scab she'd had there for what seemed like ages. Except it was gone. Probably thanks to Pink's supernanites stitching her back together at top speed. Nothing left there for her to worry at, to scratch until it bled, only for it to scab over again. Just smooth skin and the memory of a bad habit in her fingertips.

"You know," she said. "On second thought. Maybe let's call the whole thing off."

The room erupted into protests, mostly from the scientists.

"No, it's fine," she said. "You can all find another way to reach this base, wherever it is. I'll give you all my intel, no charge."

"I may have to accompany them," Vakar said quietly.

Eva's stomach seized, but she nodded. "I understand. It's your job. But it's not a good enough reason to put everyone else in danger."

Pink harrumphed. "I thought this was about justice."

"Mari and Pete can handle that without us, I'm sure."

"My brother may be there, too," Sue said. "Or there may be information about where they're keeping him. Someone might know."

"Okay, then you can go with Va—the Wraith, I guess."

"I wouldn't mind having my other body back," Min said. "This one is roomy, but it feels less . . . mine."

Min never asked her for anything. Besides those damn cats, that is. Eva couldn't exactly tell her to suck it up; it was her body, for goodness' sake.

All right, so everyone had axes to grind. Far be it from her to get in the way.

"Well then, I guess that settles it," Eva said, throwing up her hands. "But I'm still ditching Pollea. No offense."

Pollea started to protest, but Vakar put a hand on her shoulder and guided her toward the cargo bay. Eva felt a twinge of sympathy. She knew what it was like to be left out, and where that road could lead, but Pollea wasn't going to magically sprout the required training and fortitude in the time it took to get to . . . wherever.

"I'll tell you what, though," she said, mostly to herself. "The hell are we going to do with all the cats?"

Chapter 24

TUMBA LA CASA

Vakar, with a modicum of grumbling and help from Min, was able to track Mari back to a place called Pupillae in the Black Forest system.

Min charted a new course that let them drop Pollea off at a quennian outpost, along with all the cats except Mala, who settled on Min's lap and politely ignored pleas to leave. Min insisted she could bring Mala if necessary, so Eva left them to each other, muttering about stubborn goats.

They passed through the Gate two hours after that. The Black Forest system had only a half dozen planets, but three of them were big and had tons of moons. Iris was an ice giant with twenty-three moons of varying sizes, and Pupillae was the largest, a red ball of ice and rock and not a damn thing anyone could want. Besides privacy, of course.

"We don't know what to expect, so stage one is assessing the situation," Eva said. She stood in front of the holoscreen near the kitchen, which showed a rotating image of the moon. Arrayed in front of her, sitting or standing in varying stages of excitement and anxiety, were Pink, Sue, Vakar and the quennian scientists. Min was omnipresent, as usual.

"We could get there in the middle of a hot mess," she continued, "or we could be cruising in on the tail end of things and it's all high fives and happy hour."

"What if we're early?" Pink asked. She cradled her sniper rifle in the crook of one arm, the butt resting on the floor.

"They're a solid hour in front of us, if not more, but I guess it's possible. If so, we wait, then stroll in fashionably late, as usual." Eva gestured at Vakar. "The Wraith will scout ahead. Sue and I are with the scientists, and Pink and Min stay here. If things get dicey, they take off and circle back to the rendezvous point later."

"So what are we looking for?" Sue asked. She couldn't stop bouncing on the balls of her feet. It was driving Eva nuts.

"You and I are looking for your brother and *La Sirena Negra*. They"—she pointed at the quennian scientists—"are looking for the artifact. If our goals overlap, great. If not, our priorities are your brother and my ship. We find them, we pick up any nearby stragglers and we jump like a flea. Worst case, we transfer Min and Pink to *Sirena* and leave *El Cucullo* at the rendezvous point so anyone left behind has an exit strategy."

"What about Pete and the others?" Min asked.

Eva pursed her lips. "We'll jump through that Gate if we find it." She wanted to help Mari, certainly, because that would mean screwing with The Fridge, but she had to focus.

"Thank you again for your assistance, Captain Innocente,"

First Scientist Orana said. She smelled crisp, sharp as a knife. "If we can recover the artifact, our government—and possibly the universe—will owe you a debt of gratitude."

"I'm just the delivery girl," Eva said. "It's a long way from said to done. We'll stay with you as long as it makes sense, and then you're on your own."

The quennians smelled excited and scared, but mostly determined. They weren't rookies, but she didn't want to pry about their experience in combat. They'd certainly been ready to fight back on Cavus; didn't mean they were any good at it.

"Captain, sensors say there's a facility broadcasting a quarantine warning," Min said. "They're locked down until further notice with a highly contagious strain of Florxian necrosis."

Eva snorted. "I'll bet."

"Florxian necrosis is nasty," Pink said. "It usually starts as a rash in your—"

"No thank you, rash time is over," Eva interjected. "Any signs of other ships or activity, Min?"

"No, but they could be on the far side of the moon, or—"

Eva could hear the hitch in Min's voice. "Or they could have been destroyed already. They might also have landed in a shielded area."

She gave the assembled crew a last once-over. "Get your crap together and get ready to drop, everyone. Down into the cargo bay. No airlock this time; we're going to jump out the back door, guns blazing. Gird your loins and kiss your friends. Dismissed."

The scientists shuffled down the ramp, quiet but smelling up the place like a perfume store. Sue bounced over to Eva, eyes sparkling.

"Captain, I want to show you what I made," she said.

Eva bit her lip. "Is it something we can use now?"

"Yes. Definitely. I mean, I think so. Probably. Yes."

Eva followed her down to the cargo bay, where a cloth-draped hunk of something sat in the corner. With a sly grin and a flourish, Sue pulled the covering off to reveal a round-chested green bot taller than Eva, with thick arms and orange hands and what looked like a garbage can lid for a shield.

"It has no head," Eva said. "I mean, it's, very nice?"

"It's not a bot, it's a mech," Sue said. "I call him Gustavo."

Eva pondered the notion of a mech having a name and decided it was no different from a ship having one. "What's it—he—do?"

"Oh my gosh, a lot," Sue said. "He can lift up to a ton, the hands can turn into drills or an excavator bucket, he's got a sound cannon, ooh, and a flamethrower!"

"You— Wait, how did you build this?"

"You know, from whatever scraps I found lying around." Sue smiled brightly. "You'd be surprised how many nonessential bits a spaceship has. Plus I had time to scrounge while my bots were fixing stuff."

"Huh." Eva paced around it, checking out the visible components. She stuck a foot into a knee joint and hoisted herself up so she could peer inside. A pair of Sue's little yellow-headed bots looked back at her, one of them wearing goggles and a hat. The other clutched a worn-looking teddy bear.

"You sure you'll be able to handle this thing?" Eva asked.

"I've been practicing," Sue said proudly. "I only set one thing on fire last time. By accident, I mean. I set three things on fire on purpose."

"It could be really dangerous."

Sue's exuberance faded. "My brother could be in there," she said quietly. "I have to find him if I can."

Eva knew that song well. She banged on the mech's big metal belly and stepped down. "Suit up, then, and get ready to roll."

"It can do that, too!"

Shaking her head, Eva went back up to her cabin to get her gear.

Vakar was waiting for her inside, helmet retracted. He smelled like himself, but edgy. She loaded up on the last of her flash bombs and a single grenade, all that was left of the stash she'd assembled from her old life. Whatever happened after this, she'd still have a lot of work to do rebuilding all she'd lost, one way or another.

"You are sure you cannot accompany us," Vakar said.

"I'm not sure of anything." She checked the charge on her gun; it was almost full. "But if we land and *La Sirena Negra* is sitting right there next to us . . ." She shrugged. "We'll see."

He stood behind her and put his hands on her shoulders. "It seems unjust, after searching for you so long, to be parted again so soon."

Eva stifled a snort. He sounded like a romance vid. "My mom always used to say, 'Life isn't fair.' And I thought, 'Well, then I'll make it fair. I'll be the fairest damn person who ever lived, and I'll make other people be fair, too.'" She laughed. "It's not even that it isn't fair, you know? It's that it isn't anything. It just is. Life is people, and animals, and plants, and big chunks of mindless rock flying through space. And none of it gives a shit about anything else."

"Is that so? I believe many things care very much for others."

"Stop trying to ruin my foul mood by smelling delicious. Save it for the afterparty."

"Afterparty?"

She turned in his grip, smiling at him. "Oh yeah. It's in my pants, and you're the only one invited."

He smelled puzzled. "I am not sure I can fit in your pants."

"Then I guess I'll have to take them off."

Now his smell shifted; he got the picture. She sighed. Blood-thirsty mood ruined. She'd have to spend at least ten minutes imagining herself punching people to get her head in the game.

They did not arrive early.

El Cucullo flew in east of the facility, dropping low quickly to avoid the kinds of big guns that tended to be pointed sky-ward. They needn't have bothered; despite a few ships dogfight-ing overhead, the facility's cannons were silent, assuming it had any. Clearly someone had already gotten to them.

The buildings were squat, surface-hugging affairs, so small that Eva assumed there must be sublevels. Whether they were connected or not was another question. Other questions in-cluded how many troops were currently trying to kill each other, how many civilians were huddling in terror under desks making pee, and where the high holy hell was *La Sirena Negra*, because she couldn't see the damn thing anywhere.

"They must have a hangar," she muttered. "I do not want to have to run a freaking gauntlet to find my ship." She would if it came to that, but better would be to find it, steal it back from her dad quickly, and get the hell out of there without getting caught up in whatever was happening between The Fridge and Mari's people. As much as she wanted to do some damage, and as eager as she had been to get in on Mari's big mission, now didn't seem like the best time.

"I should be able to access their network from a terminal inside," Vakar said. "I will find any hangar locations and map them." The sheen on his helmet reflected her face back to her, distorted.

"Fine. Min, put us down and stay alert. Take off if things get spicy." She checked her gear again and closed her eyes, opening them to find Pink standing in front of her, lips pursed.

Pink silently held out her hands and Eva took them for the usual handshake. This time, when they bumped hips, Pink pulled her in for a rare hug.

"Stay alive, fool," Pink said.

"A smart person told me fools are protected from themselves," Eva replied, smirking.

Pink shook her head, dreads swaying slightly. "Vakar, watch her back, please."

"With pleasure," Vakar replied, smelling like vanilla and licorice.

Vakar dropped first, jumping out of the half-open cargo bay as the ship was still landing and racing toward the entrance to the closest building. By the time Eva got to him, he had the door open and was inside checking for danger.

"No guards," he said. "They've probably fallen back to more defensible positions. Turrets are deactivated."

"Got a map yet?" she asked.

"No, I am still breaching the network. We can continue moving forward in the meantime, or you can wait here for my signal."

She huffed. "I hate waiting. Let's go."

The three scientists huddled up behind her, backs to each other like a chitinous rat king. How she was going to sneak them anywhere when they smelled so strongly, she didn't know, but they didn't have the same gear Vakar did. Then there was Sue, stomping around like a giant todyk in her exosuit.

Subtlety had never been Eva's strong suit, anyway.

The next door Vakar opened led to a hallway, which led to another door. He positioned himself with his back to the control panel, gesturing to her that there were two guards to the right of the door and one to the left. She nodded and turned to the scientists and repeated the gestures.

"What does that mean?" Sue whispered.

Eva rolled her eyes, covering her mouth and then using the other hand to shoo them away from the door, back into the other room. She returned and took up position on the opposite side of the door from Vakar.

((On three,)) he pinged, then counted.

The door slid open and the two of them raced in, Vakar immediately taking down one of the guards on his side while Eva ducked behind a shipping container. It took her a few moments to locate her target while Vakar dealt with the second guard. She vaulted over her cover and landed right next to the poor guy, elbowed him in the throat and slammed his head into the metal wall.

Someone started screaming, and someone else clapped a hand over their mouth. It sounded like it was coming from a table near the center of the room. Eva tiptoed over and hunkered down, gun pointing at the ground.

Two people crouched underneath, probably the underwear-pissing scientists she'd been expecting. One of them was a mess, anyway, but the other, unpleasantly familiar face stared back at her with the kind of scorn she reserved for human supremacists and puppy-kickers.

"If it isn't my old buddy Miles Erck," she said. "How's it hanging?"

"Well, actually, fuck you," Miles spat. The woman gasped and hid her face.

"Strike one," Eva said. "Three strikes and you're out. My friends are looking for an artifact that came in recently. Ancient. Proarkhe. Stolen. Any idea where it might be?"

"Stolen?" cried the scared one.

"Shut up, Emle," said Miles.

"Totally stolen," Eva said. "Tell me where it is, oh wise paleotechnologist, and you can stay right here until everyone is finished killing each other. Or go somewhere safer, which I'd recommend."

"Well, actually, I said fuck you."

Eva yearned to break his nose.

"I've been well fucked recently, thanks," she replied. "But sadly, it is you who will be fucked in an entirely figurative fashion if you don't get polite in a hurry. And that's strike two. Artifact. Where."

"It's near the central core," Emle said.

"Emle!" Miles nudged her hard.

"She'll kill us, Miles!"

"I will," Eva said. "I'm very naughty. Where's the central core?"

"Two buildings over. You have to use the tunnels on the lower sublevels to get between buildings." The more Emle talked, the more the woman calmed down.

"And to get to the sublevels?"

"The elevator is that way." The woman pointed.

Miles fumed. "Emle, you idiot, how could you—"

"Strike three," Eva said, and kicked him in the face. He dropped like a sack of protein powder, and Emle shrieked again.

"Hey, hey, look at me." Eva stared Emle in the eyes and made shushing noises until the shrieking stopped. "His mouth is too big for his fists, and he'll have a mild concussion, but he'll be fine. Try to get out of here if you can. Get a job working for someone other than The Fridge."

"The Fridge?" Emle said. "You mean the kidnappers? No, this is—"

"It's The Fridge," Eva interrupted. "You've been lied to. Good luck not getting dead." She got up to leave.

"Wait," Emle said, crawling out from under the table. "Should I get a gun?" She looked over at the dead guards.

"Your call," Eva replied. "But if you'd had a gun when I found you, you'd look a lot like them right now."

Emle blanched and retreated under the table. Eva left her trying to wake up Miles fucking Erck, and called the quennian scientists in now that the room was clear.

"Tunnels on the sublevels," Eva repeated. "How many sublevels does this place have?"

"Six," Vakar said. "I have breached their network. Would you like a schematic?"

"Hit me." Eva's commlink pinged and she pulled up the map of the place. Each building looked roughly like a giant screw driven into the ground, with rooms and tunnels branching out from the center. The middle screw was the largest; it had a big central room that was no doubt the core Emle had mentioned.

"Any way to confirm the artifact is where that lady says it is?" she asked.

Vakar was quiet for a few moments. "There are files for a number of active projects at this facility, but each has a code name and separate security protection."

"Try checking where the alarms are going off right now. I'm guessing they'll show some kind of trajectory."

Another pause. "Interesting."

"Secrets are for sharing, mi vida."

"There are several places where the facility was breached, with the main bulk of the incursion centered around the middle building, which is the largest. Secondary teams were successful in buildings one and two, but another team was apparently repelled in building four."

Eva wrinkled her nose. "The next building over?"

"Yes."

She shrugged and punched the panel to summon the elevator. "We don't have time for detours." The elevator didn't open, and she frowned. "Must be on lockdown. Vakar?"

He did something with his commlink and the system powered back up with a low whine. The elevator doors opened and they all piled in. It was a freight elevator, spacious enough to allow for movement of large items, though perhaps not big enough to smuggle out this artifact of theirs. Eva wondered how they would manage that when they found it.

It was also a very slow elevator, worse than the ones on Nuvesta. Eva started to whistle until Vakar put a hand on her arm and shook his head. She considered dancing but decided against it.

The doors opened onto the fourth sublevel. A security desk sat at the far end, protected by impact-resistant transparent polymers, as evidenced by the lack of scratches and cracks in an otherwise trashed room. The remains of a security turret sparked on the floor, fallen sideways, but the room was unoccupied.

They passed through the open door to the connecting tunnel, which showed no signs of a fight. Sue had to duck into the body of her suit to avoid hitting her head on the ceiling, but the tunnel was as wide as the freight elevator. At the far end they hit a pair of closed doors, which Vakar immediately began to hack.

"Another security room?" Eva asked. He shrugged assent, and she gestured at the scientists to hug the walls behind Sue. If the doors were undamaged, the turrets inside probably were, too.

She wasn't wrong. As soon as the doors opened, a cheerful computerized voice said, "I see you!" and a stream of projectiles shot straight up the center of the tunnel.

Eva squeezed off a few shots at the turret's sensor, but her rounds weren't strong enough to penetrate the material.

"Let me, Captain," Sue said. "Bots, lunchtime!"

All of Sue's bots came rushing out of nooks and crannies in the mech, more than Eva could have imagined would fit. They raced toward the turret, dodging and weaving as the bullets rained around them. Eva provided cover fire, and Vakar followed suit.

Like a wave of giant yellow ants, the bots swarmed over the turret, knocking it onto its side. It continued to fire, but now it was flopping around on the floor, a victim of its own recoil. Some of the bots had tiny hammers, and many of them carried welding torches. In the space of a dozen seconds, it was all over.

Another security turret fell out of a hole in the ceiling, landing on its face but nonetheless humming to life as it unfolded its legs and rolled, turning its big red eye on them.

Sue stomped on it with Gustavo and stuck a drill-hand into its eye. It shuddered and deactivated with a sad "ah" sound.

"Reinforcements are not forthcoming," Vakar announced. "Security has been ordered to abandon posts and converge on the central core."

Eva examined the hole the turret had fallen through. She had assumed it was a shaft or pipeline for turret delivery, but it was literally a hole, oval-shaped, about three meters long by two meters wide. The edges were bright green and blurred, which was weird, but not as weird as the fact that the room on the other side was sideways, and couldn't possibly exist in the space that the location of the hole seemed to indicate it did.

"We're all seeing this, right?" she asked.

"It looks like a Gate," First Scientist Orana said.

"A Gate in the middle of a ceiling?" another scientist—

Volucia—said. "Impossible." They began to argue among themselves about physics and scalability.

"Sue." Eva held out her hand. "Give me a bot."

Sue whistled and one of her tiny minions climbed out of the mech and shuffled over to Eva. She picked it up gingerly.

"Sorry," she said, and tossed it straight up into the hole.

Instead of flying up and falling back down, as soon as it passed the edge of the hole, it kept going and arced away to the left, disappearing from view. There was a soft thud of impact and a squeal, and then a few seconds later a pair of tiny yellow hands gripped the edge of the hole, and a tiny yellow head peered down at them.

"It's a portable Gate," Sue whispered. "They made a portable Gate."

The scientists' arguments erupted into speculation and theory, all of them smelling indecently excited.

Eva, meanwhile, did a careful sweep of the room. Her grounding in the technology of the Gates was geared more toward their use than their underlying principles, partly because no one had any clue how they actually worked. Until now, apparently. But normal Gates, the kind that hovered out in space in seemingly random places, were much bigger and encircled by metal rings that maintained their stability and let users set coordinates to change their destinations. If this didn't have a ring, then there had to be some other mechanism controlling it.

On the floor next to the door was a bullet-riddled corpse. A strange-looking arm cannon encased most of its arm. White with black parts, including a glowing purple-pink power source that reminded her of those energy cubes from the temple. She knelt to examine it, aiming it at the wall and gently trying to pull it free.

It triggered, shooting a ball of green light past Eva that

hit the wall, stretching instantly into an oval hole of the same shape and size as the one on the ceiling. Which was now gone, interestingly, leaving no trace it had ever been there.

Almost no trace: a pair of tiny yellow hands hit the floor, along with a tiny yellow head.

"Oh no, Seven!" Sue cried, climbing awkwardly out of her mech to pick up the pieces.

Eva walked over to the new hole and peeked through. The rest of the little bot's body had fallen over on the floor, which was about ten centimeters from the edge.

The room beyond was two stories high and fifteen meters across, and in significantly worse shape than the one they stood in. Not designed to repel armed incursions, she imagined. The walls were pockmarked with impact craters and covered in scorch marks that smelled fairly fresh. The pools of blood under the various bodies were also disturbingly fresh-smelling.

"Incredible," Orana said. "That device was able to create a Gate—a controlled tear in the very fabric of space-time—but what powers it, and how did it trigger? What is keeping it contained rather than spreading?"

"And how was the other Gate created?" Volucia asked. "The one on the other side?"

"Don't touch it," Eva said. "I'll be right back." And with that, she jumped through the hole.

From this side, the hole was the same glowing green oval, except of course it showed the room she had just left. It was situated on one of the walls and surrounded by bullet marks, which probably explained what had happened to the person on the other side.

Eva had been expecting a lab, but this looked more like an obstacle course with movable components—platforms, half walls, pits and even conveyor belts. Observation windows lined one of the walls near the ceiling, presumably for monitoring the progress of whoever was running the course. But who were they training, and why?

One of the corpses had a cannon thing like the one in the other room. That made sense: presumably someone had to make an entry hole while another person set up the exit hole. Time to test the theory.

This former person was easier to disarm; the device slid right off. Eva examined its controls. Hand grip, simple triggering mechanism. No apparent switch to disable it or turn it off. She slid it onto her left arm and felt the weight, about on par with a rifle. Could be used with one hand, probably made for two.

"Everyone get back," she shouted at the Gate in the wall. Didn't want to have someone else lose their extremities, or head. Sure enough, they had clustered around to see what she was doing, and Vakar had to shoo them away.

Eva aimed just to the side of the existing hole and fired the cannon. The same green sphere of light shot out of it, hitting the wall and flattening into a hole. The existing Gate vanished as if it had never been, leaving a perfect oval of empty wall space surrounded by impact craters. Creepy.

Pausing to scoop up what was left of Seven, Eva climbed back into the other room. The scientists and Sue stared at the cannon in awe, while Vakar continued impassively reflecting things with his stupid armor.

"Get the other one," she told him. "Carefully. I don't want to find out what happens if you hit someone with this thing." She also didn't want to leave it with The Fridge, though she imagined they had the schematics somewhere.

As she watched Vakar, her arms broke out in goose bumps. Portable Gates. Two guns, paired to each other somehow, each capable of opening one end of a wormhole instantaneously.

On the one hand, their usefulness was limited, since you had to physically get someone to where you wanted the other Gate to be. On the other hand, once they got there, you could move almost anything through from one place to the next in an almighty hurry. Instead of having to sneak a whole team across enemy lines, you'd only have to move one person. That one person would be carrying an entire potential army in a small, lightweight device.

It had much more practical applications, too, but she knew how people thought. Maybe some of these scientists were imagining galactic peace through resource relocation, but she doubted the upper echelons of The Fridge were quite so altruistic. And while these holes were relatively small, if they were able to harness the power to make Gates big enough to move a whole spaceship . . . Eva made a disgusted noise and shook herself like a wet dog.

"All right, people," she said. "Let's finish crashing this party."

"Wait," Vakar said. "I have found something else."

"We don't have—"

"We must make time for this, I believe."

Eva gestured at him to lead the way, conscious that every moment that passed could be putting *La Sirena Negra* out of her reach.

This had better be worth it.

"Me cago en diez," Eva said.

The room looked like any other low-ceilinged warehouse, except instead of cargo containers, it was filled with row after row of cryo storage pods. Many of them were empty, but if the first row was any indication, there had to be at least two dozen people held here in stasis.

And if she didn't get them out, they might very well stay that way, assuming the place wasn't blown up before someone else found them.

"This is barbaric," First Scientist Orana said.

"On the contrary," Eva said. "It's civilized as fuck. Civilization is just bullshit."

Sue, meanwhile, was stomping around from pod to pod, presumably looking for her brother. Eva hoped she found him, thinking with a pang of how she had intended to rescue Mari much like this, once upon a time.

"We cannot leave them here," Vakar said.

"No shit." She hefted the Gate cannon. "I guess I should run back to *El Cucullo,* open up a hole, and we walk all these popsicles through in a hurry."

"Or I could return to the ship while you remain here."

She stared at her reflection in his helmet. There it was again. The line. Captain and crew, boss and subordinate, one person telling the other what to do, the other having to obey.

Except he wasn't her crew anymore, was he? Vakar had his own ship, his own mission, and he didn't have to take her orders for shit. So this was just two people having an argument, and they had to hash it out like anyone else.

"Which of us is faster?" she asked. "Who can get to the ship first? Because once the Gate is open, we can come right back through and be here in a second. But it has to get done right in the first place, or we're all screwed."

Vakar cocked his head to the side. Considering.

"I am faster," he said.

"You're sure?"

"Yes." He didn't sound happy about it, though.

Eva shot a Gate at the nearest wall. The other side showed the security room they had left a few minutes earlier, still empty.

"We can retreat back there if we have to." She resisted the urge to hug Vakar, her skin prickling all over with bad feelings. "You waiting for an invitation? Hurry up already."

He touched her arm briefly with a gloved hand, then raced off.

Eva blinked back tears. Stupid. Focus. Get it together, Captain.

"Open these iceboxes, now!" Eva barked at the scientists. "I want every single one of these meat popsicles conscious by the time that Gate opens."

She found Sue in the far corner of the room—or rather, she found Gustavo, apparently empty. Sue was curled up inside, crying silently.

"Sue," Eva said softly. "We'll find him."

Sue didn't respond. Eva got it, she really did, but now wasn't the time.

"We need to help the people who are here," Eva told her. "You can do that."

"What's the point?" Sue whispered.

"The point is, you have the power to stop other sisters from feeling the way you do right now. But you have to get up. Or you get to look in the mirror tomorrow and know that you did nothing."

Eva left her there, because what else could she say? Either Sue would get up, or she wouldn't. Eva wouldn't judge her either way. Meanwhile, she had to help open the pods.

The scientists weren't well versed in the systems, but after a few minutes of frustrated interaction with virtual intelligences, they figured it out.

Eva watched one person after another wake up, no doubt feeling much as she had when Mari freed her. Some were confused, some afraid, others angry or aggressive. There were a couple of humans, a trio of kloshians, a quennian, a dytryrc . . .

One of the pods contained someone who looked so much like Pholise, Eva grimaced. Same coloring, same features, same delicate neck folds. At least the tuann would be able to sleep easier tonight, assuming everyone got out of this alive.

The hole in the wall still showed the security room from earlier. How long ago had Vakar left? Should he have made it to *El Cucullo* by now?

As if in response, the Gate changed and Vakar jumped through. Eva had only a glimpse of the outside of the building, which seemed to be taking heavy fire from ship-based weapons.

As soon as he made it through, he shot another Gate at the wall next to the first one. It created a strange mirror effect that made her vaguely queasy.

"Where's *El Cucullo*?" she asked him.

"Gone," he said.

Eva sucked in a breath. "Okay, we planned for that. Things got hot, they had to move. We'll have to find another way to the rendezvous point." She cursed mentally, not wanting to alarm the still-defrosting people accumulating around her like a shitty birthdate party.

"I may be able to offer an acceptable alternative," Vakar said.

"Yeah?"

"I have located *La Sirena Negra*."

Chapter 25

TRAEME LA BULLA

The central core of the compound was one massive room with floating catwalks of varying sizes crisscrossing it. These led to different alcoves, some of which looked like hangar bays or storage areas, while others were walled off with glass like offices or control booths. The ceiling consisted of a large round door that opened like an iris, and was currently shut except for a tiny hole in the center just big enough to admit an average-size human.

A battle raged all around, with squads of guards and soldiers facing off from opposite sides of the room, or platforms on different levels, or right up in each other's faces. Their uniforms suggested the troops were human military, of all things, with a few others mixed in, some military, some merc, and even some BOFA.

At the center of it all, hovering in midair in some kind of stasis field, was the stolen Proarkhe artifact.

At least, Eva assumed it was the artifact, since she had been blind when they found it. The thing was shaped like a box, just how the quennians had described it, about three meters high, five meters wide and one meter deep, with strange markings along the front like the ones from the temple. It seemed to be made from the same kind of metal, too, but the color was closer to a deep blue or black.

"So," she said to Vakar, "how are we going to get that giant thing down and sneak it out without becoming incredibly porous?"

"Perhaps we might use that," Vakar said, pointing with the cannon-arm.

"The Gates it makes are too small."

"No," he said, gesturing with the pistol in his other hand. "That."

Eva followed his gesture. Sitting pretty as a picture in a hangar on one side of the room, behind a wall of security guards, was *La Sirena Negra*. She grinned like a kid at Christmas.

Vakar shot at a guard charging toward them. "I sense a plan forming," he said.

"Let me orient some goals at you," she replied. "One, we open that door up there in the ceiling. Two, we deactivate that stasis field around the artifact. Three, we get my ship, get the hostages, get the artifact, and get the hell out of here. Four, pants party."

"I feel there are more implied steps that complicate this plan immensely."

"When is anything we do not complicated?"

She spared a glance at the absurdly large crowd of hostages, scientists and Sue awaiting her and Vakar in one of the access tunnels nearby. They'd decided it wasn't safe to leave them in the cryo room, in case the attacks outside got worse, but at this point it was rocks and hard places as far as the eye could see.

"Start figuring out the door control situation," she told Vakar. "If we can't get that open, we're toast anyway."

The hole in the ceiling grew from the size of a person to the size of a medium todyk. It jammed, then opened wider, then jammed again.

"Looks like someone else has a similar plan," Eva muttered.

"Remote access to the controls has been disabled," Vakar said. "I am attempting to reactivate them, but we can reach them manually at the control center there." He pointed at an outcropping three stories up, where two concentrated forces were exchanging fire.

Eva hefted the Gate cannon. "Let's test the range on this thing." Carefully, she aimed at the wall above the outcropping and fired.

The ball of green light shot out, flew straight as a laser, and flattened itself into an oval that showed the now-empty cryo room.

"Got anything fun we can drop on them?" Eva asked. "No, wait, don't answer that. I know the best thing. Shoot at the floor."

A few seconds later, the guards were briefly surprised when a round green mech fell on them from nowhere. Then they were too busy being roasted by a flamethrower to be surprised.

Eva followed Sue to help clean things up, kicking a few burning guards over the edge of the platform and shooting the others who were still moving.

What a damn mess. How many of these idiots knew they were working for The Fridge, and how many were just sending the money home to family?

"I should have known it was you," a sour voice said. "You're subtle as a hammer on glass."

Pete emerged from the control room, trailing two of his

people—the kloshian and Nara in her giant armor. His weapon was lowered, but the others were aimed right at Eva.

"Just making sure you get that door open," Eva replied coolly. "Wouldn't want my ship to stay trapped in that hangar."

"Your ship?" Pete scowled. "Now is not the time, Eva-Bee. We need to get the—"

"Artifact?" she interjected. "Sounds good. Vakar is working on deactivating the stasis field, unless you can do that from here, too."

"Jaedum is taking care of it." He eyed the Gate cannon. "What the hell is that?"

"Shortcut." She shot a Gate at the nearest wall and poked her head through, looking up at Vakar. "Sending Sue back to you. Might want to make room."

Sue stared at the hole thoughtfully. "I'll have to move quickly or I'll fall right back down. Gravity is—"

"Yes, great, go." She turned back to Pete. "Once the door is open, we get back to my people and I send us straight over to the ship. Surprise, pew-pew, we get inside and get moving."

"And the artifact?" He gestured at the giant box hovering in its midair prison.

"Open the cargo bay door, fly underneath and deactivate the field. Drop it in, close up shop and jump like a flea."

"And how do we get Jaedum back in after he deactivates the field?" Pete asked.

Eva hefted the Gate cannon meaningfully.

The kloshian—Sanana? Sania? Sanannia, that was it—spoke up. "That all sounds surprisingly cogent."

"Surprising after all the good things Pete has said about me?" Eva grinned. "I can throw in a few crazy antics if you'd prefer."

Sanannia didn't respond, didn't even bother to smile.

"Nara," Pete said, "stay with Jaedum. Keep the guards off him while we get the ship."

The bodyguard raised a hand—which was also, at present, a plasma cannon—and went back around the corner.

Meanwhile, more guards had poured in from the elevator opposite where Eva had come in. She wondered how many there were to begin with. They had to run out at some point, right?

Jumping back through the Gate, she careened into Sue and Gustavo, nearly falling back into the hole. The change in orientation gave her flashbacks to Conelia.

"Incoming," Eva said, after she recovered her balance. "Scoot."

Vakar was already firing on the guards, and she joined him. "We have to get up to the ship," she said, checking that Pete and Sanannia were through. They were; Pete fired on the guards as well while Sanannia ducked behind Sue.

"Stand clear," Eva said, and aimed at a spot in the hangar near *La Sirena Negra*.

Before she could shoot, a familiar voice boomed from the loudspeakers. "Attend me, worthless muck-eaters. I have come to your inferior outpost to apprehend the human captain Eva the Innocent!"

Eva froze. "No," she said. "No. No me diga."

"Him again?" Pete asked.

The voice continued. "The might of the Glorious Apotheosis and the Gmaarg Empire stands ready to obliterate you at the slightest provocation! Deliver unto us our desire or bathe in a torrent of plasma!"

She resisted the urge to smack her forehead with her gun. "Okay, so, we should probably hurry before he blows us up."

"Didn't you say you—"

"Yes, I thought he was dead, but clearly I was wrong. Doesn't matter! We go now, quiet as mice. Vakar, Sue, you're on guard duty while we make a path for you." She shot a Gate next to her ship and dropped silently through the hole, landing behind the row of guards, who were now looking around in confusion.

"Orders?" one of them said.

"Hold position," the squad leader answered. "They have to come through us to get the ship."

Right. Eva suppressed a snicker as she crept toward the airlock. Unfortunately, when she tried to open the ship remotely, she remembered Pete had changed the codes.

"Do you smell something?" a guard asked.

"Only a lump of shit who won't stop asking stupid—wait, yeah, sort of like old rubber tires . . ."

((Pete,)) she pinged. ((Unlock door.))

He was a hair too slow. Just as he and Sanannia came through the Gate, one of the guards saw them, shouted and opened fire. Eva dove back through the Gate to avoid being hit, while Pete and the kloshian raced to the relative safety of the ship's umbilicus.

And the damn door in the ceiling still wasn't open wide enough.

"Vakar, I think your skills are needed. Sue, sit tight." Eva fired the Gate cannon at the platform where the control center was, grabbed Vakar and pulled him through with her. They slid out because of the angle, landing in a tangle atop each other.

After all the running and screaming, that was kind of nice, even if she couldn't smell him.

"Eva?" said a voice behind her. "How? What?"

"Moment ruined," Eva said, getting to her feet. "Welcome to the party, Mari."

Her sister came around the corner, scowling. Her face was roughed up and she favored her left leg, but that didn't stop her from stomping over and smacking Eva in the chest with her palm.

"What have you done?" Mari said. "You brought the whole damn gmaargit armada down on our heads!"

"In my defense, we both thought he was dead," Eva said.

"Cease your pathetic countermeasures, vermin!" Glorious boomed. "My military splendor is upon you. You shall fall to ruin wailing for your broodmare's embrace!"

An explosion shook the building. The lights flickered, then stabilized, and a string of curses emanated from the panel where Jaedum was working. The kyatto emerged a moment later, holding his right hand, ears flat against his velvety head.

"Stupid power surge overloaded the board," he hissed. "Have to deactivate the stasis field manually now if we want to get that damn thing out of here." He gestured at the artifact with his injured claw.

"At least you got the door open," Eva said amiably, watching the iris widen.

"Should have made sure the board was properly grounded," Vakar told the kyatto.

Jaedum snarled. "Course I did; I'm not a damn rookie. Why don't you stick to shooting things and leave the thinking to me, ghost boy?"

Eva swallowed a sassy reply. "How do you deactivate the stasis field manually?" she asked.

Jaedum pointed at the generator floating midair in the middle of the room, above the artifact. "Open the panel on the left side, press the big red button."

Mari stepped in front of her. "Don't even think about it. This is my mission and you've already done enough damage. Get back to your ship and get off this moon before the Gmaargitz Fedorach blows it up."

A squad of guards decided it would be a good time to float up to their level on a levitating catwalk and start shooting. Everyone ducked behind the corner of the console area. Everyone except Nara, all two meters of her in that massive armor, who ran toward the gunfire and returned it with gusto.

"Vakar?" Eva said.

"Yes?"

"Open a Gate in the wall here."

"That will leave Sue and—"

"I've got it," she said. She stared up at his unreadable mirrored face. "Trust me."

Would he? Could he? Because right now, she barely trusted herself. If this didn't work—no. It had to. No do-overs in a firefight. People were counting on her, and she'd already failed enough for one lifetime.

Vakar opened a Gate next to hers. His silence said enough.

"Make sure everyone gets on the ship when I open the way." Eva leaned out past the edge of the console until she had a clear shot, aimed the Gate cannon at the stasis field generator, and fired.

Without another word, she raced to the other Gate and leaped through it backward.

For a disorienting moment, Eva found herself falling through the air, away from the generator and the Gate she had made.

She fired the Gate cannon at the wall next to *La Sirena Negra* and flicked on her gravboots, which yanked her back toward the generator, her stomach flipping from the whiplash. Since her Gate had moved, she was now able to stick to the side of the machine.

She'd done it. Her crazy-ass maneuver had worked. Now all she had to do was hit that manual bypass button and—

Sadly, at that moment she had a great view of the mostly

open door above her. Hovering a hundred meters away was a gmaargit fathership, its giant death ray powering up.

"Me cago en la hora que yo nací," she said, scrambling to find the access panel. A glance told her that Vakar had figured out the Gate logistics and was hustling everyone onto *La Sirena Negra*, but if they wanted this artifact, they'd need to take off and get over here quickly.

If they were smart, they would leave you here, her inner voice said. And you would help them. You let Glorious kill all those people the last time—

"Cállate, coño," she muttered. ((Hurry,)) she pinged at Vakar.

With a familiar whine, her ship lit up and took off, and Eva's heart nearly went with it. Whoever was flying it didn't so much as scratch the paint coming out of the hangar, and dropped down in a maneuver that would have made Min sigh with envy. The cargo bay door opened, but she couldn't see who stood inside.

((On three,)) she pinged, ripping open the access panel. Big red button. She looked up again at the fathership, with the most annoying fish-faced jerk to ever walk the galaxy up there somewhere. She'd be flattered that he was still so obsessed with her, but it was less about her than it was about his fragile ego.

Eat me, she thought, and hit the button.

The stasis field around the artifact shut off with a low hum, and the huge box fell without a sound. *La Sirena Negra* shot forward to catch it.

And missed.

The artifact seemed to tumble in slow motion, end over end, toward the floor. It clipped a floating catwalk, sending the platform careening into the wall, where it cracked and spat electricity. But the artifact itself kept falling, falling, until finally it landed with a loud, echoing thud.

Eva could practically hear the scientists screaming. Probably Mari, too. She had to get down there and get the stupid thing somehow.

Sending up a prayer, she shot a Gate at the roof of *La Sirena Negra*, which hovered below her, and dropped into it. This took her back to the original platform where they'd left Sue and company, though Eva flew out so fast she hit the wall opposite the hole. Struggling to her feet, she staggered to the end of the platform and shot a Gate at the ground near the artifact.

With a running leap, she dove through the hole next to her and came out in a roll.

"You will acknowledge my dominance or perish!" Glorious screeched.

Another boom rocked the station as Eva was getting up, sending her stumbling into the artifact. Without thinking, she threw up the hand holding the Gate cannon for balance, and it smashed into the side of the mysterious metal box. The purplish-pink power gauge inside abruptly went dark.

Three things happened at once.

One: Eva thought, Mierda, I broke it. Two: *La Sirena Negra* shot into the sky so fast it made a sonic boom.

And most importantly, three: the artifact next to her whirred to life and began to transform.

The box slowly unfolded itself, one piece at a time, like a cat waking up from a nap. Except once it was finished, instead of a cat, Eva faced a robot bigger than the biggest todyk she'd ever seen. It was humanoid, with thick arms and legs and a broad rectangular chest that looked almost the same as the box it had once been. It had no mouth, but it did have two glowing red eyes that stared down at Eva with no apparent emotion.

It spoke—she assumed it was speech, anyway—in a voice like modulated noise.

Eva had never been so afraid in her life. She inched away from it, her eyes flickering from its huge bulk to the fathership looming overhead with its weapon preparing to fire.

The artifact spoke again, the sound rattling her teeth with its volume, then turned away from her and raised an arm.

Against the wall a meter away, a Gate appeared, triple the size of the ones she'd been making, but with the same green glow around the edge. On the other side, Eva glimpsed a black sky empty of stars, and an enormous city crafted entirely from the same metals that were in the temple where the artifact was found. The artifact stepped through the Gate, which popped out of existence with a splash of light.

Eva didn't realize she'd backed up to her own small Gate until a pair of hands reached through and grabbed her, pulling her in just before the fathership fired its massive laser straight down into the facility.

Chapter 26

CALABAZA, CALABAZA, CADA UNO PA SU CASA

You're sure I'm not dead?" Eva asked.

"If you inquire again, I will begin to doubt my own senses," Vakar said.

Her head rested in his lap, which was attached to the rest of him, which sat on the floor of *La Sirena Negra*. Eva stared at the place where a Gate had been a minute earlier, and which was now the paneling of the cargo bay.

"I never would have thought to shoot a Gate through a Gate," she said. "I can't believe that worked."

"I was not certain it would, either, but the alternative was—"

"If it hadn't worked, everyone would be dead," she said quietly.

If the scientists, freed hostages, and assorted soon-to-be-former crew of the ship could hear her, they gave no indication.

Everyone appeared to be about as shell-shocked as she felt, with the quennians almost uniformly smelling like a mixture of anxiety and relief.

"Where's *El Cucullo*?" Eva asked.

"We are on our way to them now."

Relief washed over her like a cold shower. "And Pete?"

"Flying the ship."

Bastard. "Mari?"

"I believe she is using the comm system in your quarters to contact someone named Schafer."

"No way." Eva finally remembered where she'd heard the name before: Schafer was the human war hero Leroy used to worship. He probably would have peed himself for the chance to talk to her. The thought of her sister being linked to that big shot was disconcerting, to say the least. That explained some of Mari's secret mission stuff.

Vakar stroked her head gently. "Would you care to receive medical attention? I am told Sanannia is well versed in first aid."

"In a minute," she said, closing her eyes and taking a long, deep breath as she snuggled closer to him. "As soon as everyone decides I'm okay, the yelling is going to start, so we might as well enjoy this while we can."

Eva sat in the mess, drumming her fingers against the table as a room full of people argued with each other about what had gone wrong. Most of it kept cycling back to her, which was fine; she'd given up any dreams of a hero's welcome long ago. You only got parades and medals if you hit all the mission objectives. Getting home alive was lower on the success ladder than dying gloriously in battle, for some reason.

"—the greatest archaeological find of the past millennium!" First Scientist Orana was saying. "And now we'll never know what it was."

"A giant robot," Eva said. "So big."

"But was it a virtual intelligence, or an artificial one, or—"

"You have to give me those Gate guns," Mari interjected quietly.

Eva shook her head. "Finders, keepers."

Really, she didn't want some massive organization to have them, Fridge-fighters or not, hero commanders or not. Mari would probably try to steal them later, which was why Eva had asked Vakar to hide them. Still, if Mari's intelligence raid had been a success, she probably had the plans for them somewhere anyway. It was only a matter of time before more were produced.

The thought did not comfort her.

"Why don't you get the hostages back to your boss," Eva said. "Someone has to take the credit for busting them all out. And I'm guessing you're better equipped to transport a bunch of random people to their respective homes, anyway."

Mari waved dismissively and stalked out of the room. Eva found herself surprisingly bereft of the urge to punch her sister, even after all that had happened. Mari thought she was doing the right thing, fighting the good fight, all that motivational-poster mierda their mom was always sending them q-mails about. And maybe she was right, and Eva was wrong, and what The Fridge was doing with the mystery Proarkhe tech was so profoundly terrifying that they had to be stopped no matter what.

They'd find out soon enough, either way. Eva thought of that strange metal planet without stars and a knot tightened in her stomach.

Pete came to stand next to her other elbow. "So you're taking the ship back, eh? What's an old man like me supposed to do for a living?"

Saddest attempt at a guilt trip ever, Eva thought. "You can stay on board if you want," she said, but they both knew she didn't mean it. "Otherwise, you can have *El Cucullo* back. Sue has worked miracles with what little we had."

"Fair enough," he said. "What are you going to do now?"

"What indeed," Eva replied.

A few hours later, they rendezvoused with Pink and Min at the quennian military station where they'd left Pollea and the cats. Poor girl smelled like incense in a stinky bathroom, she was so upset, but it transitioned into cinnamon and almonds as Vakar showed her to his bunk on *La Sirena Negra*.

Tears streamed down Min's face as she returned to her ship, her body, and Eva squeezed her arm gently before leaving the girl to privately reintegrate with all the systems. It wasn't as if Min was ever alone, not really, not unless she wanted to be.

At the end of their standard handshake greeting, Pink bumped Eva's hip hard enough to make Eva stumble. "You've got more lives than all these damn cats combined," Pink told her.

"And I've got you," Eva said. "That's like five extra lives, at least."

Pink punched Eva's arm and went to check on her med bay. Her grumbling was audible from the mess, as familiar and comforting to Eva as an old shirt.

The cats acted as if nothing had changed and they'd been there the whole time. Such was the way of cats, according to Min.

The scientists were dumped at the station with arrangements to get back to their colony ship, and promises to answer any questions they might have later about the disastrous archaeological expedition on Cavus or the Fridge incident on Pupillae. They smelled disappointed as they left, and not a little sour.

Mari escorted the hostages to what Min said was the same BOFA ship they'd run into way back on that Fridge planet a year earlier. Likely explained what had happened to the lab there, though Eva did wonder how Miles Erck had gotten out. Whether he'd made it out of the other base with that poor girl Emle was another story. She hoped it ended happily, one way or another. Emle didn't deserve to be saddled with that jerk, in life or death.

Eva never did get to meet Schafer, though. That was heroes for you.

And so it was that Eva found herself, finally, walking the corridors of her ship, touching the panels and plates that were hers again, listening to the familiar old creaks and whines and hums of the black outside trying to get inside and failing. She had no idea what she would do now, beyond finding creative ways to make The Fridge sorry for existing, but she and her crew would figure it out together.

They always did. Okay, maybe not always, but from now on.

She opened the door to her room and was greeted by the smell of licorice and anise, with a hint of lavender. Vakar sat on her bed, palps twitching, and she almost regretted giving up the much more spacious cabin on *El Cucullo*.

"So," he said, "I suppose now you can explain what you meant by a pants party?"

"I think it's easier to show you," she said with a grin, closing the door behind her.

Want more Eva?

Turn the page for a sneak peek
at the next book in the series:

PRIME
DECEPTIONS

Chapter 1

KICK THE PUPPIES

Captain Eva Innocente ran through the snow, trying to ignore that her pants were on fire.

It wasn't actually snow so much as white stuff that looked like piles of frozen water crystals, but was instead a highly flammable form of methane precipitating peacefully from the sky of the aptly named planet Kehma. She also wasn't actually running, more of an aggressive hobble that wanted very badly to be a run, but her left gravboot was randomly malfunctioning and sticking her to the ground, so she kept having to send a deactivation command through her commlink to get moving again.

Her pants were definitely on fire, though, blue and magenta because of the methane. Her spacesuit protected her from burns, or she would have been more worried about it. And while it would have been funny to note that the fire started immediately after she lied to someone, right now she was focused on not getting shot by that person and his accomplices, who were chasing her.

Eva darted behind a pillar-like rock formation as a bolt of plasma seared past her head. She would have loved to get her own pistol out, but she needed both hands to carry the package she'd gone to Kehma to steal. Well, steal back, since it had been stolen in the first place. Regardless, she had no hands with which to defend herself, so she had to rely on others.

((Help,)) she pinged at Vakar, who was supposed to be providing cover fire. Her quennian partner was much faster than she was, given his functioning boots and longer, back-bending legs. She'd lost track of him in the snow, which was now falling as tiny blue flames as the bits stuck to her legs burned higher and brighter. The air around her shimmered with heat, and she was glad her nose was protected by the bubble of her isohelmet, because she was sure it smelled like spicy farts outside.

No answer from Vakar, maybe because of weather interference, unless the Blue Hounder mercenaries behind her had signal scramblers. The doglike bipedal truateg definitely had expensive plasma rifles, no doubt courtesy of their suppliers at The Fridge. Working for an intergalactic crime syndicate had its perks, which Eva was a little salty about. Why did the bad guys always get better stuff than she did?

A shot tore through the air so fast it left a trail of blazing purple-blue, coming from in front of her instead of behind. Either she'd been flanked, or—

A second later, the sonic boom reached her, and Eva grinned. Unless the mercs had added sniper rifles to their arsenal, that was definitely Pink. And if her co-captain had arrived, that meant *La Sirena Negra* couldn't be far behind.

Eva darted from behind her cover toward another rocky pillar, lurching forward and cagando en la mierda every time her gravboot stuck. The methane-fueled fire was up to her chest now, making visibility even more difficult. She shifted the device so most of its weight was on her right side; the damn thing was heavy, and bulky, and she hadn't expected to be carrying it while running and being shot at. Another plasma bolt narrowly avoided her, sizzling against the rock as she ducked behind it. She thanked the Virgin these mercs weren't better shots, though come to think of it, that was a little odd. People who got paid to shoot things to death tended to be pretty good at it, or they didn't get paid for long. Unless they were herding her . . .

The click-whine of a rifle being armed next to her head made her freeze. As much as it was possible to freeze while on fire.

"Give back the cargo," the merc said. His voice came through her translators as whiny despite his broad, jowly features and beady eyes.

"Wasn't yours in the first place, mijo," Eva said. Why hadn't he shot her already?

"Who hired you?" he snarled, a line of drool falling into his collar. "How did you learn about this facility?"

Ah, information. The real currency of the cosmos.

"A little bird told me," Eva said.

He pressed the muzzle of his rifle to the spot where her iso-helmet met her suit. "Do not speak in idioms, human. Answer my questions or die."

"Can't answer questions if I'm dead, mijo," Eva replied. "Nice rifle, by the way, you get that out of a catalogue with your parents' credit line?"

The merc made an angry horking sound. "I earned this, you hairless whelp. I've been a mercenary for longer than you've been alive."

"And you haven't retired yet? Qué lástima, you must not be very good at it."

"Enough!" the truateg shouted. "You and your pack, playing at a profession you barely understand. It makes my testicles itch."

Eva almost snarked at that, but something moved behind the merc: the palest of shadows, silent as snow.

"When I was your age," the merc continued, "we had respect for our elders. For the mercenary code. You don't even have a proper uniform!"

"Times change," Eva said. "Oye, could you hold this for a second?"

She thrust the package at the merc, who grabbed it reflexively. His rifle swung away from her and she activated the present Vakar had gotten her for her last birthdate: a set of sonic knuckles that formed glowing gold rings around her fingers. Her first punch landed in the truateg's gut, the second on his shoulder, and by the third Vakar had stepped up to wrench away the rifle and drop the merc with a blow to the back. Eva deactivated her knuckles and took the stolen package back, giving the half-conscious truateg an extra kick in the junk for good measure.

"Where are the others?" Eva asked.

"Gaining ground." Vakar took the package from her, his shiny metal armor making him nearly invisible as it reflected all the whiteness around him. "We should complete our evacuation."

"Did you sabotage their ship like I told you to?"

"I would have reached you sooner if I had not," he replied. "Their navigation systems will be installing a false software update for the next half cycle at least."

"Dios mio, that's evil," Eva said, grinning. "Vámanos, let's get out of here before I turn into carne asada."

((Location?)) she pinged at Min.

((Look up,)) came the pilot's reply.

La Sirena Negra roared in, its dark hull obscured by the sticky methane snow coating the shields. Min brought the ship to a stop so that it hovered a meter above them, breaking some of the stone spires in the process. Eva and Vakar raced over to the emergency hatch, which opened to reveal a tight space with a ladder that slid down to meet them.

"You first," Eva told Vakar. "Get that damn thing inside or we don't get paid."

He shifted the package to one side and began to climb awkwardly with his free claw. Just as Eva started to join him, her gravboot stuck to the ground again. This time, it refused to obey her mental command to deactivate, so she had to release the ladder and crouch down to examine the stubborn thing.

A bolt of plasma streaked past, followed by a gargling howl from the truateg. Coño carajo, Eva thought, staying low and frantically jabbing at the manual release on the outer sole of the boot. Still not responding.

"Worthless feces licker!" shouted one of the mercs. "Taste my vengeance!"

"Tastes like chicken!" Eva shouted back. Not that they knew what chicken was.

A sonic boom overhead told her Pink was providing cover fire, buying her a few plasma-free moments. The methane flames completely coated Eva now, but she still couldn't get her damn gravboot free. With a frustrated groan, she activated her sonic knuckles again and punched the ground around her foot, breaking up the pale rock into gravel-sized pieces. There just needed to be enough left to trick the boots into sticking to them, instead of the solid parts underneath—

A searing pain in her thigh made Eva hiss and bite down hard. Somebody had finally hit her. Unfortunately, that meant her suit was compromised, so she didn't have long before the methane flames worked their way in as well.

Eva punched the ground one last time, and finally her grav-boot shifted. *La Sirena Negra* hovered above her, with Vakar now dangling upside down from the ladder as he reached his free claw out to her.

Grunting, Eva jumped awkwardly with her good leg and grabbed his arm with both hands. Shots sizzled through the snow around her as the ship shifted, her injury making her scream.

Vakar did the galaxy's most insane sit-up and hoisted her into the emergency access, the hatch closing beneath her as soon as she was fully inside. He released her gently and she collapsed onto the floor, breathing heavily.

((Jump,)) Eva pinged at Min. The pilot's response was nearly instant, the whine of the FTL drive preceding the stomach-wrenching sensation of artificial gravity compensating for sudden acceleration. Eva could picture Kehma receding behind them as they flew off into the black, toward the nearest Gate, a few hours away.

They'd made it. And they had the package they'd gone to retrieve, which meant they'd get paid. Despite the pain in her thigh, Eva felt cold with relief.

No, not just relief; also the fire extinguishers coating her in chemicals to stop her from burning up the ship. In moments, she was covered in pale blue gel, slippery as a dytryrc during mating season but no longer aflame.

Eva deactivated her isohelmet, which dropped a load of the gel into her black hair. Vakar retracted his helmet as well, releasing mingled smells of incense and licorice; he was worried about her.

"I'll be fine," she muttered to Vakar, tugging off her busted gravboot and throwing it against the hull. "But I'm definitely going to need a new pair of pants."

Eva sat in the med bay, trying not to squirm as Pink's mechanical eye scanned her for injuries beyond the shot to her thigh. Pink had already patched that with a quick-healing compound and numbing agent, and covered it with the usual self-adhesive bandages and a thick mesh designed to restrict movement. Other parts of Eva ached, from muscle to bone, but how many of those complaints were new was debatable.

"You'll live, again," Pink said finally, sliding her eyepatch down. "You're lucky they didn't hit an artery."

"I'd be luckier if they had missed entirely," Eva grumbled.

Pink turned around and rummaged through one of the cabinets. "I'm not wasting the good nanites on you, so you have to take it easy for at least a week. Elevate the leg when you can, pain meds every six hours. And of course, you remember your buddy—" She pulled out a cane and handed it to Eva. Its height was adjustable, but they both knew it was already on the lowest setting for the ship's second-shortest crew member.

"How can I forget good old Fuácata?" Eva muttered. "Anything else, Captain Jones?"

"I'm Dr. Jones right now, sass mouth," Pink said. "We still need to have your weekly psych session later. But we should get everyone in the mess to chat, yeah?" She peeled her gloves off and tossed them in the recycler, then gave Eva her arm to help her off the exam chair.

Eva sent a ping to the rest of the crew as she hobbled down the corridor of *La Sirena Negra* to the mess room. The smell of espresso mingled with incense and anise; that meant Vakar was already there, he had made coffee for her, and he was worried but otherwise in a good mood.

"Look at you, smiling like a fool," Pink said, elbowing Eva gently.

Eva scowled, but she couldn't sustain it. Especially not when she saw Vakar waiting, out of his shiny Wraith armor for a change. His pangolin-like scales were freshly scrubbed, and his face palps angled toward her as she entered. The smell of anise shifted to licorice, making Pink groan and roll her eye.

"Are you well?" Vakar asked, his blue-gray eyes staring pointedly at her cane.

"Claro que sí, mi cielo," Eva said. "This is temporary."

"She has to rest," Pink added, pursing her lips and giving Vakar a meaningful look that made him smell grassy, bashful.

There went Eva's plans for later. She sat down at the head of the room's big communal table and let Pink prop her leg up with a stool, then accepted her taza of coffee from Vakar gratefully.

"I'm here, Cap!" Min said cheerfully through the ship's speakers. Eva had assumed as much, since Min pretty much was *La Sirena Negra* as long as she was jacked in, which was always. Still, it was good to be sure. The pilot's human body had been in the bridge last time Eva checked, with one of the resident psychic cats asleep in her lap. Probably Mala, the unofficial leader of the pack.

That left one more crew member still unaccounted for.

((Mess, now,)) Eva pinged at Sue.

((Coming,)) the engineer pinged back. A few moments later Sue ran in, her black hair spiked at odd angles like she'd accidentally run a greasy hand through it. Her pink shirt was smudged and streaked with brown, and two of her tiny yellow robots clung to her tool belt, making shrill noises.

"Sorry, Captain," Sue said breathlessly. "I had to replace a resistor for the aft shields. Min said they were drawing too much power."

"Your bots couldn't handle it?" Pink asked.

Sue's cheeks flushed and she stared at her boots. "I sent Eleven and Nineteen to do it, but they started arguing and I had to separate them."

The bots' shrill noises increased in volume, and Sue grabbed one in each hand and brought them up to her face. "Leaky buckets, knock it off already," she said. "Don't make me put you in time-out!"

Eva didn't know what "time-out" meant, but the bots shut up, so it had to be a serious threat. For tiny robots, anyway.

Sue settled into her chair as Eva's mind wandered. Sometimes it seemed like the last six months had been one firefight after another, between sparse cargo delivery and passenger transport jobs. Fucking with whatever was left of The Fridge had been her crew's top priority, and thankfully Vakar's bosses were all too happy to subsidize their endeavors. She also got to keep or sell portions of any ill-gotten goods they recovered from their raids, or in situations like the one on Kehma, they returned stolen items for a hefty bounty from the original owner.

It wasn't an easy life, but more and more often, Eva was starting to feel like it was a pretty good one. Even the food was better than it used to be. She took a sip of her espresso, savoring the sweet bitterness; Vakar had used her stash of real beans instead of the replicator.

"So we got what we came for, and now we drop it off and get paid," Eva said. Min gave a little cheer of "Jackpot!" while Vakar's smell gained a brief almond spike of delight.

"Also, we pissed off the Blue Hounders and The Fridge," Pink added. "It's like asshole Christmas up in here."

"Feliz Navidad," Eva said. "Min, how long until we reach Atrion?"

"About a quarter cycle," Min replied. "Unless you want to refuel somewhere first."

Eva shrugged. "Anyone have a layover request?"

Sue shook her head, Pink twirled her finger in a circle and Vakar's palps twitched, but he said nothing.

"If we can make it to Atrion, and their fuel prices aren't ridiculous, let's just get this job done." Eva knocked back the last of her coffee. "Nice work, amigos. Take a break."

Sue wandered back toward the cargo bay, holding one bot in each hand and scolding them quietly. Eva stood and hobbled over to put her taza in the sanitizer, wondering whether she should grab a snack or head straight to her cabin. Vakar appeared at her side, laying a claw gently on her arm.

"Would you like assistance returning to your room?" he asked, smelling like vanilla and lavender under all the licorice.

Eva grinned, raising an eyebrow. "I'm sure Fuácata wouldn't mind the help." The snack could definitely wait.

"I said rest, woman," Pink called from the doorway. "Don't make me confine you to the med bay. I have a bunch of remote patients in my virtual queue, and I don't want to waste my very expensive time patching your sorry ass twice."

Vakar wagged his head in the quennian equivalent of a shrug, while Eva snorted. But as soon as Pink was gone, they shared a look and Eva burst into laughter.

"Come on," she told him. "There's more than one way to rest. I can think of at least three and I'm not even trying."

Eva woke up four hours later with a throbbing pain in her leg, to the sound of Min pretending to be an alarm through the speakers.

"Qué pinga," Eva said sleepily, raising her head off Vakar's chest.

"Sorry to bother you, Cap," Min said, "but you've got a call on the new emergency frequency."

Mierda, Eva thought. That could only be one of three people, and she wasn't in the mood to talk to any of them.

"Should I go?" Vakar rumbled.

"Nah, I don't wanna move," Eva said. "Min, audio only, please."

A holo image projected from Eva's closet door into the dim room. At first it crackled with static, but it quickly resolved into the face and upper body of her sister, Mari. Her brown hair was tied back in a ponytail, and unlike the last time Eva had seen her, she wore a dark red spacesuit with extra armored plating over the chest. Her expression was neutral, controlled, like she'd done a bunch of deep-breathing exercises before making the call. Which she probably had, given how good Eva was at getting on her nerves.

"Eva?" Mari asked, her neutral expression immediately slipping as a crease appeared between her brows. "Are you there? I can't see you."

"I'm here," Eva replied, slapping Vakar's claw as he ran it up her bare thigh. "It's been a while. What do you need?"

The furrow smoothed out. "What's the passcode?" Mari asked.

Eva sighed and consulted her commlink. The key generator Mari had made her install spat out a long string of letters and numbers, which she dutifully repeated.

"And what's your favorite . . ." Now Mari pursed her lips and narrowed her eyes at Eva. "This doesn't make any sense."

"What?"

"Favorite food."

Eva hmmed wistfully. "Paella. So good."

"You're allergic to shrimp, boba."

Vakar's palps tickled her face and she stifled a giggle. "Pink has been giving me a lot of allergy meds," she said. "Really strong ones."

Mari closed her eyes. Eva could almost hear her silently counting to ten.

"My turn," Eva said. "What's your favorite, uh, Mesozoic species?"

Mari smirked. "Ah, see, someone who didn't know me well might assume it was equisetites, because of the ribbed stems, but actually it's baculites because they—"

"Ya, basta, I know it's you because no one else is this boring." Eva reluctantly sat up and swung her legs over the side of her bed, wincing as her injured thigh protested. "What do you want, Mari?"

Her sister's face grew serious again. "My superiors need to speak with you. In person."

Now Vakar sat up, too, smelling as curious as Eva felt. She knew nothing about Mari's bosses, except that they thought it was totally fine to throw Eva to the proverbial wolves if it meant taking down The Fridge. And now they wanted to talk?

"I thought you didn't want me anywhere near your business?" Eva asked, barely concealing the salt in her tone.

"I don't, but I'm not in charge."

Eva's smirk died quickly. "What do they want from me?"

"That's not for me to say," Mari replied, smoothing a stray hair against her head. "But if you'll agree to meet with them and discuss their offer, I'll send you the coordinates."

Secrets, as usual. Great. "I assume I'd get paid for whatever this is?" Eva asked.

"Absolutely. A fair rate, possibly including fuel subsidies."

Eva wrinkled her nose at Vakar, who blinked his inner eyelids pensively. He smelled minty, but otherwise noncommittal. No help there.

"I have to discuss it with my crew," Eva said slowly. "I'm not the only captain anymore, and either we're all in or we're out."

"How egalitarian of you," Mari said. Her features had settled into a mask again, and her gaze flicked up like she was looking at something Eva couldn't see. "I have to go, but please let me know within the next cycle. We're running out of time, and options."

"Right, I'm never the first pick for the spaceball team," Eva muttered. "Call me back in an hour; I'll have an answer for you then."

"Bueno. Cuídate."

The holo image vanished, plunging the room back into darkness except for the dim light from the fish tank above her bed. Vakar's sister, Pollea, had taken care of Eva's fish while Eva was indisposed—okay, no need to be euphemistic, it was while Eva was in cryo after being kidnapped because of shit that was basically Mari's fault. But Eva had gotten her ship back, and her fish, and added a few new creatures to the tank for good measure, including the orange-shelled snail currently stuck to the glass, and the hermit crab digging through the substrate. She hadn't worked up the nerve to add live coral or anemones, but she figured she would get there someday.

That, of course, depended on whether she lived long enough to see "someday" for herself. Her leg throbbed as a reminder that nothing was certain, that every fight she walked into was a roll of the Cubilete dice, and the other side might get a Carabina first.

For the second time that cycle, Eva pinged everyone to meet her in the mess, then sighed. Her thigh bandages were intact, but definitely in rougher shape than they should have been for someone supposedly resting an injury.

"Pink is gonna be mad at us," she told Vakar.

"It is probable," he agreed, tickling her shoulder with his palps.

"Eh, worth it." She grabbed her nearest article of clothing off the floor. "Help me put on my pants so she doesn't see it yet, and let's get this party started."

Min's human body joined them in the mess, since it was time for a meal anyway. She was using the hot plate to make gyeran-jjim for herself and Sue, so Eva settled for reconstituting a vague approximation of picadillo along with the last of the instant rice. Pink shoveled her own rice and fake red bean concoction into her mouth quickly enough to give Eva a stomachache from watching. Vakar wasn't hungry, and he already knew what the meeting was about, so he sat at the table and waited with a patience Eva found admirable, if baffling.

Eva explained the situation briefly as everyone ate. The first to respond when she finished was Pink, who pushed her empty plate away with a look like she'd bitten a lemon.

"Mari is a liar and an asshole," Pink said coldly. "And her bosses were good with her busted-ass plan that fucked all of us over. That's two strikes already and we don't even know what they want."

"We cannot trust them," Vakar agreed. "However, some of our goals are in alignment overall."

"We all hate The Fridge," Sue said, blowing on her food to cool it. "And it seems like they have, um, you know . . ."

"Money?" Eva supplied. "Resources? Information?"

"Yeah, all of that, pretty much."

"Food?" Min asked, poking what was left of her fluffy egg substitute. She'd gotten way more interested in eating once their options had improved.

Eva gestured at Min with her fork. "That, I don't know."

Pink leaned back in her chair and crossed her arms. "If this were any other client, you'd tell them to go piss up a rope. Is the risk worth what we might get out of it?"

"Mari did say they'd pay us well," Eva said. "Maybe even a fuel allowance."

"Ooh, a fuel allowance, says the liar." Pink nodded sarcastically, her eye wide.

"We do need fuel," Min said. "I mean, I do. The ship me."

Vakar smelled like ozone with a hint of incense—uncertain, concerned—but there was also an undercurrent that reminded Eva of night-blooming jasmine. Thoughtful, which meant he wasn't entirely opposed to the idea. She considered his angle, and what he might stand to gain from it.

"You want to know more about them," Eva told him. "Mari's people, I mean, whoever they are."

Vakar shrugged in the quennian equivalent of a nod. "As a Wraith," he said, "I have been tasked with documenting the activities of the entity known as The Fridge, and disrupting them. Your sister is employed by yet another organization whose identity and motives are unknown, but whose reach appears extensive. Under the right circumstances, they could be a valuable asset."

They certainly seemed to have reached right into The Fridge itself, if Mari was any indication. How many more spies did they have, and how much information might they be willing to trade?

Pink shook her head, her dreads swaying slightly. "So assuming we agree to meet with them, then what?"

"We see what they want." Eva shrugged. "Worst case, we turn them down and walk away."

"Worst case, they blow us up and melt down the scraps," Pink muttered.

Sue spoke up then, in a quiet voice. "Sometimes good people do bad things," she said, staring down at her empty plate. "They think the reasons are good and important, and it will all work out in the end. It's not smart, maybe, but it's . . . it happens."

Sue was thinking of her own past, no doubt. Her brother, Josh, had been kidnapped by The Fridge, after which Sue had robbed a few banks and an asteroid mine in the hopes of paying off his ransom. But Josh was still missing, and none of their Fridge-busting fun had turned up any leads so far. Looking at the dark-haired girl, just out of her teens, Eva would never have believed she was capable of such a thing. Sue could barely curse properly, though Eva was trying to teach her.

Then again, the same things could be said about Eva, or Pink, or anyone else on the ship. Eva most of all, given some of what she'd done back when she worked for her father. She had enough regrets to fill their cargo hold, and more.

Eva didn't seem to be the only one following that plutonium exhaust trail of thought, so she cleared her throat to bring everyone back to the table.

"Vote time?" Eva shifted her butt, wincing at the pain that shot through her leg. "I say we check it out, with another vote to decide whether we take whatever offer they make."

"I also believe we should investigate," Vakar said.

Min brushed her faded blue hair out of her face and smiled. "Fuel sounds good to me."

Sue hesitated, then said, "It can't hurt. Can it?"

"It certainly can," Pink said. She rolled her eye. "I feel like I'm having to be paranoid enough for all y'all, but whatever. At least we're being foolish together."

"Look at it this way," Eva said, "if you're right, we can burn them for good."

"If I'm right," Pink said with a scowl, "we're the ones who are gonna be hosed."

Eva really, really hoped Pink wasn't right this time.

ABOUT THE AUTHOR

Valerie Valdes is a Cuban-American speculative fiction writer whose work is inspired by video games, cartoons and decades of accumulated pop culture references. She enjoys crafting bespoke artisanal curses, deliciously painful puns and medium-burn romances with a main course of butt-kicking.

Valerie was raised in the suburbs of Miami on a steady diet of Spanglish and stacks of library books. She lives with her husband, two children and cats who are probably not psychic.